Jonathan saw the one thing he needed: all five remaining bows were empty of arrows.

He ran at the archers, his sword singing as it cut the air. The first man tried to parry with his bow, and Jonathan laughed as the bow cracked and the man fell beneath his sword. The other archers had time to draw sturdy oak clubs from their belts, and rather than fleeing they spread out and surrounded him. For a moment he feared they were too many for him, and he could not find space or time to attack any one without leaving himself unprotected from the others. Then his training returned to him and he began to fight with more skill. The fight was a wild dance, one against four, iron against oak, eyes in all directions, all threats seen, all blows blocked or dodged – while all the time he was looking, looking for an opening, a chance to be on the offensive. A chance came, not to strike with full force, but to deliver a lightning slash. There was blood, an oak club dropped to the ground, a man running for his life. Only three against one now. Jonathan felt their fear, and his victory approaching. But then, in one of the fleeting glimpses the fight allowed him, he saw one of the men step back and set an arrow in his bow.

And he knew the archer must be stopped, at any cost...

About the Author:

Homeschooled from first through twelfth grade, Ari Heinze holds astronomy degrees from Caltech (B.S. 2001) and the University of Arizona (Ph.D. 2007). He's passionately interested in astronomy, but equally so in storytelling. Even in early childhood he entertained his two younger brothers with stories, and now, besides writing with obsessive delight, he invents stories for his own children: Petra, Eleazar, and baby Brogal, born in January 2010. He and his beloved wife Jane live in Houston at present, but plan to move to a more starry and adventurous locale when they have opportunity.

Favorite Books of the Author:

Fiction: *Cry, the Beloved Country,* by Alan Paton
Green Dolphin Street, by Elizabeth Goudge
The Jacobite Trilogy, by Dorothy K. Broster
Jane Eyre, by Charlotte Bronte
The Lord of the Rings, by J. R. R. Tolkien
The Napoleon of Notting Hill, by G. K. Chesterton
Northanger Abbey, by Jane Austen
The Space Trilogy, by C. S. Lewis
Till We Have Faces, by C. S. Lewis

Nonfiction: *Confessions,* by St. Augustine
Desiring God, by John Piper
The Reason for God, by Tim Keller
Jeremiah, by the Prophet Jeremiah
Galatians, Ephesians, Philippians, and *Colossians,* by St. Paul

Bright Against the Storm

THE EPIC OF KAROLAN

THE FIRST BOOK AMONG FOUR

Ari Heinze

SOLI DEO GLORIA

Cover art by Ari Heinze
Published by Hopewriter Publishing
ISBN: 978-0-9825543-2-6

CONTEXT WITHIN THE EPIC OF KAROLAN

This is the first book in ***The Epic of Karolan***. It tells of the adventures of Jonathan the blacksmith and Sir Ilohan during the time preceding the great war between Karolan and Norkath, and of the love that was between Jonathan and Naomi the shepherdess, whom he left behind in Glen Carrah.

The second book, **Ashes of Our Joy**, describes how Ilohan and Jonathan acquitted themselves in the Norkath War and its aftermath.

The third book, **Rain, Wind, and Fire**, tells what Naomi did during the Norkath War, and what was the end of Jonathan's search for her. It tells also how a great and unexpected danger arose to threaten Karolan, and what was done to guard against it.

The fourth and final book, **Darkness Gathers Round**, describes how the danger came upon Karolan, and how it was resisted with great heroism. It concludes the story of Ilohan, Jonathan, and Naomi, and others, no less significant, who were caught up in their adventures. For at the last, though darkness gathered round, their stories did not end in darkness.

To explore Karolan further, or learn when books two through four will be available, visit http://www.hopewriter.com/Karolan.html.

Acknowledgements

Thanks to my dear wife, Jane, for supporting me in writing and publishing this work, for believing it was possible even if I didn't, and for invaluable suggestions and insights at every step of the process. Thanks also for all the spirited discussions about points of editing -- that was some of the best fun in the whole project.

Thanks to my parents, Dan and Judith, and my brothers, Ky and Dar, for being my first readers, and for making me believe I could write something publishable.

Thanks to Daniel Song for detailed editing suggestions for the whole series.

Thanks to my endorsers, especially Louis Markos, who gave me the first endorsement despite my flakiness in getting him the manuscript. Your praise of my work provided great encouragement at a time when it was much needed.

If I start naming those who shared with me the adventures I have drawn on to write my epic, this page will never be enough – but thanks to those who stood with me on icy mountains, hiked to hidden valleys, ventured into baked but splendid deserts, and dared enough heat and cold, hunger, thirst, and danger that my portrayals of these things have some taste of the reality.

Thanks to those whose love helped me dream of Ceramir, and whose courage and faithfulness helped me dream of heroes.

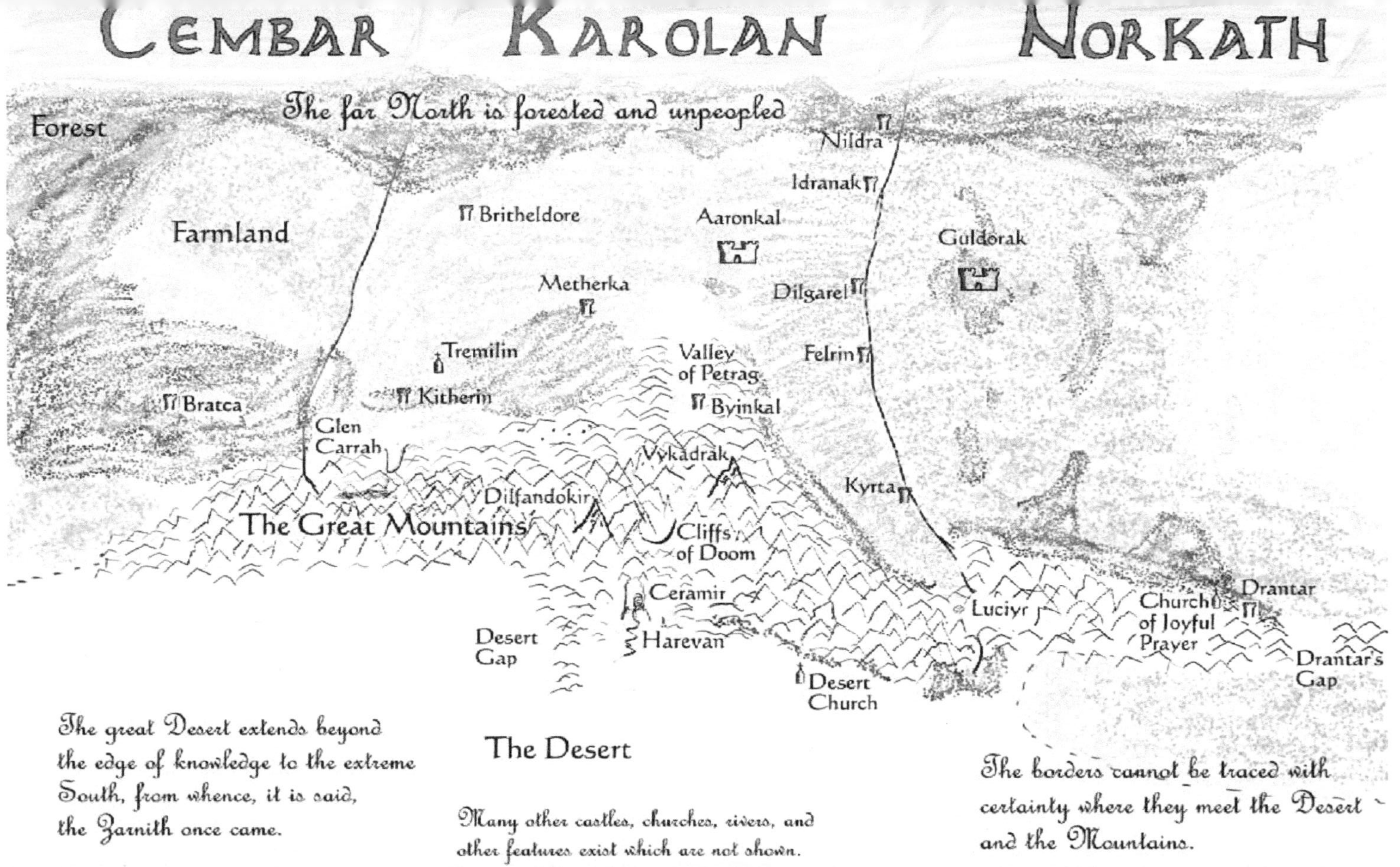

CEMBAR KAROLAN NORKATH

The far North is forested and unpeopled

Forest

Farmland

Britheldore

Aaronkal

Nildra

Idranak

Guldorak

Metherka

Dilgarel

Tremilin

Valley of Petrag

Felrin

Bratca

Kitherin

Byinkal

Glen Carrah

Vykadrak

Kyrta

Dilfandokir

The Great Mountains

Cliffs of Doom

Ceramir

Luciyr

Church of Joyful Prayer

Drantar

Desert Gap

Harevan

Desert Church

Drantar's Gap

The Desert

The great Desert extends beyond the edge of knowledge to the extreme South, from whence, it is said, the Zarnith once came.

Many other castles, churches, rivers, and other features exist which are not shown.

The borders cannot be traced with certainty where they meet the Desert and the Mountains.

To my parents:
Joyful amid the broken world,
Brave and skillful as Kindrach,
Faithful and fearless as Eleanor,
And more full of the good handiwork of God
Than I could ever write.
It is because of the childhood you gave me
That I grew into a man who could imagine Ceramir.

Chapter 1

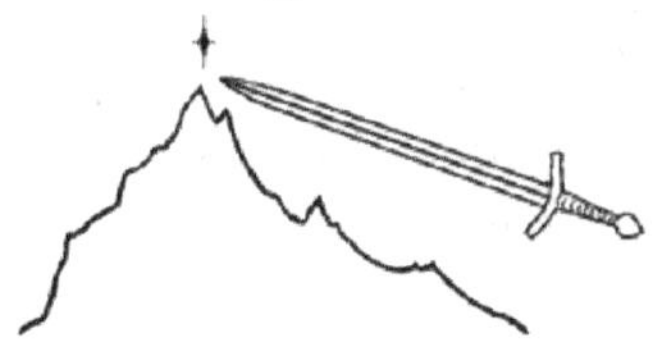

The Fear in Children's Eyes

THE YOUNG MAN KNELT BETWEEN TWO CANDLES ON THE cold stone floor. Beyond the thick walls of the chapel he heard the rising wind and the first drops of rain. Thunder boomed in the unseen sky, and rain poured down, taking all comfort from the world. The candles flickered in a draught under the door, and his prayer lost words and faded into silence. His mind was full of questions, and he felt deeply alone on this his night of vigil.

Tomorrow he would become a knight. That much he knew, and it filled his heart with joy and amazement. Himself, a knight! For this he had worked hard and waited long, almost his whole life. But what, in these days, would be the duty of a knight?

In his training he had learned much of the ancient lore of knighthood, but of the present his tutors had said little – they had left him to reach his own understanding of it. Only recently had he awakened to the dire foreboding that lay across the land. He had seen it in the faces of farmers met upon the road, of merchants at their work, and even of children who played in the autumn leaves beside the roads. He knew a cause for anxiety: the king was old and had no son. But the king was still strong, and could appoint a successor. There had to be something else that made people afraid – something he did not know, something he had never been taught. What was it? The question arose unbidden in his mind, again and again considered and left unanswered: a riddle in the lonely night.

He turned his thoughts again to the morning, when he, Ilohan, an orphan without known lineage, who might have lived and died as a beggar child in some small village, would become a knight. All this he owed to the mercy of Queen Sarah. When a child who could not yet speak, he had been found the only survivor of a band of knights and ladies that had been ambushed and slaughtered in the mountains. The queen had taken him in – and persuaded King Thomas to have him raised as a ward of the throne, and trained to knighthood.

Ilohan had overheard some in the royal castle of Aaronkal saying that this was Her Majesty's tenderhearted foolishness, and that he was only a servant's child. He hoped he might be the son of one of the dead knights. King Thomas had often told him not to worry about his lineage. "The child of a knight is no different from the child of a peasant," he had said. "Either can become a true knight, or a craven. It is a man's choices that make the man." Ignoring what anyone might say, the queen had loved Ilohan as her own son, and he had called her mother.

Queen Sarah had died four years ago, and slowly he had learned to live with the emptiness her passing had made in his heart. The question of his lineage troubled him little anymore – certainly not now, on the eve of his knighthood. The thunder boomed again, and the cold stone dug into his knees, bringing his thoughts back to the present.

A long time had passed since the beginning of his vigil, but it would be longer still until dawn. He looked around the dark chapel. The candles cast circles of light on the rough-hewn floor, polished by the feet and knees of many worshippers. Their light fell short of the ceiling, but barely illuminated the near walls and the altar in front of him. He could dimly see the carving on the altar, of Christ and the angels coming on the clouds of heaven. He suddenly found joy in being in this holy place, at this secret hour, alone.

The candles flickered in the draught. The darkness seemed to come in under the door as tangibly as the wind, so that Ilohan was aware of both the warmly lit chapel and the cold and rainy night outside, as if he could experience both at once. He began to pray again. Wind roared in the oak trees surrounding the chapel, and bowed their branches down to scrape the roof. The black sky rumbled and the dark rain fell on the worried land, while the young man kept the vigil of his knighthood.

"Lord God, guard my life, and keep me true to the vows I make tomorrow. May I draw my sword only to fight for the helpless, and against evil. Keep me from falling into error, and keep my hand strong and my heart pure. Give me wisdom to fight only when I must, and then – give me courage! Help me do my part to lift the darkness that has fallen upon Karolan, and make me loyal to my king and my land until I die. When I face pain and hardship, show me how to bear them as a true knight should. Bring me through –"

His prayer was suddenly broken by a thing he could not fight or comprehend. He was not attacked – the chapel floor did not gape beneath him – but without warning, without perceptible cause, he fell into darkness and terror as into a freezing river. Everything he knew was lost to him. He could see nothing but blackness, and feel nothing but overwhelming fear. It crushed his chest and froze his heart. It sent his mind reeling in hopeless confusion. Darkness. Loss of light and loss of hope: no reference point, no handhold. He remembered nothing of the past, and could not guess what would happen next. His thoughts spun wildly and fixed on nothing. He felt that he was falling into the Abyss, never to return – unless he was already there.

Darkness. Loss. Confusion and despair. He reached again for something, anything in his desperation. "How... what is this thing... what came before...what was I doing... why?" He dimly remembered that he had been praying – and he grasped at the idea as at a straw. "God!" he cried. "If you are there, save me from the Darkness!" There was no answer. The darkness roared. Terror surged around him like an overwhelming river. He began to lose his last hope. "God!" he cried again. "If you will not bring me out, come to me and help me in the Darkness!"

Nothing changed, but his terror faded. It faded even though he still could not move, or see, or feel, or comprehend what had seized him. An idea came to him in the darkness: the idea of Karolan, the land that was his home, whose hearty people and hills and streams he loved. Ilohan found he could not frame words, but he tried to offer up his love itself as prayer. He felt that fear was still lying in wait for him, but that prayer shielded him from it. The idea of the people of Karolan narrowed to one man, whom he had not thought of for months: Jonathan, a young villager in a remote glen, who had once thoroughly beaten him in a fencing match. Still unable to frame his own words, he used Thomas's: "The child of a knight is no different from the child of a peasant... it is a man's choices that make the man."

Horror of the blind darkness all around weighed on him. His prayer faded, and fear began to return. This time he felt a strong sense of falling, of a prison, or perhaps even a shelter, cracking open. The terror reached a crescendo and then broke. He lay again on the floor of the chapel, gasping and covered with cold sweat. His candles were still burning. The Darkness was over.

* * *

Jonathan awoke from dreamless slumber to see the light of early morning coming through the window of his family's cottage. It shone clear on the clean-swept wooden floor and log walls. The only sound was birds singing, welcoming a new day with joy. He realized with surprise that he was awake before his parents, and that he should get up and light the forge.

He slid his feet reluctantly from under his blanket and stood. He took bread from the kitchen, and drew cold, clear water from the well behind the cottage. He stood in dewy grass and watched the dawn while he ate and drank, letting Glen Carrah remind him that it was good to be alive.

The glen sloped upward in glorious bounds of golden grass, guarded on either side by steep spurs of the mountains. Far behind it, the great mountains themselves towered in misty glory. They seemed to beckon to Jonathan this early morning, but also to defy him as they always did. Birdsong rained out of the clean blue sky, though the singers were too high to be seen. Other birds winged to and fro in the mist above the glen. The first rays of sunlight streamed over the mountains on Jonathan's left, and turned the mist to shafts of golden light. He raised his cup of water, as if in toast to Glen Carrah: the most beautiful place in the world.

He finished his meal and stepped into the smithy, a small, walled yard behind the cottage. He coaxed a flame from yesterday's coals, shoveled new charcoal and ore into the furnace, and pumped the bellows. Slowly the charcoal kindled, and the furnace grew dazzling yellow inside with the heat. He took a half-formed sword from a chest by the wall, and plunged it into the midst of the blazing charcoal. The walls of the open courtyard shut out the sight of the glen, and the ground beneath his feet was lifeless with black ash and slag. Still, the sky was bright blue above him, and over the roar of the furnace and the rhythmic hiss of the bellows he could still make out the singing of the birds.

The bar of iron grew intensely bright. He drew it out to work it on the anvil. It felt slow and awkward. Molding a smooth and lovely sword with blunt hammer-blows seemed impossible. It always did at first. But as blow after blow fell, and shower after shower of sparks sprayed outward, he remembered the pattern he never really forgot.

Bang, bang, bang, the bright sparks fell and he was completely absorbed in his work. Hammer until the iron glows dull, heat it again to sparking brilliance, hammer again. Turn the blade, bang, bang; pump the bellows, bang, bang; and gradually the impossible is done. What was a crudely tapered iron bar becomes a sword blade, glowing dull red on the anvil.

This sword was smooth and straight, thin at the edges where the grinding wheel would make it razor sharp, thickest and strongest near the hilt, sturdy and lethal to the point. Jonathan tempered it carefully, plunging it again and again into a barrel of cold water, first briefly, then for longer intervals, intently watching the play of iridescent color on the surface of the metal as its temperature changed. The edges of the blade must be cooled quickly: they would be hard and sharp. The center must cool more slowly, to be tough and strong. On his first attempt something seemed slightly wrong, so he re-heated the blade and tried again. At last it was done, and he reached his bare hand into the barrel to recover the quenched blade. He drew it out and raised it above his head. It was dark and blotchy, not yet sharpened and polished. But it was already a sword.

Jonathan put his gloves back on and grasped the bare iron hilt with both hands. He swung the blade hard and fast, a glancing blow at a wood testing block that hung from a projection on the wall. The sword rang true, a musical note that joined the birdsong. He stepped back and swung harder, blow after blow that set the heavy wood target swinging. He loved the feel of the sword in his hands. He loved knowing that the strength he had earned swinging a blacksmith's hammer also enabled him to wield a knight's sword. His blows sent chips of wood flying in all directions, and the blade he had tempered did not break.

Jonathan suddenly became aware of a presence behind him. He turned around to see his father, Barnabas, standing at the entrance to the smithy. The master smith of Glen Carrah was smiling, a hint of laughter in his face. The brown homespun shirt he wore could not hide the strong, tough muscles of his arms. In one hand he held a heavy bucket of ore he had not bothered to set down.

"Good morning, Father," said Jonathan.

"Good noontide, Son. The morning is already gone. I see you have made use of the time. Still, I sometimes wonder if you do not spend more effort testing your swords than making them."

"You have often told me that we must never send the king flawed swords," said Jonathan. He changed his stance suddenly, and lifted his blade, knowing that his father would instantly recognize one of the guard positions of the swordsmen of Karolan.

"Very well then, let us test it," said Barnabas. He opened the chest, took up another half-finished sword, and swung it into a guard stance of his own.

Jonathan attacked hard. Barnabas blocked all his strokes, and nothing Jonathan tried could get through his father's defenses. Finally Barnabas' sword was slightly out of place, and Jonathan saw his chance and swung hard. His blade was knocked aside with a wrenching blow. His own effort to parry never even came close, and his father's sword stopped short a handbreadth from his head.

"Your blade is sound," said Barnabas, panting.

"How did you do that, Father?" asked Jonathan, equally out of breath.

"Son," said Barnabas with a smile, "always make sure your enemy's mistake was an accident, before you attack. But it was a well fought match, and your mother has prepared our noon meal inside."

They walked out of the smithy and through the clean lush grass together. Father and son had had such sword matches for as long as Jonathan could remember, and he knew they were both very skilled. His father still won most of the time, but he no longer won easily.

The two men stood looking out over Glen Carrah for a moment before going inside. The sun had burned away the mist, and was blazing high in the south, above the great mountains. The grass shone in the light, and waved in the cool wind. Jonathan opened the door of their cottage, and he and his father stepped into the kitchen. Good smells met them – of stew and bread, fresh-cut oak and tanned leather. Jonathan's mother, Hannah, turned to greet them with a smile. She had already set steaming goat's meat stew and fresh bread on the table. Oak shavings from a plow she was making lay deep on her work bench at the other side of the room.

"It's been a lovely morning," she said, as she took her seat at the table.

"It certainly has," said Barnabas. "I've been down into the town to get ore, and everything is bright and washed with the rain last night. They had a hard time bringing wagons along the muddy roads from the mines, but they made it sometime last night and brought in some of the best ore I've seen in weeks." He and Jonathan sat down, and all three bowed their heads.

"Our Father in Heaven," said Barnabas, "thank you for the food that you give us. Thank you for our lives, our work, and our land. Make us yours, and be our helper and protector whatever happens to us. Thank you that you are able to bring life out of death. Amen."

Jonathan had heard his father pray like this thousands of times, and though he respected his father, he thought the prayers were foolish. He rarely spoke his thoughts aloud, but today he said, "Father, why do you thank God for his power, that he is able to bring life out of death? Did he decide to be powerful for your sake, any more than I decided to be born your son? And why should I believe that there is a God who can bring life out of death? Is it not more noble to love the life and beauty that we see and know, preserve it and treasure it as long as we can, but form no groundless hopes of bringing life out of death?"

"I thank God for his power because the wandering preachers from Tremilin and the other great churches do it," said Barnabas.

"But you do not know why!" said Jonathan. "You do not test what they do to see if there is good reason for it, and you do not test what they teach to see if it is true. When they say that God brings life out of death, you believe without thinking."

"No!" said Barnabas. "I listen to the ancient stories, the stories the travelers brought to Karolan. You have heard them too – their words ring with power and truth every time they are told. Could men have written such things, could they have told them and passed them on in such words, if they had not seen them and did not know that they were true? I know they could not. Jonathan, I know how men use words when they lie, and when they speak truth. Have you seen me cheated in our trade? I tell you, I know that the stories are true, and there is life in believing them. Will you not take the life God offers you? If you will not, there is only death in the end. You will not find any other defense against death, and there will be no limit to your loss."

Jonathan saw the sorrow in his father's face, and was silent. He did believe in inevitable loss, and suddenly the fear and pain of the loss stabbed him. How comforting must be the foolish hope of his parents' faith! But he did not hear truth in the ancient stories, as his father claimed to do. Their faith was not for him, and he did not need it. He loved justice and honor, goodness and beauty. In peace, a true man should treasure what was good and beautiful, and rejoice in it. In war he should defend it heroically – but true heroism must not ask for hope that what it saved would endure.

Jonathan forced his fear away. The loss was in the distant future, and to dwell on it was to weaken the love and delight that were so vitally important now. He loved life, Naomi, his parents, and Glen Carrah. He loved the hope of future adventure and victory. He would love all these long and happily, and see his dreams fulfilled, before he faced the irrevocable loss.

He ate a spoonful of his mother's rich stew, and the wind from the glen blew through the open windows. His thoughts flew back to the present, and the steady peace he felt dismissed from his mind the idea of endless loss. His father was speaking.

"The king has ordered twelve more swords by the end of next month," said Barnabas, "He is filling his armories at Aaronkal with weapons."

"Does he expect war?" asked Hannah.

"He is making every preparation for it," said Barnabas.

"Is there any word yet of the king's appointing a successor?" asked Jonathan.

"Nothing but wild rumors that one knight or another is likely to be chosen," said Barnabas. "Obviously the king himself has not yet spoken."

"But why should war come?" asked Jonathan. "We are making swords, the whole village is worried, but no one will say why. I know only that it is Norkath, not Cembar, that they fear."

There was a long silence. Jonathan looked from his father's face to his mother's and then back again. He felt that his mother wished to speak, but would not.

"What do you know of Prince Kindrach?" asked Barnabas at last.

"Was he not a son of King Thomas who died in childhood?" asked Jonathan.

"No," said Hannah. "He lived to be a man – a prince of whom all Karolan could be proud. Then he vanished, and few now dare to speak of him."

Jonathan wondered if the prince had been killed by something horrible, so that even years later people were afraid to talk about it. But no – the Knights of Karolan feared no horror. They would have avenged him. Another explanation suddenly came into his mind. "Prince Kindrach was suspected of treachery," he said.

Hannah stood, and her eyes flashed. "No!" she said. "He was only accused, never suspected. He would have died gladly rather than betray Karolan."

"It was reported," said Barnabas, "that before his death, the prince gave Karolan to King Fingar of Norkath: that he pledged that Fingar, rather than he, would succeed King Thomas. This was the lie."

"Fingar's lie," said Hannah.

"Yes," said Barnabas, "Fingar's lie, with which he now hopes to stir his people to war with Karolan. When we fight to resist his conquest, he will say we are traitors to the pledge of Kindrach, prince of Karolan."

"Then you think we will be invaded?" asked Jonathan. Desire for adventure and glory leapt up in his mind like a flame, burning away his fear.

"When King Thomas dies, yes, I think we will be invaded," said Barnabas slowly. "But the people of Karolan are sturdy iron, and it may be that war will only re-temper, and not shatter the blade. Perhaps it is time we were tested again."

"And whatever comes," said Hannah, "we have God, who can bring life from death."

Jonathan could hear fear in her voice – but also her mastery of the fear as she comforted herself with her faith. There was a long silence. The sun cast squares of warm light on the clean, smooth floor. The wind carried the healthy smell of the drying autumn grasses of the glen. Hannah spoke again, and her hands shook with the intensity of her desire, "Oh Jonathan, my son, why cannot you believe? The Glen you live in, the love you rejoice in, the sky above you and the strength of your hammer coming down, all these tell you of the God who brought life out of nothing! Why will you not believe that he exists and can bring to you life that is not lost by death?"

"Mother, must we speak of this again?" asked Jonathan. "I grieve to see your pain, and if the things you have named are from God, I do owe him all my allegiance. But what could prove to me that they are from him? Mother, I love you, and I am sorry, but I will keep my own faith. I believe that life is a priceless treasure, but not eternal. It will someday be gone forever. The true way to live is in love and in desperate rejoicing at the treasure as it slips through our hands, never to return. We must fight for the beautiful and true, and defend them from ugliness and pain as long as we can – but in the end we will be defeated. That is how I intend to live my life: I will protect what is good, admire what is beautiful, and fight what is horrible. I will watch with a noble sorrow as everything I loved is lost to me, and at last I lose even myself."

Hannah made no reply, and in the silence Jonathan was haunted by his own words. He wanted to walk – or run – a long way through the beauty of Glen Carrah. He looked again at his mother and saw that the desperation had left her face. He embraced her and said, "I am sorry, Mother." She smiled with a hint of hope in her face, but sadness in her eyes. "Would you like me to go to the mountains and hunt for a goat for our dinner?" he asked her.

"Yes," she said, smiling fully now, "I will invite Naomi to eat with us tonight."

"The loveliest woman in the world," said Jonathan. "Mother, I will surely bring you back a goat." Naomi was more than beautiful, Jonathan thought, as he took the crossbow and arrows from the wall of the smithy. She was strong and free and loving, a girl worthy, and more than worthy, of the glen that was her home. Worthy of Glen Carrah: in Jonathan's mind, it was the highest praise.

In a moment he was running across the glen, reveling in his strength and freedom, his mind full of Naomi. He ran up toward the sun and the south. The tall grass brushed his legs and gleamed gold in the sun ahead, as he ran toward the light with joy.

Back in the house Hannah watched him go, delighting in his strength – and grieving for him. She turned and found herself in the arms of her husband. She felt his strength, and the strength of the deep love they shared. Trusting each other, sharing both their sorrow and their joy, they walked out of their house hand in hand and stood in the sunshine, watching their son run up the glen until he disappeared behind a swell of grass. Finally they went into the smithy together, and Barnabas put into her hands the cold iron parts that she needed for her work.

After Hannah went inside Barnabas stood alone for a long moment. He heard her begin to sing at her bench. At last he opened the furnace and peered into its glowing interior. The iron had melted out of the ore that Jonathan had put in that morning, and it lay in a dimly glowing heap at the bottom of the furnace. He heated it until it was bright orange, then took it out and began to hammer. He bent, crushed, and folded the iron with blow upon blow from his heaviest hammer. Gradually the impurities, the slag and ash, began to squeeze out of it and shatter into sand on the anvil. The sparks flew out in bright showers to darken his leather apron with tiny burnt dots. He enjoyed his power to refine iron with the strength of his hands and the heat of his forge.

As he fell into the strong and lovely rhythm of his work, he wondered if men are like lumps of iron on an anvil, only to be refined with fire and force. Perhaps a man could only be strong and bright after he had been through a lot of firing and hammering. He believed that he had been through some, though not enough to finish the task. He was still much less than he wanted to be.

The greatest example of his frailty was his failure to pass on his faith to his son. Of course he had not failed alone: he and Hannah had tried together and together they had failed. It was heartbreaking to them both. Yet there was still time, he told himself as he pumped the bellows and looked up at the blue sky. Jonathan would leave the house of his father soon, but he would not escape the reach of God.

Chapter 2

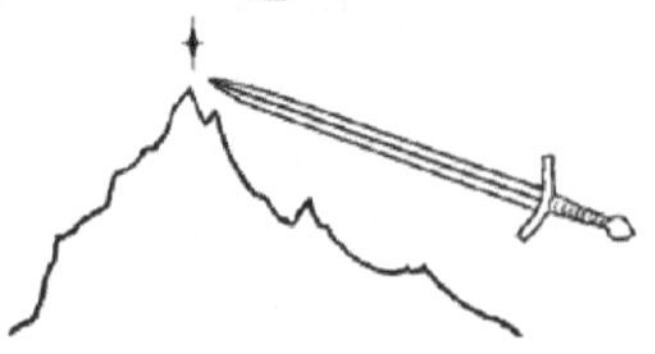

A Strange and Useless Quest

HANNAH HAD FINISHED SHAPING THE OAK HANDLES OF A plow, and they fitted perfectly into the iron sleeves of the plowshare that Barnabas had given her. She slipped iron bands heated in the fire up the sleeves until they jammed, and then tapped them into place with a mallet and rod. As the iron bands cooled they contracted over the metal sleeves and crushed in on the wood. The long oak handles would remain attached to the plowshare as long as the wood and iron lasted. She was pleased with the plow. It would help a farmer in bringing forth food from the earth – in fostering the quiet wonder that supported all human life.

She took two pairs of sheep shears, and walked briskly out the door, taking the lane toward Joseph and Naomi's cottage, which was at the foot of the glen, a little east of the rest of the village. The grass there was shorter and greener, the flowers more common, and the air quieter and warmer.

As she went, she thought of a pile of things she had left on her bench and turned her eyes from as she went out the door. They were arrows. In her mind she saw her son and husband engaged in fierce archery while the arrows of the enemy rained down in return. Jonathan might find joy in making a strong sword, and excitement in the thought of war, but Hannah saw only the pain and death, the tragedy and horror. When she made arrows – when she demonstrated with her own hands that war was a real possibility for which they were preparing – she felt sick.

Joseph's door was open when she arrived, and a small fire burned on the hearth. The welcoming room was empty, but the low voice of someone singing could be heard from an adjacent room. It was a sad but peaceful song, a song of hopeful mourning, not meant to be overheard. Hannah knocked on the door of the room. The singing stopped, and Joseph's voice invited her in. Another fire was burning in the fireplace there, and Joseph was stuffing a mattress with sweet smelling hay. In the corner lay a lamb a few months old, one of its forelegs bound with a splint.

"A good day to you, Hannah," said Joseph, looking up.

"And to you," replied Hannah, "I thought you would still be with the flock."

"I left the flock with Naomi," replied the shepherd, "and brought this lamb back to keep it safe. It is young and runs wildly. It fell off a rock and broke a leg this morning."

"And you also came back to do something else," observed Hannah, glancing at the mattress and the cheerful room. A wooden cup filled with flowers was on a table beside the bed, and a newly washed wool blanket hung across the windowsill to dry.

"Refill Naomi's mattress with new straw? Yes. And make her room as beautiful as I can."

"Some would say you spoil her," said Hannah, smiling, "but she is worthy of it all."

"Yes," said Joseph. "She is the only daughter of her mother." He turned his face away, but his voice was steady as he spoke,

"There can be no higher praise." As he rested his hand against the side of the window, Hannah noticed the thin, worn gold ring that he had never taken off. "She was kind and beautiful and brave," he said, his voice controlled, "she loved me as I thought no one ever would. I loved her as I did not know I could love. Her loss was like a sunset in my life. The bright and beautiful warmth sank into the west and was gone." There was a silence during which the lamb mewed contentedly and shifted its position on the floor. The shepherd turned toward Hannah again, and she could see no tears in his eyes. "The night also is beautiful and precious," he said, "and while I have Naomi, can I truly say the sun has set?"

"Barnabas and I will be honored if you and Naomi will eat with us tonight," said Hannah, "and I have brought the sheep shears you ordered from us."

"Thank you," said Joseph, "Naomi and I will certainly come. As soon as I finish this mattress I will pay you for the shears."

* * *

Jonathan had run far up Glen Carrah, nearly to the point where it faded into the stony feet of the great mountains, before he found a flock of wild goats. He stalked them carefully. His first arrow missed and shattered on stone behind the goats, but his second killed one where it stood. He skinned and gutted the goat, then washed the meat in the Carratril, the stream that ran through the glen. He walked back toward home with the Carratril murmuring beside him. It ran swiftly and smoothly here, bluer than the sky, between low, grassy banks. Farther down there were waterfalls and rapids that could suck a swimmer down and batter him to death. A little before he reached that point, about a third of the way down the glen, Jonathan decided he would swim today, as he often did. He took off his clothes and in one quick motion dove into the icy bliss of the laughing water.

It was cold and strong and wonderful. He drifted downstream for a moment, until he reached a large boulder that sat in the middle of the Carratril. He swam down and caught a rough edge of it below the surface, and felt what no swimmer in a pond or lake can feel: the swirling force of water rushing by faster than the fastest man can swim. Many times he surfaced and then went back down. On the surface he would lie on his back with his hands gripping the rock, letting the current run beneath him and bear him up while he stared into the deep blue sky. Then he would return to the cold darkness below and let the stream flow all around him.

The cold began to sink into his bones, and he let go of the rock to swim to shore. Immediately he was swept away by the current, and found himself drifting downstream toward the rapids. While clinging to the rock he had forgotten how swiftly the current would take him when he let go. He raised his head above water and saw that he was about to be swept into a narrow chute that ended in something that looked almost like a waterfall, studded with jagged rocks. He began fighting his way across the current toward shore. He was not fast enough, and he felt himself being sucked into the chute. He reached out desperately and caught an edge of the last boulder upstream of the rapid. The power of the river was tremendous, but with a great effort he pulled himself out of it and lay gasping on the rock.

He looked down at the swift water, beautiful and richly colored in the sunshine. He heard the roar of the waterfall below and the gurgle of the chute just beside him. He did not like to think what his fate would have been if he had not caught the rock. It was a pointed reminder that his strength was not limitless, however he might feel on a bright afternoon. He lay on the rock for a long moment, turning it over in his mind. But as he got up, he laughed, for his strength had been enough, and even if he had gone down the chute he was sure he would somehow have escaped harm. From a standing position it did not look so threatening. He walked upstream and recovered his clothes and the bow and bag of meat. He resolved as he dressed that next time he would dive off the rock and use the speed of his dive to make it to shore more quickly. His wet skin dried in the sun as he continued down the glen.

* * *

Naomi's sheep were already restless as the sun began to sink behind the foothills of the mountains. They were no longer eating, but were milling around and making anxious noises, knowing they must be in their fold before dusk. She had little difficulty in coaxing the flock to start ambling toward home. They went slowly along through the short green grass. Naomi liked the feeling of it as it brushed against her hard bare feet.

It was peaceful work, but slow, and while she enjoyed the lovely afternoon Naomi was longing to run free in the Glen, unencumbered by the sheep. She looked at her flock again, reminding herself to be grateful for them. There were thirty-seven sheep this year, and all except one lamb were with her. They were hers to care for, and from them came her and her father's daily bread. She must not be impatient with them.

Joseph could tell all the sheep apart and call them by name. Naomi could not quite do this. Many days she did not go out with the flock, but worked at home with the wool. She knew every step in the long labor of turning it into cloth or clothes. She liked to sing to herself in the quiet house, and see the stuff in her hands yield to her will and take the form she desired. But she would always stop in the early afternoon and run up to see her father and the flock – and she often ran farther, high up into the glen in joy and freedom. She loved the beauty of the world.

Her father was waiting for her at the open door of the sheepfold when she reached it. Joseph called the sheep by name as they filed in under his hand. Naomi only counted, arriving at the correct total of thirty-six.

"We are invited to Barnabas and Hannah's home tonight for supper," said Joseph.

She would see Jonathan, then. Suddenly she felt more alive, and the world seemed more beautiful, than it had a moment before. "Will you mind if I run in the Glen now, and meet you there later, Father?" she asked.

"Run with joy, my daughter," he said.

Joseph watched her go, wondering what it would mean to give her away in marriage. The final sunset of his life, after which he would be hard pressed to find any joy in the night? He hoped not, and thought not, though it would be hard. "God be with you," he whispered after her, and believed he would indeed be with her. She would raise children who were as much her daughters and sons as she was her mother's. He would see God bring to full bloom all that was now only lovely possibility in her life. That was a night he could bear with courage.

As his daughter disappeared into the sunlit grass, he sang quietly the love song that he had once sung to her mother, when the whole world was blazing with the joy of his love for her.

You came to me across the autumn field.
The sun was shining on your warm brown hair.
My longing deeper than I knew, you healed,
Beloved, with your strength and joy and care!

More lovely and more blessed than the harvest,
More precious than the life-rich golden grain,
Your love for me of all gifts is the greatest
Save one that undeserved I'll ever gain!

Deep running as the roots that lie beneath us,
Rich growing as the grain that shows above,
Forever I will faithful be to your trust;
Unending shines the beauty of our love!

Together we will sow and reap life's treasure.
Together we will stand the pain of loss.
The love we share there is no way to measure,
Nor on such gold can there be price or cost.

* * *

The Glen was still lit to rich color by the setting sun as Jonathan turned away from the Carratril toward his home. He was tired, and the sturdy cottage of weathered wood and gray thatch looked very beautiful in the low sunlight. It still seemed far away, separated from him by a wide expanse of windblown grass. Suddenly he saw a figure running, far away to his right, a brown form against the gold of the Glen. It came closer, and he knew that it was Naomi.

Tired no longer, he set down the bow and bag and ran. He ran as though his feet would leave the land and he would take wing like an eagle. His feet whipped through the grass, and its living health and sweet warm smell surrounded him. In the warm wind and the golden sunlight the lovers met, and Glen Carrah swirled around them in approval of their joy. To them both the wild grain of the glen was gold – gold they could smell and feel and taste and hear, living gold to which none mined from rock could compare. Jonathan held Naomi in his arms, and loved her more than anyone else on earth. She was worthy of all the love he could give. He would love her, care for her, protect her and delight in her. The life they would live would be filled with glowing joy that would mock the inevitable loss in which he believed. His thoughts of death and hope's ending were swept away like a grain of dust in the Carratril.

He knew that she gave him her love in return, and it was a treasure he could never be worthy of. She hugged him tightly, her brown hair swept around his shoulders in the wind, and because of her life and joy and beauty it seemed to him that he held the soul of Glen Carrah in his arms.

* * *

The cloud cover over Aaronkal began to break in the late afternoon. A rift opened in the western sky, and glowed from gray to gold to a line of white-hot brilliance. The clouds drifted apart and the sun shone on the dark gray castle walls. The warm light poured kindly on the green field before the castle, except where the long, turreted shadow lay across the grass. Ilohan stood in the shade and watched five knights ride off the field, going back to their different castles. They had come to see his knighting, and to try his strength in friendly combat. He had fought them all with honor, and to four of the five he had lost. They had commended his courage, and his chivalry, and he was grateful to each of them for coming. But now he was tired in every bone, and sore and bruised as well, and he wished he could have acquitted himself better.

He turned and walked wearily up the stairs to the castle gate. He told himself what he knew, that the combat had been the least of the important things that had happened that day. Beating stronger and more experienced men after a night with no sleep was not the point of knighthood. The central fact of his new life was not his strength but the use he had vowed to make of it. He had been honored with the challenge of holding to the Code of the Knights of Karolan. That was what mattered.

King Thomas was standing beside the throne in the Great Hall of Aaronkal when Ilohan entered it. Seeing that he was in earnest conversation with Tulbur the Steward, Ilohan was about to withdraw, but the king beckoned him forward. As he approached, the king brought whatever he was saying to Tulbur to a hasty conclusion, but Ilohan could not help overhearing some words in the echoing silence of the room: "Fingar's wrath will be cruel, but… …all the people dare hope for, and more. If not… …disaster will be complete."

The king raised his head as he dismissed the steward and beckoned Ilohan again. His thick gray hair and beard looked august as carved stone, while the rich crimson of his robes glowed in the sunshine and his crown flashed the light. He looked strong and commanding, determined to lead the country forever and well worthy to do it. He smiled, and looked straight into the eyes of his ward. "Well come, Sir Ilohan," he said. "May the blessing of God be upon you."

Ilohan felt that the words were deeply meant, and carried real power. The look the king gave seemed to encourage and strengthen him. He walked forward, bowed, and said, "And also upon you, Your Majesty."

The king walked slowly to the throne and sat down, and Ilohan came and stood before him. "I am sending you on a quest, Sir Ilohan," he said. "You will depart tomorrow at daybreak and go to a certain lake east of the Mountains of Karolan, and make a careful search all around the lake. After this you will journey on to a village to visit a certain person. When you have stayed there some days, this person will bid you to return, and you must make all speed to back Karolan and report to me what you have found. You must choose for yourself one companion to help you on your way. The name of the lake is Luciyr, and the village is called Harevan. I will give you a map to help you find them."

Ilohan stood silent, trying to understand, but failing. He wondered if the king was sending him on a strange and useless mission, or if it only seemed so to him because he was too tired to think. He did his best to reply out of his exhaustion. "Yes, Your Majesty." There was another long silence as he tried to frame a question that would not sound absurd.

"What is it, Ilohan?" asked the king.

It was one of the puzzles of Ilohan's life to know when to treat King Thomas as his king, and when to treat him as his foster father. Now the king had called him merely Ilohan, not Sir Ilohan. His name sounded like his own again, and the familiarity was comforting, though he had felt an incredulous joy each time he had heard the title of knighthood. The king's kindness seemed to call into his mind clear words for the questions he had been unable to frame before. He addressed him as familiarly as he ever dared, using a title that was a compromise between Father and Your Majesty. "What shall I look for at the lake, Sir?" he asked, "And whom am I to meet at the village?"

"Your success depends on not knowing too much at first," said the king, "but I can tell you a few things. At the lake you are to look for signs of a group of people who died many years ago: bones, perhaps, or weapons. You are to do your best to determine if the people were executed, or died fighting. If you can, carry away some tokens from among the things you find – but when you reach the village, conceal them carefully and say nothing of your mission, until one who knows what you were seeking tells you to reveal what you have found. At the village, go first to the cottage whose garden has the most flowers." The king smiled. "One more thing I must tell you, dear Ilohan," he said, "the quest on which I send you is a hard one. Remember that I love you, hold to the Code of Karolan, and be ready for anything."

"Thank you, Sir," said Ilohan. "I will try to be ready, and to acquit myself well. May I go to my chamber for the night?"

"Yes indeed," said the king, "I will send a page up to you with supper. Sleep well, and rise early to start your journey." Ilohan bowed and walked out of the throne room and up the stairs to his tower chamber.

He paused at his south-facing window, looking out toward the great mountains that bounded Karolan on that side. He could see them sometimes, on sparklingly clear winter days, but now a golden haze hung over the land beneath the suddenly clear sky. The mountains were invisible, but he could see the green grass fields stretching out around the castle, changing to golden grain farther away, and finally to scattered woods in the distance.

The memory that the king had ordered him to choose a companion slashed like a sword thrust through his haphazard musing: a decision insistently clamoring to be made. Should he choose Sir Benther, his closest friend among the Knights of Karolan? The picture of Benther as his companion came into his mind, and seemed stubbornly wrong. Yet many, likely including Benther himself, would assume that he could choose no other. It was a difficult problem – unless the idea that he should not choose Benther was only a fancy that he should ignore.

He was on the point of going to seek another audience with King Thomas to ask his advice, when he realized that his eyes had unconsciously fixed on the woods of the distant horizon. His thoughts flew instantly to the chapel that lay hidden there, where he had held his vigil. The windblown boughs of those oak trees had groaned and scraped against the roof all night. He remembered unwillingly the strange fear that had overwhelmed him, which had led him near the end to an idea... a name... Jonathan of Glen Carrah. The mental picture of Jonathan, a peasant blacksmith, as his companion seemed as strangely right as that of Sir Benther had seemed strangely wrong. He did not trust this feeling, and suddenly sat down on his bed in confusion.

His eyes closed and his head fell forward. He felt too tired to analyze events; he would merely take them as they came. He was a knight – tomorrow he was going on a quest. Tonight he would sleep. The question of his companion faded from his mind.

A page brought his dinner on a wooden tray, and he ate it sitting at a table by the window. The sun sank into a warm haze as a peaceful autumn evening stole across the land. His exhaustion blessedly removed his capacity for anxiety. He finished his dinner, stumbled into bed, and quickly fell asleep.

Chapter 3

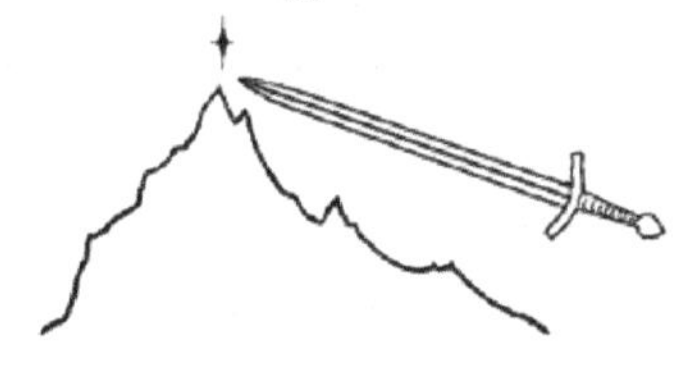

Lovers' Promises

IN THE COTTAGE AT THE FOOT OF GLEN CARRAH, HANNAH had put most of the goat's meat up in the chimney to smoke slowly, while what they would eat that night roasted on a spit over the fire. Jonathan and Naomi sat in chairs by the hearth.

Hannah looked up as Barnabas came in, bringing the sword Jonathan had finished that morning. It was now fully ground and polished, razor sharp and gleaming. She did not like to have it in her kitchen. He met her glance and was about to remove it, but Naomi looked over at it and asked to see it. He gave it to her. "The blade is bright and does not waver," said Naomi after a moment, turning the sword over and over in her hands. "The edge is straight and sharp. The hilt and cross-guard are joined in a smoothly-flaring weld with no discoloration." She looked up. "It is perfect."

"Of course," said Jonathan with a smile. Naomi stood and walked to the far wall. She raised the sword above her head, and swung it down in a swift motion. Even Hannah, who could not forget its purpose, thought it was beautiful as it flashed the light from the fire. Naomi let its point strike into the worn oak floor.

"For the rescue of Karolan," she said. "At Aaronkal there are a thousand swords. Let Norkath beware."

"I hope Norkath will consider our strength, and fear it," said Barnabas. "But Fingar may think his own the greater, and only time will show if it is true. You have appraised that sword like a true swordsmith. How did you know so much about it?"

Naomi smiled at Jonathan. "The one I love has told me of his craft," she said. "I have listened well. When will you bind the hilt?"

Hannah looked at her, standing there as gentle and as beautiful as ever, holding in her hands an instrument of death. Hannah understood the draw of war, the bright swords raised in the sun, the flags flying and the troops charging, but she knew too well what followed. There was nobility in the defense of a realm, in the valiant stand and the heroic death, but the price was bitter beyond counting. Thousands were wounded, thousands more dead. The lives they had had were lost, their loves bereaved, their work over, their places vacant. Heroes who died in battle won glory, maybe, but it was no substitute for what they lost. There was no glory for those they left behind – no matter whether the land was conquered, or saved at fearful cost. And yet she did not forget Barnabas' words of the morning: "The people of Karolan are sturdy iron, and perhaps the blow will merely temper, and not shatter, the blade." She could not imagine any benefit, any 'tempering,' that would be worth a war, and she fervently hoped that invasion would not come. But there was the sword, and there was her duty to be kind both to her husband and her guest. She went to Naomi and said, "I will bind the hilt now if there is time."

"May I?" asked Naomi.

"Certainly," said Hannah. She took a long leather strip from the bench, along with some glue. "Lay the leather evenly, spread glue under each layer, and wind tightly." Naomi took the glue and leather and sat down by the fire. Hannah found she could enjoy the peaceful scene: four people sitting around a hearth after a good day's work. Yet the sword still troubled her, flashing the firelight as it turned in Naomi's hands, while the beautiful shepherdess prepared it for lethal use.

The goat sizzled over the fire and gave out savory scents. Jonathan drank a long draught of well water from a pitcher. There was a knock at the door, and Hannah rose to let Joseph in. He was about to take a chair, when he noticed how Naomi was occupied. "Daughter!" he exclaimed. "What are you doing with that sword?"

She stood up, shame and distress in her face, "I am sorry, Father," she said, "I was binding it for Jonathan. I had forgotten that it would displease you."

Joseph looked at her in silence for a moment. She had nearly completed the work. "Finish the binding, Naomi," said Joseph, "I know you have done it as a kindness." He sat down and placed a jar of ewe's milk beside the chair.

"Thank you, Joseph," said Hannah, taking up the milk. Even as she worked to arrange the supper, she was aware that Naomi finished the sword and gave it to Barnabas, who went out to lock it in the chest. He returned, and the atmosphere in the room relaxed. Soon Barnabas, with a mischievous sparkle in his eye, was telling a story about Horntheld, a farmer in the village.

Barnabas glanced around the room, trying to draw each one into the fun of his story. "Hannah makes plows that cut through any soil grain will grow in, and turn up big rocks like it was child's play," he said. Hannah blushed and hung her head at his praise. "But Horntheld said the plow she made for him broke when it hit a rock," he continued. "He refused to pay for it. I went to his field to see what the rock was like, and found out the truth. He plowed into a bedrock ledge that any fool would have known was there. His oxen made kindling out of the plow before he decided something was wrong. I got the money from him the day he hired miners with pickaxes to take that 'rock' out of his field."

The meal was ready with the story's ending. Barnabas cut slabs of roasted goat's meat onto thick pieces of brown bread for each of them. Joseph poured his fresh foamy ewes' milk into their wooden cups, and they sat down to eat. Barnabas said a simple prayer that would not, he hoped, contain anything Jonathan thought nonsensical. "God, you have given us all that we love and have and are. Help us be grateful for all your gifts, and continue to bless us whether in peace or in war. But we pray that it will be peace. Amen." Barnabas saw no sign of concern in Jonathan's face after the prayer. Joseph, however, looked troubled, and Barnabas thought the shepherd had moved suddenly – even shuddered – at his mention of war.

After they had eaten the bread with meat, Hannah brought out more brown loaves and a bowl of honey. The dark gold of the honey glowed in the firelight, and with the fresh bread and milk it seemed good enough for a king's table. When the meal was over, Joseph brought out a shepherd's pipe and Barnabas a fiddle, and they sang around the fire.

They began with harvest songs, and then sang a few that fit no occasion in particular, but were well loved. At last Joseph put away his pipe and Barnabas played alone while they all sang the song of Nirolad the Great, an ancient king of Karolan. The song told how Nirolad heard that the horde of Dradrag, warlord of the Zarnith, was coming from the wild desert of the south to invade Karolan. Nirolad mustered a small army and led his men far up into the valley of Petrag, which he believed led to the pass the Zarnith would use to come over the great mountains. They waited day after day for the Zarnith to swoop down on Karolan to pillage and burn, but they never came. Finally they learned that Dradrag had turned back and gone to raze the land of Cembar instead. The dreaded warlord had said, "The Mountains of Karolan turned back my host, before which all armies and nations tremble. Man can conquer man, but no man can conquer stone." When Nirolad heard this, he and all Karolan rejoiced, because they knew for the first time that they could never be attacked from the south: the mountains were impassible, even to the fearsome Zarnith.

The song of Nirolad was composed by an ancient bard of great skill. The words and music seemed to carry the essence of Karolan as nothing else could: the lovely land, the hardy, courageous people, and the incomparable peaks that guarded them. It ended with defiance of all would-be conquerors and an account of the glory of Karolan in the later years of Nirolad's reign. The music lingered in the cottage when the song was over, and in the comfortable silence the fire crackled softly. It was good to remember that Karolan had been threatened before, and that there had been no war and no defeat. But Norkath lay to the east, not the south.

Naomi stood in the silence. "May Jonathan and I go for a walk in the glen?" she asked. Joseph and Hannah smiled, and Barnabas got up to open the door for them.

As they were leaving, Joseph called after them, "Enjoy the stars and take care." They walked out into the dark evening. In their hearts they both laughed tolerantly at the warning. Take care? In Glen Carrah on an autumn night there was no harm or pain. The ground was soft, the wind cool, and the stars bright. There was no fear in earth or sky. Jonathan and Naomi walked together beneath the starry heavens, strong and free, with no discord or distrust between them. With each other and with their Glen they were safe.

They ran in the darkness. The wind and the grass rushed past them. Far up the glen away from the cottage they flopped on the grass and lay there breathing hard, sucking the cool sweet air into their lungs and blood, looking into the depths of the sky. The band of misty light that the Karolans call Ceranim, the Cloth of Stars, hung in the west and arched its soft glow down behind the snowy mountains in the south.

"So beautiful," said Naomi. "How can men think of war while such stars shine?"

Jonathan wondered too, for the night seemed a holy thing that could not be violated by death and violence. "Greed and lust of power," he said. "Fingar of Norkath will not look at the stars, but instead at the land, gold, and slaves that he could gain from Karolan. But he will fail as Dradrag and many others failed. We will stand."

Naomi thought of what Fingar wanted, and the luster of the stars dimmed. She could see Karolan in flames, its mines looted, its farms captured, and its people sold as slaves. Then she saw in her mind a band of men without a leader, standing between Karolan and such a fate. They seemed very weak and frail, and the lust and greed of Norkath rose in power to destroy them. One of them was Jonathan, and suddenly she saw war with Hannah's eyes and was afraid.

"What is adventure?" she said, wondering what was the good or joy that she or anyone else had ever seen in war.

"It is the good that comes when men and women go beyond their strength and yet endure, or hope beyond their doubt and are rewarded, or attempt the impossible and do not fail," said Jonathan. "Adventure means being safe from things that are not as wonderful or terrible as they ought to be."

"Perhaps it comes from absolute commitment," she said. "Is it the reward of those who are true at any cost? If you are willing to leave safety behind, perhaps you find that all your heart desires is ahead."

"I think it is not always like that," said Jonathan, thinking of the morning's conversation. "Something could be an adventure to me, and good, even if through it I lost all that my heart desires – as long as I myself stayed true."

"True to what?" asked Naomi.

"True to justice and honor."

"Why will you be true to justice and honor if you believe in utter loss?" asked Naomi. "Would you really choose to lose all that you love, if you could retain it by some small dishonorable or unjust action?"

"Yes," said Jonathan. "I would rather be true. I do not know why, but it is the foundation of my life. I love justice and honor, truth and beauty."

"And you may have to choose between being faithful at the cost of everything you love, and betraying your foundation – rejecting an adventure that justice or honor requires," said Naomi. "That is not where I draw the line in my life."

"Where do you draw it?" asked Jonathan.

"I draw it between ashes and stars, between dust and gold, between hatred and love," said Naomi. "I make my choice between horror and beauty, spite and honor, despair and joy, death and life, Hell and Heaven, Satan and God. It is an easy choice. The foundation of my life is the rock that upholds the whole world."

Jonathan considered this in the silence that followed, while the grass rustled softly and the thousand stars shone in the measureless sky. He loved her, and though he considered her faith foolish, he was awed by her boldness. What he took to be a fantasy, she had made the foundation of her life – and he knew her too well to think her commitment was only words. She would hold to it, at any cost. "Will you never have to choose between loss of what you love and denial of your faith?" he asked her.

"What I love best of all can never be lost," she said.

"I am not the one you love best of all?" he asked.

"No. Would you want me if, believing God to exist in all his glory, I loved you better than him?"

He answered her truthfully, "No. But why do you believe that he exists to claim such love? I would need to be very sure of his reality, before giving him my soul as you have done."

"Look up," whispered Naomi. "Is it not enough?"

"I see the stars," said Jonathan. "But to me they are only the glory of the world, not of God. Everything I love and delight in is the splendor, the beauty, the truth of the world. These things show me that life is wonderful and precious, but they do not show me that God must be real."

Her hand reached across the grass and found his in the darkness. "You will not always be blind," she said. "Someday you will see."

The confidence and power in her voice frightened him. She was sure he would fall into the hands of God – absolutely sure – and he did not want to. Yet even as he thought this he saw its folly. If her God were real, of course he would surrender to him – as she had said, there would be no other choice. But he was not real – there was no God into whose hands he might unwillingly fall. He also had a faith, and for him it was enough.

Naomi, for all her beauty and goodness, was foolish in her confidence.

Suddenly she released his hand, interrupting his thoughts, and got to her feet. "Someday," she said, and he could hear a smile in her voice. Instantly she was running again, swift in the starlight. He leaped up and followed her as fast as he could go, with the night air like a rushing wind in his face. She turned east to meet the Carratril, and raced up to the top of a rock outcrop that overlooked the stream.

They sat together on its summit. The water rushed and gurgled in the darkness far below. They could look down to the north and see the glen spread out below them, dim, gray, and lovely, fading in the distance into the rest of Karolan. Their village was a tiny cluster of warm lights, set on the dim earth that stretched out to where the horizon showed black against the starry sky. Their eyes followed the brilliant patterns of the stars up over the earth, and it seemed from their high viewpoint that Karolan was safely held beneath a canopy of sky and stars so big that they could not comprehend its vastness. A shooting star flashed like silent lightning, breaking up into fragments of golden light as it passed overhead.

"Of this you may be sure," said Jonathan to Naomi as they sat there, "I will always love you."

"I believe you," said Naomi, "but even if your love for me someday ends, my love for you will not." The air was almost still, with only the softest breath of wind. Their feet were bare, and the rough rock was good and solid beneath them. In the distant village a light went out of a window.

"If war comes, you will fight?" asked Naomi.

"Of course," said Jonathan, "for you, for Glen Carrah, for Karolan. I will fight, and my father will fight as well. There is nothing else we could justly do."

"If Karolan falls..." began Naomi.

"It will not fall," said Jonathan. "Our king is wise, and he will have prepared an army twenty thousand strong to meet Fingar when he comes."

"But if he dies..." Naomi began.

"Fingar will not come until he dies," said Jonathan, "and he will not die until his kingdom is ready for war."

"Jonathan, he cannot tell when he will die. And you do not know that we will stand. We will hope, we will pray, we will fight. But I fear we will fall."

Jonathan moved toward her and hugged her in his arms. "You did not fear that at supper tonight, Beloved. I truly believe that we can stand. But why are you speaking like this?"

"I..." She paused, searching for words to say something that was difficult for her. "I want to ask you something. If all the worst happens, but you are not killed – if our lives are shattered but not destroyed, will you look for me?"

Jonathan suddenly saw the world she was seeing. Karolan fallen, its army scattered, its countryside overrun by Norkath soldiers, everything in confusion. She wanted a promise that in such a world, he would seek for her and find her. And, now that he considered it, he longed for the same assurance from her. That their love would outlast the storm.

He knelt beside her on the rough rock. "Naomi," he said, "I promise, with all my heart and soul, that I will be true to you and find you. If I am alive, though all the world be in ruins, I will not rest till I have found you. Will you make the same promise to me?"

She saw herself searching a great battlefield, looking at the wounded and the dead, alone and forlorn on the site of Karolan's disaster, hoping against hope that she would find him alive. She shuddered. "I promise, before my God whom I trust for his help, that I will seek you and find you, my Jonathan." They embraced on the rock outcrop above the Carratril.

"Jonathan," said Naomi when they were again sitting side by side, "if my father will not fight for Karolan, will you hold it against him?" It was hard for her to ask this question, and she waited anxiously for his answer.

"You are his daughter," he said. "On this basis alone I would consider him a good man. But I consider him so on his own account as well. If he will not fight I will think that he is wrong. But I will not think less of him or honor him less because of that."

"Thank you," she said.

He looked back at the mountains. There was no haze in the night air, and he could see them with piercing clarity, their peaks outlined by the whiteness of eternal snow. They seemed more real now than they had in the misty dawn, but even more remote, more unfathomably huge. "Naomi," he said, "not all adventures are war. Do you long for other adventures?" She had before, he knew, but tonight she had a new perspective.

"Do you mean besides life?"

"I had not thought of life as an adventure,"

"If I have given all I have and am to God, and pledged to follow him completely, it cannot help but be a kind of adventure," said Naomi. "There is always something in it of attempting the impossible, of hoping beyond doubt and not being disappointed. God is kind and good and holy, but not predictable, not safe: I can never know what he may ask of me. And I must love and follow and hope, no matter what."

"Sometimes I long for something outside the life I have, even though it is very good," he said.

"Perhaps that means you are to have it," she said. "I think that in a way I want it too. But I do not seek it eagerly. Perhaps it is because tonight I think an adventure will not merely give you a chance to go beyond the life you have known and then return. I am afraid it will shatter your life and carry you off into completely unexpected things. You will be free, and everything will be new and exciting. But I do not want our life here to be shattered. When my faith is strong, I dare to say I want whatever God will give me. But I do not ask him for more than this Glen, this land, this life."

"I want more," said Jonathan. "I want to go high, high into those mountains, and see where Dradrag the Zarnith was turned back and Karolan was saved. I want to see other lands and other peoples. I want to fight for the rescue of Karolan, for the protection of Glen Carrah, and most of all, Beloved, for you. I want to do things I had not dreamed of doing, and see things I did not dream existed." The Carratril chattered in the darkness, as Jonathan paused. He continued in a different tone of voice. "But through all this, if it happens, I will love you, and return with joy to Glen Carrah, the most beautiful place in the world."

Naomi was a little frightened by his desire, and its intensity made her think it would be fulfilled. "Would you be content if none of this happened?"

"With you to love me? Naomi, do not imagine that any of this compares with my love for you. I will be content, and more than content – joyful beyond measure, in your love, and in living with you in Glen Carrah, if none of this happens."

"My heart tells me that some of it will happen, and I am afraid. It is as though this golden life were broken, and a hole into a howling darkness opened, and you rode through."

"If justice and honor call me through, would you have me remain back?"

"No. Of course I could not. But Jonathan..."

"What is it, Beloved?"

"It may be that there will come a time when you desire an adventure, when justice and honor do not call you to it. It may be that then I would desire to hold you back, believing God would not have you go."

"Are you afraid of such a time?" he asked.

"Yes."

"Is there any comfort I can give you, Beloved?"

"No... Wait – perhaps there is – yet it is much to ask."

"Ask it, Naomi, best loved in all the world!"

"I ask you to promise, that, if the time of which I spoke should ever come, and I see that justice and honor do not call you, you will listen to me and not go."

"Even if I think that justice and honor do call me?"

"It is not likely that we will disagree. But yes – even then."

There was a long silence while he considered. It was indeed much to ask. But he loved her deeply, and trusted her to the core of his soul. "To you, and you alone, I dare to make that promise," he said.

"Thank you, Beloved."

They sat for a while in silence, the night wind ruffling their hair, little knowing that their promises could affect the destiny of realms.

* * *

The fire burned low, and the candles on the table outshone it. To Joseph it seemed that he, Hannah, and Barnabas sat in a circle of warm light, while behind them was only darkness.

Barnabas had told him his reasons for believing that war was almost inevitable, and now in the silence all faces were grave. The shepherd felt sick, as though a nightmare had risen up to darken the waking world.

"War," he said, shaking his head. "I am no man for war. I herd sheep, I heal them and love them, and they supply my needs and my daughter's. I cannot strike with the sword. I could not face the hell of a time when those bearing the image of God set out to maim and kill one another on a battlefield. It would destroy me. I tell you, I cannot be a fighter. That is not the task I have been given to do, and I cannot even bear the thought that others may be given it." There was a silence as he looked at the other two. He felt like an animal, hemmed in by hunters and brought to bay. Yet these were his friends. Even in his distress he could see pity in their eyes.

"What of the defense of Karolan, and of Naomi, my friend?" asked Barnabas in a gentle voice. "Will you let other men defend them?" Joseph saw Hannah wince at the uncompromising words, but he knew the question was one he must face in the end. He sat still for a long moment, and then slowly lowered his face into his hands and groaned.

"How can I?" he whispered. "But how can I not?" A log snapped in the low fire, and fell into red coals. Joseph lifted his head from his hands. He looked first at Hannah, and then at Barnabas. "You are asking me to leave Naomi, and the glen, and go into Hell," he said quietly.

There was a long silence. Then they heard in the distance the sound of laughing voices, pure and clear and joyful, immeasurably far from Hell. A moment later Naomi and Jonathan came through the door, hand in hand, their faces flushed from running and their eyes bright with joy.

Joseph stood, looking at his daughter. Would he let other men defend her? He did not know, but in that moment it seemed to him better that the mountains should fall than that harm should come to her. He bade his friends farewell as quickly as courtesy permitted, and he and Naomi went out into the night. Barnabas clasped his hand in parting. "You are a brave man and a true one," said the blacksmith. "I do not ask you to do more than you see yourself called to. God be with you."

Joseph turned and spoke no word until he and Naomi reached their cottage. Then he simply wished Naomi a good night as she went into her room and closed the door. She noticed the low fire and the flowers by her bed. Then she lay down and smelled the fresh hay in her mattress. "Father..." she sighed as the warm sweet softness held her. "God, if ever any daughter was loved by her father, I am. Bless him with more blessings than he ever hoped for, and give him a deeper joy than he has ever known."

Chapter 4

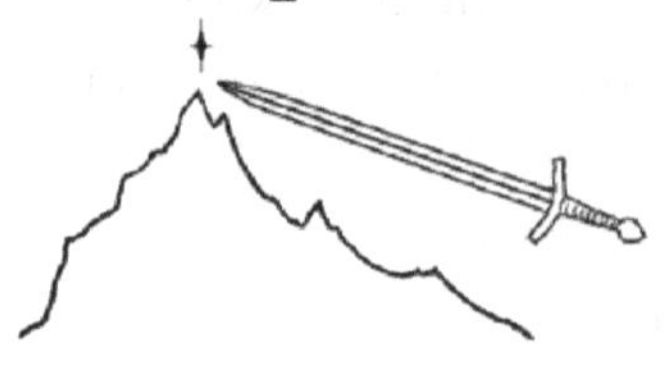

The Road to Glen Carrah

KING THOMAS HAD GIVEN A BANQUET IN HIS GREAT HALL at Aaronkal. Knights, stewards, bishops and ambassadors had feasted far into the night. Throughout, the king had sat regally at the head of the table and been a perfect host. Now he stood at the door of the hall, bidding his dinner guests goodnight as they bowed and departed. He nodded to the loyal knights of many towns of Karolan, and was just as courteous to those whose loyalty he did not trust. He received from the ambassador of Cembar the final assurance that no slaves were held there, and attentively listened for one last time as the ambassador of Norkath explained that nothing was further from King Fingar's mind than war with Karolan. At last they were all gone, and he was finished with listening to their lies or commending their truthfulness, and finished for the night with being to all of them the strong and wise king of Karolan. A servant closed the great doors, and held a torch to light the king to his bedchamber. He went there with a firm step, and with his head erect. He entered, and the door was shut behind him.

He waited for a moment and then sank onto his bed and lay against the pillows. He removed his crown, and set his royal robe aside. The iron faded out of his body, and the command faded out of his face. Had anyone looked in on him then, they would have seen an honest and faithful old man there on the pillows, but also one who was worn and weary and sick at heart. He looked at his bright crown, as it sat there on the table, and gave a long sigh. "How long, O Lord," he asked, "how long must I keep up the fight?"

His eyes strayed to the picture of Sarah up on the wall, a good likeness painted by a master artist. She was smiling, strong and cheerful. Her face was lined, but it was not old. She had never been old. "It was not thus when you were here," he said to her, "then it was not this bitter fight. O Sarah, Sarah, how long these years have been!" The candles flickered on his table, for his windows were flung open to the night. "Sometimes," he said, "I think there is no strength to carry on."

He turned, as if spoken to, to the small wood cross below the picture. "I know, Lord," he said, "You found it in Gethsemane. I know I will have it in the morning, and as many mornings as I need it. But you have prepared a place for me, and I long to go there, and find rest."

One candle blew out in a sudden gust of air, and the king started as he saw something sitting on the stone ledge of his window. It raised its broad brown wings and flew into the room to perch on his chair. "So it's you, Skykag," he said, "bringing good news I hope?" He reached out his hand and unwound a scrap of parchment from the great talons of the golden eagle. He read it carefully, holding it close to the candles. "Yes indeed," he said at last. "I commit him to your care. It is time for the great risk to be taken."

He rang a bell, and rose from his bed to put on the robe and crown again. He put forth the effort of his will to become again the strong king of Karolan. He brought a quill and a piece of parchment from his table, and wrote:

All is now completed.
He starts with the sunrise.
He is true – love him well.
Thomas of Karolan

A servant gave a low knock at the door, "You called, Your Majesty?"

"Yes. I require some meat for Skykag."

"Yes, Your Majesty."

He wound the parchment tightly around the eagle's foot, in place of the other one, and secured it with a bit of string. The servant brought some strips of meat on a silver dish, and Skykag devoured them hungrily. The king once again took off his royal robes and his crown, and sank into his bed. He took a long look at the majestic eagle, proud and beautiful, with eyes that reflected the candles in their dark depths. Then he blew out the candles and composed himself to sleep. The window framed the stars. The eagle sat preening himself for a few moments in the darkness, and then with a sound from his great wings and a brief black silhouette against the stars he was gone.

The old king sank into a peaceful slumber, and in his dreams he had no need to fight. He stood in a garden to the south of the mountains. Their snowy peaks showed above green leaves and bright flowers, and below a deep blue sky. More flowers spangled the sun-dappled grass at his feet, and birds sang in the trees. He looked up a green garden path and saw Sarah coming toward him, strong and smiling, bringing hope and strength with her. So she had always been.

*   *   *

A page came to wake Ilohan in the darkness before the dawn. "Your horses and provisions have been made ready, Sir," said the page.

"Thank you," said Ilohan, "I am awake now, and will depart soon." He went to the sill of his deep-set window and leaned out. There was no hint of dawn as yet. Far away to his left the Morning Star blazed with cold fire, a brilliant challenge in the dark sky. He remembered his need to choose a companion, but he now saw the decision was already made. If he had wanted Sir Benther, he would have had to ask him the night before. He could not wake his friend now and ask him to be ready for a weeks-long ride immediately, and he dared not delay the departure the king had arranged for him. He would ride for Glen Carrah and ask Jonathan; it was only partly out of his way. If Jonathan would not come, he would call at the castle of some trustworthy knight along his route, and ask for his company, or, failing that, the company of some loyal man from his household.

He clothed himself, and buckled on his sword in the darkness. He was a knight! This was the morning of his quest; he had been sent on an errand by his king. He took his helmet and shield from their places on the wall, and left his tower room without looking back or considering how much might happen before he returned there. He walked down torch-lit stairways and through silent halls. The guard at the doorway of the Great Hall raised his spear in salute as he passed. Then he was out in the cool night air, mounting his horse, with the black bulk of the castle behind him.

Suddenly he saw an old man standing beside the page who was holding his reins. He looked once, then twice, then realized it was King Thomas, without his royal robes or his crown. "Your Majesty..." he gasped as he dismounted again.

"I have come to see you off, my son," said King Thomas.

"But..."

"I know. You have not seen me like this before, and now I do not look like a king, but only like a weary old man."

"Sir..." said Ilohan, with a broken voice and tears forming in his eyes.

King Thomas grasped his arm with strength. "Take heart, my son," he said, "I am weary and I am worn, but I shall have strength and life enough! Now go, in the strength God has given you!"

Ilohan stumbled forward and embraced the old king, with his eyes overflowing. Here in this unforeseen and unequaled time he abandoned the practice of a lifetime. "Father," he said, "I love you."

"I know, my son," said the old king, smiling, "and I love you and always will. Now go! Farewell, and the blessing of God be upon you. You help me and Karolan more than you know. Farewell!"

Ilohan found himself riding away with no memory of the instant of parting. When his vision cleared and he looked back, Aaronkal was only a black silhouette across dew-silvered grass, far away beneath a cold moon that cared nothing for the earth. The mighty citadel of Karolan seemed as frail as the body of her king.

His eyes were dry now, and the sword at his side clinked with the walking of his horse. Beside him was a riderless animal, tied to his and ready to be the mount of whomever he chose to be his companion. He was a knight on his first quest.

He spurred his horse to a gallop. The other horse kept pace evenly: both were marvelously trained. The night air blew like a great wind in his face. Trees and dim gray fields flew past, glimpsed briefly between hedges. All was silent and still except for him and his horses, riding fast through a sleeping world.

Slowly, slowly as the wings of a newborn butterfly unfold, faint color crept into the gray world, and dawn washed over the sky. The Morning Star faded into a pinpoint of light against the blue. The world was bright with cold twilight colors: grass was green again, the road pale, the horses red-brown. Farmers led their cows out of the barn; shepherds went to their sheepfolds to see if all had passed safely through the night. Birds sang. Warmth leaped into the world as the east horizon glowed red. Men looked up with hope, their faces catching the rosy glow. Then the sun rose like a trumpet call and the world was awake. For a moment it lit the land with warmth and freshness so that it seemed all was recreated and Eden lived again, and then full daylight came. Paradise was lost, but promise remained. Children laughed in the little villages, blacksmiths got out their hammers, maids milked their cows, and Ilohan slowed his horses to a trot.

It was a long bright day. He traveled through Karolan, the land he loved, first the fertile lowlands around Aaronkal, and then fair hills where pastures, farms, and woodlands alternated. When evening came he found himself in a less inhabited part of the country, where the soil was poorer and farms were difficult to keep. He passed a castle of light gray stone, strong and great, but poorly kept, with the rusted drawbridge down and a few cows drinking from the shallow moat. From the top flew the flag of Karolan with the seal of the Knight of Metherka. Metherka was young, Ilohan remembered, and the king did not trust him – though he had spoken highly of old Metherka, the current knight's father.

Farther on Ilohan passed a few poor farms cleared from the dense forest. He noticed up ahead what he thought was another, but the ground looked black and strange in the twilight. As he got closer he realized it had been burned. The little farmhouse was a pile of charred wood and the crop was ashes. Bandits, he supposed. His heart went out to the family who, even if they had escaped with their lives, must have lost everything.

Suddenly there was another mounted knight in the road. He had appeared from behind the trees by the burnt farm, riding quickly into the road to block the path. He raised his spear in salute, and spoke. "Hail, Sir Ilohan. Well come. I have had to ride hard all day to catch you."

"Sir Benther?" asked Ilohan incredulously.

"Yes indeed, my friend. You left before I could bid you farewell."

"I thank you for your courtesy. But, friend, surely you have not ridden all day to say farewell?"

Benther's courtly manner faded, and he spoke earnestly, "Ilohan, you have been my friend ever since we were children together at Aaronkal. You were knighted and I rejoiced with you. Then the king sent you on a mission and commanded that you choose one trustworthy companion, and you left before I even knew you were going. Is this the treatment my friendship has deserved? I have come here to ask you to take me with you."

Ilohan sat silent for a moment, his weary horse motionless beneath him. The riderless horse stood nearby, a silent witness to the king's command. At last he spoke, choosing his words with difficulty, "Benther, you are a true friend to me, and I did not mean to keep from you the knowledge of my quest. And I am sorry also that I have not chosen you as my companion. Please believe me when I tell you that I love you as a true friend, and always will. You are a brave and true knight. It is not for lack of friendship or confidence in you that I have chosen another. Please believe these things of me, and believe that I have a reason for my action. I ask you to bid me farewell in undiminished friendship."

The other knight's expression was hard to see in the failing light, but as Ilohan watched anxiously it seemed to him that his friend was tormented between two conflicting desires. Then he turned his horse abruptly and rode away, and Ilohan was not sure of what he had seen. Benther stopped and turned when he reached the middle of the burned field. He spoke coldly. "Sir Ilohan," he said, "you have insulted me. I will not permit you to go on your way unless you take me as your companion. If you will not accept this we must decide the issue by jousting."

Ilohan was shocked. "Sir Benther, in saying this you make yourself seem unworthy to receive what you ask. Will you hinder the king's messenger to serve your own ends? My friend, you are better than this. Bid me farewell and turn back to Aaronkal, I pray you. I must ride on my way."

"Ride on your way and I will block the path. If you will refuse me, you must conquer me."

"Sir Benther, what has come over you? What you are doing is not just, it is not knightly – it is not even in accord with the Code. Come to your senses, and do what you will not regret."

"Dare you accuse me of breaking the Code? All I have done I had need to do. Now come; you must unhorse me or be unhorsed yourself. Are you ready?"

Ilohan was desperate as he saw Benther out in the field preparing to charge. "Benther, there is no guard on my spear!"

"Then come at me with your naked point; I dare you! You must, or be unhorsed as you stand."

"My friend, you give me no choice but to fight you. Alas! In the king's name, then!" Ilohan lowered his sharp spear, designed to kill, not blunted for friendly combat. He released the riderless horse, put his shield into position, and charged across the barren field. He almost dropped his spear as he realized with anguish that the enemy bearing down on him was his long trusted friend. Thoughts rushed through his mind in the last moment: he had jousted with Benther many times and had usually lost; he must not lose now, but how could he bear it if he won? His spear was still leveled when the awful moment of impact came.

There was a terrific crash and his shield was ripped away from his grasp with a blow that wrenched his arm and bruised him. He was flung back in the saddle as his spear took an impact that snapped off the point. Then suddenly all was quiet. He was still mounted. His horse had stumbled to a halt, and close ahead of him was the edge of the woods that bounded the little field. He turned his horse, and saw Benther's charger standing in the field, the saddle empty. On the ground he saw his own shield, Benther's spear, and the body of his friend, lying still beneath his shield on the ash.

In an instant Ilohan was kneeling at his side, taking off his helmet and peering anxiously into his face. To his great relief he could see no blood, and Benther stirred abruptly and sat up. At first his breath came in painful gasps, but soon he was breathing more easily and seemed to have escaped serious harm. "I'm terribly sorry, my friend," said Ilohan. Benther looked into his face with pain and confusion.

"I... I don't know," he said. "I didn't want to. I... I'm sorry, Ilohan. It's all... all perplexed and horrible. Nothing is good in the world anymore." He stood up heavily. "You need not think you have injured me; I am as sane and well as I had any hope of being." He mounted his horse with some difficulty. "Happiness and understanding left me many days ago," he said. "See if you can find it in your heart to forgive me. I wish I knew. Farewell." Ilohan stood stunned as he rode away. At the edge of the field Benther raised his voice in an anguished cry, "Forgive me!"

"I forgive you! Have hope, friend!" Ilohan called loudly, with as much assurance and strength as he could muster.

The night was late by the time Ilohan reached a small village with an inn. He dismounted and knocked at the door. A wizened old innkeeper opened the door for him, and, obviously impressed with his two great horses and his knight's shield and sword, provided him and his animals with everything he could desire. As he ate alone, the fight with Benther passed through his mind again and again, and still he could not understand it. What had driven Benther to such a strange betrayal of friendship? Could it be only hurt pride at not being chosen? Ilohan himself was hurt and angered by his friend's betrayal, but he also pitied him. He worried that his own strange choice of Jonathan as his companion was wrong: if he had chosen Benther back in Aaronkal, none of this would have happened.

Before he was any closer to understanding, he became too tired to wonder anymore. When the bright crescent moon rose he was deeply asleep on his hay mattress, dreaming of the old times when Queen Sarah held him in her arms and all the world was safe. He had known that danger existed then, somehow, but as he leaned his child's body against the woman who was mother to him, he had believed that it would never touch him, but only pass by in the night.

Ilohan awoke with the sun shining brightly through the wooden shutters of his window. Memory of the previous day returned to him, and with the thought of Benther came a deep uneasiness. Then, as he flung the shutters wide to the bright day, he almost laughed at his confusion. He understood nothing – his whole journey, if not his life, was one great mystery. But his life belonged to God, and he was fulfilling the errand of the king. That was all that mattered. The innkeeper gave him a good breakfast, and he rode off with a hopeful heart.

He rode through forested, rolling hills, watered by creeks that splashed and swirled through banks of green moss and fern. Many times the feet of his two horses beat a hollow rhythm on wood bridges as he passed. The land was very different from the flatter country that he knew around Aaronkal, and it was beautiful. Farmers here might find the soil too poor for grain, but the trees flourished. Some of enormous girth grew beside the streams, the water swirling around great, thirsty roots. Ilohan wondered how old they were – whether some had already been tall when Nirolad the Great went out to fight the Zarnith. As afternoon wore on, the path began to tend upward, and the trees became sparser. He was coming to the windswept prairie land that washed its waves of shining grass against the foothills of the great mountains.

He reached it when the sun was sinking in the west, ahead and to his right. The grass shimmered in the wind and the light, and his strong horses picked up their pace. The stone road dwindled away to one of dirt, covered with drying grass stems. It was kind to the horses' feet, and made Ilohan feel that he was riding like the wind through a world at once bright, soft, and wild – as beautiful as a lovely dream, but piercingly real. He startled a herd of deer resting beside the path, and they leaped away through the grass as if winged, with the sunlight gleaming on their antlers.

Chapter 5

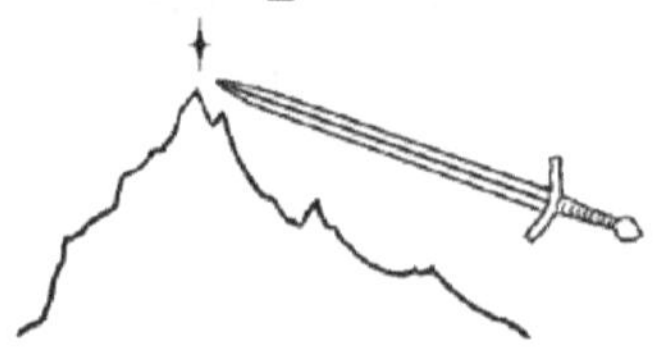

The Knight and the Shepherdess

JOSEPH AND NAOMI SAT ON THE FLOOR OF NAOMI'S bedroom, leaning their backs against her newly filled mattress. The sheep were in the fold, and they had had their supper. The fire burned quietly before them, warming their outstretched feet. "May you tell me what you and Jonathan spoke of last night, my daughter?" asked Joseph.

"Yes, Father. We talked of adventure, and of faith, and," she hesitated an instant, "and of war."

He had thought long of war in the warm clean day out in the pasture, so he did not shudder at the word. Neither did he wish to speak of it. "What does Jonathan think of adventure?" he asked.

"He says it very well; I will not repeat it quite the same. He says adventure is the surety of all things being either as terrible or as wonderful as they should be. To him it is the turning away from known safety for some good cause, the enduring and challenging of something hard and worthy. He seems to think there could be good in it, even if it destroys him."

"Do you think differently, Naomi?" he asked.

"Only in two ways. I think, because of my faith that he does not share, that my life with God will always have something in it of adventure. He thinks of adventure only as something beyond his present life."

"What is the second difference?"

"He desires an adventure beyond the life he knows. I have before, but now I am afraid. I am happy with our lives as they are."

"You mean that you are content with the adventure of the life you have known, and you do not want to look outside it for another?"

"Yes."

"What if you must go outside the life you know; what if God places in your hand an adventure whether you want it or not? Could you accept it with trust?"

There was a silence. Naomi took a deep breath and released it. Then she spoke slowly. "Knowing that my life is God's, I can trust him for all that comes into it. If I thought that I could have an adventure that would only take me out of what I have known for a while, and then bring me back, I could accept it with joy. But the adventure that I imagine will shatter this life, and never return me to it." She was silent for a little while, as was he. When she spoke again, it was as one making a solemn vow. "If that adventure comes, I will accept it with trust. I cannot say I will accept it with joy, but I will accept it with trust. And with hope. Alas for this golden life! I fear there comes an adventure that will break it."

"That is the kind of adventure you foresee?" asked Joseph.

Her whole form stiffened, and she turned toward him with eyes full of pain. "A shattering kind? Yes."

He passed his hand gently over her forehead as though she were a child. She relaxed at his touch, but all he could do in words was tell her she was not alone in her fear. "I also foresee that, my daughter," he said.

*　　　　*　　　　*

A blue-white lightning bolt blasted across the open sky down in the prairie land of Karolan. The jagged tendrils of dazzling light glowed in Ilohan's sight after the lightning faded, and the thunder seemed to echo off the clouds. He got up with a jump, in no mood to admire the thunderstorm that had waked him. He folded his blankets, stuffed them into his saddle bags, and put on a hooded cloak that offered some protection from the rain.

He waited for a while, leaning against the lonely tree where he had tied the horses. The rain came down in sheets, blown by the strong prairie wind. The black sky bore no hint of dawn, and since he had awakened from a sound sleep, he had no idea how much of the night was left. Finally he mounted his dripping horse, and set out across the windblown grassland.

It was a miserable night, more like early winter than autumn. Now and then he dismounted and ran beside the horses for warmth. He passed through the village of Tremilin, with its small castle surrounded by sleeping houses, but it might have been a town of ghosts for all he saw. He passed its church and bell tower, fabled in the poetry of Karolan as the most beautiful in the world, without a second look.

Gray dawn came at last, but it remained a wet and misty day, and even at noon he did not take off his cloak or cease occasionally running beside the horses to get warm. Early in the afternoon he reached the end of the prairie lands and began to climb steeply into a range of hills. Twisted oaks bounded the path on both sides as it ascended in long switchbacks. The grassland below vanished in the fog, and soon a few hundred feet of steep hillside composed Ilohan's entire visible world. He found it a strange, disorienting experience: as if he and a small, ever shifting sphere of oak trees and sloping rock were all that mattered, hung in a mist-bounded bubble above a world that no longer concerned them.

The path stopped climbing and began to run west along the high ridges of the foothills. Soon he reached a part of the ridge where the trees and bushes were sparser, and lush grass grew between them: the soil was better here. The gray wall of the castle of Kitherin loomed out of the mist in front of him, but a cheery light shone from a tower window, and a guard called out a hearty greeting from the parapet as he passed. The mist-blurred lights of a large village glowed on the hillside beneath the castle, warm and homely in the darkening fog.

He rode on for a long time, as the foggy twilight deepened. He began to wonder if he had missed Glen Carrah in the fog. It seemed possible. He was tired and cold, and made up his mind to seek a night's lodging at the next human habitation he found, rather than camping in the foggy foothills with wet blankets.

It was already almost dark when he noticed a warm glow in the mist ahead, and came upon a well built cottage, with a lighted window thrown open upon the road. Ilohan knocked, and the door was opened. The face of the man who opened it was weatherbeaten and gentle, but there was something compelling in his brown eyes – truthfulness, perhaps – or a love unusually free from greed. Ilohan found it hard to look away. "I – I seek a place to stay the night," he stammered.

"I am Joseph, a shepherd," the man replied. "Come in and be warm; you are welcome. I will take your horses."

Ilohan stepped gratefully into the firelit room, and Joseph took his horses. The knight stood in front of the fire, his wet clothes steaming. Returning, the shepherd helped him off with his wet cloak with a slightly awkward courtesy, bade him sit down, and handed him a wooden mug full of warm ewe's milk from a pot simmering over the fire. Ilohan drank it gratefully, and thanked the shepherd formally after the manner of a guest in the Great Hall at Aaronkal.

Joseph thought about his guest while he drank. He was very young to be a knight, and knights seldom came to remote villages like Carrah. After a long silence, he asked the knight what brought him to Glen Carrah.

"This is Glen Carrah, then!" said Ilohan. "I thought I had passed it in the fog."

"No, you have reached the glen," said Joseph. "It begins a short walk from here; we are nearly at its foot."

"I am looking for Jonathan, son of Barnabas the blacksmith."

"He lives in the next cottage to the west. He and his father are hard at work making swords for the king. Is your business with him connected with that?"

Ilohan answered slowly after a pause. "No. I have come for... another reason."

"Your reasons are your own, Sir Knight," said Joseph, "but if this one may be told I should like to know it. I am no stranger to Jonathan the blacksmith." In the silence that followed Joseph could hear singing coming faintly from the direction of the Glen, but if the young knight noticed he made no sign.

"I have an errand from the king," said Ilohan at last. "I wish to ask Jonathan for his company."

"An errand from the king!" exclaimed Joseph. "And Jonathan to accompany you!" He paused a moment. "Once again, Sir, your counsel is your own. Yet I should like to know why you have chosen Jonathan and come so far from Aaronkal to find him."

"I met him only once, and that time he beat me fairly in a friendly fencing match. He seemed to me absolutely trustworthy, as well as strong and skilled in swordplay. He told me that he longed for adventure, longed to see distant lands. Yet these are not the real reason."

Joseph's next question hung implicit in the silence.

Ilohan wondered how he could answer that question. The real reason was what had happened to him during his vigil in the chapel. Had that been a dream? A vision? A delusion that had made him waste three days' journey? "In darkness," he said slowly, "I think God put his name in my mind."

He had scarcely finished speaking when the door toward the Glen opened to admit the shepherd's daughter. Her brown hair was running wet behind her, and her clothes dripped water on the floor. Yet even now, as she came in laughing from the brisk evening outside, she was beautiful. Ilohan had seen many court ladies in their fine clothes, and he had thought some of them very lovely. But Naomi of Glen Carrah seemed so richly alive and happy that in that moment he thought he had never seen anyone more beautiful.

"The sheep will have a good washing with all this rain, Father," she said. "I had to watch them closely to see that none wandered in the mist." Then she noticed the stranger. Ilohan saw her free, happy movements stop almost as if she were frozen. She studied him for a long moment. "Have you come to find Jonathan?" she asked at last. "Do you want to take him away with you?"

"Yes, my Lady," he replied, startled that she had guessed his unlikely purpose.

"Oh," she said, sitting down suddenly on a wooden chair. "He will go." The laughter left her face. She stared with sober concentration at the floor. Her hair hung long and damp behind her, and Ilohan no longer thought her more beautiful than any other. He drank his ewe's milk silently, and knew that she loved Jonathan well. At length she spoke again, earnestly, looking into his face with such intensity that he turned away and gazed into the fire.

"Sir Knight," said Naomi, "I love Jonathan. I cannot with a calm heart see him depart without knowing the reason. Please tell me of your errand."

"Lady," said Ilohan, "this is but the fourth day that I have been a Knight of Karolan. As soon as I was knighted, King Thomas sent me on a quest, without revealing to me more than a little about its nature. I am commanded to go to Lake Luciyr, in the eastern part of the Mountains of Karolan, and make a thorough search all around the lake for some traces of a group of people who died there many years ago. I am to try to determine whether they died by execution, or in battle. After this I am commanded to continue on to the south side of the mountains, to the village called Harevan, where I am to be a guest at the house whose garden contains the most flowers. After some days there I am to return with all speed to Aaronkal, and report to the king all that I have found. The king bade me choose a loyal companion, and I searched my heart and found there was no one with whom I would rather dare such a journey than your beloved, Jonathan of Glen Carrah, the only blacksmith I have ever known who beat a squire at swordplay."

Naomi smiled at the praise of Jonathan. "Truly," she said, "you will find no one more worthy of your trust than Jonathan, and you will find few his equal in strength or skill. But it still surprises me that you should choose him. You must know many fellow knights who would have accompanied you."

"I have had little to recommend their faithfulness to me of late, my Lady," said Ilohan.

"Forgive the question of Jonathan's beloved," said Naomi, "but who are you and who are your people?" Ilohan heard the old shepherd's breath catch suddenly in shock at his daughter's boldness, but she did not seem aware of it. The intensity of her love was written plainly in her face, and Ilohan was not offended.

"I regret that I can give you but a poor answer," he said. "The utmost extent of my memory does not reach before the time when King Thomas and Queen Sarah took me in as their ward. I know nothing of my parents. I was found as a child too young to speak, the only one left alive of a group of knights and ladies who were overcome and slaughtered by bandits. The king and queen gave me every gift that parents' honest love can, preserving only such formality as was needful between their Majesties and my humbler station. They gave me my name: Ilohan. Now I am the least of the Knights of Karolan, an honor toward which I have labored since my seventh year. I hope by the blessing of God, and the help of Christ my Savior, to prove worthy of the honor, and true to the Code."

"It is enough for Naomi of Carrah, Sir Ilohan," said Naomi, "and may the blessing of God rest with power on your journey. I grieve to see my beloved depart, but you are worthy to be his companion. I will not dissuade him from accompanying you."

Now Ilohan was taken aback – by the calm confidence in her voice, as much as by her words. "I have been on trial these last moments!" he exclaimed. "You would have dissuaded Jonathan from joining me had my answers not satisfied you! Is it proper for a shepherdess to try one knighted by the king?"

"Judge for yourself what is proper, Sir Knight," she said. "Power may be used for good and faithful purposes – even if it is the power of a shepherdess's request over that of a knight."

"I ask your forgiveness, my Lady," said Ilohan, "my speech was ill considered. Indeed, perhaps I should feel honored to have been found worthy in the court of Naomi the shepherdess."

"I forgive you freely," said Naomi, "and I ask permission to tell Jonathan of your invitation."

"I grant it with thanks," said Ilohan.

Naomi stood. Her thoughts were in turmoil, and she was anxious to escape before she showed it. "Daughter," said Joseph as she reached the door, "please tell Barnabas and Hannah that we will be honored to have their company and Jonathan's at supper tonight."

"Gladly, Father," she said, and flinging open the door she ran into the night.

As her eyes adapted to the dimness, she saw that the fog had lifted. The last remnants of blue twilight glowed through rents in the clouds. Her clothes, which had begun to dry out before the fire, were soaked again as she ran through the wet grass. She shivered, but ran on: accustomed to being out in the cold, she knew that running would bring warmth soon enough. When the warmth came she slowed to a brisk walk.

But Naomi did not go to the home of Barnabas and Hannah. She went far up into the glen, crossing the Carratril by jumping from rock to rock, as she and Jonathan often did. She knew her errand did not admit much delay, but she desperately wanted to seek a lonely place, and to spend at least a little time there. She sat down in the gloom beneath two huge boulders by the Carratril, and put her head between her knees. Even Joseph, who knew and loved her so well, had not guessed the depth of her sorrow. She closed her eyes and let the strong gusts of wind press against her, like the caresses of Glen Carrah trying to comfort its child. She was glad of this lonely place, where none could see her grief.

"What are you grieving for?" she asked herself angrily. "It is a short errand, likely to be an easy one; Jonathan will return safe and soon, having had but a taste of adventure. The howling darkness that you feared – what is there of that in the errand Sir Ilohan described? It is a simple quest, a simple quest..."

The cold of the rock behind her sank through her wet clothes, and the comfort she had gained by running began to depart. She welcomed physical discomfort as a fit companion for her sorrow, which was not eased by her arguments and self criticisms.

She raised her head and looked into the dimness of the rock face in front of her. "Alas," she said, "all the reasons in the world avail me nothing when my heart tells me they are false. This is no light and trivial mission for a young knight. This is surrounded by secrecy, and has greater weight than it appears. An armed knight of Karolan does not need a faithful companion for an easy errand, and my heart's foreboding will not prove false. Oh Jonathan, Jonathan, would I could justly dissuade you! If you venture out of the life you have known, who can say if you will ever return to it?"

She shivered and coughed in the cold darkness. The wind hissed around the rocks and sighed in the wet grass. "At last I will do what I should have done first," she said.

"Father," she prayed, and paused. The single word was a comfort to her, implying that God loved her as Joseph did. "Father, you know the stars by name and you keep the souls of those who love you. You know my fears for Jonathan, my love.

I pray these may prove false, as doubtless such forebodings have before. Please guard Jonathan, and keep him, and return him to me in joy and safety. Have mercy on your people in Karolan, and preserve us from invasion by Norkath, and from the war that threatens us. Do not take from us the blessed life that you have given, but let us praise and thank you for it all our days. Oh, Father, save my beloved! Bless him and shield him, be his Guard and Helper day and night. Do not let evil befall him." She spoke the last words with great fervor, bringing herself almost to tears, which were rare with her. After that she was silent for a long moment. Her grief was eased, but the cold sank deeper into her bones. At last she spoke again.

"Father, you have loved me though I deserved no love, and saved me though I deserved not salvation. Thus I dare to ask yet mercy upon mercy. Oh Father, because of your great love, for the praise of your endless grace, open the eyes of Jonathan my beloved. Break the blindness and pride that hold him back. Make him see you in your glory; let him come to know your love. Let there be between him and me, and him and you, no longer any barrier. Do not let him perish by scorning your gift!" The last sentence was a fervent cry, blown away on the wind. With the failing of its echoes Naomi was on her feet again, running haltingly across the glen, stiff from sitting still in the cold.

She took an indirect route to the cottage, a long curve down through the wet glen, so that before she arrived she was running evenly, and was warm again. The wind and rain had washed the traces of tears from her eyes.

"My father and I would be honored by your company at supper," she said breathlessly to Hannah and Barnabas when she entered, "and... and I would speak with Jonathan alone."

Before they had a chance to reply, Jonathan himself came in from the forge. The look on his face told her he had seen her run up, and had come in to see what was amiss. Her plans to speak privately disintegrated, for she found she could not bear to let him wonder even for a moment what she had to tell him.

"Jonathan," she said, still out of breath from running, "I bring you good news. The adventure that you longed for has come to you – a knight asks your company on a quest. His name is Sir Ilohan; he sought shelter in our home an hour ago, and you all are invited there for supper."

Jonathan heard her words, and understood them. Joy kindled within him, slowly, like golden sunshine that brightens on the land at the breaking of clouds. His mind filled with visions of adventure, of valiant fights, of unimagined places and great challenges dared with boundless courage. What he had dreamed of but scarcely hoped to have was his. He felt like leaping up and shouting for joy. Ilohan, the squire he had once beaten in a fencing match, had remembered his strength and come back as a knight to ask his aid. He would serve him well, better than well. He would be a faithful companion; his help would never be lacking if he could give it. Who knew what great things might befall them? He strode rapidly across the cottage to his mother's work bench and put his hand on its rough wood, as if to assure himself that it was there and that this moment was really a part of his life. Then he turned and looked back at Naomi.

She stood where she had been standing when she told him the news, beside the door facing him. She had not moved. He missed something of the joyful freedom that was usually apparent in her demeanor at a glance. Then he looked into her eyes.

Her pain was written in them: darker than Jonathan had ever seen them, loving but not laughing, barren of the stars that he had never before seen extinguished. She would have hidden her pain if she could, that he might feel free to take the adventure that was offered to him – but what she had hidden from her father for a moment, she could not hide from her beloved.

For a long moment stillness and silence reigned in the little cottage. Naomi's sodden clothes dripped on the floor. The puddles glistened in the firelight. Above the muffled patter of rain on thatch Jonathan could hear the furious sizzle of drops hitting the glowing forge outside. His gaze moved slowly around the familiar room, and came to rest on his parents. Them, too, he would leave behind if he took the knight's offer. Could he leave his father to make the twelve swords alone? Did he truly desire to leave everyone he had ever loved and go away to follow a dream?

Suddenly Naomi coughed and shivered, and the spell was broken. Hannah, angry at herself for not acting earlier, was instantly at her side taking off her sodden cloak. "Why, child, you must be freezing cold. Come in by the fire and I will get you something dry to wear. And of course we will dine with you and your father tonight." Hannah led Naomi into the room where she and Barnabas slept, where another fire was burning in a smaller fireplace. Motioning the shepherdess to sit on the bed, she quickly removed her wet clothes and gave her others that had lain on a bench before the fire.

Naomi was grateful for Hannah's warm, dry clothes. She knew how to keep herself warm and well through long wet days in the pasture, rejecting the leather cloaks Joseph sometimes wished she would wear, but tonight sorrow had made her cold. "You have been very brave tonight, child," murmured Hannah as she put a cloak around her shoulders, "you have called a thing that grieved you good news, that you might not hinder your beloved from following his desire. You have shown courage and love." Hannah smiled sadly, "Soon I must do the same. Is he a trustworthy man, this Sir Ilohan?"

"Yes," said Naomi softly, "I tried him with questions, and he is trustworthy indeed. So I have no cause... no cause to hold Jonathan back."

In the kitchen Barnabas and Jonathan also spoke together, as they sat on either side of the hearth. Barnabas saw his son's eagerness – and his doubt. "For many years you have hoped for this, Jonathan," he said.

"Yet now that it comes, can I rightly accept it?" asked Jonathan. "Is there after all any reason for my desire?"

"Wanting your courage tried and proven is no evil thing, Jonathan," said Barnabas. "Nor is helping one who comes to ask you for your aid."

"You consider that I am free to go, then?"

"Consider in your own heart what is the right choice," said Barnabas. "Where do you think duty calls you? I have done harder things than making twelve swords in a month, and your mother has borne greater sorrows than watching her only son ride away on a quest."

"Naomi has faced no greater pain than she feels now, at telling me that I may leave her," said Jonathan.

"The decision must be yours alone, my son. The pain will not only be Naomi's. But a love that costs the lover nothing is hardly worthy of the name. If the pain runs deep, the love that accepts it runs deeper still."

"I am glad I am your son, Father."

"And I am glad I am your father."

Jonathan rose, and went to his bedroom.

Barnabas stared into the glowing heart of the fire, until his eyes stopped seeing it and made strange shapes and images lit by a rich warm light. "Father," he said, "let what I said be what I should have said."

A moment later Jonathan returned wearing dry clothes in place of the damp ones that had seen the hard day's work before the steaming forge. Naomi and Hannah emerged from the other room dressed in leather cloaks, and soon they were all walking the wet road toward Joseph's cottage. They arrived just as the shepherd was setting out his bread, honey and milk on the table before the fire.

Ilohan looked up to see them enter. He had been sitting on the hearth, fighting to keep himself from sinking into a warm slumber, but as he stood to greet the man he had come to find he woke up a little. Jonathan seemed even stronger and more full of life than he remembered.

Ilohan was hungry enough to eat the simple food gladly, and he noticed the others, too, had little time for conversation at first. Then Jonathan looked up with a twinkle in his eyes. "Have you yet found any place more beautiful than Glen Carrah, Sir Ilohan?" he asked.

"Did we not cross swords at our last meeting, because I would not agree there could be no such place?" asked Ilohan. "And you conquered me, but did not change my mind – for until we have seen the whole world, how can we know?"

"Ah," said Jonathan, still smiling, "we can only look, and listen to our hearts, and – if need be – draw our swords. Shall I challenge you again? But now that you are indeed a knight, I could never conquer you."

Ilohan laughed, but wondered: would he defeat Jonathan if they fought again? He had gained in skill and strength, but so, he suspected, had the blacksmith.

"Fighting about the beauty of a glen," said Joseph, shaking his head and smiling. Then his face suddenly darkened. "May the Knights of Karolan never have more to fight about."

"If it is a civil war, infighting about the royal succession, that you fear," said Ilohan, "I would say there is little chance of it."

"No," said Barnabas, "let us hope there is honor and loyalty enough in Karolan to prevent that. But in every village in Karolan they are saying war with Norkath threatens."

"Then the villagers know more than at least one of the knights of the realm," said Ilohan. "We are at peace with Norkath. What makes you think war threatens?"

"Your training must have been hard, with no leisure to gossip with villagers," said Barnabas, "but it is strange that none in Aaronkal informed you of this. Twenty years ago the pride of Karolan, Prince Kindrach son of Thomas, vanished under suspicious circumstances near the border with Norkath. King Fingar of Norkath claimed that he had been captured by a Norkath raiding party, and under threat of death abdicated his royal position to Fingar. He was then executed. Fingar claims that he has the right to succeed King Thomas as ruler of Karolan."

Ilohan was stunned. One of the questions of his vigil was thus answered. He knew now the half rumored fear that placed its uneasy mark on man, woman, and child in Karolan. Why had he not been told before? He could not believe evil of King Thomas, but he suddenly wondered if for some reason the king had intentionally kept him ignorant of recent history. But perhaps it was only that in Aaronkal none dared repeat rumors that hinted of dishonor to the king's dead son. Ilohan's thought returned to the news itself. "So Fingar claims that the prince of Karolan, under threat of death, abdicated to him – and even after that Fingar executed him," he said. "Is he brazen enough to hold that as lawful claim to the throne of Karolan?"

"What has the Code of the Knights of Karolan to say of a promise made under threat of death?" asked Barnabas in a level voice. His face was stern, with a hint of reproach.

The young knight bowed his head. "I am corrected," he said. "It is true that the word of a Knight of Karolan must be kept, even if given under threat of death. Yet still Fingar's own story makes him a knave: murdering the prince even after he had abdicated."

"Of that there can be no doubt," said Barnabas. "Fingar of Norkath is a knave. And yet in his story of Prince Kindrach's death he has a fearful weapon. He can stir his own troops into fury with the cry that they fight in a righteous cause, while at the same time he will call the defenders of Karolan traitors to Prince Kindrach's pledge."

Then Hannah spoke, low and clear. "The prince would have died a thousand times rather than give Karolan to Fingar. Fingar is a liar, and the fear he casts over Karolan is founded on a lie. None who knew the prince could doubt him thus."

"Even so, may not the best of men sometimes falter?" asked Ilohan.

"You speak truth without experience," said Joseph, surprising Ilohan by his sudden entry into the conversation, "a man may never say he is above failing. But when the proven faithfulness of a life has burned bright and strong for many years, you may suspect the rivers of flowing upward before you expect that flame to go out."

"I am sorry," said Ilohan, who felt foolish at this second time he had been contradicted in a short conversation. Peasant inhabitants of a remote village these people might be, but they were far from ignorant.

"Do not be sorry," said Barnabas. "It is not wrong to test with skepticism the rightness of a cause, before committing twenty thousand lives toward its success. But that is the king's decision, and he seems already to have made it."

"What do you mean?" asked Ilohan.

"King Thomas is filling the armories of Aaronkal with weapons," said Barnabas. "In the last year I myself have made for him almost two score swords. He must have thousands of them at Aaronkal by this time, as well as countless bows and arrows and other weapons. He is preparing for a war as terrible as any Karolan has ever known."

There was a long silence. Ilohan could not doubt the blacksmith's words. He seemed implicitly trustworthy, and must have had many chances to question messengers from the armories of Aaronkal, as well as other craftsmen who were making weapons for the king. The threat seemed very heavy to the young knight, and he wondered what part his own mission had in the king's preparations for war.

"Jonathan," he said at last, "whatever threat lies on the land, I must carry out the quest on which the king has sent me. He bade me choose one companion, and there is none I would rather have than you. Will you come with me?"

"If I do," said Jonathan, "I hope I will prove worthy of your trust. What can you tell me of your mission?"

"I must journey to a lake called Luciyr, far to the east in the great mountains. I will search around the lake carefully for any trace of a group of people who died there long ago, and I will try to determine if they were executed or defeated in battle. If I can find any tokens of their fate, I will carry them away. After that I must go over the mountains, which are low enough to be crossed at Luciyr, and find a village called Harevan. There, I will stay at the house with the most flowers in its garden, but I must conceal whatever I have found carefully from the people of Harevan, until I am asked to reveal it. When my host bids me return, I will report all I have found to the king."

"It is a strange quest indeed," said Jonathan, looking disappointed. "It does not seem to promise much adventure."

"How will you find the lake and the village, Sir Ilohan?" asked Barnabas.

"I have a map from the king," said Ilohan. "Here it is." He drew a folded parchment out of a leather envelope in his cloak. Joseph cleared the bowls of honey and cups of milk from the table, and Ilohan spread out the map. It was intricately drawn with colored inks, and the great title 'Karolan' at the top was illuminated with gold leaf.

Barnabas looked at the map carefully. Neither he nor the others from Glen Carrah could read, but he knew many of the places without needing to read their names.

"It will take you many days to ride to Lake Luciyr," he said, "it is far up in the corner of Karolan which extends out toward the east and south, very near the border with Norkath. The mountains are lower there, but I did not know they could be crossed anywhere west of Drantar's Gap. I know nothing of the land south of the mountains, but I am told it is a great desert. I think, Jonathan, that should you accept this quest it will not disappoint your desire for adventure"

"Yes, the land south of the mountains is a great desert," said Ilohan. "It is from there that Dradrag led the Zarnith horde – five score thousand warriors – in the time of Nirolad the Great. The Zarnith! Every nation under heaven trembled at their name. It means 'children of the desert' in their own language. The sages at Aaronkal say that someday they may come again."

"It will be a hard ride across the desert to Harevan," said Jonathan, looking at the map. Harevan was opposite Glen Carrah, and the route around the eastern mountains was many times farther than a direct cut across the great Mountains of Karolan.

"Yes," said Ilohan, "but the pass above Lake Luciyr is the first point in the east where the mountains can be crossed. We could never cross them here, or anywhere else east of Cembar and west of Luciyr. Even Dradrag gave up trying to cross them. He lost a score of thousands from cold, exposure, and falling during the attempt to scale the Cliffs of Doom. And I do not need to tell you what he said when at last he accepted defeat."

Every man, woman and child in Karolan knew that. The letters ran beneath the great symbol of the Stone, Sword and Star on the banner of Karolan: "Man can conquer man, but no man can conquer stone." It was the ancient motto of the realm, for the Karolans saw themselves as the stone, stubborn in their fierce desire for freedom, unconquerable as the awesome peaks that guarded them.

They looked carefully over the map for a few more moments, and then Ilohan refolded it and returned it to its place. "Now," he said, looking straight into Jonathan's eyes, "will you come with me?"

Jonathan sat back in his chair and looked carefully at the face of each one there whom he loved. First his father. Barnabas's eyes held a deep twinkle, and Jonathan read in his father's face only joy in the opportunity had been given. Next his mother. She returned his gaze steadfastly. There was no joy in her eyes, but only a steady determination to do what was right: to let him go, however much it hurt her. Next Joseph. The shepherd did not even notice Jonathan's gaze. He seemed troubled, but not about the quest. Finally, with a deep breath,

Jonathan looked at Naomi. He felt as if he had gazed into the face of an angel, or of a martyr. Her selfless love shone from her eyes, and despite her fear and pain, she wanted him to go. She would not have him refuse his dream for her sake.

At last Jonathan turned to Ilohan, letting out his breath with a noiseless sigh. "I will go," he said. The young knight smiled.

Hannah turned to Ilohan. "When would you leave, Sir?" she asked.

"On the morning of the second day from this," said Ilohan, "if that can be."

"Certainly," said Barnabas. "Until then, will you do Hannah and me the honor of being our guest, since Jonathan is to be your companion?"

"I would, with thanks," said Ilohan, "but I have two horses also."

"I will lead them across for you now," said Joseph. "There is ample pasturage for them near the other cottage."

"It is settled then," said Barnabas. "Let us go to our beds. Tomorrow you will lack nothing that a blacksmith can supply."

Chapter 6

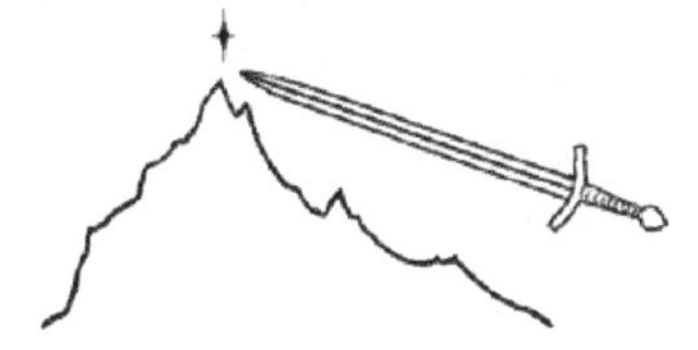

With Home and Joy Behind

THE NIGHT CLEARED AND BECAME COLDER, AND THE WEE hours of the morning came on with a swift wind ruffling the grass of Glen Carrah and fanning the stars to brighter flame. Barnabas and Hannah slept dreamlessly in the familiar peace of their home, safe and known even when shrouded in darkness. But when the crescent of the waning moon rose, brilliant in the black night, and cast a square of light on the wall above their bed, they suddenly came wide awake. With this sudden alertness in the dead of night, their thoughts ran different paths from those they were accustomed to, paths that ran opener to each other's knowledge and closer to the concerns of their hearts. Hannah was the first to speak.

"Is all well with you, my love?" she asked.

It was no meaningless courtesy, but a real question. He was silent for a while, not finding it easy to answer. "Much, but not all," he said at last.

"What things are not?" asked Hannah.

"Although I am glad of Jonathan's quest, and I am sure he will do well, I think it may prove to be more dangerous than it seems. Then there is the war. I do not want to face war again, but I think it will come, and the cost will be high. If it comes while Jonathan is away, he will have to find his place in it without the guidance I expected to be able to give him. I fear for his life, and his soul, since while he has no faith they would both be lost together. I fear for you, also, that I will ride away to battle and not return, and leave this world without having loved you as well as you should be loved."

"Do you really believe there is anything incomplete in your love for me?" she asked.

He could not answer that. His love, or the expression of it, seemed inadequate to him, but he could not explain it in words. "I do not know," he said.

"Know this, then," said Hannah. "I do not believe there is. Let go your fear of being less than you should be. You love me as the man you are – do that as long as we live and I will always rejoice. You are enough, and your love is enough. The God we love makes us enough; abandon yourself to him and stop fearing."

He drew her close. "Thank you," he said. "I am sorry."

She was glad he had trusted her with his fears, and wanted no apology. She was silent in his arms, and she felt there was more peace in him than there had been before.

"My love, what was it like for you when I went out to fight before?" he asked her.

"It was terrible," she said. "I felt as though my soul and my strength had ridden away to war and left me. Every day I wondered if you were still alive, and if you were in great danger. And every day I prayed such prayers for your safety as I had never prayed before for anything. I had two consolations. The first was that God had heard my fervent prayers for you. The second was that, wherever you were, you were acting with love for me, and with honor and justice. I always trusted you absolutely for that."

"I was always true to your trust," said Barnabas. "More than once, when the night fell around us and we felt naked and blind in our camp in the forest, the only thing that held me in hope was the thought of your prayers."

"You could have been attacked at any moment?" she asked.

"Yes," he replied. "For days we all knew that at any moment we might be attacked and certainly defeated. Yet what I remember most in the faces of the men, and in my own heart, was the bewilderment. We did not know what to do. If we had been attacked, our duty would have been clear. While we were only threatened and surrounded, we did not know what to do. All that kept me through those dark nights was one small, bright picture. It was the picture of you on your knees, faithful and courageous and loving, praying to a loving God, who could somehow refine the greed and madness, the hate and evil, out of the hearts of mankind."

"Why was it a picture of me, Barnabas?" asked Hannah. "Why not just God alone?"

"Because if I picture him alone, I do not see his mercy. I see him good and just, holy and free above the world, and I fall in awe-struck, utter silence. I want him to destroy all that is unworthy of him. Let him destroy Norkath, and Fingar, and horror, and fear – and me, and all else that is stained with evil. This is what my heart cries when I picture him standing alone. But when I pictured you kneeling before him, I knew he did a greater thing than the destruction of all that is not worthy of him. Some of it, he made worthy."

"I thought my prayers were answered on the cold and dreary morning when you came riding back from Dilgarel all wet and weary," she said. "I see now that they were answered every day, the whole time you were gone."

"I will never forget that cold morning," said Barnabas.

"Neither will I," said Hannah. "I think for us it was brighter than the sunniest day that has ever been."

Though the light wind through the moonlit window bore an autumn chill, both of them felt warm with the memory of that joyful homecoming. In their eyes were the ghosts of tears that had fallen hot and fast twenty years before; tears of thanksgiving and of joy.

But presently Hannah spoke in a changed voice, gratitude now mixed with doubt and anger. "Barnabas, why were you called? Why were you ordered to leave all you loved and invade Norkath? Did the king accomplish what he had hoped? Was it worth the risk of your life?"

Barnabas was silent for a moment, and then he spoke slowly. "I do not know. The king was driven half mad by the disappearance of his son, yet I can scarcely bring myself to think that even then he acted wrongly. He mustered a small army as quickly as he could, and we marched on Fingar's citadel before he had any chance to raise an army in response. We surrounded the castle, and Fingar allowed the king to enter it. He went cautiously, intending to return before nightfall. He did not return, and had it not been for the old Knight of Metherka we should have despaired of ever seeing him again."

Hannah listened eagerly in the moonlit darkness, for she had never asked her husband about those dark times before. "What did the Knight of Metherka do?" she asked.

"He rode up to the gate of the castle with a hundred Karolan soldiers and a battering ram, and shouted that he would break down the gate unless King Thomas was released. Fingar bargained with him, offering in the end to let the king walk every day upon the parapet of the castle. Metherka agreed, saying that if ever the king failed to appear by nightfall, he would break down the door and sack the castle. Five days later, while we were still trying to think of a way for the king to escape, some of the knights of Norkath gathered a huge army and surrounded us. All our lives hung by a thread, especially the king's. But as long as we surrounded Fingar in his castle, his knights were reluctant to attack us. Although they could have conquered us easily, they feared we would sack the castle and kill Fingar before they killed us. It was during those terrible nights, fourteen long, long nights, that the only bright spot in my whole dark and treacherous world was the knowledge that you were praying for me." He hugged her close as he said it.

"What happened at the end of the fourteen days?" she asked.

"I don't know. For once it was not my watch, and I had drifted into a troubled sleep. Suddenly there was a shout, and I got up trembling and weak with sleep, expecting the worst. Then I realized the cries were shouts of joy – the men were yelling, 'The king, the king!' They stopped suddenly, and the knights and commanders ran through the camp, waking their men and giving orders in a whisper. The orders were to leave camp, taking only our weapons, and leaving the tents, supplies, and fires as they were. Soon we were marching through the woods in the darkness, following the gleam of a tiny torch and the rumor of the king's name. We surprised the Norkath army and fought our way out of the trap; they were in disarray and did not know what was happening, but it was still a desperate fight in the dark forest. As soon as they found out what had happened they gave chase, with their fastest cavalry. Since we were retreating on foot they overtook us easily, and hunted us back and forth across the fields of Norkath, shooting at us from the shadows and harrying us as much as they could. We marched with desperate haste all night, and when morning came we saw the main force of the Norkath army not far behind. In the heat of the day, when all were weary and those who carried the wounded were falling behind, we sighted the border castle of Dilgarel. We made for it with renewed strength, hoping that for some reason the Norkath army would stop at the Karolan border.

The king was bringing up the rear. I was with him. He sent the men carrying the wounded on ahead, and gathered a small group of soldiers around him. I was carrying a wounded man, but I gave him to another soldier so I could stand with the king. We hoped to hold back the Norkaths long enough for most of the men to get inside the castle. A few knights begged the king to flee to the castle himself, but he would not do it. By the time the gate of Dilgarel was open and they started carrying the wounded inside, we were already exchanging arrows with the vanguard of Norkath.

Suddenly we heard a tremendous blast of trumpets from the direction of Dilgarel. The king ordered us to retreat. As we fled, the banners of the Army of all Karolan came into view above the trees in front of us. The Karolan battle cry was like the sound of a great storm, and the knights of Norkath did not dare to lead their army across the border. We raised a great shout when we realized that we were safe, and we retired wearily behind the fresh Karolan army.

We had invaded Norkath a thousand strong, but a quarter of us were dead. The new army, which Tulbur the Steward had mustered, numbered a score and five thousands. They had waited uneasily at the border until spies brought news of our escape from the Norkath trap, just in time for them to march to Dilgarel and cover our retreat. We camped watchfully at the border that night, and the next night, and at sunset on the second day Fingar himself arrived at the Norkath camp. He and King Thomas signed a peace treaty in the castle of Dilgarel that night, and the next morning the armies dispersed. I came straight here."

The story had taken both their minds far away from the safe wooden cottage at Glen Carrah. Its spell gradually lifted, and they noticed again the warm blankets around them and the square of silver moonlight on the floor. A wisp of flying cloud drifted across the moon, and its light dimmed. At the same time the wind blew cold and gusty through the open window, and they drew the blankets close around them.

"It is strange," said Hannah, "that you never told me that before."

"At one time I thought it strange that you had never asked," said Barnabas.

"Did the king find out what became of Prince Kindrach?"

"I do not know. I only know he must have assured himself that the prince was dead, or he would never have given up searching for him."

"There are so many things about the story that we do not know."

"Yes. That is why I cannot bring myself to say King Thomas was wrong to do what he did, though it cost so many lives. I do not know what he knew."

Barnabas got up to close the shutters against the cold wind. They pulled the blankets over them again, and the rustling of the grass began to lull them to sleep.

"We know almost as little about the story of the past as about the story of the future." murmured Hannah sleepily.

"They are tangled together and we cannot see the thread." said Barnabas.

"Yet somehow now I am not afraid of the story's unfolding," said Hannah.

Barnabas himself was almost asleep, and it was nearly in a dream that he heard what Hannah added just before she drifted off.

"I am sure it has a happy ending," she whispered.

* * *

Ilohan woke from an utterly unremembered sleep to see Jonathan's room illuminated by the colorless light of early dawn filtering through shuttered windows. He lay still a while to enjoy the deep peace his sleep had given him. Then he slipped quietly out of Jonathan's bed and opened the door of the cottage. The Mountains of Karolan met his gaze. Ilohan let out a long breath of awe and leaned against the door frame. The great peaks towered behind their foothills, jagged with crags that looked as hard as iron, crowned with eternal glaciers wherever snow could stick to their tremendous flanks. He saw them across a huge gulf of air, sharp and clear, as the rising sun lit their edges with golden light. The size and distance staggered him.

He heard bare feet on the floor behind him and turned to see that Jonathan had risen from his bed of blankets before the fire. "They are beautiful, are they not?" said the blacksmith, "Do you think anyone will ever conquer them?"

"This morning I would not make you defend the beauty of your glen," said Ilohan, "I would concede your claim that there is no place on earth more lovely. And no, I do not think any man will ever come over those mountains. They must be for the angels alone, not for men."

"Well said," said Jonathan.

The mountains and the glen soon became only a backdrop to busy preparation. The day passed quickly for Jonathan, but also uneasily. He did not know how to meet the eyes of his parents, and every familiar thing around him seemed to cry out for a last farewell. He realized how comfortable and at peace he was in his home, and how many things he would miss.

He was happier when he and Barnabas were absorbed in their work over the forge, repairing Ilohan's broken spear. Better still was when Barnabas asked Ilohan for permission to test his sword. The young knight, who had been watching the blacksmiths' work with interest, readily agreed.

Barnabas swung the sword against their wooden target, not very hard at first. The blade rang with a note that seemed slightly false to Jonathan. Barnabas swung it harder and harder, until suddenly the sword shattered with a loud crack.

All three men stood still in the sudden silence. Bright shards of the sword littered the smithy. "I... I had no idea that could happen," gasped Ilohan at last. "The target was only wood."

Barnabas shook his head. "That could have happened to you in battle," he said. "Your blade was not true. I have heard of such things – smiths who are careless, or lazy, taking the king's gold and sending back faulty work."

Ilohan wanted to say something, but the words would not come. He was thankful he had not had to fight with a defective sword – but what was he to do now? He could not continue his quest with an empty sheath. He suddenly noticed what Barnabas was doing.

The blacksmith had taken a new sword from the chest and was swinging it at the target – but with blows much harder than the one that had shattered Ilohan's old blade. Fragments of the wooden target were flying off in all directions. Finally the blacksmith stood still, looking up and down the blade. "Still flawless," he said, and handed it to Ilohan. Without thinking, he slid it home into his sheath. The fit was perfect.

Ilohan suddenly realized that Barnabas expected him to keep the sword. He began to thank him, but stammered over the words. He wondered if he should offer payment. Barnabas silenced him with a gesture.

"Not all smiths work alike," he said. "I have only settled the score against my craft." Ilohan saw in Jonathan's face the confidence that there was no blacksmith like his father in the whole of Karolan.

All through the day Jonathan half expected to see Naomi running over the Glen to him, but she did not come. When the sun sank below the mountains in the southwest, silhouetting them against a golden sky, they finished their work and went in to the kitchen for dinner. Somehow, along with her usual work, Hannah had found time to repack the saddlebags of both horses with loving care. Jonathan smiled when he saw the neat bundles, knowing she had thought of everything he would have and more. After dinner they sought an early rest as the stars came out over Glen Carrah.

* * *

Jonathan awoke with all his usual morning thoughts: look at the dawn, get breakfast, start the day's work at the forge – and then suddenly he remembered. He heard hurried sounds outside, and realized that he was the last one up. A moment later he was standing beside the horses in the cool gray of a cloudy morning. Hannah held the reins, while Barnabas and Ilohan made last minute adjustments to the saddlebags. Joseph and Naomi stood to one side, looking uncomfortable. At last the moment of departure came.

He embraced his mother; she held him tightly for a moment and then released him. "I love you," she said, "whatever comes do not forget it."

Barnabas gave him a quick, strong hug and looked him in the face. "Your choice was right," he said. "I love you, and am proud of you. Go, and seek what God offers you!"

Joseph shook his hand firmly. "You are honest and true," he said, "God be with you."

Then Naomi was in his arms, strong and warm. When she looked up at him there were tears in her eyes, but joy was in her face. "Go," she said, "be the adventurer you were meant to be. In everything you do my prayers will follow you. I know you will return with great honor. Remember your promise."

"The sun will forget to rise before I forget. Though all Karolan be ashes I will seek you and find you, Beloved. Farewell."

Half believing he was still in a dream, he mounted his horse awkwardly and rode away from all he loved. Ilohan rode at his side down the stone path, and Carrah disappeared into the light mist behind them.

* * *

"I tell you it was wrong! What I did was stupid, unjustifiable, a betrayal of friendship. There was no excuse for it. Say what you will, I know it was wrong." Benther the son of Tulbur the Steward turned on his heel and stalked out of his father's room at Aaronkal, slamming the heavy oak door behind him. The young knight stomped heedlessly down the broad stone stairways and out the great gate into the night. He found a hidden reentrant of the outer wall and slouched against the stone. It had been cloudy all day, and the night was starless. Benther felt at home in it, for it matched his black mood, and concealed him.

His loyalties were savagely torn, and every day of his life he seemed to face an impossible choice. Whenever he thought honor called one way and one way only, he felt that was the one way he could not go. Then he was plunged into the same black dilemma again. He wanted to deny it all, to go back to the way things were six months ago, when there was still joy in the world.

His thoughts wallowed in the gloom. Sometimes he would shake himself and try to think that perhaps things weren't quite as bad as he thought; perhaps the worst parts were only imagined. Surely that was it, surely it was impossible things could be so black. He would prove it was so tomorrow.

Benther went back into the castle, made his way into his darkened chamber, and flung himself on his bed. He sank into a sleep in which there was no peace. In his heart of hearts he knew his comforting thoughts were an empty dream. The impossible was true, and a worse disaster than any he had ever considered was falling upon him. When morning came he rolled over with a groan and got up. He sat on the edge of his bed and planned out in his mind another miserable day in which he had no expectation that either relief or any useful guidance would come to him.

* * *

Jonathan also was miserable, when he awoke wrapped in a blanket, lying on a leafy forest floor beside the ashes of a campfire. He had known that leaving Naomi, his family, and his home would be hard, but it was harder than he imagined. He seemed to have left all joy – even the joy of adventure –

behind him in Glen Carrah. Yet his decision was made, and he would abide by it. He struggled out of his blankets and folded them neatly for traveling.

Ilohan, who had woken first, smiled as he handed Jonathan half a loaf of bread. Jonathan made an effort to return the smile, but the taste of his mother's bread made him more homesick than before.

He was deeply troubled by a feeling that he had needed to leave his home, and that he could never come back and live there as he had before. He felt he had to find his own way and make his own new home. These were the ideas that had come to him during the first two days of their journey – days, for him, of silent, thoughtful riding. Try as he might he could not persuade himself to dismiss his thoughts. They rang true in his heart, and their truth lay heavy on him, sapping his strength with a feeling of irreparable loss.

Jonathan found he had eaten and packed while lost in thought, and now they were riding off into a thin, cool mist: this day starting just as the previous two had. The mist was colder, however, and the forest soon gave way to barren rock with only an occasional stand of pines. The only sound was the ringing steps of the well-shod horses: Ilohan, like Jonathan himself, was silent, absorbed in his own thoughts.

Ilohan knew of Jonathan's sadness, but did not share it. His plans had gone well, and he was off on his first quest, with the king's blessing. He was patient with the long days of their journey, but he felt a calm expectancy. Though he did not know the purpose of his mission, he now believed it to be an important one, and he imagined countless possibilities.

The only thing troubling Ilohan was Jonathan's despondency. He guessed that in mourning all he had left behind, the blacksmith had forgotten the good hope of adventure ahead. He wanted to encourage his companion.

"Jonathan, what is it that makes one smith's sword strong, while another's is weak?" he asked.

Jonathan heard the question and stirred himself out of his misery to answer mechanically, "The weak sword is made out of poorly refined iron, with some of the slag still in it. Or it may be that the blade was badly tempered."

"Which was it in the case of my old sword?"

"There was no slag in the blade, so it must have been the tempering. The edges of a sword are cooled quickly, to be hard so they will stay sharp. The shaft of the blade must cool more slowly, so the sword can bend but not shatter. A good smith plunges the sword in water many times to temper it, for a very short time at first, then longer later on. Sometimes he reheats it a little. There are subtle colors that move across the metal after it stops glowing, which show if the tempering is going well." This time Jonathan relished the words he used to describe his craft. He loved to think about the hot loud hiss of a blade being quenched, and the shifting colors of heated iron.

He continued, "Almost all the iron ore in Karolan comes from the stone valley of Petrag, which must be quite near us now, just a little lower in the foothills. Gold and other metals are mined there too – in fact, I have heard that hundreds of years ago the miners were required to pay a yearly amount of gold into the treasury at Aaronkal, but they were angry with the king in those days, and said the gold had run out and they could pay it no longer. It is said they went on mining and setting aside the king's share, however, storing up a vast treasure that they will reveal whenever a king arises who seems to them to be worthy of it."

"I have heard of that legend," said Ilohan, "and indeed in my education as a knight I was taught a good deal about the valley of Petrag, source alike of our weapons and our riches. It was when Garthan was king of Karolan that the miners stopped paying the royal share of gold into the treasuries of Aaronkal. It was a brave deed and a good one, for Garthan was evil. So much is true, but at Aaronkal it is said that the treasure hidden until the coming of a worthy king is only a fable."

The misty morning had given way to a bright noon, the first cloudless day they had seen on their journey. They had been trending downward for some time, and now it was less cold. The sky was rich blue, and stands of aspens flanked the road, their yellow leaves flickering in the breeze. Jonathan looked about him and saw the beauty of the world, and suddenly he accepted his adventure. He knew the pain he felt would not depart. To imagine that it might would have mocked the love from which it came. But as he looked at the living gold of the aspens shimmering against the azure freedom of the sky, he knew he would go with the blessing of those he had left behind, and live this adventure to the full.

They left the groves of aspens, and the road ran straight before them through a wide meadow. Jonathan spurred his horse to a gallop, and he and Ilohan raced across the meadow together. At the end of the meadow the road began descending, and a wooded valley came into view on the left.

Ilohan looked out into the valley, and marveled again at the vastness of clear air in the mountains, so that he could look across such a vast gulf and see everything – tiny with distance, but perfect in detail and glowing color. Their road dropped far into the valley, and then turned east again and led along the mountain foothills at a lower level. Here they were again in a forest, and streams were more common than they had been high up on the barren stone nearer Petrag. They talked together as they rode, and sometimes laughed.

They camped that night in a small clearing beside a stream. Jonathan swam in the cold, clear water but Ilohan only bathed his feet in it. They ate their dinner beside a small fire, and then, wrapped in blankets, lay down by its coals to sleep. The trees overhead were dimly visible in the dull red glow of the coals, and behind them shone a thousand stars.

Chapter 7

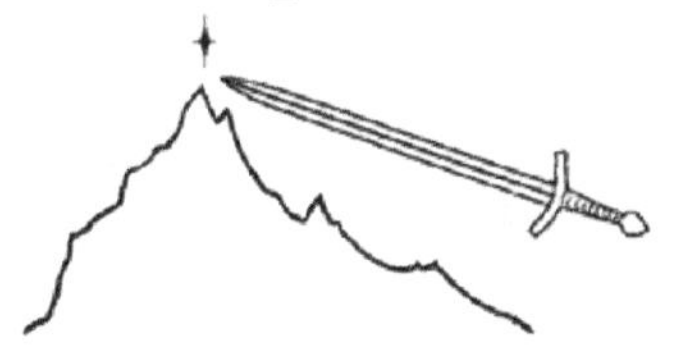

The Cottage and the Unreaped Field

ILOHAN WOKE VERY EARLY. DISTURBING DREAMS lingered in his mind, dreams about old bones and broken, rusty armor that told of dire deeds long past. He had gone to sleep thinking about the first stop of their journey: the search around Lake Luciyr, and he continued to ponder it as he lay uncomfortably watching the cold dawn. At last he got up, shook Jonathan and went to wash his face and hands in the stream.

They ate a quick breakfast in silence, and then mounted their horses. As they rode away, Ilohan suddenly said, "How long would it take for a sword to rust away in a forest?"

Jonathan considered. "I do not know," he said. "An ill kept sword can rust for the life of a man and yet be re-polished bright and sharp, but I do not know if one could last so long if it were left out in the rain and sun." Jonathan thought for a further moment, and then, realizing the purpose of Ilohan's question, asked, "Have you any guess what we will find at Luciyr?"

"None at all. I only hope we find something, so that I can have some discovery to report to the king."

"Who knows? Perhaps finding nothing is the very discovery he hopes you will make."

"I do not know. I wonder, too, why he could not tell me more about Luciyr; what it is that he thinks may have happened there, and why it is important to know."

"What do you make of those two up ahead?" asked Jonathan suddenly.

Ilohan looked up sharply and saw the two figures Jonathan had mentioned. They were both on foot, clad in green and brown. They carried longbows in their hands and had stout oak clubs at their belts. They looked dull and drab, standing there on the light stone path through the vibrant autumn forest. Ilohan felt a twinge of uneasiness as they drew closer to the archers, and wished that he or Jonathan had a bow. As the strangers did not move from the center of the path, they brought their horses to a halt a short distance from them.

"Hail, friends," said Ilohan.

"Hail, Sirs," said one of the bowmen, "we are looking for one Sir Ilohan. Do you know where he is?"

"Why do you seek Sir Ilohan?" asked Ilohan.

"We have a message for him from the king."

"I know that Sir Ilohan is on this path," said Ilohan, "but I do not know whether to direct you east or west to find him. If you are indeed honest men seeking our help, not bandits holding the road against us, lean your bows against that tree while I consider."

One of the archers looked very hard at Ilohan's face. "It is not our habit to lay down our weapons in the presence of a strange knight," he said. The next instant the peace of the lovely wood snapped with a crack. The archers had pulled back arrows in their bows with movements too quick for sight, but Ilohan had doubted them. His own sword was in his hand

and his shield raised across his chest in the same instant. He spurred his horse forward with a cry. The first arrow twanged from a bow and rang off the shield. The startled horse reared in terror and caught the second arrow in its shoulder.

Ilohan struggled to regain control of his wounded horse. One of the archers was almost under the horse's hooves, and he dived to the ground and rolled away just in time to escape being kicked. The other man, however, drew a second arrow back in his bow – then fell beneath a terrible downward stroke from the sword of Jonathan. Even in that moment of crisis Ilohan was astonished at his companion's strength – and horrified by the instantaneous, bloody death of his enemy.

The arrow meant for Ilohan had flown harmlessly into the sky. Jonathan spurred his horse forward to pursue the surviving archer, who was just getting to his feet in an attempt to escape into the woods. The young blacksmith leaped from the saddle, threw him to the ground, and stood over him, the bloody point of his sword trembling an inch from his throat.

"Lie very still," said Jonathan, his voice shaking from the shock of his first deadly fight, "and answer all our questions truthfully. Otherwise I will kill you, just as you have sought to kill my friend."

Ilohan had managed to quiet his horse. The animal did not appear to be seriously wounded. He realized that Jonathan alone had defeated both the archers and saved his life. He dismounted and walked over to where Jonathan held the surviving archer at swordpoint. "Was it the king who sent you?" he asked, keeping his voice cold and steady.

The archer hesitated. Jonathan's sword point trembled nearer. "The truth," said Jonathan.

"No. It was... a knight who said he had the king's orders. Met eight of us in a tavern in the village of Aaronken... offered a princely sum for your death... described –"

"Up!" cried Jonathan suddenly, moving his sword to allow obedience. The archer began to rise, trembling, but as soon as his head was well clear of the ground Jonathan knocked him senseless with a savage blow from the flat of his blade. "We are attacked again," said Jonathan, pointing down the path with his sword. There, coming arrogantly up the lovely, wooded path, was a contingent of six archers clad in the same drab clothing as the two at their feet. They were already within bowshot, but they advanced slowly as if to be sure of their aim before they shot.

Ilohan looked from side to side. The forest was too thick to ride through. Guarded by his shield, he could try to ride the archers down alone – but they would kill his horse and then run through the woods to surround him. "We must fly!" he cried, leaping on his horse and slinging his shield across his back. Jonathan was beside him, mounted and galloping in an instant. Arrows whistled past them, but all went wide, and they were soon out of range.

Jonathan looked back, then reined in his horse. They could not continue their flight, he thought. The quest, the adventure, lay in the other direction. Ilohan also stopped, far ahead of him. "Are you mad?" asked the knight. "We will be in range of them again in a moment.

"I know," said Jonathan. "But we must find some way to get past them and continue east."

"We can ride a long circuit through the woods," said Ilohan.

"But they are thick for half a day's journey at least," said Jonathan, "and the archers may take to the woods themselves to hunt us. I have another plan. You must go through the woods – alone, on foot. I will take the horses along the path."

"But they will kill you! They are already preparing to shoot at us again!"

"Sir Ilohan," said Jonathan, "if you trust me to mean you no harm, you may trust me also to guard my own life. If these things are true, let us fight as though we were mortal enemies for a moment, then you must fall from the saddle and race through the woods."

"I see," said Ilohan. "But first wipe from your sword the blood of their comrade!"

Jonathan did so, then cried out, "Death to the traitor!" and crossed swords with Ilohan in furious mock combat. In a moment Ilohan fell from the saddle and raced away through the woods. Jonathan turned and began riding up the path toward the archers, leading the horses.

"Help! Kill the traitor!" he cried. "He has already killed two of your comrades. I was with him until I understood, but now I am with you. Death to the king's enemy! Death to the traitor! "

The archers stopped walking. Some of them looked uncertainly into the woods with arrows strung. The others leveled their aim on Jonathan, their faces dark with suspicion. Stifling the sick fear he felt, he waved his arm in a gesture of irritation. "Fools!" he cried. "You have no time for doubt! The traitor is escaping. Think of your reward!"

He reached the archers and dismounted without being shot, and immediately pushed his bluff still further. "You!" he said, pointing to an archer, "Guard the horses and bring them along down the path; he may try to escape on them. The rest, follow me! Justice to the traitor!" With that cry he raised his sword and plunged into the woods. Crashing noises behind him told him that the archers were following. The absence of an arrow in his back told him they were fooled, at least for the moment.

For a short time that seemed forever he stumbled through the bright autumn forest with no eye for anything except what blocked his path. Then at last he saw and heard Ilohan running through the woods on his left. "There he is! After him, men!" he cried, and immediately struck off in the wrong direction. To his great joy the archers followed him; it seemed none of them had noticed Ilohan. Then he heard a cry: "No! He is over there!"

Jonathan turned and sprinted in the direction Ilohan had gone. He ran as he had never run before. His bluff had held for a time; now he had to discard it and make the most of the chance it had given them. He had to catch Ilohan before the pursuers started shooting. The archers followed him quickly, but they were no match for the runner from Glen Carrah. He raced downhill toward the path, bounding over fallen trees and bushes in terrifying, exhilarating leaps, as though he were a stag or a winged creature. He reached Ilohan's side while the archers were still out of range behind them.

"They're both traitors!" came a shout from behind. "Kill them both!" The plan was exposed, but it seemed possibly to have succeeded. Ilohan and Jonathan ran for their lives as the pale stone of the path appeared ahead of them. A few arrows whistled through the trees around them, but none were close. To Ilohan's great joy the horses now came into view on the path close by. Then he saw the guard.

Jonathan also saw him: the fatal flaw in his plan, blindingly obvious now that it was too late. But the guard did not seem to understand! He had no arrow on the string. Full of hope that they would escape after all, Jonathan sprinted ahead. He was within a few strides of the path when at last the guard lowered his bow to shoot. In the instant he had to react he saw a large, dead tree stump at the edge of the path. He swerved and ran into it with a fearful impact.

Ilohan saw it happen. The stump shook as Jonathan hit it, and the blacksmith sank toward the ground as if dazed, grasping at the stump for support. The guard let his arrow fly directly into the dead wood, and stood gazing at it a moment in surprise. Ilohan sprinted faster, ignoring the protests of his burning lungs. The guard might draw another arrow in an instant, but with a bold, desperate move that instant might never come. The young knight put all his strength into a running bound that took him over Jonathan's head, up to the top of the tree stump, and off the other side. As he fell he saw that the guard had drawn another arrow, but was still aiming into the undergrowth, unaware that his enemy was about to fall on him out of the sky. Ilohan's sword came down with the full weight and force of his fall, and reduced the man to a broken wreck before his feet struck the stone. Heedless alike of his jarred ankles and the bloody demise of his foe, Ilohan pulled Jonathan out from behind the tree and yanked him to his feet just as the first arrows flew out of the forest. To his surprise and joy he found that Jonathan could stand. In an instant they were both mounted and spurring their horses to a gallop.

The wind rushed in their faces, the muscles of their horses moved beneath them with warm power, and their hooves pounded the path like thunder. Neither of them felt what they had half expected to feel; the deadly sting of an arrow from behind. It took them a few moments to realize they had actually escaped. Their pursuers were on foot, and they had left them far behind. They were panting raggedly, lungs on fire, reeling in their saddles from exhaustion. Yet when they turned and looked at each other as their horses galloped neck and neck, it was not weariness or fear they saw in each other's eyes. They had faced death together, and would not go on with life and friendship unaltered. Their eyes were bright with victory, but also with a new depth of respect for one another.

*   *   *

The clouds of a gathering storm filled the sky east of Glen Carrah that evening. In the west the sun broke through and sent its warm, bright beams washing over the golden grass and gray rock. Naomi knelt in the midst of her flock and prayed, her head bowed, not seeing the glowing earth blaze against the threatening sky. She was pouring out her heart to God, asking him to bless and protect her beloved. She was praying for Jonathan as she had promised him she would. At last she got up and opened her eyes. She caught her breath in wonder, for the colors of the world seemed refined and intensified to something of more than mortal beauty. Her sheep shone white like stars in the heaven of autumn grass; the green of the oaks that bounded the field was dark and rich, and the mighty mountain spur stood out bold with the rugged, enduring majesty of stone.

She had prayed longer than she had realized, and when she saw how low the sun was, she took up her crook and began coaxing the sheep back toward their fold. The sun gave one last gleam of blazing light, and then disappeared behind the blowing clouds. The storm shadow surged across the landscape and swallowed it all in a moment. Naomi shivered slightly as it reached her, as though its darkness was the threat of some dire calamity, rather than the promise of nourishing rain. She did not understand this, for even in her childhood storms had never frightened her.

The sheep submitted to her hurrying, and moved along in a huddle at a good pace. Soon they were filing into the sheepfold. As always, Joseph counted them as they went in, but tonight he did not say their names.

At supper he lit no candles, and seemed content to sit in the gloom of the gathering storm. Before the meal he bowed his head to pray as always, but raised it after a long pause, having said nothing. Naomi lit the candles herself, and stoked the fire so that the room looked like a home and not a cave. She sat and ate, slowly and calmly, looking at him lovingly now and then, but saying nothing.

She knew what distressed him, but she did not know how to lighten the load. The curse of war had lain heavily on him ever since the day of Ilohan's arrival, and tonight he did not even eat. Her concern over his distress kept her thoughts away from Jonathan's absence. She was grateful, for she might yet learn how to ease her father's pain, but the other sorrow had only to be borne.

The candles burned unsteadily as gusts of wind blew round the house. In the stillness Naomi could feel the storm awakening, calling to the earth to get ready. Over the low hissing of the fire she heard the sound of distant thunder. "Father," she said in a low and earnest voice, "war may not come, and if it does you will do all that God wants of you. Please eat something and do not be so sorrowful."

The shepherd raised his head and looked at her, with the hint of tears sparkling in his deep eyes. "Thank you for that, my child," he said, "I wish I were as sure as you." He reached out his rough hand slowly, and took the glass of ewe's milk that was before him. He set it back on the table half empty, and got up from his seat. He placed his hand on Naomi's shoulder as he paused by her chair. "You are a treasure from God," he said in a hushed voice. Then she felt a gust of storm wind, heard the door shut behind her, and knew he had gone out into the darkness. With a sigh she put away the food he had not eaten, blew out the candles, and went to lie down in her own dark room, alone. Around her Carrah brooded in the stormy gloaming, and then the rain came roaring down.

* * *

Far east of Glen Carrah and far beyond the reach of the storm that was drenching Joseph, Ilohan and Jonathan pushed steadily on through growing darkness. The last twilight was fading from the star filled sky, and a faint glimmer of the path was all they could see in the forest gloom below. Their journey became like a wild dream: swift passage through the half-seen forest in the teeth of a cold wind. Jonathan could feel his soreness with every jolt, and his lungs still burned from the strain of the desperate chase in the forest. He rode on silently, guessing that Ilohan was in little better shape despite having escaped collision with a tree.

The long night wore on, and the winter stars began to rise in front of them. They flickered brilliantly through the trees, brighter than the stars of other seasons, their light somehow impregnated with cold. Jonathan thought it strange to see them in the fall: they were the stars of crisp, freezing nights when Glen Carrah was a blanket of sparkling snow. As he rode through the darkness his mind formed pictures of past winters. Naomi, bundled against the cold, chattered happily to him in the smithy and held out her hands to the glowing forge. His tempering water froze solid, and hot swords cut through the ice like knives through cheese – and had to be retempered in water before they were strong. He was a small child going with his mother far up the glen, to what seemed the end of the world, to go play with the small oak sled she had made him.

In the cold gloom of the nighttime forest he ached with homesickness and longing. Yet he could accept the pain: it was born of love, and the adventure was his, rightly chosen. The fight in the forest had sealed his commitment. He knew now that the quest was a true adventure, and that Ilohan would not be able to come through it without his aid. His heart leaped as he realized that he would not have traded his place in the saddle for any other in the world.

Ilohan suddenly halted his horse, and Jonathan looked around him. The winter stars shone high. Both horses hung their heads down in exhaustion. At their feet a trickling stream made a soft splashing in the night. "I feel," said Ilohan, "that even if we are pursued we must sleep before we can fly farther."

"Surely they have left off pursuing us by now," said Jonathan. "We are well mounted, and they must have seen it is hopeless."

Ilohan dismounted and wavered on his feet. "If they are on foot, their pursuit is indeed hopeless," he said. "Nonetheless let us camp out of sight of the path."

Jonathan wondered how this could be necessary, but he was too tired to disagree. He stumbled into the woods after Ilohan until the last glimmers of the white stone path were lost in the darkness behind them. They tethered the horses to a tree by feel, and rummaged in the packs until they found some bread and smoked meat.

Ilohan found it odd to eat in total darkness, yet somehow strangely satisfying. By faith he would bury his teeth in a half-seen lump of something, and find out by taste and smell that it was food. When they had finished the last mouthful, they hastily unrolled their blankets on the leafy ground and sank into deep sleep.

Ilohan awoke when the sky was bright with pale blue dawn, cold and lovely, well before sunrise. The hollows of the wood were filled with mist, and birds sang in the trees, but he was very sore. With an effort he got up and folded his blanket. He led the horses to the stream, and they drank deeply. Soon they were hungrily eating lush grass that grew along the banks. He set them free to get their breakfast, and buried his own face in the stream for a long drink. The water was cold and fresh, and when he raised his dripping head to look around, shivering with the chill of the water, the morning looked brighter. He heard a rustle behind him and saw that it was Jonathan, looking tired and disheveled.

"Must we start so early?" he grumbled.

"I do not know," said Ilohan, "but I want to have seen the last of those archers."

"Why do you still fear them?" asked Jonathan. "Do you think they can have got horses?"

"I do not know," said Ilohan, "only –"

"Only what?" asked Jonathan.

"I keep thinking," said Ilohan, "that the reward they were offered to kill me may have been much more than the price of a few horses. This stretch of road is remote, but it would take them no more than half a day to reach an inn or a farm. And we were so close yesterday! Without your quick planning I would be dead today, and the king's quest would have died with me."

"I am sorry," said Jonathan soberly, "I see that we must start at once. And do not forget that you saved my life as well. If you had not leaped at that guard, he would have come around and pinned me to the stump like a goat's hide hung up to dry."

They ate a hurried breakfast from the bread in their saddlebags, and set off down the path. The sky before them kindled with the colors of the dawn, and the sun first peeped redly through the trees, then rose higher and dazzled them with its white-hot brilliance.

After midmorning the trail began to descend steadily. At first the forest around them remained more or less unchanged: the same mixture of tall oaks, sycamores, aspens and other trees that they had seen the day before. But as they descended farther, the trees grew smaller and thinned out. Beneath them the undergrowth grew lush and green, dappled with the sunshine they let through. It became a blanket of tangled vines and bushes, as high as their stirrups in most places, and above the horses' heads in others. They looked at the sunny woods with delight. Autumn though it was, the healthy green brush was sprinkled with yellow flowers. In the midst of the innocence of nature it was easy for them to forget that they might be hunted. The feeling that they would always escape, no matter what, was strong in both of them.

The sun began to lower in the southwest, behind them and on their right, and the white light of midday dimmed to the golden radiance of a hazy afternoon. They passed from the forest into a wide hillside meadow, and a distant vista opened on their left. The farmlands of southeast Karolan stretched out below them as far as the eye could see. The standing grain, white for harvest, seemed to glow with warm color in the sunlight.

Ilohan caught his breath as he saw it. It seemed to him that it was the very heart of Karolan that he saw: the grain planted by hardy and industrious hands, the fertile land drinking in the rain often falling on it. Every one of the farmhouses and barns that dotted the landscape, each square in the vast patchwork of fields, represented a little cluster of lives: of hope and heartache, shared labor and shared delight.

This was Karolan, his country, the country on which the shadow of fear had fallen. The fear came upon him in a cold wave, and he could imagine the fields burning, the barns and houses razed, and the people being herded together to be sold. He shuddered, for there seemed to him nothing between the land and that fate. As the sun sank behind them his thoughts became prayers, and as he prayed he became more and more certain that only God could save Karolan: his hand must guide the wild rush of events, when the trap of Fingar's deceit and treachery was sprung.

Ilohan rode silently, intent on his thoughts. He paid little heed to his surroundings, though he was aware that the path stopped descending before they reached the fertile plains. The weather, too, forced itself upon his notice when dusk fell accompanied by heavy rain. They donned leather cloaks, but did not find them wholly proof against the cold, steady downpour. They pressed on in silence far into the night, thinking of archers behind. Death and danger seemed far more real in the cold darkness.

Ilohan wondered if riding all night gave them the best chance of escape, or if they should make camp and then try to hurry on faster after whatever rest the uncomfortable night would afford. There seemed no inns on this stretch of the road, or he would gladly have taken the risk to sleep warm and have the horses well cared for. For a time there had been the occasional glimmer of firelight, or whiff of wood smoke, from a hillside farm, but now even these had ceased. The path began to climb steeply, and seemed to bear southward as well. The night grew colder as they climbed. There came a time when they were almost too tired to keep shivering.

Suddenly they saw a light ahead, the low warm light of a fire or candles shining on a partly shuttered window. Ilohan heard his own exclamation of surprise and delight echoed on Jonathan's lips. Yet as they turned into a side lane and approached the light, he felt an unaccountable misgiving, so strong that he nearly turned back to the road. "I fear it is no good thing that keeps a bright fire burning so late," he said, "Most would have closed the windows tight and slept long ago."

"Even brigands might give us a warm place to sleep, and not dare attack armed men," said Jonathan.

"There may be more dangerous things than brigands," said Ilohan. "If we knock at that door, henceforth our lives are twined with those within. Even if they are innocent, there may be danger in that."

"I wish to risk that, rather than continue this journey in the cold and dark, with horses stumbling from weariness," said Jonathan.

"My heart warns me that these are not empty words I have spoken," said Ilohan. "Nevertheless we will knock. I too wish to sleep warm and dry, and not all dangers are evil."

Even the act of dismounting seemed a blessing to them, as at last they stretched their sore, stiff legs. The cottage was well built though very small, and the light was shining through a window to the right of the door.

The outdoor noises of wind and rain made anything happening inside difficult to hear, yet Ilohan thought he caught the sound of low, strained voices in the cottage just before he knocked. There was a strangely long wait – so long that he began to turn away – and then at last the door opened.

A girl of about thirteen years peered timidly around it. There were dark circles about her eyes, and her face was scared and thin. Ilohan suppressed an impulse to kneel to speak to her, as one kneels to small children so as not to tower above them. "We are weary travelers seeking nothing but a dry floor and a fire," he said, "will you offer us hospitality for the remainder of the night?"

"Send them away, Jenn," said a hoarse woman's voice from within.

"No, let them in, child," came the low voice of a man, flat and despondent, "whoever they are they can do us no more harm." Jenn opened the door just enough to admit them, and disappeared behind it.

Jonathan tethered the horses to a tree that would offer them some shelter from the rain, took two saddle bags, and followed Ilohan in. He shut the door against the wet night, and looked around. On the right side of the room there was a hearth with a low fire. Before it stood a table of rough, gray wood, and two chairs. The woman whose voice they had heard sat facing them, with a look of resignation on her weary face. The girl called Jenn sat in the other chair, with her back to them. Both wore rough gray dresses, and looked very thin and cold. The hair of the woman was gray before its time. On a bed against the wall lay a gaunt man who seemed utterly spent. Jonathan thought, as he saw him, that he would rather die than see anyone he loved look so hopeless.

"I am Tharral the farmer," said the man in a tired voice, "I would give you welcome if it were not a mockery. I offer you only what you asked, for I have nothing else to give."

Jonathan and Ilohan pulled the damp blankets from their bags and laid them and their cloaks by the fire to dry. They lay down on the clean wood floor with their saddlebags for pillows. The warmth that gradually seeped into them made them feel they had stumbled into paradise. They must have seemed asleep, for the conversation they had apparently interrupted was renewed.

"Please try once more. Please! For me, for Jenn, for the memory of Harl, try again." The woman's hoarse voice was pleading, and she was near to tears.

"I cannot, Mer," said Tharral. "You and Jenn are stronger than I even now, and you cannot hold the scythe. Thinking that I could is a dream..." After a moment's pause he repeated in a sobbing whisper, "Only a dream."

"Then what are we to do?" cried his wife.

"We can only do what I have already said. You and Jenn must go, up the road toward Luciyr. You are well now, only starved, and perhaps you may find someone to take you in. If by a miracle you find saints among men, then you may ask them to send for me, and perhaps they will do it. Otherwise you must try to forget me. This is the only way."

"I will not leave you," said Mer with flat finality.

"You must, for Jenn's sake if not for your own. Would you have her starve before your eyes?"

"I will not leave you either, Father," said Jenn in a small voice.

There was a long silence. The rain had lessened, but a mournful wind moaned around the house and sighed in the standing grain. Suddenly Mer looked at the two young men asleep before the fire.

"Thar!" she said suddenly, "They could harvest the grain for us!"

"If we asked them for help we should have to tell them about the plague," said Tharral, "and then they would fly as if death itself pursued them. No, we must send them on their way as soon as may be."

"Wait," said Jenn softly, "they are awake."

"What will become of us now?" said Mer in a voice of quiet wonder that did not match the words.

Ilohan sat up with an effort. His heart was in turmoil, swirling with fear, anger, and pity so entangled that he could not tell them apart. Yet the decision of his spirit was clear. He opened his mouth to speak, but finding no words, he reached into his saddlebag, brought out all the food he had there, and laid it on the table. "I offer you all that I have," he said. "I pray it is enough to save your lives and preserve your courage and love."

Jonathan sat up as well. He wanted to run away and preserve his life from the plague, but it would be dishonorable to desert Ilohan. Worse than that, even if he had not promised to be Ilohan's companion, it would be dishonorable to let fear keep him from charity to this poor family. He had claimed honor as the foundation of his life, and could not abandon it. Yet he felt the full power of Naomi's question: "Why will you be true if you can lose all that you love?" He had no answer, but he would not cease to be true.

Tharral, Mer, and Jenn sat still as if frozen with shock. They made no move to approach the food. "Friends," said Ilohan, "I rejoice that God has permitted me to serve you. Please accept the gift as though he had brought it – indeed, he has brought it, for I have only been his agent."

At last Tharral found a voice. "You know we have had the plague?"

"Yes," said Ilohan. "We heard it all."

"You will not fly from us?"

"Not now," said Ilohan. "We are already at risk, since we have entered and lain down before your fire. Our danger may not be much increased by staying, and if we stay we can help you." He paused and anger came into his face. "Yet I do indeed wonder why you admitted us, and spoke no warning, though you knew our peril."

"I do not think you are in any peril. I do not now have the plague; it is only that my strength never returned. I called you in because I wanted to offer one last charity before my death." Suddenly Tharral broke down in tears – tears that seemed immeasurably happier than the dry-eyed despair that had preceded them. "I am sorry!" he cried. "I am sorry I admitted you, and yet I thank God I did." He struggled out of his blanket and slumped weakly into a kneeling position. "Oh God," he wept, "I see now that you are good after all, and have not abandoned us. Please forgive me, and do not let this be only a dream!"

Jenn grasped her chair in her thin, cold hands and pulled it closer to the table with a trembling effort. She reached out for a loaf that Ilohan had placed there. She tried to tear off a piece, but lacked the strength. She brought it to her mouth and bit off a small bite. She chewed intently for a long time before she swallowed. She looked at her father, still kneeling in an attitude of prayer beside the bed. She looked up at Ilohan, now standing beside the table. His face was alight with joy, and the fear and anger had faded. "Are you an angel?" she whispered.

"No, child," he said, "but I could not be happier if I were."

* * *

Ilohan stood regarding the rough stubble of Tharral's field, warmly lit by the setting sun. The wheat stood here and there in awkward sheaves – all the accomplishment of a day's work that had left him and Jonathan exhausted. Two thirds of the field remained uncut.

The young knight, however, was not dissatisfied. He was confident now that they would be able to finish the task. Even today they had threshed some of the wheat, out on the stone path, and Mer had said it was enough to make bread for many days. Ilohan knew he and Jonathan would have to stay at least one more full day, but he would not leave until they finished harvesting the field, and until they had threshed enough grain to last the winter. He hoped that later Tharral would grow strong enough to thresh what remained – laying in ample grain for sale and for seed at spring planting.

For now, Ilohan smiled as Mer and Jenn walked through the field, touching the sheaves with a kind of awe. Even Tharral found the strength to leave the chair from which he had directed most of the work, and with tentative steps he made his way across the stubble of the field he had known he could never harvest. The joy in their faces, and the tears of thankful wonder in their eyes, were to Ilohan payment hundredfold for the hard labor.

Tharral, Mer, and Jenn returned to the cottage to escape the cold of falling evening, leaving Ilohan and Jonathan to continue the work as long as there was light for it. They were finishing the binding of a sheaf, clumsily in their inexperience, when Jonathan suddenly froze. Before Ilohan had time to ask what had startled him, he cried, "To the horses!" and began running across the scythed field. Ilohan glanced round and followed instantly, forgetting weariness in a desperate sprint. The archers, whom he had nearly forgotten in the joy and labor of saving a family from starvation, had found them again. In his lightning glance he had seen them turning off the main path, already within bowshot.

He saw Jonathan reach the horses and draw his sword. There was no time to untie them. "Slash them free," he panted, "slash them free and ride!" His own sword was strapped to his saddle. He grasped the hilt and tore it from its sheath, but at the same instant there was a burning pain in his right shoulder. He spun around, clutching at the saddle for support. Fire seemed to run up and down his arm, and he struggled to hold his sword. The archers were in the field, a very short distance away.

"Our next shot will not be so merciful," said an archer who had stepped to the front. "Do not move or try to flee, for that will only hasten it." They drew up in a body a few paces from where Ilohan and Jonathan stood motionless. Ilohan's blood ran down his arm and dripped onto the path, but he was beginning to master the pain. The wound might heal well, he thought – if only he were not about to die. An archer with a bandaged head came to the front, and drew his bow back to the head of the arrow.

"Your companion struck me when I lay defenseless beneath his sword, yet I recovered," he said. "By rights I should kill him first in vengeance, but it is your death that will make me rich forever." Ilohan raised his sword across his body, futile though he knew it was. The shrill hiss of the arrow split the air – and Ilohan found to his astonishment that it had not touched him. Instead, as if the world had suddenly reversed itself, the archer who had planned to kill him was lying at his feet with an arrow through his chest.

Jonathan, being unwounded, understood more quickly. He had seen Tharral, supporting himself against the frame of his door, take careful aim with a crossbow and then shoot. He had seen the would-be murderer of Ilohan take an arrow through his chest and send his own harmlessly over the knight's head. He had seen the door slam shut immediately afterwards as five arrows whistled into its wood. And then he saw the one thing he needed: all five remaining bows were empty of arrows.

He ran at the archers, his sword singing as it cut the air. The first man tried to parry with his bow, and Jonathan laughed as the bow cracked and the man fell beneath his sword. The other archers had time to draw sturdy oak clubs from their belts, and rather than fleeing they spread out and surrounded him. For a moment he feared they were too many for him, and he could not find space or time to attack any one without leaving himself unprotected from the others. Then his training returned to him and he began to fight with more skill. The fight was a wild dance, one against four, iron against oak, eyes in all directions, all threats seen, all blows blocked or dodged – while all the time he was looking, looking for an opening, a chance to be on the offensive. A chance came, not to strike with full force, but to deliver a lightning slash. There was blood, an oak club dropped to the ground, a man running for his life. Only three against one now. Jonathan felt their fear, and his victory approaching. But then, in one of the fleeting glimpses the fight allowed him, he saw one of the men step back and set an arrow in his bow. Jonathan knew he must be stopped at any cost. With a shout he broke away from the other two and attacked the lone archer with terrible force.

An oak club struck his head with a great crack, and he fell to his knees. It seemed to him that he had killed the man who had tried to draw an arrow. He struggled to his feet and turned around to meet the remaining two archers. He wondered why they had turned away from him and seemed to be fighting someone else. It was strangely difficult to see things in the evening light, although it was not yet very dark. He stepped forward and leveled a savage blow at the neck of one of the archers. The stroke went wide, wounding the man only slightly in his upper arm. Jonathan was shocked that he could have missed such an easy stroke. Suddenly there was an archer in his face, swinging his oaken club. Jonathan parried his blows, and at last broke the club with a tremendous stroke of his sword. The man hesitated a moment, holding half of his shattered stave. Jonathan raised his sword for another blow, and the archer turned and fled. The blacksmith's last stroke caught his thigh heavily as he ran. Heedless of his injury, the mercenary kept running and soon disappeared into the darkness.

Jonathan turned to meet his remaining enemies. To his surprise he saw only one man, and he had a sword rather than a longbow or a club. Jonathan stepped toward him to fight, but as he advanced he heard the man say something. Jonathan knew when he heard it that something was wrong. He had not understood what the man had said, but he knew that it was Ilohan. He had been ready to fight his own friend. He dropped his sword. The night around him seemed to be filled with roaring and rushing, and he felt himself falling and being carried away in some terrible current. He was filled with fear, and cried out to Ilohan for help, yet the sound of his voice formed no words in his ears. He fell into darkness.

Ilohan stood alone beneath the blue twilight, with his sword in his left hand. His blood still ran down his arm and dripped into the gray stubble of the twilit field. At his feet lay Jonathan, his friend. Scattered about the field were the bodies of four of his enemies: the one that Tharral had shot from the doorway, two that Jonathan had mortally wounded as they drew their bows, and one other that he himself had killed when the man, already wounded by Jonathan, had rushed at him with a drawn dagger. Of the other two mercenaries, one had run away despite being badly, perhaps even mortally, wounded, while the other had escaped with a thigh wound that had seemed less severe.

The young knight felt miserable in every way. He was wounded, he had just fought a horrible, desperate fight against men fiercely determined to kill him, and now Jonathan, who had fought for him, had fallen at his feet injured he knew not how.

Chapter 8

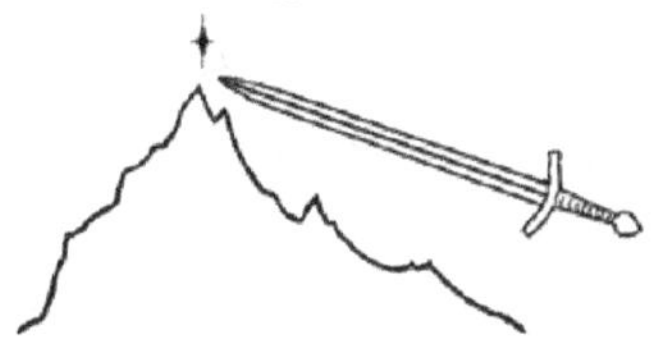

Dreams of Hope and Rescue

NAOMI AND HANNAH SAT CLOSE TO THE FIRE IN HANNAH'S cottage, while a gusty wind moaned and sobbed around the walls. Hannah worked quietly, making arrows beside the fire. The work troubled her, as always, but the shadow was lightened by Naomi's silent presence.

Presently the shepherdess rose and threw open the door to look out. The fire hissed and flickered in the sudden draft, and Naomi had to throw all her weight against the door to force it closed. "The mountains are so clear that it is frightening," she said. "The wind blows cold from their peaks, and makes the sky so deep and blue I can already see stars." She returned to sit by the fire, her hair tangled by the wind.

"Before you looked out, were you praying for your father, or my son?" asked Hannah.

"Both," said Naomi, "but chiefly Jonathan. I wish I understood Sir Ilohan's mission! I am sure it is important, but even he does not know why. If the quest matters so much... I am afraid someone will try to stop them."

"You have been giving your fear to God?"

"I have tried to, tried to commit Jonathan to God's care. But I am still afraid. What if despite my prayers he still lets harm befall him?"

Hannah placed a hand on her shoulder. "I cannot believe that he would," she said.

"But has he not done such things in the past?" asked Naomi. "Prince Kindrach was the bright hope of all Karolan, and yet he was lost. And –" Naomi hesitated, and then said reverently, "even my mother, Abigail. She died though my father would have given his life to save her. She died, though if she had lived I would have had her to love and be loved by all the years I can remember." She paused again, and Hannah saw in her eyes the memories of all that Joseph had told her of her mother. Naomi continued, "God did not save them. How can we be sure he will save Jonathan?"

The question hung in the room. The wind whistled around the house, and despite the well-made walls the cold seemed to come through.

"God never promised to protect him," said Hannah slowly. "And surely he does many things that we do not understand. Yet he has promised to work all things together for our good; for your good and mine, and the good of all who love him. It is not in me to believe that Jonathan's death on this journey could ever be for my good or yours. I believe he will protect him."

"Yet Jonathan does not love him," said Naomi.

"No," said Hannah. "Jonathan does not love him. Kindrach did, and your mother Abigail did, but Jonathan does not. That is why I believe he will be protected. His death could not now be for his good, and I believe that God will have him yet." She spoke the words with fervor, hoping with all her heart that they were true – demanding almost fiercely of her God that they must be true.

"He will not always be blind," murmured Naomi as she sank to her knees beside Hannah's chair. "Someday he will see." Hannah took her hands, and together they poured out their love for Jonathan: a fervent prayer too deep for words.

Naomi forgot the cottage, and the fire, and even the touch of Hannah's hands, and she seemed to be alone in cold twilight, alone yet unafraid. Hope grew strong in her heart, and it seemed to her that God showed her a time when her beloved would see him. Jonathan would come to her in the gloaming, and she would no longer be alone. Darkness came in her vision – darkness that was more than night. But though the darkness gathered round her and Jonathan, she saw that nothing dimmed the brightness of their joy. They were triumphant. "And there shall be nothing more to separate us," she whispered. Suddenly she was back in the cottage, chilled from the coldness of the vision, but clearheaded and at peace. Hannah was looking down at her with a strange expression, but she said nothing.

They heard footsteps at the door, and got up together to greet Joseph and Barnabas as they entered. The two men came gladly in from the cold, and laid their thick cloaks beside the fire. They had been working together at the sheepfold, enlarging the shelter and preparing it for winter, using nails Barnabas had forged. Naomi did not know what they had talked of as they worked, but it seemed to her that the shadow upon her father had lifted a little, and that there was new hope and joy stirring in him. He ate his food with enjoyment, and talked about the sheep he cared for, and the day's work.

When she walked with him back through the cold night to their own cottage, the vision she had seen, if it had been a vision, still lingered in her mind. As she lay down to sleep she whispered to herself, "Though darkness gathered round us, still nothing dimmed our joy."

* * *

Tharral, Mer, and Jenn gave no thought to why Ilohan had been attacked. They had no suspicions or fears for themselves, only love and care for their benefactors. Their home, where the plague had come with its terrors and taken a son, was no stranger to pain and grief. Weak though they were, they did all they could for the two young men, and did it well.

Ilohan hardly understood what happened after he staggered up to the door, half carrying Jonathan and half dragging him. Somehow, sometime later he found that the arrow had been removed from his shoulder, his wound had been dressed, and he was lying on a blanket by the fire, with Jonathan beside him. He started to sit up, but Mer moved to restrain him. "Be still," she said, "you are hurt, and there is no need for you to move."

"Is Jonathan alive?" he asked, lying still as she had said.

"Your friend is alive and breathing," said Tharral, "but he has been struck hard on the head, and we do not know when or if he will recover."

"Alas," said Ilohan, "He saved my life." He looked suddenly at Tharral, "As did you. I give you my deepest thanks. It seemed a miracle to me that you could shoot an arrow. How did you do it?"

"There was a crossbow, which," Tharral paused for a moment, his lips shut in a firm line, "which belonged to my son Harl, whom we lost to the plague. When we heard your shouts, Jenn looked out the door to see what was wrong. She told us, and immediately we took the bow down from the wall and began trying to load it. I held it steady, and Mer and Jenn together turned the crank. By a great effort they loaded it, and then I opened the door and saw that if we were not too late we were at least none too soon. I prayed and shot, and I thank God I did not miss. Mer slammed the door shut before me, or I should not have lived another instant. And somehow, though greatly outnumbered, you and your friend drove off the enemies. That seems at least as much a miracle as the crossbow shot."

Ilohan lay quietly for a moment. His shoulder throbbed with a dull ache, but it was nothing like the pain he had felt during the fight. He looked toward Jonathan. "It was a miracle with too high a cost," he said. "Jonathan did most of the fighting, because I was wounded. He has been sadly rewarded for his courage and faithfulness."

"He must recover," said Jenn, her voice trembling, "surely he will recover. But then... But then I have said that before... poor Harl..." she covered her face with thin hands and cried.

There was a silence, and the air seemed filled with sorrow. Suddenly Mer glanced at Jonathan, and she smiled through her tears. "But Jonathan will live!" she said. "Look, he is awake."

Jonathan opened his eyes and looked around the room. It was strange to him. He could not remember how he came to be there. Nor did he recognize anyone in the odd grouping of people around him: a well-dressed young man with a shoulder wound, and an old man and woman and a girl all clothed in coarse gray. It seemed like a dream to him, and he half thought it was one. Yet he had always had the power to awaken himself, when once he knew a dream for what it was, and with a surge of hot fear Jonathan realized that he could not be asleep. This impossible, unreal situation was actually happening to him, in the only life he would ever have, and there was no waking to a world he understood. He tried to remember things, and remembered his life in Glen Carrah clearly, even down to individual days and events. But he did not remember ever leaving there, or ever knowing the place or the people that he saw. He did not even know his age or what season of the year it was.

"What – what is happening?" he asked tremulously.

"You were struck hard on the head in a fight," said the old woman, "it is no wonder if you do not remember it. But you are among friends now, and all will be well with you."

"Where am I? Where is Glen Carrah?"

"You are in the cottage of Tharral, Mer, and Jenn, five days' hard ride from Glen Carrah," said the young man. "You were struck on the head with an oak stave, swung as hard as fear and anger could swing it. Your valor saved my life."

Jonathan sat up and shook his head violently, trying to remember. "I have always longed for adventure," he said slowly, "but alas! – What I have lost! What will become of me if I cannot remember?" He ran his hands through his hair in anguish. In one place it was stiff with blood, and his head throbbed, but he could find no sign of an injury to the bone.

The old woman stood and touched his hands gently, pulling them away from the injury. "Your skull is sound," she said. "Leave well enough alone and you will heal easily."

"My head, perhaps," he cried, "but what of my memory? I still do not know who you are, or why I am here!" He saw that the young man was looking at him with deep concern, and seemed about to say something. Before he could speak, Jonathan suddenly put his head in his hands and said, "Wait! It may be returning!" He concentrated intensely for a few silent moments and then said, his voice still unsteady, "Are you Sir Ilohan? Did I go with you from Glen Carrah on some errand from the king?"

"Yes, yes!" cried Ilohan, "I thank God – you are remembering!"

Gradually the memories of recent events returned to Jonathan, and with a flood of relief he remembered clearly his farewell to Naomi and his parents and Joseph. He remembered his despondency of the first days of the journey, and then his acceptance of it as his adventure, rightly chosen. He remembered their flight from the archers and their arrival at the cottage of Tharral the farmer. Oddly, he remembered word-for-word Ilohan's talk of strange misgivings before they entered the cottage. The young knight's fears had indeed turned out to have some reality. As the crowning relief he at last remembered the evening fight in the stubble field before the cottage.

At first he only felt great joy that he had got his memory back, but then he recalled how desperate the fight had been and jumped suddenly to his feet.

"We won?" he cried, looking at Ilohan. "You are alive, and they are gone?"

"They are gone," said Ilohan, "two of them have fled and four have gone where they will not return. And I am alive and likely to remain so, thanks to your courage and strength and Mer's skill at dressing wounds."

Jonathan was shaken by what had happened to him. His heart was seething with conflicting emotions: relief, exultation, shame, gratitude, and pity. "I must see..." he said, and before anyone could stay him he had opened the door and gone out into the night.

At first he saw nothing, but walked blindly a few steps into the darkness. Then as his eyes grew accustomed to the night, he saw the gleam of a sword lying on the stubble. He lifted it, and felt that it was his own. The leather grip was the one

Naomi had made, and he himself had forged the blade. It was smeared with gore, so he wiped it clean on the dry stubble. He remembered now his desperate attempt to kill the only archer who was still trying to shoot, and the terrible crack of the oak club hitting his head. He remembered the few confused moments afterwards, and he shuddered as he thought of the roaring, hot darkness that had swallowed him.

With a shock he realized that he was looking at a man he had killed, whose body lay sprawled on the ground still grasping a broken bow. He glanced once at the head, then averted his eyes. In his desperate anger he had used an overhead stroke, and had split the man's skull. His stomach clenched at the horror. "There was no time to think," he whispered brokenly. "And it was no time for mercy."

He grasped the cold hand of the corpse and dragged it into the dark woods, until he found a narrow leaf-lined ditch. He threw the body there, followed by those of the other three dead mercenaries. Then he piled up the sweet smelling autumn leaves and covered them deeply. He stood back in the darkness. The dead were invisible in the lovely health of the autumn forest: the beauty of the world had covered the horror of death and evil.

He returned to the stubble field. The stars above his head were bright, and the Ceranim gleamed in the west. Naomi's words echoed in his mind: "How can men think of war while such stars shine?"

"I do not know," he said aloud, "but they can." He was angry, angry that he had been hurt and weak, and had not been able to escape unscathed as he had before. He was angry at the world where such things were possible, and fiercely angry at the darkness into which he had fallen. He felt that having once enveloped him it would always haunt him.

His vision was very clear now, and he could see the field by starlight. He picked up Ilohan's sword, and leaned it against the cabin. He plucked the arrows from the door, broke them in his hands, and flung the pieces into the forest. He picked up the great scythe, and began to cut the grain. All his anger poured out into his great sweeping strokes, and the standing grain fell before him. He did not care that he was sore and his head throbbed and it was night. His mind was clear and filled with hot anger, and when he was warm with his exertion he rejoiced in his strength. When he grew tired he bound the grain into sheaves as best he could. He found a smooth stone and sharpened the scythe to a keen edge.

He went at the grain again, for he still had no peace. The stalks fell even faster before the newly sharpened blade, and he worked on and on through the night. Now and again he stopped to gather the grain into sheaves, and then picked up the scythe to cut once more. Exhaustion narrowed the focus of his mind, until at last he found a sort of comfort in the rhythm of his work. His world became only half-seen grain in the darkness, the painful but determined work of tired muscles, the wholesome smell of harvest wheat, and the slow, silent wheeling of the bright winter stars.

He was still working when the blue light of dawn leaped up in the east and swallowed the stars, and when the cold morning woke the world and filled the forest hollows with mist. He was still working when Ilohan came out of the cottage in the strong light just before the sunrise, his right arm held stiffly against his body. But as the first rays of the rising sun caught the treetops, Jonathan bound the very last sheaf of the field of Tharral the farmer.

The rest of the morning was very hazy to him, in his exhaustion. He knew that everyone wondered at his accomplishment, and that Mer examined his head in the morning light and said that the injury had not been severe and would cause him no more trouble. He knew that they ate a hurried breakfast of smoked meat from Carrah and fresh bread made by Mer from some of the new wheat. He knew that he and Ilohan threshed many sheaves together on the stone path, and carried the grain to Tharral's tiny barn. He knew that Mer cautioned Ilohan not to use his arm for several days, and that Tharral remarked with joy and amazement on how much stronger he and Mer and Jenn had grown after just one day of good food. Then strangely Jonathan realized that he and Ilohan had said a heartfelt farewell to the little family, and were on the road again beneath the bright midmorning sun.

Ilohan, as he rode alongside his exhausted friend, knew that as long as he lived he would not forget that morning. His heart sang a song of worship to God, a song beyond any words he could speak or write. He had been saved from death, and he had seen life and love conquer hunger, hatred, and despair. He had seen Tharral, Mer, and Jenn rescued from starvation, and he and Jonathan had been rescued from assassins. He had learned again the truth of Thomas's words equating knights and peasants: their courage was like his courage, their love like his love. Even now he felt protected by the blessings they had spoken at parting, and he remembered the love in their eyes, and their happy tears. Though he had seen and understood each part of the last two days' events, together they seemed a miracle beyond his comprehension.

It was a clear, bright day. The road, which had turned from due east to southeast just before Tharral's cottage, held that course and climbed relentlessly. Ilohan knew the path was now striking out in earnest for the high pass above Luciyr, but even so he was astonished by the steady, unending ascent. It seemed they must soon reach the barren heights of the mountains and the eternal snow. Instead, they were riding through mountain pinewoods watered by clear brooks and carpeted with moss and fern.

In the early afternoon they came to a village beside a deep blue lake. Ilohan consulted his map, which told him Luciyr itself was still far ahead, and then he stood still a moment lost in admiration. The cabins of the village clustered close to the shimmering water, and all around it majestic pines lifted their crowns against the sky. He would have asked Jonathan if it was as beautiful as Glen Carrah, but he had mercy on his tired companion and said nothing.

As they left the lake behind, Ilohan was sobered by the thought that this was where Jenn and Mer might have come seeking shelter, after a journey that would have cost them the last of their strength. He wondered what welcome they would have received. He was deeply grateful that they had rescued them, and that it would never matter.

Such thoughts were still in his mind when evening found them even higher, climbing a thinly wooded spur in long switchbacks. He wondered if there were other families in Karolan in desperate straits, to whom no unexpected rescue would ever come. As his horse trudged along the dusty trail, he felt in his heart a great desire to rescue them all; to see in a thousand worn faces the same wondering joy he had seen in Tharral, Mer, and Jenn. "God," he whispered, "do not let them die. And if I can help them, do not let me fail to do it." He rode for a moment in silent thought, and then went on, "Please make me able to help them. Please give me power to bless them. There is nothing else I would rather do."

They crested the rocky ridge and looked back northwest across Karolan. Ilohan caught his breath. There were mountains and hills to the limit of vision in all directions. On the left, the impassible peaks that had guarded Karolan from the Zarnith stood black against the sunset brilliance. Below, the valleys had fallen into hazy shadow, but the peaks of mountains and foothills caught the rosy light and glowed above the shade. The fertile flatlands were lost in the distance, and for all Ilohan could see they might never have existed. He pondered this wonder: a land so big that from one part of it you could not see another, even from a mountaintop.

It seemed incredible to him that this could still be Karolan, and that long ago Nirolad and the other ancient kings had dared to imagine this vast place as one nation, ruled by one man. In one sense the power wielded by the king was dizzying. In another, he was weaker than any other man, because other men might accomplish their tasks but his was too great ever to be done. He could never truly rule the land. He could only guide some of its people and try to do them good rather than harm. Ilohan thought of King Thomas, of the enormity of his task and of the kindness he had nonetheless always shown him. He remembered their parting, and thought he understood better the reason for the king's deep weariness. The breathtaking view blurred before his eyes, and he blinked away his tears.

Jonathan followed Ilohan wearily as he turned and rode into the shadow on the far side of the ridge. The blacksmith longed only for the end of the day's journey, and a chance to sleep. He looked ahead to see a towering ridge of treeless mountains, their peaks whitened with a dusting of snow. It looked utterly impassible, and Jonathan stared up at it in dismay. With great relief he heard Ilohan suggesting that they camp by the stream in the valley before them, and attempt the ridge in the morning. He ate as quickly as he could, and then lay down to sleep before the last light had faded from the sky. Jonathan awoke a few times during the night, and each time he rejoiced in the new strength and life that his rest had brought, and promptly fell back to sleep. He did not get up until it was bright morning, and the sky above the valley was brilliant blue. Then he leaped to his feet, rested and well, strong and ready for adventure.

He felt a soaring excitement as they left the wooded valley floor behind and mounted up the great rock face of the mountains. The trail was narrow, hewn in long switchbacks into the nearly vertical stone. They had to dismount and lead the horses, and a cold wind gusted in their faces, intensified by the sheer wall of the cliff. Jonathan knew that his dream was coming true: he was seeing places he had never known existed, and doing things he had never expected to do.

They ate their midday meal sitting on the path with the wind blasting them and their feet hanging over a terrific gulf of air. They pressed on as soon as the meal was done. They had not gone far, however, when Ilohan stopped so suddenly that Jonathan bumped into the knight's horse. "What do you see ahead?" Ilohan called back to him.

Jonathan carefully made his way past Ilohan's horse to stand beside his friend. "Nothing surprising," he said, "only more rock."

"But do you see any more trail?"

Jonathan looked again. They had about twenty paces more of the trail, and then they would walk off into air. He looked around for any sign of a new switchback, or any continuation of the trail, and saw none. "Now I understand why you stopped," he said.

Ilohan shrugged. "I suppose there is nothing to do but go cautiously to the edge and see how it appears from there. I hope we will not need to back the horses all the way down."

Jonathan slid back past Ilohan's horse, and took the reins of his own. They moved slowly along the cliff face for a little distance, and then suddenly he heard Ilohan call back, "All is well! The path does not end." The next instant Ilohan and his horse vanished, and Jonathan was left staring at what, to him, still looked like the end of the path only a few steps ahead. He went on, wonderingly, and then suddenly stopped.

A high, narrow crack opened in the rock face, and the trail turned into it. The rock on which he stood was rubble that the makers of the path had shoved into the crack to make a smooth place wide enough for a horse to pass. The great, cold stone walls on either side soared to unmeasured height, and between them he could see a narrow strip of blue sky. Ahead the path lay through the mountain. Ilohan was already pressing forward, and Jonathan followed him in wonder.

Slight windings of the crack soon hid the opening behind them, and only the cold light of the strip of sky far above illumined their way. The sound of wind whistling over stone came to them from high up, but where they walked the air was still – and cold. The chill of the rock seemed to come straight from the frozen heart of the mountains and sink into their bones. Ilohan paused, and Jonathan saw him pulling on his leather cloak. He did the same.

The path was uneven. Sometimes they had to coax the horses gently through parts that were like rough stairways up or down. Evening came on quickly, and pitch darkness fell in the crack while twilight still showed dimly in the sky above.

"The trail is smooth here," came Ilohan's voice back to Jonathan out of the blackness. "Let us continue on as far as we can." Jonathan could not see his hands in front of his face. He followed the slow footsteps of Ilohan's horse, hoping that soon the high rock walls would open and they would pass out into a star-filled night.

Instead he heard a loud scraping sound ahead, and the next instant he bumped into Ilohan's horse. The horse whinnied in fear. Ilohan called, "My horse is stuck; the crack must have narrowed. I think we will have to sleep here, Jonathan."

"Yes," said Jonathan. "Morning light will help. But what if we cannot get the horses through at all?"

"It would grieve me to leave them here to starve," said Ilohan. "However, we must, if we cannot get them through. Perhaps we could buy new horses from somewhere, even from Norkath, before we cross the desert."

"We must sleep now, whatever happens later," said Jonathan.

"Yes, thank God," said Ilohan.

They had again the strange experience of eating in total darkness, and then they laid their blankets over the rough rock and went to sleep watching the stars wheel slowly across the narrow slit of sky.

Ilohan woke to see that the sky above was already the blue of full morning. He looked around at the place he had slept in but never before seen. It was odd to experience by sight the things he had only felt and heard the night before. He stood up and looked back at his horse. "Why, he's only jammed by the saddlebags," he said to himself with cheerful relief.

What had seemed an insurmountable obstacle the night before was a simple problem in the morning. They tied the saddlebags up over the horses' backs and continued on their way. About midday the rock underfoot changed to mud, and the crack got wider. Soon afterward Ilohan saw light ahead.

The light was dazzling, brilliant green, and he blinked as they approached it. Then suddenly he stepped out of the crack and into the blinding brightness of a sunny day.

Jonathan and Ilohan stood together on short, thick green grass. The ground beneath their feet was damp. Behind them lay the great peaks and ramparts of the mountains through which they had come. In front of them the meadow fell away in a long, gentle sweep to a stand of stately pines and aspens surrounding a lake. Beyond that the ground sloped up again to another ridge. In every direction there were mountains: the lake lay in a lovely bowl of green meadow, ringed about by soaring peaks of stone.

The lake itself was a sparkling sheet of azure, the perfect crescendo of the splendid beauty of that valley. Ilohan remembered that a poet had once written, "The waters of Luciyr hold in a moment the cloudless skies of a thousand years." The valley was a masterpiece, a fragment of Eden graciously restored to the weary world.

"Luciyr," said Ilohan. "We have come to this place to look for the remains of the dead. How anyone could die or kill here is beyond my understanding."

Jonathan looked at him and smiled. "Sir," he said, "to me Glen Carrah will always be the most beautiful place in all the world. Yet if I had seen this first I would not have challenged your claim that there might be a place as lovely."

Jonathan unbuckled his sword, dropped the reins of his horse, and ran like the wind down the great green slope. He reveled in his strength, and in the beauty that surrounded him. He leaped headlong and somersaulted and tumbled down the grassy slope until he came to a stop and got up laughing.

Ilohan came on more slowly leading both horses, but his heart too was brimming with joy. The purpose that brought them here was grim. Yet the staggering beauty of the place seemed to blast the grimness from his mind. He could no more be somber upon arriving in the valley of Luciyr than sing a dirge to the stars.

Chapter 9

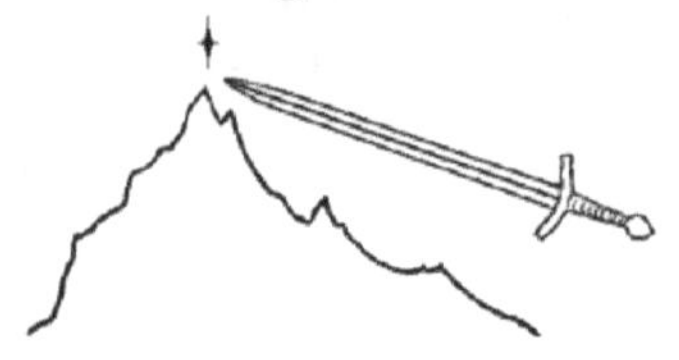

The Warrior on the White Rock

BY THE AFTERNOON OF THEIR THIRD DAY AT LUCIYR, THEY had searched all around the lake several times. They had found nothing. They sat together beside the ashes of their fire in their camp on the west side of the lake. The view was glorious, as always, but they spared little attention for it.

"We have looked everywhere," said Jonathan, "surely if anything were here we would have found it."

"We do not even know what we seek," said Ilohan. "It might be very subtle. I believe we should keep searching."

"But we have gone over every single patch of land within a hundred paces of the lake. If even a silver ring or a single bone were there we would have found it. Would the king have us spend a year here and search the entire valley?"

"It is at least a lovely place to spend the days," said Ilohan, "come, there is still daylight enough for one more search around the lake."

"I will follow you, however unwillingly," grumbled Jonathan, "but I am sure now that we will find nothing."

"Try not to be sure of it," said Ilohan. "Even if you think you are looking, it is very hard to see something if you are sure it does not exist."

Jonathan did his best to believe there might be something. He followed Ilohan around the north side of the lake, keeping close to the shore and scanning the ground carefully. In most places it was rocky soil, but here and there it was covered with pine needles. There was not a single pile of needles on the perimeter of the lake that they had not sifted. By the time they reached the east side of the lake, Jonathan was confident that whatever Ilohan might say, there was nothing to be found – but as long as the knight searched, so would he.

Ilohan stopped on top of a huge, light colored rock that jutted out into the lake. They had spent little time searching this area because the barren surface of the rock could conceal nothing. On the lake-ward side the rock fell vertically a few times the height of a man to the water's surface.

"We may as well pause to admire the setting sun," said Ilohan as they stood there. It was indeed worth looking at. Great spires and ramparts of the westward mountains were silhouetted black against the bright sky, but gilded here and there with white fire from the afternoon sun just above their peaks. The clear waters of the lake shimmered below. Ilohan lay down on the smooth warm rock and peered into the water. Jonathan remained standing, squinting into the brilliant west, his mind full of hard-edged black silhouettes and dazzling pearly light. Suddenly he heard a low exclamation from Ilohan.

"Jonathan!" Ilohan cried. "Do you see something shining in the water over there?"

Jonathan looked very carefully where Ilohan pointed. The water was little more than waist-deep there, and he could see the sunlit pebbles on the bottom almost as though they were in air. "I can see nothing but rocks," he said.

"It is very small," said Ilohan, "and I do not know how to point it out to you. But there is something there, and if I take my eyes from it I am afraid I will not find it again. I have no idea how we might recover it. The water must be as cold as ice."

"I doubt it is any colder than the water of the Carratril, the stream that runs through Glen Carrah," said Jonathan.

"Likely not," said Ilohan, "but who would dare swim in that?"

Jonathan enjoyed the shock in Ilohan's face as he rapidly took off his clothes, climbed down the rock, and leaped into the frigid lake. He swam fast until he was far beyond where Ilohan was pointing. When his exertion had warmed him, he turned and swam back toward the white rock until his feet touched the bottom. "Now I can stand still for a while," he called to Ilohan, "where is it?"

"Very near you," he said. "Come a few steps closer to me, and then a few more to your right."

Jonathan followed these instructions, stepping very slowly as he was still quite far from shore and the water was up to his shoulders. The pebbles were thinly coated in mud, which swirled up from his feet and clouded the clear water.

"There!" cried Ilohan, "You must be nearly on top of it now, although I can no longer see it."

Jonathan went under and felt around the pebbly bottom with his hands. His breath ran out, and he surfaced without finding anything. He held up empty hands.

"Try again!" said Ilohan. "There is certainly something there."

Jonathan dove under and searched again. Suddenly he shuddered as he felt something slice smoothly into his hand. He knew that he had touched an extremely sharp blade. He felt very cautiously around for it, caught hold of it and drew it from the water. It was a great sword. He held it high above his head for Ilohan to see, heedless of the blood that flowed from a deep cut in his left hand. The sharp, almost unrusted blade shone in the failing sunlight, and the hilt was overlaid with gold.

* * *

They were much merrier later that evening, as they warmed the last of their goat's meat over the fire. Ilohan had bound Jonathan's hand in cloth, and thanks to the sharpness of the blade it would heal quickly. They examined the sword in the firelight.

"What does the blade reveal to a master swordsmith?" asked Ilohan.

"I am no master, not yet," said Jonathan, "yet I think this blade would puzzle me, even if I were."

"How is it strange?" asked Ilohan.

"In at least two ways. First, the lack of rust. If the blade has been here for several years, it should have rusted more than that. It may be made of a metal that the smiths of Karolan do not know. If it is iron it must have been there only a few months. The second is this notch." He pointed to a deep notch in the edge of the blade. "I have never seen a notch as deep as that in an unbroken blade. The force of the blow that did it must have been terrible. I do not think that either I or my father could deliver such a blow. There are also these tiny marks, which are like the marks made on a sword when very hard blows are parried. The last thing that puzzles me is how a blade like this ended up so far out in the lake. It might have been thrown, but this is the gold hilted blade of a king or a prince. Who would throw away something so valuable? Yet how else could it get so far out in the lake?"

"Difficult questions, indeed," said Ilohan, "Does the deep notch in an unbroken blade mean it must be stronger than the iron swords made in Karolan?"

"Perhaps. I do not know."

"Is there a way to test it?"

"To test if it is stronger than iron?" asked Jonathan. "Of course – but if it is not, the test will destroy it."

"I think it is worth that risk," said Ilohan.

Jonathan took the sword in both hands and stepped up to a boulder at the edge of their camp. The blade sang in the air as he slashed it down to strike the rock. Sparks flew from the stone, and there was a deafening clang – but the sword did not break. Jonathan struck the boulder again and again, each time harder than the last. His last, mightiest blow split a large flake of rock from the boulder, and the sword fell ringing from his stung hands. He picked it up unbroken and took it back into the firelight. The blade was almost imperceptibly dulled where it had hit the rock. There was no other damage. "This sword is stronger than iron," said Jonathan quietly.

They slept on the mystery of the royal sword, and as soon as the sun rose high enough to shine into the lake they were back at the huge white rock. Jonathan was in high spirits, and he played with the sword as he stood on the smooth stone. He fought for his life against imaginary opponents, killed them and then in a mad flourish of victory pretended to throw the sword far out into the lake.

He stopped and turned to see Ilohan watching him with amusement. "I do not think that even a mad knight would throw away his sword," Ilohan said.

"Then what did he do?" returned Jonathan. "Something threw it out into the lake."

"Yes," said Ilohan slowly, "something did." He looked up at the blue sky, and seemed deep in thought. Suddenly he turned to Jonathan. "Did you say that the deepest notch was made by a very strong blow?" he asked.

"Yes," said Jonathan, "so strong that it is hard to believe anyone could strike such a blow."

"Strong enough to throw the sword thirty paces out into the lake?"

"Yes indeed," said Jonathan, "provided it was knocked out of the hand that held it."

"Suppose the knight was forced up against the edge of the rock, fighting for his life," said Ilohan. "Suddenly he parried a tremendous, almost superhuman blow, and it knocked the great sword out of his hands and far out into the lake. What happened to him then?"

"He died," said Jonathan, sobered by the picture that came suddenly into his mind. "The next blow… a blow hard enough to notch that sword… He was broken, and died where he stood."

"Yes," said Ilohan, "but where are his bones?"

Jonathan looked around the bare face of the rock. Nothing could be hidden there. He ran to the edge and looked down into the cold clear water. At the very base of the rock the pebble bottom gave way to smooth gray mud. There was no sign of the remains of the unfortunate knight. "I think I know where they are," said Jonathan, "and I have no objection to another swim."

He swam fast and far to gather warmth, and then returned to the base of the rock to start searching. The mud was very soft, and about a foot deep. His footsteps churned the waist-deep water into hopeless murk, and he had to submerge and feel through the mud with his hands. Fruitless moments in the icy water chilled him, and he had to swim fast again to warm himself. He had started searching at the south end of the great rock, and by the time he was two-thirds of the way to the north edge he began to think he would find nothing. He dove into the cold mud yet again, and this time he met something smooth and round, like a twig. He shuddered, reminded himself that it might be only a twig after all, and then surfaced to examine it. As soon as the water was out of his eyes he saw that it was no twig.

"I found a bone!" he called to Ilohan. "It is large enough for a man's arm, but it is cracked in the middle."

"Broken!" exclaimed Ilohan. "Are there any more bones?"

Jonathan placed the bone gently on a rock ledge, and ducked back under the icy water. His hands met bones all through the mud near where he had found the first one, and he pulled them out and laid them on the rock. Before long both he and Ilohan had no doubt that they had found the remains of a man. Jonathan searched grimly through the silt, submerging time after time and always bringing up more bones. Finally his hands lighted on a smooth, round object. "The skull at last," he thought, with a mixture of horror and satisfaction. Even before he surfaced he had a hint of something wrong: an edge or ridge that should not have been there. When he stood and looked at what he held, he recoiled. It was a human skull, as he had expected. But it was split from scalp to jaw, and he held its halves. He remembered another man who had received a similar blow, and for a moment all the beauty of Luciyr seemed to him a mockery and a lie.

He submerged once more, and brought up nothing. He dressed himself and carried the bones reverently up the rock to Ilohan.

Ilohan looked grimly at the skull. "The next blow," he said. "He had lost his sword, and there was nothing he could do."

"Nothing," said Jonathan. There was a long silence.

"He was fighting on top of this boulder," said Ilohan at last. "Then he lost his sword and got his ferocious deathblow. His body fell at the base of the boulder, and the years covered his bones with mud."

"It seems so," said Jonathan, looking around the valley to clear the dark pictures from his mind. "But, after all, it is only a guess. Can we learn any more from the bones?"

"I was taught, once, how the skeleton of a man is assembled," said Ilohan. "Perhaps I can remember." He stared at the pile of gray bones for a long moment, and then began to lay them out in the shape of a man. Jonathan marveled at the knight's knowledge, and at the intricate framework of the skeleton. He stared at his own arms and legs, imagining the bones beneath his flesh, understanding their form for the first time.

At last Ilohan stood. "That is as complete as I can make it," he said. "Both bones of one forearm are cleanly broken. There is no other injury, except to the skull. Many of the small bones of the hands and feet are missing, and perhaps a few of the vertebrae – that is, the parts of the backbone."

"I could easily have missed those smaller bones down in the mud," said Jonathan. "What does the skeleton tell us about the man who died here?"

"He was a man of ordinary height," said Ilohan. "And, by all the signs, he died in fierce battle with a pitiless foe. Thus is answered one of the king's questions: whether those who died here were executed or killed in battle."

"Yes," said Jonathan. "There is the sword, too. Executioners would surely have kept the sword. If it was thrown into the icy water during the battle, it is easier to see why it was not taken."

"Who was he? Whom did he fight, and why?" muttered Ilohan as if to himself. He strolled to the edge of the rock and peered into the water. His demeanor changed instantly. "Jonathan," he cried, "look!" Jonathan ran to the edge of the rock and looked eagerly into the lake. The mud he had stirred up had settled, and there, in the muddle of turned sediment that he had created while digging for the skeleton, he could easily see a gleam of metal.

Jonathan ran to the water and waded along the rock without bothering to take off his clothes. He was able to reach the bright object just before the clouds of muck obscured it, and he reached for it with both hands. He found two pieces, and brought them out together. The object was unmistakable. It was a crown.

It was split down the center, just as the head it had adorned had been. Jonathan held it silently for a moment, slowly grasping its implications. A king had died here, fighting for his life. A royal crown. A royal sword. "Ilohan!" he called. "I think we have found our answer." To his surprise Ilohan did not reply. "Ilohan!" he called again.

*   *   *

A moment before Jonathan found the crown, Ilohan had been lying on the white rock, eagerly watching his friend approach the treasure. But the sound of horses behind him had brought him to his feet. In the next instant he was standing on the rock with the great sword held in both hands. Riding toward him, down the steep earthen shore of the wooded lake, came five knights with swords and spears. He recognized the insignia on their shields, and knew that they were knights of Norkath. He had a little time to think, because the horses had difficulty negotiating the steep, forested slope. He felt weak and sick, and his shoulder throbbed. He knew that Jonathan had left his sword at the camp, and could not help him. He was sure beyond a doubt that the knights had come to kill him. The cries of his friend came to him from below, but he did not heed them. The knights dismounted and ran toward him with their swords raised.

It was five against one, and he was wounded. He knew he would die, and the king's errand would fail. He was weak, weak, and he could not fight. Then suddenly his anger rose against himself and against the world. Weakness meant nothing, excuse was evil; he was called to live in a broken world and must endure it. He raised his sword with a cry, and they were upon him. For an incredible moment of clashing steel and wild motion he kept all five of them at bay.

He could only delay the inevitable. He parried two strokes at once and saw another sword raised that he knew he could not block.

At that moment Jonathan's voice came roaring up to him, so loud it seemed to shake the world, shouting a single word: "Jump!" Without an instant's thought Ilohan jumped. He felt the air beneath his feet. He saw the knight's bright sword slash empty space where he had been, and saw the astonished looks on his enemies' faces as he escaped them. Then his stomached clenched terribly as he fell. Mastering his fear, he held the sword well away from his body, closed his eyes tight against the splash, and hit the water feet downward. Though the water was waist-deep, it hardly seemed to break his fall. He crouched and rolled to absorb the impact just as if he had fallen on dry ground. He had a momentary impression that he was outside himself, watching a person named Ilohan smash himself to pieces against the shallow pebble bottom of a lake. Then suddenly he was at the surface, spluttering, gasping with the cold, uninjured as far as he could tell. He struck out for the opposite shore, half dazed and desperate. With a sudden sick feeling he realized that the sword was gone – he would never now be able to show it to the king. He heard splashing behind him, and turned around to see Jonathan following him swiftly.

His friend came up beside him, swimming a sidestroke with his head above water. Something long and shining was trailing through the water at Jonathan's side. "I have the sword," said Jonathan, "you must swim faster. They are coming around by land."

"I will try," gasped Ilohan.

Jonathan delighted in the wild rush through the water, even though their situation was desperate. The forested land would slow the knights with their horses as they rode the long circumference of the lake, he thought, while the camp he and Ilohan had to reach was on a promontory of land, only a short swim away. Laden though he was, Jonathan reached the land before Ilohan. He burst out of the water, encumbered with his wet clothing, cold, and out of breath. The Norkaths were not yet in sight. He threw his and Ilohan's blankets, and anything else of their belongings that he could grab in a moment, into the saddlebags of both horses. Holding the reins, he looked northward along the shore, and saw three of the Norkath knights rapidly approaching. He spun round and saw that Ilohan was running toward him and would be mounting his horse in only a few strides. In a flash he leaped onto his own and they rode away. They quickly broke through the belt of trees into the open meadow, and spurred their horses to a gallop.

"Hunted and fleeing again," called Ilohan.

Jonathan looked back. "Yes," he said, "but we have a good lead, and these knights do not have bows. Do you know which way that village is from here?"

Ilohan looked around. The southern half of the valley was before them, and they could ride where they willed in the great bowl of rippling grass. But it was a bowl, closed in by mountains on every side. Ilohan scanned the mountain barrier – gray, immense, and rugged – trying to find some sign of the pass, or to remember from his map where it was. Even in their danger he could not help feeling a surge of wonder at the grandeur of the mountains. Yet he saw no way out, short of climbing their great, sheer sides.

He looked below the mountains, and scanned the shimmering beauty of the meadow. Two small black dots, very far away, moved slowly against the bright green grass. For a moment he gazed at them in idle curiosity, and then suddenly he realized what they were. "Jonathan!" he called. "The other two knights are ahead of us!"

"Yes," said Jonathan when he had looked, "they want to cut us off. Shall we fight them, or can we get past?"

"Alas," said Ilohan, "how can we evade them, when we do not even know our own path?"

"Look!" cried Jonathan. "There is a path ahead!"

The wind was piercingly cold on Ilohan's wet skin and clothes, as he squinted into it to look where Jonathan was pointing. He saw a line of beaten grass, and followed it with his eyes. It changed to a narrow path of bare earth, and then, almost lost in the waving grass of the far distance, he saw that it was bounded by two rows of stones.

Ilohan and Jonathan galloped down the path side by side. It led them straight toward the figures of the two mounted knights. Ilohan unbuckled his spear and set it in its rest.

"You are wounded," said Jonathan. "Can you do it?"

"If God wills I can," said Ilohan, "and I must as you have no spear."

"Nevertheless there are two knights," said Jonathan. "I will take one and you may have the other." Ilohan wondered how Jonathan could fight a mounted, lance-wielding knight without a spear, but there was no time to argue. The two Norkaths kept apart at first, ignoring Jonathan and trying to cut off Ilohan's chance of escape. Jonathan spurred his horse forward and came between Ilohan and one of the knights. The knight leveled his lance on the blacksmith and spurred his horse forward.

Ilohan's assailant charged also, and the young Knight of Karolan gritted his teeth for the impact. He remembered this moment from many tournaments, and from his fight with Benther. Many times he had heard the thunder of his horse's hooves and seen his enemy's lance level on his shield. Most of those times he had been unhorsed. That had only meant disappointment and a long, uncomfortable discussion with someone about what he had done wrong. This, for the first time, was life or death. The moments before impact seemed to last ages, and yet too soon they were gone. He did everything he had been taught to do, and as the last instants passed the confused thoughts of his mind became a prayer.

His shield was struck, a crunching sideswipe that wrenched his arm and made him reel in the saddle. His own spear took a strong, square impact on the Norkath's shield and unhorsed him. Then he was galloping over the grass again, panting, wondering, but victorious. Before him the path led unobstructed to where it disappeared behind a huge outcrop of rock. With a sudden shock he remembered Jonathan and turned to look behind him.

He saw that, for reasons he could not imagine, the Norkath knight had killed Jonathan's horse rather than killing Jonathan himself. Ilohan was just in time to see the great animal topple and send his friend rolling on the grass. Jonathan got up immediately, sword in hand, but the Norkath, who had let go of his lance, did not attack. Ilohan wheeled his horse and galloped back to his friend. Jonathan leaped onto the saddle behind him, and they galloped away up the narrow path. The Valley of Luciyr vanished from sight behind the rock outcrop. The path changed from bare earth to jagged gravel, and they found themselves entering a steep, barren valley. Cold gray cliffs rose high on either side.

"I fear your horse will be exhausted, and they will catch us," said Jonathan.

"But we have escaped from Luciyr," said Ilohan, "which seems to me a miracle. Perhaps we may hope for another. In any case, there is nothing to be done but ride as hard as we can."

"You should leave me behind," said Jonathan. "I can climb these cliffs to escape, and then make my way back to Karolan. You will ride faster without me, escape the knights, and continue the quest. There are no miracles. There is only the honor, wisdom, and strength of men."

"I cannot leave you," said Ilohan. "It is against the Code of the Knights of Karolan."

Jonathan was silent for a long time. Ilohan wondered if he had offended his friend by refusing his offer. Perhaps his plan had been a wise one after all. But the Code of the Knights said, "If a knight accepts companions on a journey, he may not abandon them, except they willingly part in a place of safety, or they die." It was a comfort, at least, that Jonathan did not argue.

Looking back, Ilohan saw their pursuers just entering the valley, tiny with distance. All five were there, and so he knew they had regrouped, taking time even to help the one he had unhorsed regain his mount. That had given him and Jonathan a substantial lead – though the blacksmith was right in saying the double-laden horse could not hold a fast pace forever. In any case, they could not make plans until they reached the pass, when new terrain would come into view that might offer hope of throwing off the pursuit. Escape from Luciyr had seemed impossible, but they had done it – how?

"How did you escape being speared?" asked Ilohan suddenly of Jonathan.

"I thought the sword we found could cut a lance in one stroke," said Jonathan. "I found that I was right."

Ilohan thought about the thick, cured oak lances of the Norkath knights. "You broke your enemy's lance with a single blow?" he asked. "You are a mighty warrior, my friend! But why was your horse killed?"

"I could only cut downward," said Jonathan. "The piece that I broke off the lance hit me across the chest, I think, side-on, so that it did not wound me. It was all too fast to see. The other part, with the knight still driving it from behind, must have been knocked down toward the horse's neck or chest. Alas. It was a noble animal, and our loss is great."

Ilohan could see in his mind Jonathan rearing up in the saddle and slashing forward and down with staggering force, breaking the lance at the desperate last moment before collision. It was easy to imagine the splintered end knocked toward the horse's unprotected chest, and the blunt point driven into the creature's heart: a horrible, bloody impact.

Ilohan also thought he understood the Norkath's reluctance to engage Jonathan on foot. The knight had not been eager to put anything else in the way of Jonathan's terrible sword strokes.

The light suddenly dimmed, and Ilohan looked up. Windblown clouds covered the blue sky and dimmed the sunlight that even without them could not have reached the valley floor. There began to be patches of snow against the walls of the valley, and the air felt thin and cold. It tingled in his lungs as fresh, cold fire, too cold to breathe deeply. His clothes had dried, for the most part, but nonetheless he was cold. Behind him, Jonathan was rummaging in the saddlebags. He brought out only a single leather cloak, and stopped.

"Yes," said Ilohan. "We have, I guess, only one cloak now – and have lost many blankets and much food as well. If we can live through this night and reach the desert, we will not need the cloaks or blankets. The food we will miss – but what are you seeking for so frantically?"

Jonathan had begun searching through the bags at a furious rate, twisting himself into all sorts of awkward positions as he tried to reach every corner without falling off the horse. He stopped suddenly again. Ilohan heard his sigh of relief.

"I was searching for the crown, of course," he said. "I could not remember, but I must have put it in your saddlebags in my haste, so we have not lost it."

"The crown!" said Ilohan. "What – was there a crown with the bones?"

"Yes," said Jonathan. "I had forgotten that you did not see it."

Ilohan looked over his shoulder and down the long, rocky slope. The knights were gaining on them but they still had a substantial lead. The sun on the eastern cliff top was golden: evening would fall soon, perhaps increasing their chances of escape if they could but reach the pass. The tired horse knew what had to be done, and had no need of his hands on the reins. "May I look at the crown?" he asked.

Jonathan gave it to him, and he held the pieces in his hands. It was a circlet of gold, set with rubies. It was a little wider than one finger all the way around, but the metal band was thin so it would rest lightly on the wearer's head. The metal was smooth and cold in his hands, and he could feel the hard edges of the gemstones. He turned the pieces over to look at what had been the inside of the circlet.

"There is something written here," he said. "Inside, where no one could read it if the crown were being worn. The words must be intended for the wearer alone." He held the pieces close to his face to make out the lettering in the failing light. "The inscription is marred by the blow that cleaved the crown, and I think one word is missing."

"What does it say?" asked Jonathan.

"As your…so shall your strength be," Ilohan read. He handed the pieces back to Jonathan and took the reins in his hands again.

"I have not heard of that blessing being connected with the royalty of Karolan, Norkath, or Cembar," Ilohan mused aloud. "But it seems to be a very private message, so that proves nothing. The great Crown of Karolan worn by King Thomas at Aaronkal is also a circlet, but it is wider than this and the metal is thinner still. It is set with diamonds as well as rubies. Beneath the largest diamond in the front is the engraved emblem of the Stone, Sword, and Star. There is no emblem on this crown."

"It cannot be Prince Kindrach's, then," said Jonathan, "for surely the Stone, Sword, and Star would be engraved on the prince's crown."

"Prince Kindrach!" said Ilohan. "I was not thinking of him. The ancient things, of which I was taught in detail, come more quickly to my mind. Why was I not taught of Kindrach, of the recent past? Was it folly in my tutors, forgetting that I was young, and could not know all the history they had lived through? I do not think so. I think King Thomas told them to be silent on these matters. It was strange – yet still I trust him."

"Indeed, I am sure the king did you no wrong," said Jonathan. "But do you think, then, that the crown could be Kindrach's?"

"As you say, it lacks the emblem of Karolan," said Ilohan. "But it is still possible it could be his. The queen's crown, an even circlet set with diamonds, also lacks the emblem."

"What is the blessing of which you spoke?" asked Jonathan.

"'As your days, so shall your strength be,'" said Ilohan. "It is a blessing that God once gave to a people he loved, the people of Asher the son of Jacob, as is told in the Books of the Travelers. It is a very great blessing. It is possible that Karolan or Norkath uses those words to bless its king. They could be written on the inside of King Thomas's crown, for all I know."

"How can you be sure that the missing word is 'days'?" asked Jonathan.

"I am not sure of it," said Ilohan, "but if it were, it would become a blessing that I recognize."

"What does the blessing mean to you, who believe in God?" asked Jonathan.

"I think it means that, by God's help, the strength of those he loves will be enough for the times in which they live, no matter how hard those times are," said Ilohan.

"If a man is strong enough to stand the times he lives in, he will stand," said Jonathan. "If not, he will fall. How could it be otherwise? It seems to me there is no meaning in the words."

"There is very great meaning in the words of the blessing," said Ilohan simply.

"What of the wearer of the crown?" asked Jonathan. "His strength was not sufficient for his fight."

"A man is not blessed by God simply because he wears a crown inscribed with a blessing," said Ilohan. "Yet, also, the defeat of the knight on the rock is not enough to prove the blessing was not truly his. I do not think it was ever meant to promise escape from death, only the strength to bear it in the day that it comes."

Jonathan looked behind them. "Sir Ilohan," he said, "I do not believe in God, and I seek from him no promises that my strength will equal my days. Yet I hope that together you and I will be strong enough for this day. I know your horse is tired, but if we are to live he must go faster."

Behind them they could hear the five Knights of Norkath getting closer, shouting to each other as they came. Ilohan leaned forward and whispered to his horse, and dug his heels into its sides. The exhausted animal sprang forward, and Ilohan and Jonathan leaned low over its neck. The gravel rattled beneath the horse's hooves, and the icy wind blew in their faces. Ilohan knew horses well, particularly his own horse, and he was sure the valiant animal would not carry them much farther. The long uphill ride, doubly laden, had taken a heavy toll on its strength.

The steep sides of the valley shrouded them in a premature dusk. All around them was sculpted stone and broken rock, barren of growing things. The high mountain wind whistled thin and cold among the jagged rocks. The speed of the long chase had increased, but behind them the Norkath knights were still closing the gap. Then suddenly Ilohan looked ahead and gave a great cry.

"The pass!" he said, "We have reached the pass!"

The horse seemed to gain new life when they reached the level ground, and they flew along through the cold air and the deep shade of great cliffs that still continued on their right. On their left, the ground fell away steeply. Soon the path was only a narrow ledge hewn out of the cliff, which below them dropped sheer to a large lake that looked almost black in the evening shadow.

The path was barely wide enough to ride on, and Ilohan slowed his horse. The Norkaths also slowed when they reached the path along the cliff, but somehow they were still closing the distance. Ilohan was searching his mind for some plan of escape. He thought of a desperate fight on the great cliff, far above the blue-black water, and shuddered. The horse stepped on a section of path that shifted beneath its hooves, and he gripped the horse more tightly in an involuntary reaction of terror. The stone was loose there, as if that part of the road was no more than a huge boulder waiting to slide down into the lake and render the route impassible.

Jonathan noticed the unstable section of the path as well. Without giving Ilohan any warning, he pushed himself off the back of the horse and landed with both feet on the stone path. "Wait but a moment," he cried, "and I will stop them."

He lifted a large rock from the path, and ran down to the section that was loose. He raised the boulder above his head, and smashed it down on the path before him with all his strength. It splintered into shards that careened off the cliff wall and fell far, far down into the water with great splashes. Nothing else happened. Jonathan glanced up at the knights. They were nearly upon them. He ran back to get another boulder, and smashed it with all the force he could muster against the loose section of the path. This time there was a crunching, scraping sound, and the whole section of the path slid toward the lake, leaving an impassible, sheer cliff face in its place.

Yet Jonathan had accomplished more than he intended. The rock on which he stood had seemed solid, but it gave way with the rest and his feet were over the edge of the cliff before he had time to react. Terror clutched at his heart, but he spun round as he fell and caught hold of a sloping edge of rock with his hands. He hung there for a moment, his feet dangling over the great drop to the lake. He could feel his hands slipping, and he moved his feet frantically, trying to find some purchase on the smooth cliff face below the path.

Just before he lost his hold, he felt a hand come over the side of the path and grasp his wrist. It was Ilohan's. "Alas," said the knight, straining to pull him back onto the path, "I cannot lift you – yet no! I must."

Jonathan grasped Ilohan's wrist with his own hand, and, with his other hand still gripping the edge, pulled upward with all his might. His head came up over the edge, and he tried to swing his feet up onto the path on his left. The swinging motion pulled Ilohan outward, however, and nearly caused him to lose his footing as well. Jonathan stopped instantly. They strained together, trying as hard as they could, yet the hard, smooth rock did not give them the holds they needed. Ilohan had one hand in a crevice on the cliff wall. This was necessary to hold himself in, but it meant he could not use his full strength to pull Jonathan over the edge. Jonathan scrambled and struggled, but his great strength was useless without a secure hold, and he feared to pull Ilohan off the path as well. Something clattered on the rock wall just above them. It was a Norkath lance, thrown like a javelin.

Ilohan then took a desperate risk. He leaned against the cliff wall and caught hold of Jonathan with both hands. He pulled as hard as he could, and Jonathan came up over the brink and got his feet on the path at last. Yet Ilohan was pulled away from the cliff wall. For a few instants they teetered between the safety of the firm rock wall and the gulf of cold air beyond it. Jonathan tried to sacrifice himself and save Ilohan by pushing him back against the wall, but Ilohan would not let go of his hands. Time seemed to stand still as they balanced on the edge. Then together they toppled off the path and plunged toward the dark lake.

The pure terror of the moment was uncontrollable. There was nothing but empty space beneath their feet. Ilohan let go of Jonathan's hands, and they pushed each other away so that they would not strike one another when they hit the lake. The cold air rushed fiercely past them. They heard the triumphant shouts of the men of Norkath far above. Then they struck the water.

Cold as ice, hard as iron. An impact too violent to be called a splash. The water roared deafeningly in their ears, and they plunged deep into the darkness. Jonathan's lungs cramped in the penetrating cold, and all the air had been dashed out of them by the impact. With a rising, desperate fear of drowning he began to struggle up toward the surface. All his strength, all his intense love of life and desire to live, would not save him if he could not reach the air. The realization was terrible to him. He might indeed die, and the ultimate loss that in Carrah had seemed so distant might now be as near as the icy water pressing in on him from every side. His strength was ebbing fast as his lungs cried out for air. Then – oh blessed moment! – his hands and then his head broke the surface. He filled his lungs with the icy, life giving air, and when he could think again he turned in renewed desperation and scanned the surface for Ilohan.

He did not see him. His eyes turned to the depths, and suddenly he saw his friend, still more than his height from the surface, swimming upward. Ilohan's strokes slowed, faltered, and then renewed. At last to Jonathan's great joy his friend broke the surface.

Ilohan burst out of the water and breathed a great gasp of air. He had feared he would never see the sky again, but it was there in all its glory as he opened his eyes: a deep blue expanse embellished by golden clouds. It was only a fleeting glimpse, and then he was treading water frantically in the piercing cold. Something plunged into the water near him with a violent, abbreviated splash. An instant later there was a splash on his other side, this time unmistakably that of a large rock that had fallen a long way. Ilohan looked back at the dull gray cliff face to see the Norkath knights gathering more rocks, and brandishing their lances. "We are attacked, Jonathan!" he cried, "We must reach the further shore!"

"On, then!" called Jonathan. "Swim as you have never swum before!"

The water was so cold that Ilohan thought it must freeze them; surely it was too cold for a man to swim in and live. It had numbed his skin instantly, and the cold quickly sank deeper. He felt the water was trying violently to suck the last vestiges of heat from his body.

They swam as fast as they could, making for the shore ahead, where the path might continue. Rock after rock hurtled down toward them from the Norkaths above, making ferocious splashes that sprayed the icy water high into the air. They paid little heed to these attacks – dodging was out of the question. Finally the splashes ceased: they had passed out of range, and escaped their pursuers for the moment. Whether they could escape from the deadly cold was another matter. What they would do if they reached the shore, with no possessions but their dripping clothes, was a question neither Ilohan nor Jonathan had any leisure to consider.

Chapter 10

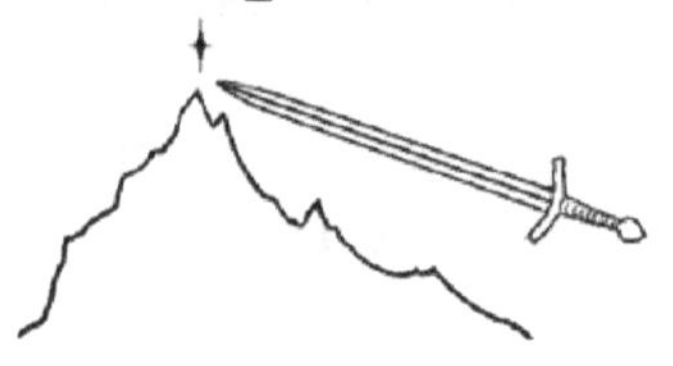

The Anthem of Karolan

BARNABAS BROUGHT HIS LARGEST HAMMER DOWN UPON the lump of iron he was refining. The iron glowed brightly in the dusk, illuminating his hands and the hammer he wielded with dull red light. When the yellow sparks fell in showers, their sudden light played upon his face. His expression was stern and focused, as he beat his iron into purity and strength.

It was not only of his work that he thought as he labored. He thought and prayed for Joseph, his friend. He wondered if it could be that God would call him to go to war, though he hated and abhorred it. Would God send one of his beloved to do the very thing he had made him to shrink from the thought of doing? It seemed unbearably hard. He partly understood the depth of Joseph's horror of war and bloodshed, but he knew that he would never understand it fully. There was nothing like it in his life – nothing that he hated the same way Joseph hated war.

He and Hannah had tried to tell the shepherd that if war came to Karolan, it would be his duty to fight. Yet in doing this, he, at least, had been asking Joseph to do something that he himself could not be called to do: he could not be called to face something as abhorrent to him as war was to Joseph.

Barnabas considered this carefully. The rightness of an action was not altered by its difficulty. If the only right course was impossible it must nevertheless be attempted. But it seemed presumptuous for him, a mere man, to ask another man to do something so hard, to overcome a horror he himself would never face. Perhaps God alone had the right to tell Joseph to go to war.

And yet, he and Hannah had acted in love, and even now he did not think their action wrong. They had gently tried to show Joseph that he might be called to war. They had succeeded. In a sense they had helped to give Joseph a warning, and if war came indeed he would be glad of the time of preparation. Yet the misery through which the gentle shepherd was passing grieved Barnabas. He recoiled from the thought of what would happen to Joseph if war came indeed. Again, his thoughts coming full circle, he wondered if God indeed desired the gentle shepherd to fight.

Then, as his great blows folded and crushed the glowing iron, his thoughts became a prayer for his friend. He confided Joseph to the care of God, asking him to bring the shepherd comfort. He prayed that war would not come to Karolan, and that if it did, Joseph's hatred would be lifted, so that it would not break his heart to go out to fight. Barnabas ceased praying as his blows fell on the glowing iron. He felt in his heart that God would not grant his last two requests. War would come, and Joseph, without any lessening of his horror, would have to face it. "Oh God," prayed Barnabas again, "if it must be so then stand at his side. Help him to make the impossible choice, and do what it will break his heart to do. Guard him and be with him."

Bang, bang... The bright showers of sparks lit the whole smithy with soft flashes of leaping, golden light. The iron was crushed and folded, broken and reformed, beneath the mighty hammer strokes of the blacksmith. Barnabas fell again into imagining the glowing iron as the life of a man, being purified by blow upon blow, by pain endured and suffering passed through. The refining of this iron was nearly over, and he struck with even greater force as he neared the end of his work. The sparks flew outward like the golden stars of a short-lived firmament. "My Lord," said Barnabas, his quiet voice far below the noise of his great hammer blows, "few men have ever known such a trial as will be Joseph's if he is called to war. If he must be hammered with such a blow, let it render him pure and strong indeed – a saint such as the world has seldom seen… Ah, Lord! It is not as though you have borne no greater pain than his."

* * *

The cold was creeping into his bones, paralyzing his muscles, reaching its icy fingers toward his heart. Ilohan struggled onward, but he could not feel his legs or arms. Now and then he had the sensation that he was sinking towards warm rest and oblivion, but each time he shook it off and kept swimming. He knew that if ever he did not shake it off, he would sink into the icy water and die. The feeling of warmth was an illusion, a deathtrap. Yet it was compelling, almost irresistible. Each time it came it was stronger. He grasped his left arm with his right as he swam, gripped hard as he could, but felt no sensation at all from either hand or arm. He felt hunted, weak. He was in danger from both man and nature. It seemed that nothing in all the world would help him. Now even his own body was failing him. "As your days, so shall your strength be," he thought. "Yet alas, that blessing was never spoken to me. Oh, Father, be with us now!"

He was vaguely aware of Jonathan swimming onward beside him, kicking strongly and fighting doggedly onward. "Jonathan," he called, his words blurred by his numb lips, "I am going to die."

"Not while I have strength to save you," said Jonathan loudly – but Ilohan could tell that his lips, too, were numb. "If you can swim no longer, put your arms around my neck and I may be able to pull you."

Ilohan tried this, but he could not hold on with his numb hands. With Jonathan's help he entangled his hands as best he could in Jonathan's clothing, and then he felt himself being towed along by his friend's stronger swimming. Suddenly the warm, peaceful sensation came over him with immense power. He knew he must fight it, but somehow he found that he was not fighting. He sunk into blackness.

Jonathan fought on, now and then putting a hand to Ilohan's arms to make sure his friend did not slip away and his head was still held above water. He was accustomed to cold water, and he was strong – but he had never attempted a swim like this. The dark lake seemed endless, and cold as ice. He fought against a terrible fear that rose within him. He might indeed die here. His great strength was ebbing fast: it might not be enough. Already he could not feel his hands, though he could move his fingers. The possibility that he might perish even though he was doing everything he could seemed a monstrosity to him. His heart rose against it in immense, impotent anger. He might die. He might fail. He might never see Naomi or his parents or Joseph or Glen Carrah again. He might lose it all, everything. Everything he loved, everything he had, everything he was, the only life he would ever live. All.

This was not a wild dream or a dismal imagining. This was his life, his real life, his only life.

Each time he had these thoughts they would fly through his mind in a rush of terror. Then he would silence them by force of will, shake the water out of his eyes, and keep swimming. The darkness was now almost complete. The shore in front of him was visible only as a black band of something silhouetted against the faintly starlit sky. The band of blackness was not getting noticeably nearer. His legs went completely numb, yet he could tell that he was still kicking. He closed his eyes for a moment and felt that he was back in Glen Carrah, drinking something warm before the fire. He opened his eyes again and shook his head in terror.

He fought against the desire to give up, to let go and slip into the illusion of warmth and die. He blinked desperately and peered into the darkness ahead. He did not see the strip of blackness any more. Then with a sudden leap of exhausted hope he realized that he did not see it because it had grown so much closer, towering above him into the sky. A moment later his body shifted suddenly in the water, and after an instant's shock he realized that his numb feet had touched the bottom.

Trembling, weak and clumsy with cold, he lifted Ilohan in his arms and staggered out of the water. He smelled pine; the dark band had been the trees of a pine forest that grew on this side of the freezing lake. He started carrying Ilohan forward into the forest. Pine needles rustled beneath his numb feet. He had no idea what to do. He realized that, though they were now out of the water, they might still die of cold – at least Ilohan might, if indeed he was not dead already. He stomped along with heavy footsteps, trying to pound life back into his unfeeling legs.

He was cold, alone, and without help in a land of which he knew nothing. He wanted to defy the world that seemed to have conspired to kill him and Ilohan – to do something to show the unfeeling universe that he was not defeated yet. Without knowing why he began to sing the anthem of Karolan through numbed lips that stumbled over the words. He remembered the day, many years ago, when his father had taught him the anthem, and it had seemed to him the most wonderful thing in all the world:

Against the host of Dradrag
Our fathers stood alone.
Their valor was unneeded;
No man can conquer stone.

He panted and tried to warm his lips, and then began the second verse. He liked the sound of the bold words shouted into the cold night that threatened to destroy them.

And though today in battle
Our banner must be flown,
Stands Karolan forever;
No man can conquer stone.

Somewhere far off in the darkness he thought he heard a horse galloping. It seemed to him that he should have felt fear, but he felt none. Perhaps he was too tired and hopeless to care. If it was a Norkath knight he hoped he could at least get to the last verse, and defy him to his face, before being killed. Ilohan was still and heavy in his arms. He wondered again if his friend had already died of cold. With shame, he blinked back the tears of hopeless anger that came into his eyes, and began the third verse.

Against love, joy, and freedom
The gauntlet has been thrown.
Fight on, fight on together;
No man can conquer stone.

Love, joy, and freedom. Though all the universe conspired against them, still they were worth fighting for. Love of Ilohan, held unconscious in his arms. The freedom of Karolan, that the Norkaths threatened. The joy of Glen Carrah, where he would yet run with Naomi his beloved, if only he did not die tonight. He let his tears fall this time, and through them he begun the fourth verse.

From the one who weeds the barley
To the king upon his throne,
We walk in honest free –

He stopped abruptly in the middle of the verse, for the sound of galloping was unmistakable and close. He was sure that it was only one horse, and that it was galloping on a stone path. An idea came to him out of nowhere. His heart soared with sudden hope, and he took his life into his hands and ran stumblingly toward the sound. As he ran he shouted out the last verse as loudly as he could, for the benefit of the Norkath knight if his hope proved to be false.

So you who come in conquest
Of a land never your own.
Tremble before our banners;

You shall not conquer stone!

He staggered out of the needle-carpeted pinewoods and heard his numb feet stomping loudly on a stone path that glimmered white in the deep darkness. The horse whinnied, its hoof beats slowed to a trot, and it came into view as a half-seen shape in the darkness. There was no rider. As Jonathan had hoped, it was Ilohan's horse. The horse walked straight up to him and stopped, gently nudging its unconscious master's face. Jonathan laid Ilohan on the ground and searched through the saddlebags for the means to make a fire. He found the flint and iron that he needed, and then considered wearily where the fire should be built. He knew the needle-carpeted pinewoods could catch at a spark, and he had no wish to burn the forest down around them. After trying in vain to think of a better plan, he decided there was nothing for it but the path. He checked that the gold-hilted sword was safely fastened to the saddle: if the fire brought the Norkaths, he would, at least, be able to make a last stand.

He piled half-seen dead branches and pine needles into a large heap in the middle of the wide stone path, and knelt over them. His cold hands fumbled with the flint, but at last he struck out a single bright spark. It flashed into a heap of dry pine needles, and after a moment's anxious waiting a yellow tongue of flame burned straight and small in the dark, cold woods. Light, and life. He almost cried at the beauty of it. At last it did not seem as though all the forces of nature were against them. The fire caught, and glorious red, orange, and blue flames blossomed. The light leaped and danced, bringing color that Jonathan had almost forgotten existed into the dim, cold world of that night.

Jonathan wrapped Ilohan in a dry blanket and laid him near the fire. He knelt anxiously over him. For a few moments he could not tell if his friend was alive or dead. Then at last he was sure that Ilohan was breathing, very shallowly and slowly. He lay down beside his friend, trying to make sure that he was as warm as possible, without being too hot. Slowly the feeling came back to Jonathan's own hands and feet. He looked at his calloused hands in wonder, moving them freely as if he had never done so before. He touched the rough, warm blanket around Ilohan, and marveled that he could feel its weave. He got up and patted the horse's head affectionately, and felt its warm breath.

Ilohan moved suddenly, and opened his eyes. Jonathan knelt beside him. He moved as if to sit up, but fell back on the blanket and closed his eyes. Jonathan shook him gently. "Ilohan," he said, "I rejoice that you are alive. Can you hear me?"

"I can hear you, my friend," said Ilohan, his words still blurred by the cold. "I thank you for saving my life."

"It would not have been in danger if you had not tried to save mine," said Jonathan. "Yet, surprisingly, we are both alive, and may remain so if the Norkaths do not find us."

"Where are we?" asked Ilohan. "How is it that we have a fire?"

"We are at the southern end of the lake that was almost our grave," said Jonathan. "We have a fire because your horse met us on the road. He came to the sound of my voice singing the anthem of Karolan."

"Why did you sing the anthem of Karolan at night, half frozen, in an unknown forest?" asked Ilohan.

"Perhaps I wanted to defy the cold darkness," said Jonathan. "I do not know."

Ilohan thought he knew a reason Jonathan could not. That song was the only one that would have drawn his horse, and his friend had sung it at a moment when most would not have dreamed of singing anything. God's care, then, was the reason: when death had seemed certain, God had saved them through the song. The young knight lay back in his blankets again. The fire burned low, and became a heap of glowing orange coals. Life seeped slowly back into his arms and legs, and he felt it with deep thankfulness. When at last he felt warm and could move freely, he unwrapped the blanket around him and stood up stiffly beside the fire. He swayed on his feet, and the world seemed unsteady for a moment, but then his head cleared.

"Jonathan," he said, "I am very weary, and I am sure that you are also, but we cannot sleep here in the road beside the coals of our fire. We must go to some more concealed place."

There was no answer. Ilohan walked around the fire and found his friend stretched out beside it, with no blanket over the hard stone, sound asleep. He woke him with an effort and repeated his words. "Yes," said Jonathan shortly, and staggered to his feet.

They stuffed the blankets back into their saddlebags, and led away the exhausted horse. The light of their fire was lost in the distance behind them. The stone road they followed was visible only as a barely perceptible lightening of the blackness, leading them on through the cold, scented air of the pinewood. The road began to slope down steeply. Ilohan pressed on until he was nodding on his feet, sometimes starting awake with the impact of a footfall. He shook his head hard to wake himself, and turned off the path into the dark pinewoods.

They found a hollow at the foot of a great tree, and they laid their blankets down there and tethered the horse to a branch. Before they slept, they ate hungrily of the last of the bread from

Carrah. It was hard and stale now, but delicious after the labor of that day. They washed it down with deep draughts of water from their skins, wrapped themselves in blankets, and fell deeply asleep. The pinewoods brooded around them in unseen majesty. The forest creatures sought their burrows, tunnels, and nests against the chill night. In their own hollow, deeply covered with dry pine needles, Ilohan and Jonathan were warm.

Jonathan dreamed of the adventures to come, of great fights valiantly won and journeys successfully completed. Ilohan sank into the depths of warm peace, this time no trick of the icy water but a blessed fact, and he dreamed of days gone by. He heard Queen Sarah's laughter, and felt her strong arms around him. He saw the face of King Thomas, younger and more hopeful, happy in the love of his wife, and easily equal to his great task of ruling Karolan. So, at least, he had seemed, when Ilohan the child had watched, and had known nothing of the harshness of the world.

Ilohan awoke to see the sun shining brightly through tall pines. Thoughts of his foster father and mother were still with him, and he felt a solemn responsibility to use well the chance their love had given him. He stretched his arms toward the sky, feeling deeply that despite the pain and danger in the world, the day was a gift. He had been sure that the icy water would kill him, but it had not. The day, the rest of his life, stretched before him.

Jonathan stood, brushing the brown pine needles off his clothes. He stretched his muscles slowly, grimacing, then stood straight and smiled at Ilohan. "A good morning to you, Sir Ilohan," he said, "shall we set out at once?"

"Not without something to eat, I think," said Ilohan. He searched carefully through one saddlebag, and found no food at all. He felt through the other, and found only one stale piece of bread. "It will be a hungry journey," he said, holding up the crust to Jonathan. "This is all we have."

"Alas!" cried Jonathan, "Pardon my grave error!"

"Friend," said Ilohan, shocked at the depth of grief in Jonathan's face, "what on earth do you mean?"

"I must have put all the food in the saddlebags of my horse," said Jonathan, still in the voice of one stricken with guilt.

"But, surely, it was only an accident of haste," said Ilohan. "You did not will to starve me."

"Of course not," said Jonathan, "but my error is still worthy of your anger."

"Jonathan," said Ilohan sharply, "do not be a fool! You had to pack the saddle bags in haste – you did it well, leaving little of our gear behind. You had no time to plan, and no way of knowing your horse would be lost. You have already saved my life more than once this journey. I wish, therefore, to hear no more about your grave errors."

They each ate half the crust in silence, Ilohan musing on the hungry journey ahead, but also on his companion's startling quickness to blame himself.

Presently Jonathan asked, "How many days will it take to cross the desert?"

"Seven at least," said Ilohan, "perhaps eight or even more. However, a man may starve for twice as long and still live and walk. Water we shall have, for the desert path skirts the mountains, and now and then crosses a stream. Grass, too, may grow by the streams for our horse. Since we are already pursued by Norkaths, we cannot ride east out of our way, to seek food among the farms of transmontane Norkath – and, of course, we cannot go back to purchase supplies in Karolan."

Squirrels fled chattering into the trees as they led the horse back to the path. Once found, the road led them almost due south, descending steeply through more pinewoods. They halted by a laughing stream to fill their water skins. Ilohan's horse, too, drank deeply and ate of the green grasses that still grew there.

The path soon dropped into a valley, in which at first there was a deep, cold river – flowing, Ilohan guessed, from the lake that had nearly killed them the night before. As they continued, the valley became steeper, drier, and more rocky. The stream sank into the thirsty ground and vanished.

It was mid afternoon, with the sun high in the southwest before them, when they rode down past the last dry evergreen bushes, and out through the great mouth of the valley. The cool pinewoods were far behind them, up in the mountains they had left. Ahead was the endless desert, stretching out to meet the unimaginably distant sky. A hot wind blew in their faces and parched their lungs. The desert here was not a sea of sand, as Ilohan had expected, but a wilderness of stone, barren beneath the blazing sky. The road dwindled to a dusty track across the stone. Ilohan was struck by the hard, clear colors of the naked rock.

Jonathan felt the hot wind whipping his hair, and despite the grueling journey ahead, his spirits rose. The desert was harsh – crossing it might take the last of their strength – but it was also wonderful. He had never known there existed a land of such desolate, wild freedom. It called to him to run and fly, yet he knew he could not. He could spend his strength against the desert in vain, and he rejoiced in this knowledge. Here was a place beyond him, the kind of place he had longed to see.

The hooves of their horse rang dully on the dusty gravel, and their brisk trot seemed a crawl beneath the vastness of the sky. Presently Jonathan heard Ilohan begin to sing in a low, awed voice. Neither the words nor the tune were of Karolan. It sounded to Jonathan like this:

Lo skiera scha cal whyethree
Lo hrethri scha yeen yohilee
Lon ikrok scha neared whython
Lo hrado scha Arnith thraigon

Korak srad astrailo, srad thraiah
Astrailon thro fooshgorn whyflaiah
Whyfra strai scho Zarnith sgearoth
Scha Arnith fo hreon zruboth

"What was that?" he asked when it was finished.

"The war song of the Zarnith," said Ilohan. "Seeing the great desert that was their home reminded me of it. It is a very fierce song, unforgiving as the desert, about a warfare that is very different from the warfare of Karolan."

"What does it mean?" asked Jonathan.

"This is what I was taught it means," said Ilohan:

Our banner the dust;
Our mother the sky;
Our arrows the death that has wings;
Our father the windblown, hot Desert.

None stand before us, none ever.
Before us all enemies fly.
Fly before the Children of the Desert in despair.
The Desert will swallow your bones.

"Were they ever defeated in battle?" asked Jonathan.

"No," said Ilohan, "only by the mountains of Karolan."

Jonathan looked at the distant horizon, where bare stone hills met the pale blue edge of the endless sky. "Is it known if any Zarnith still live?" he asked.

"No one in Karolan has ever seen the distant reaches of the desert from which they came," said Ilohan. "It may be that they perished many lives of men ago. Or, for all we know, they might come again in force tomorrow."

"They must have been great fighters," said Jonathan.

"Yes," said Ilohan. "But the only honor they knew was to fight bravely forever."

"Then they were the most dangerous men in all the world," said Jonathan.

"Of that I am not sure," said Ilohan.

Jonathan did not press him, though he wondered who Ilohan thought was more to be feared than a bold, determined fighter who cared nothing for the justice of his cause.

In the hot sun and dry air they grew thirsty faster than Jonathan would have thought possible. Now and then they would dismount, Ilohan would let the horse lap water from his hands, and they would jog along on foot a while to let the animal rest from bearing them. Gratefully, Jonathan watched the sun sink at last toward the horizon, in front of them and to the left. He stared in wonder at what followed, for in Glen Carrah, the sun set behind the mountains and silhouetted them. Here, the awesome peaks caught the evening sunlight, and glowed bright against the deepening blue sky. He was awestruck when the sun went brilliant red: he had never before seen it set over a low horizon. When it slipped beneath the hills, it left the sky glowing with colors that seemed to him the richest he had ever known.

When night fell, he saw above him the same stars that he and Naomi loved. Low in the south, however, were stars that never shone on Glen Carrah because the mountains blocked them. He stared at them a long time, as the horse plodded on in the darkness, marveling that Naomi had never seen them. She never would unless she came here, or somewhere where one could see the far southern sky. He had no wish for her to come to this barren place, he thought – but he would very much like her to see Luciyr.

As they continued on through the darkness, hunger began to trouble Jonathan, especially during the intervals when they jogged beside the horse. He wondered when Ilohan intended to rest, but did not like to ask, knowing his own strength was the greater. As the long, starry night wore on, hunger and weariness narrowed the focus of his mind until his whole world was the back of the horse: Ilohan's dim form in front of him, the jingling of the metal buckles of the harness, the rustling of their clothes, and the steady footfalls of the faithful horse.

He found himself jogging along almost in a dream, lightheaded with exhaustion and hunger, with no memory of getting down from the horse. Ilohan jogged beside him, head down. Jonathan looked up and saw the winter stars, brighter than he had ever seen them before. It was comforting to recognize constellations he knew by heart, but however well known, they still seemed strange, blazing above the unearthly desert rather than the snowy winter landscape of his home. He looked along the southern horizon, seeking stars that never graced the sky of Glen Carrah. He rubbed his eyes, and looked again. The startlingly bright star he had seen was still there, shining with a warm white light while twinkling furiously. It astonished him to see such a bright star for the first time; all the other stars of that brightness were well known, old friends to him.

"Do you know that star?" he asked Ilohan, pointing.

Ilohan's answer came slowly, sounding breathless and very tired. "I am not sure," he said. "It may be the star called Varilie, the Mountain Topaz. It can be seen now and then from the battlements of Aaronkal – but it never looks as bright as that."

Ilohan stopped the horse for them to remount. As they rode forward, he wondered how Jonathan could spare any thoughts for the stars. His own mind had been wholly filled with the longing for food. He told himself that knights often had to go without eating for several days, and that it was nothing. But the intense and hopeless hunger, the longing for food that simply was not there, did not seem like nothing. The hollow feeling was oddly inconstant: sometimes he felt more or less content, only a little weak and light. At other times – as now – he felt he could eat four meals in succession.

Dark hours passed in the wearying rhythm of alternate riding and jogging. Ilohan was often only half awake. A time came when he was more alert than usual, and noticed a tiny glow behind them in the east. The sky just over the hills there held a small, soft aura of warm light. He stared, wondering, for it was too small to be the longed-for dawn. Then the Morning Star rose brilliant above the desert hills, and his heart leaped for joy. It brightened as it climbed, and soon it cast their shadows, faint but wonderfully sharp, on the light sand of the trail ahead of them. "The Morning Star, herald of the dawn!" said Jonathan.

"Yes, and star of the Stone, Sword, and Star, the great banner of Karolan," said Ilohan.

It climbed high into the crystal blackness of the sky, until it seemed to pale even the Ceranim by its brightness, and then, washing slowly up the sky behind them, came the dawn itself. The desert came into clear view in the cold twilight. Then the east horizon glowed blue, blue-green, yellow, white, brighter white, dazzling white, blinding white, and at last the piercing brilliance of the sun leaped into the perfect desert sky and flooded the land with light.

"Well," said Jonathan, "we have traveled all night. Did you push on thus for fear of the Norkath pursuit?"

"Not chiefly," said Ilohan wearily. "A note on the map said we must travel at night – day is too hot – day is for rest."

Jonathan looked around doubtfully for any shelter where they might rest, but then saw that Ilohan was already guiding the exhausted horse off the path toward a rugged hill. When they reached it, they took refuge in a narrow gorge that would cast some shade. Jonathan saw a large flat rock on the valley floor. He put his hands beneath it and tried with all his strength to lean it up against the side of the gorge, where it would have given excellent shelter. When his utmost effort moved it not at all, he realized that his weariness had made him foolish: ten men could not have shifted the massive stone. They tethered the horse, lay down against the south side of the gorge, and pulled their blankets over their heads to shut out the light. Thanks to their weariness, they were soon deeply asleep.

Chapter 11

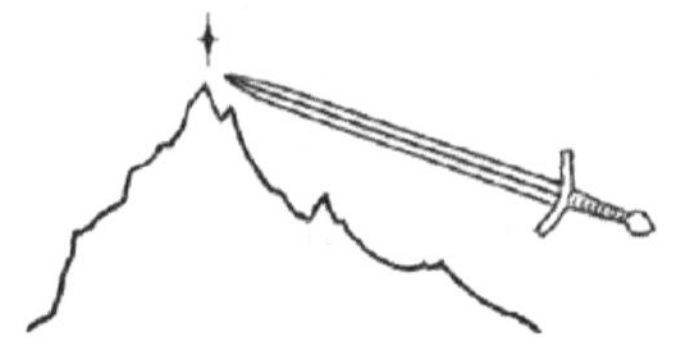

Desert Charity

IN THE AFTERNOON ILOHAN AWOKE. HE WAS STILL IN shade, but the heat was stifling and rocks dug into his back. From Jonathan's impatient movements beside him he knew that the blacksmith, too, was awake and uncomfortable. Neither spoke. When the sun sank low in the west they got up in silence, drank more of their dwindling supply of water, and continued doggedly on their way.

The desert seemed endless: beautiful and awesome, but utterly unforgiving and inhospitable. Ilohan remembered often, as the sun set and the evening darkened into night, the Zarnith curse with which the war song ended: "The desert shall swallow your bones." Yes, it could, and of them no one might ever find a trace. It was too big. It had been a vague region on a map, or a word in the mouths of his teachers at Aaronkal. Now it was an immense, breathtaking, heartbreaking reality whose realness was pounded into him with every footfall of the weary horse.

Hunger weakened them, blurred their thinking, made even the simplest actions or decisions difficult. The Ceranim wheeled over their heads, brilliant in the clear desert sky. They seldom looked at it. When they did, each felt a strange mixture of hope and dismay. The mighty swath of starcloth staggered and dazzled them. The sight of it lifted their hearts. But it was far, far above them, beyond the reach of men. The stars could give them no help, and the splendor of the heavens was beyond their knowledge. They never looked at it for long at a time.

After a look, Jonathan would turn away, admiring in his heart the beauty that, perhaps, would last forever. He would remember how Naomi loved the stars, and wonder if some strange longing called her out of sleep to see them now. He would think of nights when he and Naomi had rejoiced together in the great concourse of the sky, and their spirits had soared in awe, while the grass of Glen Carrah was soft and sweet beneath them. Then he would smile, and stare into the darkness ahead of them with renewed determination. The stars could lend no help, yet true men would carry on to the end. Nothing but death could stop them, and death would not come. Not yet.

Ilohan would turn away and pray, for strength to carry on, and for a successful conclusion to their journey. The end of their quest seemed as far away as the stars, and beneath their tireless glory he felt helpless and frail. Yet he believed that God had made the stars, and was greater than they, and yet loved one stumbling knight called Ilohan. He could think of no reason why God should love him, but he repeated to himself words from the Books of the Travelers that told of God's love, and he believed. Even now, when his thoughts were blurred and his hope wavered on the edge of despair, he believed. He did not feel God's love, but somewhere in his soul there was a certainty that was not shaken.

Varilie rose over the southern horizon, bright and yellow, and twinkling wildly. It stayed low in the south, and set again just as the Morning Star leaped up behind them. A sudden exclamation from Jonathan woke Ilohan from a doze. The sound of the horse's hooves on the ground seemed odd, somehow hollow.

"What?" asked Ilohan groggily, shaking his head to clear it.

"We have just passed a bridge!" repeated Jonathan. The words sank into Ilohan's tired mind, until he suddenly realized their importance. He stopped the horse. A bridge meant a channel – and a channel might mean... water. They dismounted shakily, and led the horse back to the edge of the ravine. It was small, not deeper than twice the height of a man. After some searching they found a way down into it. Their footsteps crunched on dry gravel: the creek bed contained no water. It was not wholly useless, however: soft stalks brushed their legs in the darkness, and they soon heard the horse grazing hungrily on the dry grass. Ilohan and Jonathan lay down in the dust beneath the shelter of the stone bridge. There was as yet no sign of dawn in the sky, but by one consent they wrapped themselves in their blankets and slept. Even when the sun rose high, the shade beneath the bridge was cool and deep, and despite their hunger they slept soundly. It was not until near sunset that Ilohan awoke.

Jonathan was still sleeping beside him. Most of the ravine was plunged in blue evening shadow, but the rocks on its eastern side caught the warm sunset light. The young knight lay still for a few moments. He felt weak and a little lightheaded, but no longer desperate for food. Water, however, they must have, for all but one of the skins they had filled on the descent from Luciyr was empty. He got up slowly, and walked out from under the bridge. The horse had grazed well during the night, and the marks of its hooves were everywhere.

In the center of the ravine, where the ground was lowest, he noticed a place where the hoof prints were dark against the light-colored sand. He knelt slowly and dug a little, feeling the sand damp in his hands. Farther down, it was wetter still. At last, a tiny pool of clear water formed in the bottom of his hole. He lay down on the sand and drank draught after draught of cool, fresh water from his cupped hands. He had not misread the map: streams from the great mountains did cross the desert road – and they did carry water, for those who did not despair at the sight of their parched channels.

Ilohan laboriously filled their empty water skins. Jonathan woke, and first he and then the horse drank deeply from the little well. The glowing sunset still lit the sky when they resumed their journey – hungry still, but with a full supply of water.

To Jonathan the stars seemed slightly veiled, perhaps with a haze of dust. As the long night wore on, the hollow feeling in his stomach worsened. He wondered how much his strength was reduced with every day he did not eat. Certainly he was weakening, and quickly. That knowledge irked him far more than the ache of hunger itself.

Blue dawn was bright in the sky when they slept in a crevice in one of the low hills beside the trail. They rested fitfully through the long day that poured its aching brightness into their shelter. At sunset they dragged themselves out of the crevice and set out again without a word.

The waxing crescent moon shone high and bright over the desert at dusk, but soon set, red and dull, behind the rocky hills on the horizon. Ilohan's thoughts were wild and confused from hunger. "God loves me," he whispered, trying to cut through his confusion with simple truth. "I go on the king's mission, with his blessing. Now another step. Now another. How weak I am! Keep walking, horse. We will make it. Keep walking."

Jonathan's mind wandered too, in the hungry night. Strange visions of himself and Naomi passed before his eyes. He saw her wandering barefoot across the hot desert with him, or swimming in the deadly cold water of the dark blue lake. Yet, through all the confusion and fear of loss which filled his thoughts, there ran the breathtaking certainty of Naomi's love. Her love was enough, he thought: no terror in the world could dismay him as long as she lived and loved him. He shook his nodding head, swallowed nothing into his empty stomach, and looked around him.

Varilie was at its highest, a brilliant point of warm light in the south. He could see the desert quite clearly in the starlight. He turned and scanned the mountain horizon to the northwest. He blinked, rubbed his eyes, and looked again. It was still there. A warm light shone out from the dark land, as if Varilie had fallen on the earth. Looking closer, he could see the dark bulk of a large stone structure behind the light. It stood on the desert floor a little ahead of them and to the right, quite near the path. The sight suddenly resolved itself in Jonathan's weary mind as a castle with a single lighted window or door thrown open.

"Look!" he cried, pointing, "Can you see it?"

Ilohan had been plodding along beside the horse, but he raised his head at Jonathan's shout. Yes, he saw it: a lighted dwelling – no, a garrisoned fortress – here in the barren desert. He turned the horse off the path without a word. Whether they were friends or foes of Karolan, the garrison would have supplies. Ilohan quickly decided to risk their possible enmity – and pay out all the money he had, if necessary – to purchase food. As they drew closer, Ilohan saw that the building was not, after all, a fortress. It was a church, or a monastery. Thankfulness filled his heart. "We have come to a place where dwell some of the servants of God," he said. "Here, of all places on earth, we can be sure of getting food."

The light shone through a window in one of a pair of great oaken doors that formed the main entrance to the church. When they reached the doors, Ilohan tugged on a rope that hung down near them, and a bell rang cheerfully inside.

One great door opened part way, and a man with a stern, bristly-bearded face looked out. "Have you come on pilgrimage to the grave of the martyr Fersenius?" he asked in a gruff voice.

"No," said Ilohan, "we are on a long journey, and have been attacked by lawless men and lost our supplies. We ask only for food and drink to continue on our way."

"Travelers," said the gray-bearded man suspiciously. "Travelers from Karolan, or Norkath. Why should I give you food?" Ilohan was shocked and dismayed that they were not offered food at once in the name of God.

"Please, Sir," he said, "we are indeed starving. We are honest men on an urgent errand. We mean no disrespect to the tomb of your martyr, and we can pay for our food if we must."

"The ordinary dole for pilgrims is a loaf of bread for each person," said the man. "What more you need, you must gather from the others in your party."

"But Sir," cried Ilohan, "we are not pilgrims. We are alone, and starving, with a long journey ahead. We need more than just a little bread." But even as he was speaking, the man tossed them two loaves of dry bread and slammed the oak door shut. "Sir!" called Ilohan, pounding on the unyielding door in vain, "We starve! It is not enough! As you love God or man, come back!" They waited long before the motionless oaken barrier. At last Jonathan picked up the stale loaves.

"The bounty of the servants of your God," he said quietly. "He is real, and from him comes all goodness – or so say the preachers from Tremilin. Here in the shadow of a fortress inhabited by his people, the evidence does not seem very great."

Ilohan took a small bite of the bread, chewed it long, and swallowed with difficulty. "God is real," he said, turning away to hide the tears of shame and disappointment on his face, "and though all his servants disgrace him, still he is good."

They ate the bread very slowly, and with much water. Stale though it was it brought them new life. Their minds were clearer, and their spirits higher, when they rode away from the church.

"Why do you believe in God?" asked Jonathan when they were on the road again.

"I know him," said Ilohan, "I have felt his love and seen his mercy."

"But I have not," said Jonathan, "and you will never be able to show me that you have. Why did you first believe? Why did anyone in Karolan ever believe?"

"Long ago in the reign of Nirolad," said Ilohan, "travelers came to Karolan from a far country, bringing the news of Christ our Savior, the Son of God. They had borne great hardship on their long journey, and when they spoke it was with honesty and authority. The king and people of Karolan believed them, and they sought for love, healing, and freedom from guilt. They sought for God, and Christ, his Son. They found them, found healing, found that the words of the travelers were true. So it was in the days of Nirolad. So it was for me."

"You believed the words of those who taught you, looked for God, and found him?"

"Yes," said Ilohan, "I did. Or perhaps I should say he found me. He opened my eyes."

"To see what?" asked Jonathan.

"To see that he had been there all along," said Ilohan. "To see that I was guilty and weak, and that he was pure and strong, and yet still loved me. To see that I had always needed him and that because he loved me I had found him."

"I do not think I am guilty and weak!" said Jonathan, shocked.

"You are not, by the measure of men," said Ilohan.

"How could there be a truer measure?" asked Jonathan.

"Do you truly think there could not be?" returned his friend.

Jonathan was silent for a long moment. "In my heart there is a measure stricter than the measure of men," he said at last. "Yet in this measure also, I am guiltless. Guiltless, I mean, save for my error which deprived us of food – but you yourself have bade me not to consider that."

"But is there nothing else – I mean, are you indeed guiltless –" Ilohan began, and then stopped, thinking. "But I do not think I like that word, guiltless. It is like saying, 'not empty'. But are you full – full of goodness – does it seem to you that you are as good as you ever want to be? Do you have hope that one day you will know immeasurable goodness, and that in you there will not be even a hint of anything dishonorable or unjust?"

Again, silence reigned for a while. "No, I am not as good as I want to be," said Jonathan at length. "And I do not see any reason to hope I will ever be perfect. But I am good – I am as close as I can come to perfect goodness, justice, and honor. Surely that must be enough."

"Is it enough for you? Do you truly think it is enough?"

"Sir Ilohan, I do."

"Jonathan," said Ilohan, "there is no one I would rather ride with on this adventure. You are honest, trustworthy, and full of courage. Yet you are blind. You hope for too little. God has put before you an adventure that leads to more goodness than you can possibly imagine. You do not set out on the adventure because you do not see it. I pray that God will someday open your eyes."

"What of the cruel gatekeeper of the church? If your God is real, why does he suffer his servants to behave thus?"

"I do not know. I believe him still, yet I do not know." There was another silence. Ilohan spoke again. "Although I do not know, yet consider this. That gatekeeper owes more to God than he could ever owe to us. We are his fellow men, whom he should have served with kindness but did not. God is his Creator, Christ is his Savior, yet he dishonored him, disobeyed him, scorned his service. It is God first whom he has wronged, not us, yet God –"

"Stay!" cried Jonathan suddenly. "There are hoof beats behind us!"

Ilohan veered the horse off the road, and stopped, listening. "It comes at a gallop," he said, "yet it is alone, and too light to be a knight's charger." He listened for another moment, then rode back onto the path. The strange rider reined in a short distance away.

"Are you the travelers who sought food at the church this night?" he asked.

"We are," said Ilohan.

"I ask your forgiveness for the welcome you received there," said the stranger. "I have come in the hope of mending it."

"We thank you," said Ilohan. The young knight relaxed, but Jonathan kept his hand on his sword hilt.

The stranger dismounted and led his horse to them. "God forbid that you should come to his church, and not receive his servants' charity," he said. "Take the horse, and all the food he carries, and go in peace."

Jonathan dismounted, and approached the man. "You have greatly improved my opinion of churchmen," said Jonathan. "May I ask who you are?"

"I am Brogal, son of Mudien of Ceramir," he said. "There are many who claim to be servants of God, but do not know him."

"Do you say, then, that the gatekeeper is one of these, but you are a true servant of God?" asked Jonathan.

"The gatekeeper is deaf, and prone to harshness," said Brogal. "Of him I will say no more. Yet it is my privilege and joy to say, with all praise to Christ my Savior, that among the children of Ceramir you will find none who claim to be God's servants but are not."

"I thank you from my heart, and would learn more of Ceramir," said Ilohan, dismounting and stepping forward.

"Where are you bound?" asked Brogal.

"To Harevan," said Ilohan.

"How long will you stay?" asked Brogal.

"Some days," replied Ilohan.

"Then inquire when you get there, and you will indeed learn more of Ceramir." Even in the starlight Jonathan could see a change come over Brogal's face, like a wave of bright wind washing across the golden grain in Glen Carrah, he thought. "Ceramir, the Cloth of Joy," said Brogal, "spend a day there and forget it if you can! Farewell!"

Before they could say another word to him he had laughed heartily and run off into the night. His free and joyful stride as he flew along the desert path reminded Jonathan of his own, when he ran in Glen Carrah.

"There goes a man I would like to know better," he said.

"I am very thankful," said Ilohan, "but I do not understand where he came from or how it was that he could give us so much aid. What and where is Ceramir, the Cloth of Joy, and what brings him here from there?"

"I do not know," said Jonathan, "but I understand very well a fresh horse and saddlebags full of food." He was looking through them as he spoke, and he brought out smoked meat, cheese, and bread. They ate sparingly of the cheese and bread, careful after their long fast, and then rode on into the night. They went faster that night than they had since Jonathan's horse was killed.

*　　　*　　　*

Joseph woke at dawn in his cottage below Glen Carrah. He and Naomi ate a hurried breakfast as the cool, clear morning brightened around them. She did not ask him why he ate so early or so quickly. When the meal was over he got up swiftly and went to the door. He turned to her and said, "I am taking the sheep up into the glen today."

She met his gaze. "Why, Father?" she asked.

"Your love has told you, Naomi," he said.

"I understand, Father," she said. "You have my prayers."

"I need them. Farewell." He was gone. Naomi opened all the windows in the house to the morning freshness. He had gone to make a decision, at last, whether he would fight if war came to Karolan. She knew his suffering so deeply that she felt it as her own. It seemed to her, as it seemed to him, that gentleness was part of his character and that fighting would violate who he was. Yet of this she was not sure. She wondered why he had to suffer now, why he could not wait to know for certain if war would come. For some reason he had felt that he could not. Her fingers wove the wool as she worked at a west-facing window, yet her eyes did not see the sunlit glen, and she poured out her heart to God on behalf of her father.

If Naomi did not see the glen before her eyes, Joseph, despite his distress, was aware of it. The sun rose above the mountains and lit the light mists that covered the glen, making it a fairyland of blue sky and golden air. The grass through which Joseph led his sheep was wet with dew at first, but it dried quickly even as the sun dispelled the mist. Far up in Glen Carrah he stopped and let the sheep graze. He lay down in the soft, tall grass and gazed at the blue sky between the waving heads of wild grain. It was odd, he thought. This place, this Glen Carrah, his home, seemed worthy of heroic defense, yet at the same time it seemed too beautiful to exist in a world where there could also be war.

"Father," he said, "how can it be right to kill? Surely it is wrong, at least for me, for whom the very idea is horrible. Yet is it not true that sometimes you have desired your servants to kill in the past, and have been pleased with them when they did it?"

The grass waved in the wind and the sheep munched contentedly. "They would destroy this," he said as he thought of the Norkath armies. "They would burn Carrah and eat my sheep, and sell Naomi as a slave. If it is ever right to kill anyone, surely it is right to kill them. Surely it is better for them to be killed, than to do such evil. It is a dark stain on the world that wars are fought, yet it would be darker still if evil were never resisted. I must let go of my hatred, and bless those who go out to fight, bless Jonathan and Barnabas. Yet I cannot go myself. Father, I thank you for the others who will go, and I ask you to bless them and give them victory. But I cannot go. You, who made me, surely know that I cannot go."

Still, he had not decided, and he knew it. He lay motionless and quiet, listening to the sounds around him, but his peace was not the peace of a decision made. Rather, it was the peace of resignation. He had given up his resistance, and today the choice would be settled, one way or another, between him and the God he worshipped.

The words he had spoken a short time ago, and had not truly considered, came back to him and he trembled from head to foot. "They would sell Naomi as a slave." Naomi, the only daughter of Abigail, his beloved. She was immeasurably more precious to him than his own life, more precious to him than all, save God alone. He had called war Hell, and even the idea of it was a torment to him. Yet for Naomi, would he not go into Hell? Was there anything he would not suffer for her?

Suddenly he considered it in still another way. Suppose he remained behind, and Karolan fell. The invaders would come to Glen Carrah, would come to his own house, would batter down the door and take Naomi and himself as slaves. Would he let them? Would he not fight them then, with his crook, his shears, his hands, anything he could, until they killed him? He knew he would. Though it would destroy him, though it would be hopeless, still he would do it. Would it not be better to fight in the Army of all Karolan, to defend Naomi and Carrah there, while there was yet a chance of victory?

Then, like a lighted door flung open in a dark night, a new idea came to him and brought great hope into his mind. He would take Naomi and fly, taker her and hide in a place where no Norkath would ever find her. Though Karolan fell, yet he would defend her, not with sword and bow that could be defeated, but with mountain and forest that no man could ever conquer. They would find refuge in the beauty of the world, and it would cover them that they might never be found. His heart soared. He did not know now where they might hide, but weeks, perhaps months or even years, lay before him to find out. Let them burn Carrah and eat the sheep and rape Karolan. What was any of that in his sight compared to Naomi? Nothing, less than nothing, utterly swept away in his love for her.

But would this course bring Naomi joy? Although his thoughts had been following a hopeful path, the question stopped them like a barrier of stone. It was not merely Naomi's safety that he valued, but her joy – not merely her existence, but her life. Would it be an act of love to take her away, and leave Jonathan, Hannah, Barnabas, Glen Carrah and Karolan itself to perish if the war were not won? Would she, with her own love and courage, even follow him in such a course? It had never occurred to him before that merely saving her from death might not be enough – might not be fully loving.

He thought of the all the people of Karolan – all the daughters, all the fathers who loved their children. Each, he realized, faced the same choice as himself. They could fly to the wild places of Karolan, the high valleys of the mountains or the barren forests in the north. They stood a fine chance of escaping, of preserving the lives of their loved ones – always providing that other men stood and fought. On the other hand, they could join the great army that would be mustered, and try to preserve all Karolan. It was a terrible choice.

Joseph took a deep breath of the sweet air of Glen Carrah. He made a conscious effort to look at the blue sky, and listen to his sheep calmly eating – then he sank back into the dark conflict of his thoughts.

If all the fathers and young men in Karolan made the choice he longed to make, the Norkaths would march in unopposed, and burn and plunder Karolan as they pleased. The Karolans would flee to every place that might hide them. Their sheer numbers would defeat them. Many would be hunted down and captured, while most of the rest would starve. Karolan would die, in dishonor. Those who sought to preserve their lives would lose them nonetheless. Flight was safety only if most did not fly. Those who fled would be traitors to those who stayed.

Still there remained the unbearable desire to fly to the mountains, in the hope that most of the men of Karolan would fight. It was likely that they would. Few if any abhorred fighting as he did; some, like Jonathan, actually hoped for it. Those who wanted to fight also more often knew how: they were the ones who practiced archery or swordplay, and had real skill as warriors. What could he do, one poor shepherd who knew nothing?

But if flying were indeed treachery, if it were evil, the absolute command of God stood against it. He must do what he could, fight with whatever skill he had, if it was evil not to fight. But was it evil? What if, instead of being treachery to Karolan to stay with Naomi, it was treachery to Naomi to leave her and fight for Karolan? But here his thoughts halted. He felt the choice closing in on him, like a wolf or a lion on a wounded sheep. For he had already concluded that to stay beside Naomi and fly with her into the mountains might not be the course of real love for her.

He remembered her own words: "Alas for this golden life! I fear there comes an adventure that will break it." He must try to protect her golden life. All the ways of escape he had tried were now closed, and his decision was clear at last.

What could one poor shepherd do? He could make the selfless choice his God required of him. He could join the Army of All Karolan when it was mustered. If all the men of Karolan made that choice, the nation might be saved. If none of them did, it would surely be destroyed.

He reviewed in his mind how the choice had been made, what had finally decided him in the end. Jonathan, he knew, governed his life by what he called justice and honor. Joseph sought a different word. Justice and honor were part of his choice: God's demand that he act justly and honorably toward the other men of Karolan. But it was love that had decided him. It was love of Naomi that made him want not only to save her from death, but also to preserve the home and way of life that she loved. But even love was not enough. Love sometimes meant only a possessive thing – a thing that would have made him want to keep Naomi close to him, and safe, even if it made her unhappy. The foundation of his choice, he thought, was love with wisdom – love with understanding – holy love.

What were justice and honor, and holy love? They were beautiful and warm, strong and bright as the sun – but hard and unyielding as stone, and sharp as a sword. Whence had they come, that he should yield to them? They had come from God, and he must follow him.

The sun was high in the sky, and it was warm on his face and body. Its light coming through his closed eyelids filled his vision with red: the red of his blood. Blood and love, he thought. The two things had been linked for uncounted ages, from the blood of the animals Abraham had cut in half when God promised unfailing love to him, up to the blood he himself had seen on the day his sun had set: Abigail's lifeblood pouring out, while for love of him she tried to bear his child. And at the center of all was the blood of God himself, raining down from a cross onto the thirsty earth.

It was God who required of him the choice he now had made, the same God whom he loved, with whom Abigail had now found rest. God had the right to require of him anything he could give. "Father, I will fight," he said. "Give me now your strength."

He felt sick with fear of the horrors he had chosen to face – but he also felt at peace. He had called war Hell, but Hell was eternal, while war was not. It might indeed seem to him like the agony of the damned, but it would end. Either he would die, or the war would be over.

He stood up suddenly and gathered his sheep together. It was well past midday and the glen was warm. He was pleased to see that none of the sheep had strayed far. He leaned on his crook at the edge of the flock, facing the great mountains. His decision did not waver, but fear and horror came suddenly upon him with great power, and the mountains seemed to waver before his gaze. The torment would not last forever, it was true, but that seemed as paltry a comfort to him as it might to a prisoner about to be torn to pieces on the rack.

He collapsed on the ground in tears. "Father," he cried, "must it be thus? Must you call me to do the one thing that, for me, is harder than any other – the only thing I cannot imagine doing? Yet I am yours. Your will be done – but be with me, or I cannot stand."

He got up from the ground and looked again at the sky, and there was comfort in its limitless blue depth. "So be it, Father," he said, "it is not today that I must fight; today I have only to live. In each day give me the strength I need for it, even up to the day when at last I will have to fight."

*　　　　*　　　　*

He sat with Naomi that evening, eating bread, milk and honey before the fire. After their meal was finished neither spoke for a while. At last Naomi said, "May I ask you what I long to know?"

"Yes, Naomi," said Joseph.

"What have you decided?"

"I have decided that I must fight."

"I know something about this decision that I think you never will, Father."

"What is that, my daughter?"

"Only this: for making it, you are a hero."

"It is what I have to do."

"What I have told you is true," said Naomi. "As I said, I think you will never come to know it. Yet I hope hearing me say it brought you joy." They sat in silence, both intent on their own thoughts, and a spell seemed woven to give each a special vision of the other.

Joseph looked at his daughter. Her unconsciousness of herself, her sorrow and concern focused on him, lent her a special beauty. When the sudden golden light of a flaring log shone full upon her face, he turned away, for her loveliness seemed to him more than mortal.

Looking at him in her turn, she saw wisdom and patience written deeply in his face, and imagined that ancient prophets or kings must have looked as he did now – but he had no suspicion of his greatness.

Joseph spoke, breaking the spell. "You must take the flock as usual tomorrow, my daughter. I will go to Barnabas and ask him to teach me how to fight."

Naomi embraced him, knowing the depth of the pain his choice cost him, awed that he had made it nonetheless. "Yes, Father," she said. "Oh Father, how I love you! If in any way I can bless you, tell me how."

"All your life is a blessing to me, my daughter. Only be who God has made you. Deeply I love you."

They parted, and Naomi went to her room to sleep. She closed the door gently behind her, and lay down on her soft, sweet smelling mattress. There, with the darkness around her, she began to weep. She could not have told the reason for her tears, but she wept quietly, that Joseph might not hear, until sleep took her.

When morning came they shared a good breakfast, and Naomi led the flock up into the Glen. As the sheep filed out of the fold she asked Joseph their names, and he told them to her. That day, for the first time, she knew them all.

When she was gone, Joseph set out to visit Barnabas and Hannah. The thing that he had to do seemed utterly impossible to him, but after each step along the road it was possible to take the next. Not even the beauty of the glen that seemed to sing around him could lift his spirits, but he whom his daughter had called a hero did not turn back.

Chapter 12

The Welcome at Harevan

ON THE MORNING AFTER THE SEVENTH NIGHT OF THEIR ride across the desert, Ilohan and Jonathan did not stop to sleep, for they knew they were close to Harevan. The mountains at this point dropped precipitously to the desert floor, and they rode with the awesome cliff walls more close than usual on their right. The trail was climbing gently, following an upward bulge of the desert. They were dusty and tired, and also thirsty, for they had found drinkable water only once since leaving the desert church. In spite of this their spirits rose as they climbed, and it seemed to them that the air grew less dry.

The sun rose high into the sky, and it was very hot. The hard light on the bright desert sands hurt their dry eyes, and the distant landscape wavered and shimmered in the heat. Yet still they hoped, with every tiny rise in the floor of the desert, that they would suddenly come in view of Harevan. At last Jonathan, peering into the heat-blurred distance, said, "Ilohan! I see a tree!"

Ilohan looked where he was pointing, and could also make out a strange projection on the horizon. It looked greenish, and seemed partly transparent against the sky, but it wavered like a windblown flame. He could not be sure that it was real.

"I hope it is a tree," he said. "Yet perhaps it is only a trick of the desert heat."

"I do not think it can be," said Jonathan. As they approached, other similar apparitions came into view in the distance, and it became obvious that they were real trees, several of them: tall, healthy, and green, in lovely contrast to the harshness of the rock desert around them. "If that is not Harevan, then at least it is water," said Jonathan, and he drank the last of the water that was in the skins he carried. Ilohan followed his example – a delicious indulgence after their careful rationing, though back at Aaronkal he would have thought the stale, tepid water undrinkable.

As they approached, refreshed and hopeful, Ilohan wondered what awaited them at Harevan. Mixed with his hope was a feeling not unlike fear. Here, he suspected, the true purpose of his journey would be revealed to him. He would like to find that the quest had been important, that he had accomplished something significant for the king – but what if it had been very important indeed, and he had somehow failed, or was about to fail?

But, he told himself, he and Jonathan had faithfully followed the king's commands as well as they could, and it seemed that they had succeeded – despite wholly unexpected opposition. There was reason to exult: they had escaped archers, knights, cold water, hunger, and weariness. They were alive, and had crossed the desert!

* * *

Eleanor of Harevan could smell her roses as she worked in her garden – the only flowers still in bloom, blossoming as brilliantly in autumn as they ever had in spring. Besides the roses her garden was dead: the lovely annuals shriveled to tangled brown sticks that she shoveled underground with her spade. Yet the empty soil she was turning was good in its own way, rich with compost, ready for the new spring.

As she worked, kneeling in the dirt, she looked now and then down the road and out east into the desert. She had watched thus for many days, always hoping, sometimes with desperate desire, sometimes with cautious patience. Any day he would come, riding in from the barren waste. She had made a thousand pictures of him in her mind, but each one she tried to erase, waiting until she actually saw him. Now she told herself not to waste time in staring, and she bent over her work, the iron tool in her fingers turning and loosening the soil… until almost without realizing it, she raised her eyes again to scan the distant path.

Two horsemen were coming, dark against the brilliant desert floor, mere shimmering specks in the distance. She lifted the crutches that lay beside her, and got slowly to her feet. Brogal, if he were returning so soon, would come alone. It might be Ilohan and his companion. It might be them at last! She limped into the middle of the road to get a better view. She leaned against one of the great trees beyond it and watched them get nearer. They came slowly, as if the horses were weary. One of the animals was larger than the other, like the powerful warhorse of a knight. Her hope rose. When they were close enough that she judged they might soon notice her, she made her way back across the road and went into her cottage.

Eleanor's friend and servant Auria was scrubbing pots and pans in a tub of water that had been heated over the hearth.

She heard the sound of the door and looked up. "Coming in so soon, my Lady?" she asked in surprise.

Eleanor did not answer at once, and Auria turned to look at her. "Is all well?" she asked.

"All is well," said Eleanor in a voice which, though calm, was filled with wonder. "Two horsemen are coming up from the desert."

Auria got quickly to her feet. "Do you think it is them?" she asked excitedly.

"I think so," said Eleanor. "Come to the window."

Auria needed no urging. She hurried into another room, where a large window opened on the road, and leaned out to look down the desert path. Eleanor followed slowly. "Two young men, weary and mounted on weary horses," said Auria, "yet each has the bearing of a prince."

Eleanor leaned out beside her. Yes, the horses were weary, and the riders looked exhausted as well, but she could see what Auria meant about their bearing. There was nothing about either of them that spoke of mockery or cowardice. They had passed through darkness and fear together, and reached the end of their journey. The one mounted on a war horse wore the garb of the Knights of Karolan, and Eleanor knew at last that he had come.

She watched him, and wondered what kind of a man he was. Fear for him touched her, for she knew pain lay in his future – but not pain only. This moment was not meant for foreboding. She loved him, and longed to bless him, and knew that she would. She wished intensely that she could fly down the desert path and embrace him with all her joy. Long ago she could have run, a score of years ago when her hair was golden and not gray. Long ago, before... She made no sound, nor did she lower her eyes, yet her vision blurred and her tears fell on the smooth wood of the windowsill. What she felt was far deeper than mere mourning for the days when she had not been lame. It could not be mere mourning, for it was shot through with joy. What it was even she herself could not explain.

"Auria," she said softly, "give them all the welcome you can, and tell them that I regret being unable to greet them at once, but that I shall see them before supper."

Auria looked at her friend. "Yes, my Lady," she said.

Eleanor walked slowly into a small room that faced the garden, and closed the door behind her. Auria went back into the kitchen, put away the clean pots and pans, pushed the wash tub into a corner, swept at imagined dust on the clean stone hearth, and then stood by the door to wait.

* * *

For Ilohan and Jonathan, the approach to Harevan was an experience unlike any they had had before. They came out of the endless, barren desert, and in among an open stand of tall, well-watered trees. Lovely green leaves blew and shimmered in the warm breeze. Green grass was soft beneath the horses' feet. High, beautifully symmetrical crowns of foliage filtered the brilliant sun and gave them shade such as they had not known for many days. They dismounted and stopped a moment to savor their delight and surprise. They had passed through the mighty desert, and come to a place of joy and life.

Finally Ilohan turned to the village of Harevan: many cottages, large and small, well and ill kept, all set on a gentle upward slope covered with grass and graced here and there by more huge trees. Many of the cottages had gardens, but there was no mistaking the one to which the king had directed him.

The roses grew in a glorious profusion of stems, leaves, and blossoms, blooming rich crimson, pale pink, pure white, and every color in between.

Before entering the village, Ilohan reached into his saddlebags, and wrapped a blanket around the crown and sword from Luciyr until they made a shapeless bundle. Only when thus wrapped did he withdraw them from the bag, and hand them to Jonathan to carry beneath his cloak – thus obeying the king's command to keep whatever was found at Luciyr hidden from the people of Harevan.

At last they approached the door of the flower-girt cottage, leading the horses up a garden path between the tall tangles of the roses. Ilohan's heart was beating very fast as he reached out his hand to knock, wondering who lived here, why he had been sent to them, and what he should say when the door was opened. He had very little time to wonder, for the door flew open even before he had finished knocking – almost as if the young woman who opened it had been waiting expectantly immediately inside.

"Welcome to Harevan," she said, ushering them in before Ilohan had a chance to say anything. "You are expected, and are honored guests. Lady Eleanor regrets that she cannot greet you herself, but you will see her just before supper. Here are cups of cool water flavored with limes; if there is anything else you desire, please tell me. Come, sit down on the hearth and rest. I will take care of your horses; they have no need to starve in Harevan." With that she went out the door, leaving Ilohan feeling very welcome indeed, but also bewildered.

"This is good," he said. "We are wanted here, and all is well. But how is it possible that they have known we were coming? It is not as though King Thomas would have sent a messenger three weeks' journey merely to announce the coming of a single knight and his companion."

"I do not know," said Jonathan, "but now that we are here, what should we do?"

"I would say, sleep – as soon as we can!" said Ilohan. "But we are very dusty and travel stained. We will need to wash before supper, and that may not leave time for resting also. "

"I wonder..." said Jonathan. "I wonder if there is any place to swim nearby. A moment in the Carratril would wash from me many days of desert traveling."

Just as he said this, the young woman reentered the room. "I have put your horses in a pen with a good deal of lush grass," she said. "They will eat better than they have for many days, by the look of them. Now, is there anything you would like me to do for you? I have already prepared beds for you in the back room of the house, which looks out toward the river."

"The river!" said Jonathan. "Is the river good for swimming?"

"It is very good," she said.

"Can you provide us with fresh clothes, my Lady," asked Ilohan, "or should we wash our own in the river?"

"Ah, I have not told you my name," she said, smiling. "You need not call a servant 'Lady,' though I thank you. I am Auria. Fresh clothes are already laid out for you in your bedroom. With them are simple clothes such as the people of Harevan and Ceramir wear when swimming. These you should use, if you swim, for large groups of people often swim together here, and therefore we do not go naked as in other places."

"Thank you, my Lady," said Ilohan. The courteous title she had just renounced had slipped out before he could catch himself, but it seemed appropriate to him. Then suddenly the cheerful, half-amusing thought of the swimming clothes of

Harevan turned his mind to the memory of the dark lake, chilling his laughter. "We have swum clothed before now, for reasons much less kindly expressed," he said cryptically.

Heedless alike of the niceties of Ilohan's courtesy, and the shadows of his memories, Jonathan had dressed in the swimming-clothes and run eagerly to the river. He stood for a moment on the bank, enjoying the feel of soft, short grass beneath his bare feet. The water was brown with mud from the earthen banks, but the river was wider and slower than the Carratril, and looked both calm and safe. He leaped in, and was shocked to find the water was barely cool to the touch. He had not known a river could ever be so warm. It was deep and clean, with a good taste when it splashed into his mouth. He lay on his back and turned his face up to the sunny afternoon sky, delighting in the caresses of the slow current around him. This was water that he could swim in forever. Suddenly he noticed that Ilohan was still standing on the bank, looking uneasy.

"The memory of the dark lake is heavy in my heart," he said. "I do not know if I shall ever swim again."

"You could not find a better cure for that memory than to wash it away in this water," said Jonathan. "And if you do not, I will come out and throw you in, counting it a kindness to my friend."

"I hope my courage will suffice to spare you that labor," said Ilohan, and he took a deep breath and leaped in. When the kind brown water closed over his head, he knew that all was well. He came to the surface, looked into the brilliant blue sky, felt the warm water around him, and laughed. Jonathan had been right. The fear of the dark lake was gone.

*   *   *

They were refreshed and clean when evening came, having both swum and slept. Auria knocked to call them for supper, and they came into the kitchen. It had been transformed into something very like a banquet hall. A large table of polished wood stood in the center of the room. The fireplace behind the wide hearth was covered with glowing coals, and above it sat many pots and pans on a metal grill, bubbling and sending out good smells. Garlands of greenery hung from the rafters, and wooden cups holding roses were set among the candles on the table. The windows were open, and a soft breeze wafted through them. There were many chairs around the table, most of them rather small. A silver plate was set before each chair.

Auria motioned Ilohan and Jonathan to two large chairs on either side of the head of the table. They heard a step in an adjoining room, and then for the first time their hostess appeared. She was of average height, and her light-brown hair was graying, but there was something in her face that caught their attention and held it. As she approached, they saw that she was lame, and leaned heavily on crutches, yet she had an air of patience and grace. She sat down at the head of the table, and smiled kindly at the travelers. "I am Eleanor," she said. "You are welcome and honored guests."

Auria took her own seat near the hearth. "As you know, I am Auria," she said. "I am a daughter of Mudien of Ceramir."

"I am Ilohan, a knight from Aaronkal," said Ilohan. "I thank you for your welcome. May your hospitality always be blessed."

"I am Jonathan, son of Barnabas, a blacksmith of Glen Carrah," said Jonathan. "I, also, thank you."

"Tonight," said Eleanor, "we celebrate your safe arrival and rejoice together in the bounty of Ceramir. Tomorrow there will be more serious matters to consider, and you will learn more of why you have come here."

"My Lady," asked Ilohan, "what and where is Ceramir?"

"Ceramir is up the river less than an hour's walk, for you, from Harevan," said Eleanor. "It is in a hidden valley at the feet of the great mountains. As for what it is, you know the meaning of its name: the Cloth of Joy."

"Your words are your own to speak or to withhold," said Jonathan, "but will you tell us no more than that?"

"You will see it soon," said Eleanor, "and you may then learn for yourselves what it is. But this much I will say now. You have heard of an affliction called pythri?"

"Yes," said Ilohan, "I was taught at Aaronkal that it cannot be cured, but kills slowly through weakening and fever."

"Tonight you will see many children who are happy and in perfect health," said Eleanor. "Among them will be two who were dying of pythri a year ago. Their parents heard of Ceramir, dared a long journey to bring them there, and there saw them healed. And pythri is not the only sickness, deadly throughout the world, that is vanquished in the Cloth of Joy."

"It was also said at Aaronkal that to linger near one afflicted with pythri is to invite the deadly thing on oneself," said Ilohan.

"Healers can indeed be infected – though afterward they may be healed themselves," said Eleanor. "The work of a healer is dangerous, like all the works of love. But there is great power in Ceramir – power that God has given to be used boldly, not hoarded in fear." She paused, her face thoughtful, and then spoke again.

"The Cloth of Joy is more than a dwelling place of physicians," she said. "What you will see with your own eyes and know in your hearts will tell you more than any words of mine. For now, ponder, if you will, another name by which it is called: the Valley of the Undismayed."

"Brogal spoke of the children of Ceramir," said Ilohan, "who are they?"

"They are all who spend their youth in the Valley, and come to love it," said Eleanor, "but Auria can tell you more."

"My Lady," said Ilohan to Auria, "if you will, tell me more of the children of Ceramir, and of Mudien. Who is Mudien? Are you truly Brogal's sister by birth, or do all the children of Ceramir also call themselves children of Mudien? Is Mudien the father of all who love the Cloth of Joy?"

"I answer the last question first," said Auria with a smile. "No, Mudien is not the father of all the children of Ceramir, yet he and my mother Imranie have many sons and daughters. And yes, Brogal is my brother by birth. As to who my father is, that, too, you must judge for yourself. He wields great power, but is kind and good – and I love him. But how do you know of Brogal, my brother? Did you meet him on your journey?"

"Yes," said Ilohan. "If we had not, we would have come very near starving in the desert." Ilohan was looking at Auria as he spoke, but Eleanor started at his words, and he turned towards her. For an instant there was horror in her eyes.

"Were you truly close to death?" she asked quietly.

"Not from hunger, my Lady, though we suffered," said Ilohan, "but we were very close to death for other reasons. We were hunted by mercenary archers on the roads of Karolan, and by Norkath knights at Luciyr and the mountain pass behind it. It is only by the great care of God in more than one desperate fight that we were not killed on our journey."

Eleanor gripped the table very hard with one hand. "Oh, Father, I thank you," she whispered, looking up. "We knew nothing of them, yet you have saved him." She turned to

Ilohan again, and relaxed. "I thank God you have reached here alive," she said quietly. "Had King Thomas or I suspected any such danger, he would not have sent you out as he did. Yet you must both have shown great bravery and strength."

"Jonathan far more than I," said Ilohan. "He defeated five of the mercenary archers alone, and stopped all of the knights by making the path impassible to them.

"Do not listen to him, my Lady," said Jonathan. "Sir Ilohan's courage is at least the equal of mine, and it is he who has the training of the Knights of Karolan."

"Sirs," said Auria, "our other guests are at the door, and it is time for the feast to begin."

"So let it be!" said Eleanor. "This is a time to rejoice."

Joyful laughter was heard at the door, and Auria opened it to admit many children, all dressed in their best and very excited. They quickly crowded into their seats around the table. Miraculously they were silent for a few moments while Eleanor prayed, giving fervent thanks for the safety of Ilohan and Jonathan and asking God's pleasure and blessing on the feast and the days to come. The children began laughing and talking again, and Auria began to serve the food.

Serious conversation was impossible for the moment, but Ilohan did not mind the noise. The children were in such glowing good spirits, and so remarkably well behaved even in their excitement, that it was a merry feast indeed. He found it somewhat overwhelming after his long, hard journey alone with Jonathan, but it was overwhelming in a good sense, setting hope, laughter, and innocence against his memories of toil and danger. The food was more varied than he had seen even in the Great Hall of Aaronkal, and he guessed that to Jonathan it must be more marvelous still. There was soup made with meat and soup made with cheese and soup made with vegetables, and soup made with all three. There were cakes with many kinds of fruit and nuts. There were delicious fresh fruits of kinds Ilohan had never seen before. There were roasted birds with good spices unknown in Karolan. There was golden cider, and clear water, and rich red wine. Ilohan and Jonathan made up for their days of starving in the desert, and their weeks of eating stale bread and dried meat. Every bite was a joy to them, and when at last the feast was over they had almost forgotten what it was like to be hungry.

When the last person had eaten the last thing they wanted, Auria cleared away the plates and bowls and cups, and piled them in the wash tub. She lowered the shutters of the windows against the dark night, leaving only a crack through which the fresh night breeze could wander in, and she blew out all but three of the many candles that burned on the table. The children gave sighs of contentment, and sat back in their chairs. The room was silent. Then one little girl near the foot of the table spoke in a worried voice, "Aren't you going to tell us as story, Ella?"

"Of course, Freni," said Lady Eleanor. "I would not invite you here for a feast and then send you away without a story. Only wait a moment longer, for it must be a good story." There was another silence. Candlelight fell on expectant faces all around the table, while the rest of the room lay in shadow.

"Once upon a time," said Lady Eleanor, "a brave knight welcomed a minstrel into his castle. The minstrel was a man of great skill, who played his harp and sang wonderful songs. When he sang songs of sorrow, those who heard him would weep, and when he sang songs of joy they would laugh and dance. When he sang stories he had imagined, they felt as if they themselves could see the things happening. When he sang truths to them they believed him. He never sang lies.

"The knight gave him a great welcome, and held banquets in his honor for three days. On the night of the third day, the knight asked the minstrel to sing a song that had never been sung before. Some thought the minstrel would have to think for a day before he could do this, but he did not think even for a moment. He said to all the people gathered in the knight's castle, 'I sing to you a story, and as I will not lie, I tell you that I do not know this story to be true. Yet neither do I know it to be false. It is a noble song, and it has never been sung before.'

"The minstrel took his harp and sang the song of the Sapphire of Mount Vykadrak. He told how the sapphire had been found by a miner of Petrag, high in the great mountains, in a mineshaft that cut through fifty paces of ice before it entered the rock. He told how the miner had brought it out in triumph, and how his fellows had envied him and wanted to cut the stone into pieces that they might each have a part of the profit. But the miner was so awed by the beauty of the stone that he said he would rather put it back in the mine than see it cut apart. He searched in his mind for a way to hide it that it might never be found. At last he decided to set it on the very summit of Mount Vykadrak, where no one else would dare to climb. He set out one morning holding the stone. No one dared to hinder him or follow him. His fellows set a watch around the mountain to see when he would come down, but he never returned. The legends of the miners say he reached the peak, and froze there, still holding the great sapphire in his hand.

"When the minstrel's song ended, all the people there could see the great sapphire, cold and blue as ice, sparkling in the miner's frozen hand as he lay dead beneath the sky on the awesome peak of mount Vykadrak.

"Now it happened that the king of a certain realm was visiting the knight in his castle at the time the minstrel sang.

The knight loved the princess who was the king's daughter, and the princess loved him. But the knight was good and brave, and the king was not, and the king hated the knight and would not let the princess marry him. Yet when the king heard the story of the great sapphire, he desired it. He thought about it all night and all the next day.

"Finally he said to the knight, 'Sir Knight, if you go to the peak of Mount Vykadrak and bring me the great sapphire, you may marry my daughter. This is the only way.'

"The princess wept when she heard it, for she was afraid that the knight would die trying to get the sapphire. But the knight tried to comfort her, and they walked together in the halls of his castle. He told her that he loved her with a great love, and that because of this he must go and try to find the sapphire so they could be married. The next day the knight mounted his great warhorse and rode away.

Eleanor stopped. Even Ilohan and Jonathan had been drawn into the spell of her story, and they suddenly became aware of the room around them again. The coals on the hearth glowed dimly. The candles had burnt low, so that although Eleanor and her listeners were illumined and seemed held in a circle of warm light, behind them the world was dark and unknown. The children sat spellbound, their faces eager in the flickering light – until at length a small, worried voice asked, "But Ella, what happened to the knight?"

"Oh," said Lady Eleanor, "You wish me to finish the story? Are you not all sleepy, and longing for your beds? I can tell the rest next time you come."

"No, no!" cried the children in terror. "Tell us now, tell us now!"

Eleanor smiled and went on with the story. She told of all the troubles and difficulties the knight met with on the quest.

She held them all spellbound again, and they could see him as he struggled up to the top of Mount Vykadrak, and feel his despair when he arrived there half dead and found no sign of the great sapphire. Then she told how he thought that it might be buried in the snow, and how he chipped away at the ice and snow with his sword and shield, until finally he found the body of the poor frozen miner, and pried the magnificent sapphire out of his icy hand. Eleanor told them how the knight was nearly frozen himself, but somehow struggled down the mountain and went back to his castle. She told how he gave the great sapphire willingly to the king, and was married with great joy to the princess. Then she told how the castle of that king was besieged and sacked by thieves, who killed him and stole the great sapphire, but how the knight and princess lived long and happy lives.

When the story was done the children breathed sighs of relief and satisfaction that it had all gone well in the end. Yet one little boy went up to Eleanor's chair. "Did the story really happen, Ella?" he asked.

"Perhaps," said Lady Eleanor. "I will never lie to you, and I tell you that I do not know the story to be true. Yet I also do not know it to be false." The children departed with many sweetly childish thanks to Eleanor and Auria, praising Eleanor's story to the skies. Auria went out with them, to walk them home to their cottages.

Eleanor stood slowly. "One afternoon's rest does not suffice for the weariness of a journey such as yours," she said. "You are safe here after all your perils: go now, and sleep without fear."

Ilohan lingered, looking at her. "You are a wonderful story teller, my Lady," he said.

"God has given that to me," she replied simply. "Sometimes I make up stories of my own that hold the children in wonder and bring them great joy. Yet the best stories are those that might be true – that are made, like the one tonight, of rumors and legends that may have more substance than people know."

"It was marvelous; it kept me nearly as spellbound as the children." Ilohan paused. "Your story has made me very curious. May I ask if you believe that the Sapphire of Mount Vykadrak truly exists?"

"Whether the story told about it is true is beyond my knowledge, but I am nearly certain that the stone itself is real," said Eleanor. "There are things far more worth finding that the great Sapphire, however."

"I know it," said Ilohan. "It was not in greed that I asked you."

"No," said Eleanor. "You are a true Knight of Karolan. Now we must sleep. There is much to be done tomorrow."

Chapter 13

A Dangerous Journey

ILOHAN WOKE SUDDENLY FROM DREAMLESS SLEEP THE next morning. He went to the window and saw that the sun was already high, shining brightly on the grassy banks and the smooth brown water of the river. He came into the kitchen, and saw that Auria had risen early and worked hard: all traces of the night's banquet had vanished. Auria, Eleanor, and Jonathan were talking quietly over a breakfast of fresh fruit and bread with honey. Ilohan joined them gratefully.

"This is an important day," said Eleanor, when they had finished eating. "Many hopes may be fulfilled in it – but there is danger also: unless they are fulfilled, they will perish forever before the night." She paused and turned to Ilohan, and he met her gaze. He felt as if her eyes pierced him, but her smile was kind. "I believe, however, that they will not perish," she said at length. Then she bowed her head and was silent once more, and Ilohan wondered if she was praying. When she raised her eyes, they were troubled.

"Yet we must begin," she said with determination. "Sir Ilohan, I must send you out again without wholly explaining your mission – but this is the last time, and it will be short. Will you carry a sealed message from me to Mudien?"

"Willingly, my Lady," said Ilohan.

"I thank you. You must not suffer any eyes but his to see the message, not even your own. Do not entrust it to other hands for any reason."

"Yes, Lady Eleanor," he said.

Eleanor turned then to Jonathan, who had risen to prepare to accompany Ilohan. "You are a faithful friend," she said to him, "but you cannot be Sir Ilohan's companion on all roads. Today he must go to Mudien alone."

"You should take your sword," said Eleanor to Ilohan, "even in peaceful lands a knight should not be without one. Here is the message for Mudien. Auria will point out the way."

A moment later Ilohan, wearing his sword, was walking briskly up a dirt path toward the mountains. Eleanor's warning about the danger and importance of this day lingered in his mind, but it was hard for him to heed it. The great trees blew in the wind and glowed with color in the sun, birds such as he had not heard for many days sang merrily around him, and at last he was going to see Mudien of Ceramir.

Ilohan met an old man upon the road, and greeted him. The old man stopped, looked at him intently, and then asked, "What is your errand from the cottage of Eleanor?"

"Have you been shadowing me?" asked Ilohan, suddenly suspicious.

"Hardly," said the man, "but a travel-weary Knight of Karolan cannot come unnoticed to a village as small as Harevan. Are you going to Mudien?"

"Why should you think that?" asked Ilohan.

"They are forever scheming together, Eleanor and Mudien," said the old man. "You would not be the first to be caught in their toils."

"Do you, then, have a grudge against the Lady Eleanor?" asked Ilohan.

"Now I will repeat your own question back to you," said the old man, "why should you think that?"

"Because you seek to make me doubt and fear her, whom I have great reason to believe is trustworthy and good," said Ilohan.

"What are your reasons?" asked the old man. Ilohan held his peace.

"Why not tell me, that I might help you see that your reasons are less sound than you have thought?" asked the old man.

"I will not," said Ilohan. "I ask you to leave me alone to go on my way."

"Ah, I have it!" said the old man. "You have a parchment concealed in your cloak. Eleanor has made you her messenger to Mudien. But do you not know that he has great power, with soldiers at his command? When you deliver the message, you will be at his mercy, and whatever Eleanor has asked of him he will do to you."

"I believe you are a liar, harboring malice in your heart toward Eleanor and Mudien," said Ilohan.

"Why not read the message, and see what Eleanor is telling him?" asked the old man. "I could help you repair the seal, that Mudien might never know – and if the message portends evil for you, there is yet time to fly."

"I have promised to deliver it unopened, and I trust Eleanor rather than you," said Ilohan. "Will you not desist from following me?"

"Behold," said the old man, suddenly stepping in front of Ilohan so that he had to stop walking. The man opened his hand, and a large diamond on his wrinkled palm flashed multicolored fire in the sunlight. "This I will give you, if you but let me read the message," he said.

"You offer me a diamond," said Ilohan quietly, "but what is the price of a man's honor? My promise stands. Step out of my path."

The old man obeyed, but followed Ilohan only a few steps behind, still spouting dark warnings against the wiles of Eleanor and Mudien. The mere repetition and persistence engendered a seed of doubt in Ilohan's mind. Could he be walking into a trap? But no – the king had sent him to Eleanor, and the king loved him. Besides, his own heart told him that Eleanor was trustworthy and good. He turned on the old man in sudden anger.

"Depart from me!" he said. "Or, at the least, be silent!"

"What will you do if I do not?" asked the old man.

Ilohan drew his sword. The old man did not react. "You are unarmed, and I would die rather than use this blade upon you," said the knight. "See, then: I have no recourse against you. Will you not desist of your own accord?"

"You could cut a stave from the forest, and beat me," said the old man, "or you could overpower me and use the fastenings of my garments to tie me to a tree."

"You are old enough to be my grandfather," said Ilohan, "or one of the venerable sages of Aaronkal, my tutors. Will you then oblige me to treat you thus?"

The old man smiled, "No," he said, "but if the day goes ill for you, do not blame me." He turned and went back in the direction of Harevan.

As Ilohan went on his way, the anger and annoyance of his encounter with the old man quickly faded. Distrust of Eleanor did not persist in his mind, and he was glad that he had managed to dismiss the malevolent old gossip without doing him any violence. The trees beside the path grew closer together than down in Harevan, but they were still tall and well spaced, with dark green grasses growing around their roots. Presently the path joined the river and ran along the top of the earthen bank, which was twice or thrice the height of a man. Ilohan rejoiced in the balmy weather, the bright day, and the blessed fact that his journey was over and he had reached a welcoming destination. He swung his right arm freely, feeling that his arrow-wound was nearly healed. He looked forward to seeing Ceramir, and hoped that there, at last, the purpose of his quest would be explained.

A sudden scream startled him. He ran forward, toward the sound. As he rounded a bend in the path, he saw three men with ugly cudgels surrounding a red-haired young woman who was trapped at the top of the high riverbank. They were advancing on her slowly, as if uncertain of what to do.

Ilohan had no such uncertainty. His sword was in his hand in an instant. "Fly, knaves!" he cried as he ran toward the brigands. Two of the men fled at once when they saw him. The third reached the woman before Ilohan could stop him. There was a brief struggle which he could not quite follow, and then with another scream she fell off the bank, leaving her assailant standing alone on the edge. He turned to face Ilohan, but at the sight of the sword-wielding knight he ran for the woods.

Ilohan ran to the edge of the bank and looked down. The woman was lying motionless on a gravel bar below. Ilohan sheathed his sword and climbed down the bank, using roots for hand holds and steps kicked into the soft, mossy earth for his feet. She turned her head as he approached, and he knelt beside her.

"I do not know how to thank you," she said. "Had you not come, they would be the ones clambering down the bank to find me here."

"Thank me later," said Ilohan. "How badly are you hurt?"

"I have twisted an ankle, I think," she said. She tried to get to her feet, but winced. "Alas," she gasped. "With an ankle twisted I cannot walk."

"I think I can get you to the top of the bank," said Ilohan, looking along it, "but then where can I bring you where you will be safe and cared for?

"I have a cottage a short way up the road," she said. "I live there with my brother. You could leave me there. He will be returning from Ceramir tonight, and then he will take care of me."

Ilohan lifted her gently in his arms, and carried her upstream to a place where part of the bank had collapsed, making it easier to climb. It was steep and difficult still, and twice he had to ask her to support herself by hanging from protruding roots with her hands, while he climbed up to a place from whence he could lift her further. She proved strong enough to hang from the roots easily, and Ilohan was surprised at her fearlessness. At last he pulled her up the final distance and she turned to sit safely on the top of the bank.

"Now," he said, panting, "your cottage is in the direction of Ceramir?"

"Yes," she said, "a short walk."

He lifted her in his arms again and set off down the path. She seemed so strong, and in such good health, that he was surprised she had sprained her ankle so badly. After he had walked on in silence for a moment, she said, "I am sorry you have to carry me so far."

"I have the strength," he said breathlessly, "You have no reason to be sorry, my Lady." There was another silence. "Do you know who they were?" he asked.

She was silent for a moment, and then said, "No one from Harevan or Ceramir would do such a thing. I have always been safe in these lovely woods until now."

"Will you be safe in your cottage, do you think, with such people around?"

"Yes," she said in a voice that was strangely soft, "I will be safe there."

Ilohan was very relieved to see a group of cottages in the woods just ahead. He saw a straight, smooth sapling lying across the path just ahead of him. In the center of the path stood a guard, dressed all in green and holding a spear.

"Halt!" said the guard as he approached. "Who are you and why do you come this way?"

"I am Sir Ilohan, a Knight of Karolan," said Ilohan, "and I must bring this lady safely to her cottage, and afterwards go on to Ceramir to deliver a message to Mudien."

"Are you loyal to the Code of Karolan?" asked the guard sternly.

"Yes," said Ilohan, "and with the help of God I always will be."

"What if he should ever fail to help you?" asked the guard.

"I do not believe he ever will. It is not as though he would desire me to break the Code."

"How can you be sure of that?"

Ilohan's arms were very tired now, and shook a little as he stood there speaking to the guard. He thought it would be discourteous to the woman to lay her on the ground, however, so he held her and tried to think as fast as he could how to answer the strange challenges of this unwelcoming gatekeeper.

"I have promised before God to hold to the Code," he said, "and the rules of the Code are in accord with the rules of God."

"How do you know the rules of God?" asked the gatekeeper.

"They are written in his books, which the travelers brought to Karolan in the time of Nirolad. Also his Holy Spirit places their echo in the hearts of all mankind."

"Can a man be sure that if he keeps the Code, he is doing all that God desires of him?"

"No," said Ilohan breathlessly, "for God wants more than rule keeping. He desires love and allegiance, lives fully given to him. Now let me through, lest my strength fail."

"Live in Ceramir and in all the world according to what you have said," said the gatekeeper. "Require not from God the explanations of his commands, and often he will give them. You may pass."

Ilohan stepped quickly over the fallen sapling. "Which house is yours?" he asked the woman.

"That one," she said, pointing.

Ilohan staggered to the door, which opened at a push, and carried her inside. The cottage was clean and well made, but seemed rather bare. Ilohan went into the second room and laid her on a bed he found there. Then he leaned against the wall to rest, and shook out his tired, cramped arms. Gradually he caught his breath, and smiled, glad that he had been able to carry her so far. He looked around the room, at the smooth, light wood walls, the large, half-open window, and the woman who lay still upon the bed.

She was very beautiful: lovely of face and hair, slender, strong, and full of life. She seemed to him kind and generous, as well as honest. Yet as he recovered from his exertion he began to feel uneasy. There was something he wished he did not see about the way she lay there, so still – something of self-conscious helplessness in her demeanor. He exonerated her, held her completely guiltless, and yet he hated the black lust that rose in his own heart. He turned suddenly and made for the door.

"Wait!" she said. "I have not yet thanked you."

"I need no thanks for doing my duty, my Lady," he said.

"Yet you have perhaps saved my life," she said, "and in any case carried me to near the limit of your strength. There is little I can give you, for we are very poor, yet –" she hesitated. "Yet there is one gift that any woman may give to a man, no matter how poor she is. I know some think it is wrong to offer it thus, but how can that be true? We are alone in this house; the gift is yours for the taking. I cannot resist you, nor will I cry for help."

The world spun around Ilohan when he realized what she meant. He grasped the doorframe to steady himself. A great pleasure, like a jewel that he intensely desired and knew to be precious, was thus offered him. But it was forbidden. The woman was wrong to offer it, and he was forbidden to accept. Precious, desired – yet forbidden. Forbidden why? The words of the guard returned to him: "Require not from God the explanation…" It seemed to him that he had no explanation, no reason, for this command, and he longed to require it – to confront God and tell him that he would not obey without a reason. But that would be to scorn God and his vows of knighthood. That would be to find fault with both the divine Law and the ancient Code of Karolan, based only on his own small experience and understanding. He must not do that. He would not do it.

Yet there was the woman, full of health and beauty, and her offer stood. There was a part of him that regarded her offer as though a white swan had lighted in a cesspool, or as though a fragrant rose spat slime. She had seemed so beautiful and innocent to him that it seemed a violation of the universe that she should say what she had said. But this was the perspective only of a part of his mind. For the rest, he wanted to yield to the overwhelming temptation, to shatter the Law and Code without remorse. Long moments passed in fierce internal struggle. But in the end he was true. Ilohan of Aaronkal obeyed the God he loved, and kept the promise he had made.

"Alas!" he cried, and was gone. He poured into that anguished cry all his grief and anger at the evil within him and at the marring of her who had appeared so blameless. He was running up the dirt path in a strange and broken world he did not understand. He ran fast, afraid lest he turn around and go back. The beauty of the world held no joy any longer. No more did he consider misplaced the words of Eleanor concerning the dangers of this day.

The sun was hot and the path was bare and brown. The trees that had seemed so majestic and beautiful before now looked dark and old when he glanced at their boles as he passed. Who knew what dark secrets they concealed, what buried mysteries their ancient roots might probe? He no longer looked up to see their crowns shimmering with autumn leaves in the sun. He cried aloud as he ran, "God, how dreadful is the world you thrust me into at my birth!" Only when his lungs were scorched with the dry air did he slow down to a walk. He walked despondently, with his head down, for a long while.

A furtive movement ahead of him made him look up, and somehow he knew instantly that it meant death. His years of training for knighthood brought his sword from it sheath as soon as he formed the thought, and had he been slower he would not have lived another instant. The five knights of Norkath had been lurking in ambush and now were coming at him from all sides. The fight was hopeless, yet for a few terrible moments he fought them all. His sword flashed and rang in his hands, and every Norkath blade was blocked. His heart was still full of despair of the world, and he cared little for his life. Yet here they were, assassins, murderers, trying to kill him. Here was evil itself, ugly and real in the sunlit woods, and he would fight it till he died.

It could not last long, and even while he was completely, desperately focused on fighting he knew it. Some detached part of his mind could still realize that he was doomed. A few more strokes, a few more heart beats – "Stop!"

A voice like thunder roared out the word, and few men in all the world could have dared to disobey it. The Norkath soldiers froze, and Ilohan stood still, panting hard, with sweat running down into his eyes.

"Do you know that you are in the outlands of Ceramir, and that the people of this place consider your actions evil and worthy of death?" thundered the voice. Ilohan scanned the forest for the speaker, but saw no one.

"I have no fear of them," said the leader of the Norkaths. "We obey King Fingar, and him alone."

"Do you know that God himself has forbidden that which you seek to do?" asked the voice.

"You say he has. I do not fear you," said the knight, still peering into the woods, trying to see the one who was speaking.

"Are you resolved to dare the judgment of both God and Ceramir?" asked the voice.

"Our swords will conquer wayward peasants, and we have no need to fear the God we know," said the knight.

"Then you do not know the God who is," said the voice. "Yet if you are resolved, forget not you were warned, but continue."

Ilohan raised his sword again, tired, hopeless, despairing as he realized his hope of rescue was gone. Whoever the speaker was, he had no power behind his thunderous voice. The Norkaths closed in for the kill. Then suddenly the air filled with fierce, eerie shrieks, and the Norkaths gave way, sank down, and fell at Ilohan's feet. Even the mightiest died after only one or two agonized groans. Ilohan was unscathed.

He looked down at the dead knights. Some of them had been wearing light armor. The arrows had torn through it with startling violence. Every man had two or three shafts in his back. Not a single arrow had missed its mark. Ilohan looked around the small forest glade where he stood. Somehow the fight had shifted here, a few paces off the path, while he was too busy blocking swords to heed where his furious dodging and parrying was taking him.

The small field was covered with bright green grass, and healthy autumn brush grew around its edges. As he watched, a dozen archers clad in green seemed to materialize out of the woods. Arrows were in their bows, and Ilohan let his sword fall to the ground.

"I surrender to my rescuers with thanks," said Ilohan, "yet I request my freedom, for I have promised to deliver a message to Mudien of Ceramir."

The archers surrounded him without a word, and bound his hands behind him. Ilohan did not attempt to fight or flee. He was too confused to know what to do, but somehow he felt no fear. "Bring forth the other prisoner!" said a man who appeared to be the leader, whose voice had clearly been the one that froze the Norkath knights at a word.

Four of the other archers returned to the woods and – to Ilohan's shock and dismay – they brought out the red-haired woman he had rescued. Her hands, like his own, were tied behind her, and she was carried firmly between two archers.

The archers formed a loose circle, with Ilohan held at one side of it and the woman held at the other. "We know what has passed between you," said the leader when all was still. "We regret that it is necessary to hold you thus, but we will not judge you. That we leave to you yourselves."

"Sir Ilohan, of Aaronkal, what do you command be done to this woman for the evil that she has committed?"

Ilohan was silent for a moment. He had hoped he would never see her again. Now it seemed strange and wrong either to look at her or to look away. "I wish nothing done to her," he said at last.

"Why not?" asked the leader.

"What she has done hurt me for two reasons. One was the evil that stirred within me, to my shame and fear. That it was there is my fault, not hers. The other was the fact that she, so fair to look upon and seemingly so good, should have chosen to do wrong. I grieved to see it. It is not just that she be punished for either of the wounds she gave. I leave her to the mercy of God, and may he make her true. Free her and take her back to her cottage in peace."

"Veril, daughter of Ceramir, what do you command be done to this man in return for his deeds and words?"

Veril was crying, almost silently. The tears rolled down her face, and she involuntarily tried to raise her bound hands to wipe them. "Alas," she said, "release him and send him on to Ceramir with all speed. Beg him to forgive me. Alas for what I have done."

"Your commands will be obeyed," said the leader.

They cut Veril's bonds and carried her back into the woods. Ilohan was freed as well, and thanked his former captors graciously. They returned his sword to him, and the leader led him back to the road.

"You have resisted a temptation before which many men have fallen," said the archer. "You are worthy of great praise, for you have been true."

"I am not wise enough to live," said Ilohan. "The whole world seems to me full of confusion and dread. And my thoughts and hopes have not been pure this day, if my actions have been. Even them I now doubt. I drew my sword today in the face of an unarmed man old enough to be a venerable sage. I nearly fell when lust was my enemy, and I understand neither the law I have kept nor how nearly I failed to keep it. Praise me not. True praiseworthiness still lies endlessly beyond me."

"Then," said the archer, "you had best get started on the journey to it. Yet much which is now a mystery will soon be made clear, and the path may not be as dark as it seems."

"I thank you, though I do not understand you. Farewell."

He crossed the river on a broad wooden bridge and passed on toward Ceramir.

* * *

The morning that had held so much that was fearful or troubling for Ilohan had passed quietly for Jonathan back in the cottage of Eleanor. As soon as Ilohan had departed, Eleanor had knelt beside the table and bowed her head. Auria had quickly washed and put away the breakfast plates, and then sat silently in a chair beside Eleanor. Jonathan had decided they were both praying against the dangers Eleanor had spoken of. He wondered what the dangers were, but was confident they were not such as could be defeated with a sword, or Eleanor would not have prevented him from accompanying his friend. Perhaps Ilohan had to prove himself to Mudien, and there was danger that the mysterious leader of Ceramir might reject the young knight.

Long moments passed with Eleanor and Auria silently praying, and Jonathan silently watching them. He wanted to do something for Ilohan. Even the thought of praying for him flitted through his mind, but the honesty in his nature rebelled: he could not kneel in a mockery of reverence, and frame silent requests of a God he knew did not exist.

At last he took up a silver plate they had used at breakfast, and began to examine it, thinking of silversmiths and goldsmiths, and wondering if someday he might master their craft as well as his own. As he looked over the plate and gained some inklings of the process by which it was made, he considered the only thing he truly wished to make from the precious metals: a ring for Naomi. He put the plate away and lay down on his back on the floor. The sun through the windows was warm, and it was good to do nothing after all his journeying. He dreamed of working the gold of the mines into the semblance of the gold of the glen: a ring of wild grain wrought in gold, to encircle the finger of Naomi, his beloved, child of Glen Carrah.

A sharp knock on the door startled him out of his daydream. Auria jumped up to open the door. Eleanor remained kneeling, but looked up alertly as a tall bowman dressed in forest green entered the room. "All is well?" she asked him quietly.

"Yes," he said with a smile. "All is well thus far."

"Thank God," said Eleanor, and bowed her head again.

The archer nodded briskly and departed. Jonathan stood and watched him run up into the woods that thickened along the path to Ceramir. He admired the fearless freedom with which he bounded through the forest: almost the equal of his own, Jonathan thought. He turned to ask Eleanor what the message had meant, but found he dared not interrupt her prayer.

Eleanor was not aware of Jonathan's glance or his curiosity. She trembled with the intensity of her prayer, and thought of nothing but Ilohan and his danger. Her fear was so strong that it took all her faith to fight it. Ilohan had passed the first test that she and Mudien had commanded, the old man speaking words of doubt and evil. But with the next test, the one still to come, it seemed to her that she and Mudien had dared to do something that was God's right alone. Yet they had believed it was what he desired of them, and in that belief they had done it. Suppose they were wrong. Suppose Ilohan failed.

"Father," she cried in her heart, "forgive us if we have been wrong, and do not let him fall. Keep him safe, confirm your power in him, bring him home in love and joy. Be with him, and with us, and let all things be as you will. Keep him true forever and bless him greatly in the life that lies before him." She prayed such things for a long time.

She started at the sound of a knock on the door. In her anxiety she tried to rise, but could not. Auria opened the door and the same tall bowman entered the room. "Victory!" he cried. "We have won. We know not yet the cost, of course, but we have won." He hesitated, and Eleanor, though her heart was singing, noticed his hesitation.

"Thank God!" she said, meaning it to the depths of her soul. "But what is it that you have not told me?"

The archer knelt beside her and spoke earnestly. "Lady Eleanor," he said, "five knights of Norkath attacked him in the woods. Many of us were needed to watch over Sir Ilohan's tests, and so I had withdrawn some who normally watch the desert road. Thus it was, I think, that the knights passed by Harevan and entered the forest without our knowledge. When they ambushed Ilohan, we were hard pressed to ready our bows and our positions in time to save him. He fought valiantly, or I fear we would have been too late. As it is he is unscathed."

"Thank God! What of the Norkaths?"

"They are dead. We gave them the chance mercy required, and they refused it. They took two or three ironwood shafts each, and never breathed again. It is to be mourned that we should kill, still more that we should do it in the outlands of the Cloth of Joy. Yet truly there was no other course."

"Will he be safe now? He spoke to me of only five knights, encountered back at Luciyr, but who can tell if there are others?"

"The sons of Ceramir can tell, my Lady. Now that we are warned, nothing will move upon the desert road or through the Gate of Hope without our knowledge. Ilohan and all Ceramir will be safe. We are not dismayed."

"It will be a dark day if you ever are, Rangol," said Eleanor.

"May it never come," said Rangol, and with that he was gone, running again through the woods with joy and freedom.

* * *

The water of the river rushed white and swift over smooth rocks as it issued through the Gate of Hope. It glistened in the sun, and the sound of its splashing was a joy to hear. Over it hung the ghost of a mist, and the essence of rainbows was in the air. There was a broad path on one side of the river, bounded by bushes that were turning crimson and gold in the cool autumn days. Close by the river and the bushes rose the gray cliffs that walled in Ceramir and made its entrance a natural gate.

Many had seen that white rushing water before Ilohan. To some it was the first sight of a home that was as precious to them as life itself, and with joy mounting in their hearts they passed through the gate. To others, sick and weary, it was a last hope, the entrance to the only place on earth where they might find healing. To Ilohan it was neither of these, and yet he could not help smiling as he approached. No one had told him the name of the gate, but if he had been asked, he would have guessed rightly. He did not have certainty, nor understanding, nor joy. As he approached the gate into Ceramir, he had hope. He quickened his pace, and the roar of the river filled his ears.

A light breeze blew between the walls of rock and carried the smell of flowers that did not grow in Karolan. The shade of the bright autumn bushes fell upon him. The rainbow mist was around him. Ilohan of Aaronkal passed through the Gate of Hope and looked into Ceramir. And he knew he had not hoped in vain.

The clear lake from which the river came shimmered in the sun. The valley itself was broader than he would have thought possible above the narrow gate, and it stretched back toward the great mountains farther than he could see. It was filled with mighty trees, glowing in the bright color of their autumn leaves. Their handsome trunks and great crowns concealed the farther reaches of the valley, and it seemed that lovely mysteries might be hidden there. Colorful fallen leaves spangled the lush green grass beneath the trees. The path curved left around the lake and led up to a large house made of light brown stone and built with many windows and pillars that let in the air and light.

Ilohan could hear distant singing and laughter, but he could not see where it came from. He walked up the path, came to the door of the stone house, and knocked. The door had been ajar already, and was immediately thrown wide open by a young man whose face and manner reminded Ilohan instantly of Auria and Brogal.

"Welcome, Sir," said the young man. "Are you Ilohan of Aaronkal?"

"Yes," said Ilohan, "I thank you for your welcome. I have a message for Mudien."

"I am Karlak the son of Mudien. You will find my father on the far side of the lake, surrounded by children. He told me that you would be coming soon."

"I thank you," said Ilohan.

The lake was smaller than Luciyr, and it did not take Ilohan long to walk around to the other side. He went slowly and drank in the valley's beauty. He felt again that the mystery here was good mystery, not dangerous and distressing like the mystery of the events he had encountered on the way. "The Cloth of Joy, the Valley of the Undismayed…" he mused as he walked. "I wonder what it means to be undismayed. Certainly there are many things that have power to dismay me. Will that always be so?" The afternoon sun filtered through the autumn leaves and glowed in a light mist that rose from the lake.

He looked ahead of him and saw two boys flying through the air out over the lake. It took a moment for him to realize that they were hanging onto a long rope that was tied to a high branch of a tree overhanging the water. One of them let go with an excited shout and splashed into the lake, with the other following a moment later. Ilohan ran forward in amazement, and saw a dozen or more boys and girls standing on a tall, wide wooden platform near the water's edge. A strong looking, gray-haired man was with them. The man reached out and caught the flying rope as it swung near him, and he handed it to a boy who was standing on the highest part of the platform. A girl stepped up beside him, and without a hint of fear they jumped off the platform together, holding on to the rope. It was more than twice the height of a man to the water, and Ilohan was amazed at their daring. Yet it looked like wonderful fun. They soared out over the lake and let go one after another to splash into the clear water with cries of delight.

Ilohan climbed the wooden ladder that led up to the platform, and as he reached the top the old man turned toward him with a welcoming smile. For a long moment Ilohan could not look away from his face. He thought he had never seen such strength and freedom. There was in the man's eyes a confidence so deep that it was frightening.

"I am Mudien of Ceramir," said the man at last. "You are Sir Ilohan of Karolan. Welcome to the Cloth of Joy."

"Thank you, Sir," said Ilohan. "I have a message for you from the Lady Eleanor."

"I will receive it, with many thanks to the bearer," said Mudien.

"Here it is," said Ilohan, and gave him the parchment.

There was a hint of laughter in Mudien's face as he read the message. It was well that Ilohan had not read it, for it said:

The bearer has been convicted by certain evidence.
Please see that the sentence is carried out in full.

Mudien knew the true meaning of Eleanor's words: Ilohan of Karolan had been convicted of faithfulness, beyond doubt, and his 'sentence' would be a gift he could not even imagine.

Mudien put the parchment in his cloak. "This is a place of freedom and joy," he said. "You are welcome here, and may do anything or go anywhere you please. A room has been prepared for you in the great house. We request your presence at a banquet tonight on the lawn beside the lake, starting a short time after sunset. The Lady Eleanor will be there, as well as your companion Jonathan of Glen Carrah. Rejoice in this place, Sir Ilohan. In Ceramir you are safe from all dangers and temptations save those you have brought with you, and even those we have power to defeat."

"May I ask you a question, Sir?"

"Yes indeed."

"How much of what I have seen today was a test, and why was I tested?"

"The second question will be answered soon, but not now," said Mudien. "However..." Mudien was silent for a moment, and for the first time he seemed troubled. "Since you wish to know what was a test, I will tell you this: He who tried to persuade you to break your word rejoiced when he failed. The guard at the fallen sapling was there only for you, to remind you of the Law. She who seemed unfaithful was not, yet her tears were real. Those who lie dead in the woods below knew nothing of us, nor we of them. We gave them nothing but our arrows, and still their presence troubles us, for we did not suspect it."

Ilohan sat down suddenly on the railing of the platform, thinking hard. "It must all have been a test, all but the Norkaths. The brigands were not brigands, and her ankle was not really sprained." He stood up suddenly.

"Sir," he said sharply, "what would have happened if I had failed?"

"We rejoice that you did not fail," said Mudien with triumph in his voice. "Of failing all you need to know is this: it is great evil to choose to murder a man. However if you are not permitted to do your chosen act, the man is not dead. This is why failing a test is better than failing reality."

"How can it have been good to tempt me thus?"

"We dared to do what we have done, knowing its boldness, but believing that God desired it of us. If we have been wrong, may he forgive us. I ask you to forgive us also, for indeed it is not strange that you should be angry."

Ilohan sat back down on the railing. "I am sorry," he said. "I have no cause to be angry. If I was tempted it is because of the evil within me, and the existence of that is my fault alone. Alas that it is there."

"You have proven true, Sir Ilohan," said Mudien. "Do not forget that the evil within you is the enemy of Christ, whose Spirit is also within you, and Christ will triumph."

"I thank you," said Ilohan, "yet please pray for me, for my heart is heavy and I would not have it be so here in the Cloth of Joy."

"It will not be," said Mudien. "Look at the joy of the children."

Ilohan leaned over the railing and watched them. They were going off one at a time now, soaring out over the deep, clear lake, and falling into it with great splashes. One young boy, more lithe and strong than the others, swung his feet up as he let go of the rope, and did a full back flip before he landed in the water. Ilohan wondered how it could be that they were not cold.

"Are there swimming clothes in my room back at the house?" he asked.

Mudien smiled. "Yes," he said, "go and find them, and rejoice in this place. It is not for nothing that it is called the Cloth of Joy."

Ilohan climbed down the ladder and ran back around the lake to the stone house. The door was again ajar, but no one was there. He went inside, and was astonished to realize that a small stream went through the house, entering by means of a low stone archway in the wall. He walked through clean, silent rooms, and found a woman kneeling by an open window. She looked up when he approached. Her hair was gray and her face lined, but she did not look old. She reminded him a little of Queen Sarah.

"What can I do for you, Sir?" she asked.

"I am looking for the room that has been prepared for me, my Lady," said Ilohan. "My name is Ilohan, and I have recently arrived here from Karolan."

"And I am Imrànie of Ceramir," she said with a smile. "I will show you to your room."

"I thank you, my Lady," said Ilohan.

"You are welcome. If you desire anything, ask me or Mudien or one of our children and we will do our best for you."

Ilohan found his clothes laid out in his room, and put them on quickly. He liked the swimming clothes of Ceramir. They suited well those who wore them, and they were light and quick to dry. He ran out of the house and across the leaf-carpeted lawn, and stopped at the water's edge. The bottom was fine sand, and the water was as clear as that of Lake Luciyr. He started to wade out into it, and was astonished to find that it was warm. Not merely warm enough to swim in indefinitely, as the water down in Harevan had been, but warm to the touch, as if it had been heated over a fire. Ilohan could not understand it: a deep mountain lake, more blessedly warm than a shallow pond in summer back in Karolan.

He plunged in, and the warmth comforted him through and through. The afternoon sky was brilliant blue above him. Autumn leaves drifted in the breeze. The deep, clear water beneath him held no fear. "Ceramir, the Cloth of Joy, the Valley of the Undismayed," he thought. "Perhaps I will yet be among them."

He closed his eyes and floated on his back. He thought of what Mudien had said, of the certain victory of Christ in his life. "I will be purified," he whispered. "When I think or do evil I am acting contrary to my true identity, given me through Christ. Slowly and inevitably the one I truly am, the one God intended me to be, will triumph. Here in the warm lake of the Valley of the Undismayed, I see myself growing ever closer to the Savior I love, until at last I pass through the door of death into his presence forever."

He took a deep breath and dove down toward the bottom of the lake. He was surprised to find the deep water was even warmer than the surface, and that the bottom was far too deep for him to reach. When he surfaced for air, he realized that there must be a hot spring deep in the lake – which, of course, was the source of the warm river that flowed down through Harevan. He floated on the surface again, and felt the slight swirling motion of the water coming up from the hot depths of the earth.

His mind wandered over the events of the day and Mudien's words about them, and fixed on a phrase. "She who seemed unfaithful was not, yet her tears were real." He rejoiced that she was faithful. Nothing that day had caused him greater pain than the thought that she, who had seemed to him so honest, kind, and trustworthy, had tried to seduce him. It was a great relief to him to know that it had been a test, that she also was true.

Yet she had cried, and her tears had been real. Why? Had she considered herself guilty for what she had done, even though it was only a test? He thought she had. He was sorry for her, for he suspected that the pain of his test would hurt her far longer than it had hurt him. "You were very courageous, Veril," he said. "Please do not weep over what you have done, for wrong or right you meant it well, and are forgiven." He laughed at himself suddenly for speaking to the absent, and turned his thoughts into a prayer as he floated in the blissful warmth.

His prayer was not without requests – for wisdom, joy, purity, rescue for Karolan, and peace for Veril – yet chiefly it was a song of thanks. "I thank you, Father, for today, and for the peace and hope I feel in this place that seems a piece of Eden graciously left behind to bless the weary world."

*　　　　*　　　　*

Eleanor, Auria, and Jonathan set out for Ceramir in the early afternoon. Jonathan had offered Eleanor his horse, but she had declined, saying that as there was plenty of time she preferred to walk. Jonathan and Auria did not mind going through the sunlit autumn woods at Eleanor's slow pace.

Jonathan questioned Eleanor courteously but persistently about the events of the morning, and she answered some of his questions while firmly refusing to answer others. Jonathan learned that Ilohan had been tested, that he had proven true, and that he had been attacked by five Norkath knights who were shot by the archers who were watching him as part of the test. More than this Eleanor would not say.

Over Jonathan's shoulder he carried a bag containing the crown and sword that they had found at Lake Luciyr. As King Thomas had commanded, Ilohan had carefully hidden it – in the rafters above his bed, where Auria and Eleanor could neither see nor reach. Jonathan had found it undisturbed, so he knew that neither they nor anyone else had touched it. The bag was padded carefully with spare clothes so the metal did not rattle, and Jonathan said nothing about its contents. He ambled contentedly through the lovely woods beside the river, hoping that at Ceramir the fallen warrior of Luciyr, and the purpose of the quest, would at last be explained.

As he walked, he glanced now and then at Eleanor, and once or twice fell behind so he could watch her without appearing awkward. Her hair was long and straight, light brown mixed with gray, but her face was not old. She bore her limp with patient cheerfulness that seemed almost miraculous to Jonathan, to whom the ability to run was as precious as the light of the sun. There was something about her that he did not understand – something wonderful, but mysterious. After a while he found a way to express what he was thinking in words, but this did not dispel the mystery.

"My Lady, may I ask yet another question?" he said.

"You may," she answered with a smile, "provided I may refuse to answer it."

"Have you passed through great suffering, and emerged the stronger for it?"

The expression on Eleanor's face was strange, a kind of joy mixed with shame and sadness, and she was silent for a long moment. "Do you think I have?" she asked at last.

"I do," said Jonathan. "Something strange and strong and good has come to you, and I think that pain is the only way it could have come."

"Thank you," said Eleanor, and for a moment Jonathan thought she was thanking him for the compliment, and then he realized she was praying. "Thank you, Lord. I do not understand what you have given me, but I understand that it is good. If any power has truly come out of that dark time..." She shuddered. "Lord, please help me to use it well." There was another silence, as she limped along with her crutches. Then she turned to Jonathan again. "If you want a better answer, be patient and at Ceramir you shall have it. Yet I myself do not understand the least part of what God has done for me."

Chapter 14

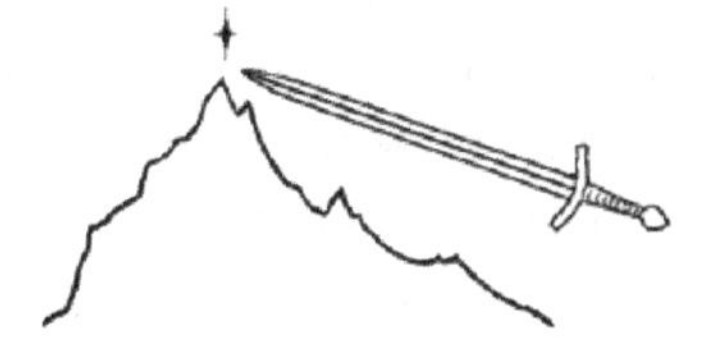

The Cloth of Joy

JONATHAN STOOD STILL A MOMENT IN THE GATE OF HOPE, looking into Ceramir. Mighty trees filled the wide valley, tendrils of mist wafted from the blue lake, and gray cliff walls towered up on the left and right. It was as beautiful as Luciyr or Glen Carrah, though very different. Here he felt a glorious sense of all-embracing welcome. This lake cried out that all who wished should swim, and the trees begged to be climbed, and the many-windowed house called out that here was rest and hope for all weary wanderers.

He hastened to find the room assigned to him and Ilohan, and put on swimming clothes. Yet after he was dressed he stood still a moment at the window, looking out with unseeing eyes. Though only a few weeks had passed, he was much older than when he had last run for joy in Glen Carrah. He had seen wounds and death, hunger and fear, cold and cruelty. Careless joy did not come to him as naturally as it once had. But he raised his head defiantly. "We triumphed," he said. "I am Jonathan of Glen Carrah. Joy and freedom are not for children only, but for all who will delight in beauty as they ought."

He ran out from the house with all the wildness of unhindered joy. He flew along the grassy, leaf bright shore. He ran through the shallows kicking up great splashes of spray that caught the sun and shone like stars as they fell. He came to the east side of the lake, where the children were playing, and leaped up on the platform with a single motion. He turned to the young man who was watching over the children. "Happy are you, to be a son of Ceramir," said Jonathan. "But is the rope for the children only?"

"Welcome to Ceramir," said the man. "I am Karlak son of Mudien. You must be Jonathan of Glen Carrah. This rope is for all who rejoice in its use. Yet there is a higher one. Few who were not raised as children of Ceramir dare swing on it."

"Where is it?" asked Jonathan.

"I will show you," said Karlak. "It is near enough that I need not fear to leave the children."

It was on the very next tree, a giant sycamore that towered up from the water's edge and extended one huge branch far out over the lake. An astonishingly high platform was attached to the tree, and could not be reached without climbing a long, knotted rope. Karlak climbed it in a flash, and Jonathan was only a little behind him. A sturdy swing rope awaited them. Karlak unhooked it, put his foot in a loop, and leaped off the edge of the platform.

He sailed far out over the water, until it seemed to Jonathan that he had crossed half the lake. On his return he slipped his foot out of the loop with a clever motion, landed back on the platform with a crash, and handed Jonathan the rope.

The blacksmith's arms were so strong that he had no fear of losing hold, but the height was dizzying. He stood still for a moment, considering. Suddenly, with a running jump and a final shove, he flew off the platform without putting his foot in the loop. He loved the cool rush of the air as he flew through it, and the lovely confusion of glowing color that he saw as he swung fast and far. Below him he saw Ilohan, swimming on his back in the warm water. Then he was flying back toward the tree, and he suddenly realized that he did not know how to keep from hitting the platform. He lifted himself as high as he could, just cleared the edge with his feet, and made a landing louder and less elegant than Karlak's. As he stood on the edge of the platform he felt more free and joyful than at any time since he had left Carrah.

Karlak turned to him with twinkling eyes. "You were born to be a son of Ceramir," he said. "You are among the undismayed."

"No," said Jonathan, remembering times during his journey when dismay had seemed to blot out all the beauty of the world. "Yet I rejoice that I am here, that there is such a place as the Cloth of Joy."

"There is much more than this to see," said Karlak. "Would you have me show it to you? The children are already going to the house to greet Lady Eleanor and pester her for stories."

"I would indeed see more of Ceramir," said Jonathan, "yet I would have Sir Ilohan come with us."

"Very well, then," said Karlak, his eyes twinkling, "we can easily ask him for his company. Have you seen how the children will swing two at a time, dropping off into the water one after the other? Are you daring enough to try the same here?"

"And more besides," said Jonathan.

They grasped the rope together and ran off the platform, giving it a push with their feet as they left. Karlak let go when they were almost at their furthest, and Jonathan followed an instant later. Empty air was beneath their feet until the thrilling terror of their flight ended with almost simultaneous splashes.

The glorious noise crashed in Ilohan's ears as he swam, and somehow he knew exactly what it was. He looked up to see Jonathan and Karlak treading water only a few strokes away.

"Greetings, Sir Ilohan," said Jonathan. "Karlak here suggests that there is far more of Ceramir for us to see, and I request your company in seeing it."

"Certainly," said Ilohan, laughing.

They swam to shore and began running up through the lovely valley, not caring that their clothes were wet and the air was cool, for their joyful running warmed them. The great trees' lush branches grew as they pleased, sometimes brushing the ground and making leafy arches over the grass, sometimes soaring high overhead from tall trunks devoid of lower branches. Here and there small hot springs gave birth to little streams like the one that ran through the stone house of Ceramir. Autumn though it was, some bright flowers still grew on their mossy banks. Wherever they ran, even well out of sight of the valley's edge, they could feel the great rock walls of Ceramir protecting them, benevolent and strong, shutting out the world that might have frayed the Cloth of Joy.

The trees grew sparser as they came nearer to the feet of the mountains. Ilohan noticed that Karlak, in the lead, had changed direction as if making for a particular destination. Then suddenly they emerged from a clump of trees and he saw it.

The sight was hard to comprehend. It seemed to be a vast, steeply tilted sheet of green leaves and branches, soaring into the evening sky like a cliff face cloaked in vegetation – but from the surrounding land, Ilohan was sure there could be no cliff there. Karlak ran forward and began to climb it, looking as if he were wading up a frozen waterfall of vegetation. Jonathan bounded up behind him and began to climb, laughing aloud when the sheet of leaves bounced and swayed under his weight.

Ilohan ran up and began climbing himself. The sheet was made of thickly matted vines, some of them thick as a man's arm, old and tangled, yet strong and living and green. Presently Ilohan realized with a thrill that they were already higher than the battlements of Aaronkal. Yet he climbed on without fear, for the woven mat of vines was so thick that there seemed no possibility of falling through.

Karlak far above them waved them on, and at last they reached the crest of the vegetable mountain. Then Ilohan understood: the vines were growing on a tree: a huge, gnarled giant, one of the very northernmost trees in the Valley of the Undismayed. He stood beside Karlak and Jonathan holding on to the tree's rough trunk where it protruded through the very top of the sheet of vines. Looking down, he saw that the blanket of vines grew not on one tree only, but on several: it seemed draped like the top of some great pavilion over the tree by which they stood, and several smaller ones on either side.

Ceramir lay below them, guarded by the tall cliffs that surrounded it. They could see the river woods and Harevan beyond the Gate of Hope, and again beyond that the immense desert stretched out to the horizon.

"You can see it all from up here," said Karlak. "In the spring these vines bloom white and yellow, and you can smell the fragrance all the way to Harevan if the wind is right. It was this blanket of living green that was first called the Cloth of Joy, and gave its name to the whole valley. Now come and look the other way."

Ilohan and Jonathan followed him a few steps to where they could get a clear view north, toward the mountains. There was no cloth of vines on that side. It was like looking off a vegetable cliff. The northernmost part of Ceramir stretched back against the mountains, farther than Ilohan had imagined. It was an immense and fertile farm. Lush gardens of many different crops were interspersed among fields of wheat and barley. As they looked over the bounty of the Cloth of Joy, Karlak described what was grown in each place, including many vegetables that were not known in Karolan.

"Among the trees in the rest of Ceramir are many that bear fruits or nuts," he said, "and close against the mountain wall we have stone barns that hold our cows and other animals. We keep as many as the fields we have to spare will support, which is no great number, but enough to supply us with all the meat and milk we require."

The adventurers listened to him, but their eyes wandered up to the cliff walls that bounded Ceramir on the north. They soared up, gray, forbidding, and dark in evening shadow. Above them the awesome mountains, still huge beyond their minds' grasp, towered bright against the sky.

Ilohan turned and looked again in the opposite direction. He looked out beyond Harevan, where the trees faded into the endless sand. The desert landscape was hard to make out, shrouded by the long blue shadows of its dusty hills. He could just discern the pale line of the desert road going west, toward the sun. Not far west of Harevan it ran between two unusually large ranges of hills, one of them practically a spur of the mountains and the other extending out as far as he could follow it into the desert. The sight of these hills, and the gap between them through which the desert road passed, seemed oddly significant to him. He would not easily forget it, he thought.

He slipped into a reverie as he stared at the blue shadows and the golden light. The confusion in his mind seemed to fade into the gulf of clear air and vanish. He had been tested; it had been hard, and he did not understand the reason, but he had not failed. Tonight something would happen – the sense of expectancy seemed to fill the valley. He believed that tonight he would learn the reason for his quest, and for the tests. There was peace in the thought that all would soon be made clear.

Then fear fell on him suddenly. "All will be made clear," he thought. "What will that mean? The quest was simply the king's business, which I have now completed, but what were the tests? I am the least of his knights – why should I be tested? Perhaps I was tested for a new, harder quest – and if that is true, I am sure my strength and virtue will not be enough, and I will fail." Vague guesses, all full of strain and dread, came to him of what the new quest might be, and he clung suddenly close to the trunk of the tree.

"Lord," he prayed, "I have been taught that you rule over all people, and that though we seem to determine the course of our lives for ourselves, in truth it is you who do it. So it is not untrue, the feeling that I now have that my life is beyond my control, that anything may happen – tonight. I have been taught that I should not fear, for you guide and guard the paths of those you love. Surely I have seen your protection and rescue. And yet, I fear! Forgive my fear, and give me peace. Be with me, and may I not fail or fall into evil in any of the trials which lie ahead of me. Though the blessing was never spoken over me, may it be true of me – the blessing on the ruined crown. May my strength be equal to my days."

* * *

The three who had mounted the sheet of vines had not noticed a solitary, bent figure in one of the distant vegetable gardens. It was Veril. She was still there later, when the open shade of evening was falling cool and gray across the fields, and she looked up from the plot of ground she had been weeding. She loved the changing beauty of the days: misty dawns, brilliant mornings, soft afternoons, and restful evenings. Yet of all times in the day she liked this best: the sun no longer shining on the valley floor, but its light still softly brightening the sky. The evenings were kind and free, connected in her mind with many happy memories, from wild children's games racing through the woods, to quiet conversations at the fall of dusk.

But there was no happiness in her tonight. The troubles of her life seemed to have intensified and gathered into a hollow pain that robbed her of all that used to bring her joy.

Though she was a faithful daughter of Ceramir, for a long time she had not been altogether happy there. She enjoyed the warm lake, the great trees, the frequent merry feasts, the swinging ropes, and the cloth of vines. Yet as her brothers and sisters had grown up, each of them had found a useful thing to do, and she had not. Auria served Eleanor down in Harevan. Brogal did she was not sure what, but something very good and helpful, somewhere out in the desert. Karlak tended the sick over at the house. Rangol led the young bowmen of Ceramir in their ceaseless vigilance over the roads that led to the Gate of Hope. Her other brothers and sisters, and all the grown children of Ceramir, had each found some way to help. Only she was left; able to enjoy the blessings of the valley, but useful for nothing.

Everything she had tried to do had failed. She had looked for someone to serve in Harevan, but Eleanor did not need two helpers and no one else needed any. She had tried to care for the animals in the barns, but though they loved her, old Pintor who managed the livestock had found her too slow in her work and too softhearted to be a useful assistant. She had tried the best and hardest task of all, the healing work of Ceramir, but at that too she had failed. She had loved the sick and injured who were brought to the Cloth of Joy from far and wide for healing, and her skill and understanding had been enough to serve them. But their pain had horrified her, haunted her dreams at night and distracted her from serving them during the day, until at last Mudien had banned her from working as a healer. "You have the skill and courage, child," her father had said, "but it costs you too much. Let this labor be for those on whom it weighs less heavily." She worked the gardens sometimes, as now, and did it well, but the young children could do that. She was no longer a child, and wanted a task beyond the tasks of children.

Her thoughts had been running on these things two months before, when without meaning to she had overheard Eleanor and her father talking together, saying something like this:

"...test is a necessity, yet have we any right to ask anyone to carry it out?"

"I do not think so..." "...any idea how it has been done..."

"None that helps us now. When I imagine myself doing something like that I tremble..."

"...sure indeed that it is what we were intended to do. There must be someone who will do it."

"Yet we have no right to ask anyone. What can we do?"

Veril had opened the door of the room where they were, and said in a tremulous voice, "I will do it."

They had told her what it was, and tried to dissuade her. Yet again and again she had asked them if they were sure that Ilohan must be tested, and they had said yes, they were. And so she would not be dissuaded. At last she had found something she could do for her father, for Eleanor, for someone. It was a hard thing, a thing they would find no one else to do. And although she, too, was afraid, she would not give in. At last Eleanor and Mudien had reluctantly agreed.

Returning to the present from her vivid memories, Veril lay back on the dirt beside the plants she had been weeding. The deep twilight blue of the sky told her she was about to miss the banquet.

She remembered how the feasts of Ceramir had delighted her as a child, and she mourned her fate. She had found a task that she alone dared to perform. Had it turned out to be the only one of all the deeds of Ceramir's children that caused harm rather than good?

It had been frighteningly easy to carry out Ilohan's test. Falling off a riverbank uninjured and then faking a sprain had been simple enough, and barely more serious than a well acted story at a banquet. Lying on the bed as she had, and saying the words she had said, had been a different matter. Somehow she had known exactly how to act and speak. She had been frightened by her own ability, by her tremendous capacity for evil. In that room she had realized for the first time how strong lust was, and how easily she could awaken it in a man. Strange and bitter that she should realize these things only after it was too late, after she had wounded a man who had been kind to her, who had believed her truly injured, and who for courtesy's sake had carried her to the limit of his strength.

She had seen that he was true and kind, had hoped with all her heart that he would pass, and had believed he would. Then she had hurt him, tempted him, wounded him. He had given a cry of pain and dismay, and had fled. What did it matter that she had thought she was doing good? She had hurt the one whom, above all people on earth, she wished might not be hurt. Suddenly she observed her own thought, and was startled. What had she just thought about Ilohan of Karolan? That she wanted to avoid hurting him more than she wanted to avoid hurting anyone else in the world? Did that mean she wanted to bless him more than she wanted to bless anyone in the world, more than her mother Imranie, more than Mudien her father, more than her dear friend Eleanor, or Auria and Rangol and her other sisters and brothers?

Yes. She realized that the answer to both questions was yes. This made no sense to her, but that did not alter its truth. Suddenly she rose to a kneeling position, confused by her thoughts, shaken and wondering. "Father," she prayed, "if I have sinned against you, forgive me. If the thoughts that I have displease you, free me of them. If it is because of my wrong that I am useless, forgive me and set me free so that I can be a blessing to someone. Keep me tonight I pray, and guide me. Bless Ilohan, please, and do not let him ever fail to be true and good. Thank you for who you have made him. Bless me and keep me."

She was resolute, almost on the point of getting up and going back into the woods to the banquet. Then suddenly she fell back on the dirt, her face buried in her hands. "How can this be, Lord? I did not seek to hurt. What is coming to me? What are you doing? Have you left me? Do you not love me? Help, Father! What shall I do? What shall I do…" She suffered dry-eyed for a moment, and then her tears came fast and hot.

* * *

The last rosy light was fading from the treetops when Ilohan left his room, dressed in dry clothes and ready for the banquet. It was a lovely, calm evening. The air in the valley was almost still, with only a slight breath stirring the highest tree branches and wafting away the mist that rose from the warm lake. A long table was set up on the lawn near the shore. The table was covered with a blue cloth edged in gold, and surrounded by many chairs. Candles in holders of polished wood, silver, and gold were on it ready to be lit. Already some of the children of Ceramir were bringing out the food in steaming bowls and on well laden plates and trays. Narrow columns made of brass and silver stood at intervals around the table. They stood about as high as Ilohan himself, and had what looked like clumps of wool at their tops. He could not guess their purpose, but like almost everything he had seen in Ceramir they seemed well-crafted, fitting, and beautiful.

Many people of all ages stood laughing and talking on the lawn near the table. Some of them carried musical instruments, a few of which were familiar to Ilohan while most were not. Freedom was in the air: fearless, joyous, undismayed. He himself stood silent, unwilling or unable to feel wholly free and safe, though the people before him clearly felt so. His inability to rest and trust even in the Cloth of Joy grieved him, made him feel foolish – but he could not escape the sense that Ceramir was too good to be true. Were not the people here yet of the human race, the same race that could enslave and murder, rape and plunder and betray?

Yet were not the people elsewhere the same race that here appeared to laugh and love so faithfully and joyfully? Why should such places not exist? But again – had he not been taught that perfection could never be attained on the earth? Here he seemed to see and hear it all around. It could not be. He could not trust a thing so beautiful.

He heard a young boy raise his voice in jealous anger, and go on in selfish crying even while his mother tried to hush him with loving words spoken firmly. She succeeded after a moment, and the peace of the lovely evening was restored. Ilohan looked up at the high treetops from which the last sunlight had now faded. The young child's quickly ended anger loomed large in his mind, though it was hardly noticed by anyone else. It had seemed a terrible, jarring note in the joyful song of the freedom of Ceramir. But it was soon over, and left no scars, while the song went on all undismayed.

True joy came to his heart then, and he felt himself smiling. Ceramir was not perfect, but real. It was flawed, like all else on the broken, fallen earth. But he had not known; he had not imagined what the power of God could weave out of lives honestly given to him. Ceramir stood, not as a flawless paradise that rivaled Heaven, but as a song of joy and praise that told of it: a herald of the day to come, not a mockery of the dawn itself.

As he approached the table with slow steps, his thoughts were all a single, happy prayer, a prayer for the freedom of the Cloth of Joy: "Father, may it be free from fear always – as free as it is tonight until the end of time."

The people of Ceramir welcomed him like a brother, as if he had been among them since his childhood. He almost felt that he had. The preparations for the feast had been completed while he watched and wondered, and soon they were all sitting down.

Everyone, young and old alike, had some bright happiness in this festal night, and whatever their private troubles may have been, they were lightened and buoyed up by the current of joy that ran like the warm river itself through the Valley of the Undismayed. Mudien and Imranie sat together at one end of the long, broad table, and Rangol and Karlak sat at the other, surrounded by more sons and daughters of Ceramir than

Ilohan had any chance of counting. He himself sat near Jonathan, close to Imranie and Mudien. Eleanor did not seem to have taken her seat yet. Several people had been carried out of the house on light beds, and set down just inside the row of brass stands. Ilohan guessed that they were sick; too weak to sit at table but well enough to be present and share some of the joy of the banquet.

Tall boys and girls came from the house carrying small, bright torches, and went up and down the table with them, lighting all the candles. Auria appeared and poured something from a clay jar on the tops of the silver and brass stands, then lit them with one of the torches. They burned high and bright, with blue and golden flames that gave off not only light but also a good deal of heat, which was welcome on the cool autumn night. The lighting of the candles and the stands changed the appearance of everything dramatically: the banquet become an island of color and dancing light surrounded by a sea of mysterious blue dusk.

"The lamps of Ceramir are lighted," said Auria in a clear voice, "when shall the feast begin?"

"Let it begin now," said Mudien, "with thanks to him who gave it."

"Father," said Mudien in the sudden, happy silence, "we thank you and love you. You have blessed us with bounty we could never deserve; often even beyond what we have hoped. Help us to love and praise you as we should. This we deeply desire. Hold Ceramir in your hand, and let it always please you. Guard it from all evil, and keep it bright and pure, as it is today because of your mighty care. Our hearts rejoice in you. Amen."

Ilohan noticed that Jonathan did not echo Mudien's 'Amen', though everyone else did without reluctance or affectation. He looked again for the Lady Eleanor, shocked that the feast had begun without her. Then he saw that she had come to her seat unnoticed, and was quite near him on the other side of the table. She was dressed in white, and a white ribbon was woven through her hair. She looked younger and more beautiful than she had before, and he rejoiced to see her.

Very few at that banquet felt ill at ease, and there were many animated conversations. Some considered eating the first priority, and did not engage in conversation until much later. These were much appreciated by the cooks, whom they honored with high praise – as did everyone else. Those who wanted just to sit and look and listen could do it, without feeling awkward. The valley seemed full of peace and freedom, and joy rested on them all like the light of the lamps.

Few people noticed when Imranie found the lone empty chair and slipped it quietly out from among the others so that the blank would not be seen. She leaned against it a moment at the edge of the island of light, knowing that Veril had not come, and wondering what she should do. She had not agreed when Mudien and Eleanor had let Veril persuade them that she should carry out the test. Yet she had allowed herself to be overruled, and now as she had expected it had hurt her daughter deeply. She sighed and went back to her place at the banquet, deciding she should not abandon it. Yet most of her thoughts and all of her prayers were with Veril, somewhere out in the darkness of a valley that to her tonight would not seem the Cloth of Joy.

Gradually the feast drew to a close. Most people had eaten all they wanted and only a few here and there were still finishing up, with one last cup of deep red wine, or slice of rich cake, or spoonful of golden honey over buttered bread. Then those who had musical instruments brought them out, pushed back their chairs, and struck up a song. It gathered depth and strength, and it seemed ancient and yet not old. It was full of the leaping life of the trees' bright leaves and the children's laughter, yet it had a dauntless joy that was like the roots that never give up growing, or the faith of Imranie and Mudien that is not shaken. Soon Karlak, Rangol, and several others got up and went away into the darkness, while many around the table began to sing:

Free of the fear that holds love back,
Bright is the joy hope brings!
We fear not sickness, sword, or rack.
The undismayed heart sings!

The music was glorious, and the words fitted into it and gave it a voice and a purpose. Ilohan felt he could have listened to it forever.

As long as Hope still stands unseen,
As long as Dawn delays,
Ceramir's joy runs bright and clean
For all who bore dark days.

He wondered why Karlak and Rangol and the others had left, and missed such a wonderful thing.

Here let the power, deep and strong,
Defy all evil things.
Healing is here from hurt of wrong,
Where the broken heart sings.

"Daring words," thought Ilohan. "Only God has such power. Yet I think his blessing rests on this place, and the song is true."

Bright may the light of Ceramir
Shine to its Maker's praise!
For he has blessed and held us dear,
Though we once scorned his ways.

The singers around the banquet table paused, while those playing the music went on. A thunderous roll of drums came from across the lake, and the deep voices of the sons of Ceramir roared across the water:

Hope, Hope,
Joy, Joy,
Praise him, for dawn shall come!

Great splashes in the darkness showed that two of them had been swinging out over the water as they sang. The singers around the table sang again; nearly everyone except Ilohan and Jonathan was singing now:

Weaver of all of Ceramir,
Savior of those who trust,
Keep this valley from every fear:
The star amid the dust!

Rangol and company roared out from across the lake, accompanied again by drums and splashes.

Faith, Faith,

Joy, Joy,
Praise God for all he has done!

The pattern continued for one more verse, and then the end of the song came with a great crescendo in which everyone sang at once.

So all whose hearts have been made free,
Sing to the Savior above,
Dance for joy as you come to see
The endless depth of his love.

Love, Love,
Joy, Joy
The best has not even begun!

Dance for the hope in the darkness.
Dance for the Dawn that shall come.
Dance for your Lord and your Savior!
The best has not even begun!

Ilohan felt that he could dance, in that place, to that music, to the glory of God, forever. And he saw that the people of Ceramir did indeed intend to dance. Some of the musicians kept playing, while the rest of them and many others ran to a flat part of the lawn where a few more lamps had been set up, and danced. Ilohan stood and watched. Some of them had cymbals or tambourines, and they all clapped in time to the song. For the most part they kept in a big circle around a lamp in the center. Sometimes they joined hands, sometimes they danced individually, sometimes in pairs or threes or fours, however they desired. Throughout the whole Ilohan could hear the words of another song, as strong and lovely as the first, although he was not sure who was singing them. The dance was beautiful and unselfconscious. He was hesitant to join in, for even in that place and time, he did not think he could dance as they did.

While he was thinking about this, he suddenly felt Eleanor's hand on his shoulder. "I know you would like to dance, Sir Ilohan," she said, "as would I, who never will again until the new dawn. But tonight there is a different task for both of us."

"What is it, my Lady?"

"Come in to the house, and you will know. Jonathan and Imranie and Mudien are already there."

Chapter 15

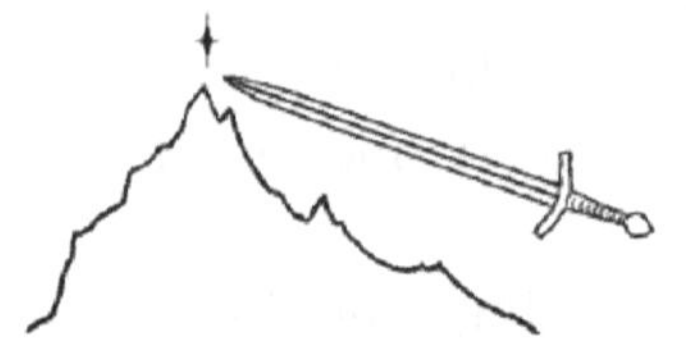

The Princess of Karolan

ELEANOR LED ILOHAN TO ONE OF THE ROOMS THROUGH which the warm stream flowed. There were many candles there, and the room with its light-colored stone walls seemed warm and bright. Wooden seats and benches lined the walls, except where a merry fire burned in a small hearth. Five chairs had been pulled into a rough circle near the hearth, and Jonathan, Mudien, and Imranie sat there talking quietly together. Ilohan and Eleanor took the remaining chairs.

As they sat down, Ilohan was struck anew by Lady Eleanor's beauty. She was dressed for the banquet, tastefully and well, but it was more than this that he noticed. She knew this was a very special night, and knew why – and the knowledge made her more beautiful. She was excited, and perhaps even a little frightened. Yet she also seemed more herself than ever, more patient, more hopeful, more radiantly worthy of trust.

A moment passed in silence, and then Mudien spoke. "We are met tonight on a joyful and important occasion. Tonight many secrets will be revealed, many hopes fulfilled, many plans considered. Yet before we begin one thing must be said. Sir Ilohan, all your life some things have been hidden from you. There was a reason for this, and it came from love and wisdom. Now all that was hidden shall be revealed. It may be that you have thought that your life was in the hands of others, whose power and wisdom you could not aid or match. Think so no longer. Henceforth those who were once your teachers may yet be your counselors, but your decisions are your own. We, like you, walk in a world that we see only incompletely. Like you we walk by faith, and like you we can stumble through doubt or stop undecided through fear. Consider us now no longer your leaders, but your friends. Together we face a great challenge, equal before God, who alone can lead us all."

"Thank you, Sir," said Ilohan.

"I request your forgiveness for the tests through which we called you this morning," said Eleanor. "That shall be the last time that we seek to hide things from you. Even now I wonder if we were right or wrong."

"Right or wrong I forgive you freely, my Lady," said Ilohan, "and my trust in God and in you makes me sure you did no wrong."

"Thank you, Sir Ilohan," said Lady Eleanor. "Now the story shall begin."

The candles shone bright and steady along the light stone walls. The fire crackled on the hearth and the stream swished softly through its channel in the floor. They waited in silence. Then Eleanor began.

"The love of Sarah and Thomas was not an easy love. It was born out of suffering for both, and matured in a life that was filled with challenge though also with hope. It was a faithful and a bright love, seldom spoken, but always deeply known.

"In the year that Konder, king of Karolan, died and Thomas was crowned, Sarah brought forth a son, the first sign of his father's strength. The king rejoiced at the birth of his child, and all of Karolan rejoiced with him.

"The people hoped that the reign of Thomas would be more peaceful and more prosperous than that of his father Konder, which had been troubled in its early years by a war against Norkath, and later by internal strife, heavy taxes imposed by the king, famine, and an outbreak of plague. They saw the birth of the new prince as confirmation that a happier age was dawning for the weary, battered land of Karolan. They praised the valor of King Thomas and the beauty of Queen Sarah, and said that the banner of the Stone, Sword, and Star would float high in honorable peace, and never again be struck down in war or rebellion.

"The love of Thomas and Sarah grew deeper as their son grew, and they raised him with wisdom and care. As he grew, the hopes of all Karolan rose, for he was strong and courageous, and in everything he proved faithful. When he rode through the land he sat as a prince should, on a great black horse, with his banner snapping in the wind and his handsome face alight with the joy of his strength and the hopes that he had for the future. Soon he was known throughout Karolan as generous, selfless and trustworthy.

"Once, when he was riding through the woods and farmlands far to the west of Aaronkal, he saw a farmer and his wife and young sons trying to rebuild their farmhouse, which had been burnt by brigands. He took off his crown and royal robe, and in the dress of an ordinary knight he dismounted to help them rebuild the cottage. His servants watched astonished at first, and then had to join in themselves for shame. They cut trees in the forest, and sawed strong new logs, and by nightfall the house was nearly done. The farmer and his family were amazed, and did not know what to say, but the prince saw that as yet there was no thatch. He would not hear of leaving them without a roof, so on they worked by the light of a full moon until they had thatched the cottage.

"By then it was very late, with the moon shining high in the sky, and the prince and his servants were tired and hungry. The farmer invited them with a tremulous voice to stay the night, but as there was barely room for him and his family, the prince declined. He and his retinue journeyed on, until they came to the castle of Britheldore. There at last he stopped to seek lodging for the night. The knight of Britheldore awoke and welcomed them warmly, but he did not recognize the prince, without his crown or royal robes, weary and disheveled from the long work. The prince concealed his royalty, and as Britheldore was very courteous and hospitable, he respected the unknown knight's desire to remain unknown.

"Despite the late hour, Britheldore had a good meal prepared for the prince and his servants, and they ate far better than they had expected to. Britheldore's daughter came down from her tower room while they were feasting. She had woken at the sound of the portcullis going up, and had dressed quickly and descended to see who had arrived. She saw the prince and the other knights, and sat down at the table to speak with them. She had no fear that her parents would rebuke her for this, because while they had taught her carefully and wisely, they had also given her great freedom. Now, in her seventeenth year, they permitted her to do whatever she wished, and trusted her not to go astray.

"The prince liked her confident manner, though her action was unusual, and somehow he and she stayed at the table talking even when all the others had gone to a well-earned rest. For some strange reason he told her about the events of the day, and about many other things in his life, as much as he could without revealing himself. He was not given to praising himself, or talking much about his accomplishments. Yet somehow he felt that to her he could speak freely. He thought that she would understand that each thing he did was less than he had hoped it would be, that every time he helped someone he saw what he had failed to do: he saw five score breaches in the wall for every one he helped to mend. Today a farmer's cottage rebuilt, yet brigands still roamed the land. A month ago a child rescued from a well, yet left to be comforted in a loveless house.

"The prince was right in thinking that Britheldore's daughter understood him. They talked of many things that night, not only of the suffering of the world but also of its joy and beauty. They walked together on the parapet of the castle in the moonlight, and watched the stars wheel overhead. When dawn began to glow in the east they were surprised, for they had not felt weary as the night was passing. They saw the sun rise brilliantly, and they rejoiced together in its strength. It seemed to them upon that bright morning that however dark the suffering in the world, it was outweighed by living joy. Those who saw them at the good breakfast that Britheldore's servants prepared did not guess that they had been up all night, so fresh and happy did they seem.

"But the joy of Britheldore's daughter was short lived, for before midday the prince took his leave of Britheldore with many thanks. She went out onto the road to bid him farewell, but as he mounted his horse she noticed that the scabbard by his saddle was empty. She asked him what had happened to his sword. He told her that he had given it to the farmer, that he might have some protection in case the brigands came again. She told him to come back into the castle for a moment, and he followed her. She led him up to her tower room, and there she opened a walnut chest inlaid with gold, and drew out a great sword.

Eleanor paused a moment in her story. None of her listeners made a sound. The music and laughter of the dancers outside came faintly through the thick stone walls. Then Lady Eleanor went on.

"The sword was broad and long, made of some silver metal stronger than iron. The hilt was overlaid with gold, and in the pommel were five diamonds set in the gold in the form of a cross. At each end of the cross-guard was a ruby. The blade was perfect, without a hint of defect, and sharp as a razor. Britheldore's daughter handed it to the prince. 'Take it,' she said. 'I would not have you ride the roads of Karolan unarmed.' He looked at her, and she read in his eyes the question of whether it was hers to give. But to her joy, he did not ask it.

"'It is a noble gift,' he said. 'Yet I value it more for the one who gives it.'

"'Take it,' she said again. 'Use it well, and do not forget me.'

"He put the new sword in his empty sheath, and it fitted well. She followed him out under the sky again. His hand was on the sword hilt as he mounted his horse, and turned to meet her gaze just before he rode away. 'We will meet again, princess,' he said. 'And you may be sure that I will not forget you.'

"He did not, and although his visits were far less frequent than the daughter of Britheldore would have liked, they were never disappointing. Many nights, beneath many different moons, they walked together on the parapet of the castle. Twice they watched the great winter stars come out of the dawn in early autumn. Twice they watched those same stars reach their peak, flashing brilliantly in black midwinter, while they gathered fur cloaks close about them and their breath smoked in the air.

"Then one spring night, in her nineteenth year, he told her that he had a confession to make, and the words filled her heart with dread. She sat down on a parapet, and tried to calm her fear. She wondered what it could be that he would say, what dreadful thing he must in love reveal, and doom the joy she had hoped for. The prince sat down beside her.

"He told her not to tremble, but she noticed that his own voice was shaking, and she wondered yet again what thing he was about to say. She begged him to speak on. He took a deep breath.

"'Once I called you princess,' he said. 'You smiled, but you did not know the reason for my words. The reason is this, Beloved: I am the prince.'

"She was silent for a long time, in the cold, while the stars wheeled overhead and the broken ice on the castle roof glistened in their light. Then at last her voice came, unsteady and filled with wonder. 'Did you mean it?'

"'With all my heart and soul, princess.'

"Suddenly she was on her knees before him. 'I have no dowry, Your Majesty.'

"He stood, and raised her to her feet. 'Beloved,' he said, 'do you understand me so little as to think I care? Do you think I want your homage, who have found my life's brightest joy in seeking your love?'

"'No,' she said, 'I am sorry.'

"'Are you willing to be my princess?'

"'With all my heart and soul, prince.'

"She smiled, and felt like dancing. He must have too, for with his sword he cleared the worst snow and ice from a space in the middle of the castle roof. His sword glinted in the starlight as he put it back into its scabbard. Then they danced, and their joy was brighter than it had ever been before. She wondered, as she looked into his eyes, if he knew that the sword had been her dowry. If she had known him then as well as she did later, she would have known that he had guessed it long before.

"In the morning they told her father and mother, who shared their joy. Then life seemed to burst into riotous blossom for Britheldore's daughter, as the preparations were made for a magnificent royal wedding, and then one lovely, breathtaking, wonderful day she found herself princess of Karolan, walking on a summer night on the battlements of Aaronkal with her prince.

"The two years that followed were good ones, blessed by God with happiness and deepening love. Yet there were times when the princess wished they could walk alone again on the battlements of Britheldore, with the ice crunching under their feet and no one but God and each other knowing they were there. The endless turmoil of court life wearied her, and the prince often had to leave her for days at a time when he visited distant parts of Karolan on royal business. Now and then it seemed to her that he was sinking into the concerns of the realm so far that he was forgetting her. That thought terrified her, and there were nights when she cried herself to sleep all alone in her warm tower room.

"Soon she and he and all Karolan had the joy of knowing that she carried the prince's child, perhaps a new prince to carry on the hope of the realm. Yet now she was prevented more than ever from following the prince on his arduous journeys, and she saw even less of him than before. He came back earlier than expected from a long journey one night, and opened the door of her chamber to find her weeping by the fire.

"Then she found his love and understanding even deeper than she had thought them. He tactfully released himself from some of his duties, and he began taking fewer long journeys, and more shorter ones that brought him back to Aaronkal by nightfall. She felt him now closer than he had ever been before, and his love was a great comfort to her as the birth of their child approached. When it came it was hard, but she was strong, healthy, and brave, and with the help of God she bore a son.

"All Karolan rejoiced. When the child was two months old, King Thomas called the people to assemble for a royal address. He gave a short speech about his hopes and plans for the future of Karolan, and then he had the child blessed and prayed for before all the people by the servant of God from the church at Tremilin. That was nearly the happiest moment the princess had ever known: standing beside her prince, hearing the blessing and prayer that were offered for her baby, and knowing that she held in her arms the new hope of all Karolan. Its memory was like a brighter joy shining in the back of her mind through the happy months that followed.

"She never again felt that the prince was drifting away from her. He had a set made of all the keys to the doors that led up to the various parapets and battlements of the castle, and often on the kind warm summer nights she and he would walk there together, having locked all the doors below them so that no one might disturb their peace. It seemed to her on those nights that once again she was fully his and he hers, and their love was deeper and better that it had ever been on the brilliant winter nights at Britheldore.

"At the end of the long bright summer, when the child was more than six months old, the prince told the princess that in the future he wanted her to come with him on his journeys to the distant parts of Karolan. He wanted her help and counsel in the things he was trying to do, and he did not want to leave her to handle alone the endless duties of court life as he had sometimes done before. She had always been adventurous, and she had a great desire to see his work and aid him in it, so she agreed with loving thanks.

"A week later they went on their first journey, starting out in the direction of southeast Karolan with a large retinue. The princess enjoyed the journey. It was nearly as comfortable, and much less wearying, than life at Aaronkal. She saw the new stone road that King Thomas was building, and the foundations of the castles that he planned to make to defend it. She and the prince conferred for hours with the men who worked on the road, and with the people who intended to make farms and build taverns and villages along it.

"It was fascinating to her to understand what was happening. A whole section of the country was coming out of isolation. Soon heavy wagons carrying stone, ore, or wood would be able to travel there. She understood how the prince could have been captivated by these things and drawn away from her, and she understood also, more deeply than she had before, how strong was his love for her. He had consciously thrust all this aside in order to bless her.

"After they had spent a week at the end of the stone road, the prince went farther southeast, where the road was merely a dirt track. The princess accompanied him, with the child and a few of the servants. The road wound far up into the beautiful and nearly uninhabited mountains. They went slowly, enjoying the days. At night they camped beside warm fires and watched the bright stars gleaming in their thousands from the clear mountain sky. One day they reached a beautiful valley with a sheer rock face on one side, and camped beside a stream. The next day the prince took the princess, the child, and one laden horse up a rugged trail that had been hewn into the cliff.

"She was a little frightened sometimes, when the wind gusted against them as it rushed along the rock, and when the blanket in which she held the baby fluttered and slapped in the breeze. Yet she kept following him, and she enjoyed the sense she had that they were leaving the world behind and climbing into the sky. Now and then she asked him where they were going, but he would only turn back and smile, and say it was well worth the journey.

"Far, far up on the rugged cliff the narrow path turned inward into a crack in the rock. The prince led onward into the heart of the mountain. It grew cold, and the princess gathered another blanket around herself and the baby. Yet they walked on far into the night, until at last they came out of the dark crack and into a moonlit valley so lovely that it seemed scarcely to belong to the world. The bright half-moon was rising over tall, jagged peaks, and pouring its ethereal light onto the soft sweet grass, the beautiful trees, and the lovely star-mirror of the lake. It was the most enchanting valley in the world, seen at its most enchanting time. It was Luciyr unmarred, between the moonrise and the dawn.

"The princess wrapped her baby lovingly in blankets and laid him in a soft place in the grass, and then they danced. The great bowl of the valley was the floor of their ballroom, and the place where the baby lay was its center. The time was of such surpassing loveliness that the princess would not have been surprised if they had found themselves dancing up the Ceranim and into heaven. Never had their love shone brighter, purer, or more secret than it shone that night. They rejoiced in their aloneness. It seemed that the whole valley was made solely so two lovers could dance in it that night, while God looked down and delighted in their joy.

"When they were tired, they took up the baby and slept beside the lake. They slept a long time into the bright morning. Finally they awoke, to see a Luciyr as beautiful as before – less ethereal, but vibrant in the morning sun. They ate a leisurely breakfast, talking quietly of this and that, and playing with the child. The huge, smooth rock on which they had camped gave a beautiful view of the lake, shimmering in the sunlight. It was a lovely, life-filled but restful time, and they were at peace. The child slept, and the prince and princess sat silently together in the sunshine and cool wind.

There was another pause in Lady Eleanor's story, and her listeners were surprised to see that the candles had burnt low, and the fire had gone down to glowing coals. But when Jonathan looked at Lady Eleanor he was even more astonished, for she was crying. The sounds of the singing and dancing outside had ceased, and a compassionate silence reigned in the room, broken only by her sobs and the light splashes of her falling tears. Jonathan gazed at her, sorry for her pain, yet full of wondering about exactly what had happened on that white rock above Luciyr. He tried to suppress the guesses that leaped into his mind, and to wait calmly for her to continue.

Ilohan felt for her even more deeply than Jonathan. He shivered, and did not know if it was from fear, or wonder, or something deeper than either that he could not name. He was afraid of what Lady Eleanor was about to say – and afraid of what his life was bringing, this life that was beyond his understanding and control. Yet even while he was afraid, he did not wish to turn back from this night, or to escape whatever terrible thing was coming.

Eleanor's tears ceased suddenly, and she lifted her bowed head without any effort to conceal them. She began again, her voice scarcely changed at all, and instantly the spell of her story was rewoven around all who listened.

"The princess heard a single footfall behind her, and then she was roughly gripped by the shoulders and pulled up onto her feet. In her panic she screamed once and clutched the baby. A long, bright sword came from behind her and was held close against her throat. She glanced cautiously to either side, looking for the prince, not daring to move her head. She could not see him. She wanted to scream again, but instead she kept a terrified silence.

"The sounds of footsteps told her they were surrounded by many soldiers. Some of them came around in front of her and stood there with drawn swords. She knew that they were soldiers of Norkath. Her baby cried, and she tried to hush him, but he could feel through her body that she was afraid, and he cried all the more. There was a short silence when none of the men moved. Then one set of slow, even footsteps came up behind her on her right. The man to whom they belonged came into view, a proud, confident man, with a wiry frame and a tanned, weather-beaten face. He was wearing a crown, and strange royal robes woven of green cloth and gold. He stopped near the edge of the rock.

"'I am Fingar, king of Norkath,' he said, 'and you are my prisoners. To you, prince of Karolan, I give this choice: Abdicate your royal position to me, and swear that after

Thomas dies I shall be king of Karolan, or see your wife and son killed before your eyes, and then be killed yourself. What is your choice?'

"The princess knew then that the prince must be held captive somewhere on her right, just too far behind for her to see him without turning her head. Fingar's voice, his arrogant and cruel consciousness of power, filled her with anger and despair, and she could not tell which was the stronger. She held her baby tightly to her, and Fingar stood as still as stone despite its wailing. Then she heard the voice of her beloved. Love and fear overwhelmed her, and her eyes filled with quiet tears. Never had she heard him speak with such strength, and she wondered if such a voice could ever be disobeyed.

"'You offer me a terrible choice, Fingar,' he said. 'Betrayal of my people, or death of her I love more than my life. Two grave evils. It would be better for you to take the dagger at your belt, and thrust it through your greedy coward's heart, than to persist in the course you have chosen. Do it!'

"The princess trembled at the power of his command, but to her awe and horror Fingar laughed.

"'You are an impotent fool, prince,' he mocked, 'as all your fathers were before you. What is your choice?'

"'It is you who are the fool, Fingar,' said the prince. 'You do not understand love. It is stronger than the Iron Fist of Norkath, stronger than the Sword, Stone, and Star, stronger than the earth and moon and sun. It is more precious than all you have gained at the cost of its loss. Do you think that I will not save my wife and child? Release her!'

"The princess felt the hands that held her relax, and the sword moved a little away from her throat. But at Fingar's next words they held her even more tightly. 'I will not,' he said.

'Here and now write me a royal decree of abdication, and after that I will release her, and you as well.'

"'Coward, full of greed and fear,' said the prince. 'She is unarmed, and holds my child at her breast. You have her ringed in with warriors who carry drawn swords. Have you any need to hold her as you are? If you release her and let her stand unthreatened in your midst, could she fly? I will seal no proclamation while a sword is at the throat of my princess. As long as you have me thus threatened, and her surrounded by your soldiers, what do you have to fear? Release her!'

"Fingar looked angry, but he was swayed by the prince's reasons, and his voice. 'Release her!' he snapped. His soldiers obeyed, and the princess breathed a long, shuddering breath and took a single step toward the lake. She knew that all could not be well, but without the iron hands gripping her and the naked sword across her neck she was far less afraid.

"She looked lovingly at her husband, who was held more or less as she had been, although by more men. She shuddered when she saw the bright sword across his throat, and the gigantic Norkath warrior who held it. But she trembled even more at the look upon his face. She had never seen him look more alive, more noble, or more free. His eyes shone, and in his face there was no hint of fear or guilt. She knew when she looked at him that he would not sign the proclamation. 'Goodbye,' he whispered to her, and she knew that only she could hear it. 'I will love you forever.'

"'Karolan!' he roared in a voice like autumn thunder. The great warrior who held him cried in pain as the prince wrenched his sword from his grasp. The Norkaths rushed toward the princess to kill her, but the prince was at her side before them. The swords clanged loudly, and the fight was brutal and terrible. He defended her with all his strength, and more strength than he had, but she knew he could not win. They were forced up against the edge of the rock, and surrounded by a half circle of Norkath soldiers. There was a terrible clang and a bright spark, as the prince's Norkath sword shattered in his hand. Yet three of the Norkaths were felled with that blow, horribly wounded, and the ring was broken.

"He dragged her through the gap. Her clothes were splashed and soaked with the Norkaths' blood. The prince's own great sword, stronger than iron, lay on the ground before him, and he snatched it up like lightning. There was a terrible crunch as the giant Norkath warrior killed their horse with a blow from an axe. But they had broken free. The lovely green grass of Luciyr stretched unmarred before them. She thought they would run together, and try to make it through the great crack in the mountain. But he knew that there was no hope that way. He turned and faced the soldiers of Fingar again, and again he protected her from them all.

"The prince was a great warrior always, but that day he fought with strength and skill that seemed beyond the lot of men. The Norkaths were trying to kill his beloved, and had there been a thousand he would have defied them all. And she stood still behind him, sick with horror and fear, upheld by blazing love, praying as she had never prayed before. Somehow the prince noticed that she had not moved. 'Fly!' he roared, in a terrible voice that she could never afterwards forget. 'Fly if you have ever loved me. There is nothing else you can do.'

"She would gladly have died for him, and even the life of her child she did not value beside his. She wished with all her heart that he had commanded anything else. Yet her ears had heard, in that terrible, compelling voice, 'Fly if you have ever loved me.' She loved him. And because of this she abandoned him. She gathered her baby in her arms and fled, running in desperation, faster than she had thought possible, faster than she ever had before.

"As she ran, she listened through the gasps of her own breath for the sounds of the fight. She dreaded them, but at the same time dreaded the thought of not hearing the end. The prince was speaking as he fought, roaring his mighty defiance to the bloody coward who wore the crown of Norkath. 'I will die without betraying them, Fingar. You have failed. You understand neither love nor honor. You tried to make them opposites and they united against you. They will destroy you.' Suddenly the prince's words ceased, though the sounds of the fight did not. The princess ran on. Her lungs burned like fire.

"She heard the vile voice of Fingar saying something that was not loud enough for her to understand. Again there was no sound but the distant clanging swords for a moment. She felt as if she could run no farther. Then there came an awful crash, like splintered iron, and she heard the voice of her beloved for the last time, raised without anger, without fear, loud enough to make the valley ring. 'Love, Foreve—' and then cut short by a sound that brought her horror unimaginable. There was a great splash, and the sound of galloping horses. The princess ran on, blinded by her tears.

Here Eleanor stopped again, partly because she was nearly blinded by her own, and partly because the sound of running feet was suddenly heard in the passage beyond the door. Eleanor's listeners had been drawn so deeply into her story that they had seemed to see the heroic prince with their own eyes. Now, the racing footfalls brought them forcibly back into the present, to face a new time, a time not yet lived, a new challenge that they would have to answer with their own new deeds.

The door burst open and Veril rushed in without closing it behind her. Her face was tearstained, and her hair had blown loose from its braid and hung disordered about her shoulders. She threw herself on the ground and knelt before Ilohan's chair, bowed her head and covered her face.

"I am sorry for what I have done," she sobbed. "Terribly sorry. I cannot bear the knowledge that I did it. I beg you to try to forgive me."

Ilohan felt overwhelmed. He was reeling from Eleanor's story, which was still unfinished. And Veril's appearance alone was enough to throw his mind and heart into a sort of chaos. "I long to comfort her somehow," he thought, "but I am afraid of reawakening my lust. But surely I must comfort her, and God will guard me." He could not bear to see her kneeling there, kind and faithful yet in agony, far from understanding how he truly thought of her. He silently prayed for help as he swiftly gathered his courage to speak. He kicked his chair behind him, knelt in front of her, and gently pried her hands away from her face.

"Veril," he said. "I hold you guiltless. I rejoice in your courage, and I rejoice that despite how it appeared you were faithful. Yet if this is not enough, know that even if I considered you wrong I would forgive you." He saw that the pain did not fade from her eyes, and he remembered her words of deep regret while the archers had held her. "Veril," he said, "you are not thinking of yourself as you truly are. You think you have done grave evil, but you have not. Your life is beyond your understanding, just as my life is beyond my own. But Veril, Christ is at work in you. Do not consider yourself less than the one God has made you. Ah! We are half-seeing souls that stumble in a reeling world, immeasurably beyond us. What a night is this! God, be with us and save and guide us!"

Veril cried freely, and tried to cover her face again, but he gently held her hands and did not let her hide her tears. Then he released her as Imranie stood behind her and raised her to her feet. Her mother led her to a bench that Jonathan had brought for her, and she sat down. "I am worthless, worthless," she said. "I live in this beautiful valley, but I help no one here. I am the only one who does no one else any good. And when at last I found a thing that I alone dared do, it was the only task in Ceramir that caused harm rather than good! Alas. I am good for nothing."

Imranie sat down beside her daughter on the bench. She drew her daughter to her, and Veril leaned her head against her mother's shoulder.

"I am just like you, Veril," said Imranie.

Veril gasped and sat up straight. "Mother," she said in blank astonishment, "surely not."

"What do I do to help and bless, Veril? Name the things if you can."

"You are the Mother of Ceramir," said Veril. "There is no one here who does not think of you as the Mother of the Undismayed, who would not come to you for comfort in their sorrow. There is no one in the Valley whose pain you have not soothed, whose fretting you have not quieted, whose wandering you have not guided. No one who comes here in the dreadful distress of their sickness, and goes away healed, does so without your prayers. You are like a beloved queen to us. There is no one in the Cloth of Joy who is more needed."

"Veril," said Imranie, "I scarcely think you will believe me when I say that I do not see that any of this is true. I seem to myself powerless to help, impotent in my prayers, futile in my attempts to comfort. When others say such things to me as you have just said, I thank God, but nearly without understanding. I walk in the way he sets before me, but it is a way of blindness to the blessings I give. It is by faith alone that I know I am not worthless."

Veril looked in her mother's face. "And you want to tell me it is the same for me?" she whispered.

"It is the same for you, my daughter," said Imranie. "You are the only one of my children who shares with me in this. I am sorry that I bequeath to you such a difficult road, and yet not sorry, for it is also a path of wonder and of joy."

Imranie continued, "Shall I tell you what I know, dear child? When the young children of Ceramir are hurt, or sad, or confused, they come to you before anyone else, save their parents – or me, perhaps. The children work in the garden three times as happily and twice as fast when you are with them. You are loved by nearly everyone in Ceramir or Harevan, and you bless them greatly even while you imagine that you help them not at all."

"You are sure of this?" asked Veril in an awed voice.

"I am sure, beloved Veril," said Imranie

"What shall I do, then?" asked Veril.

"Let your blindness keep you humble, but do not let it dismay you," said Imranie. "Seek to do whatever good you can, but do not try to be someone other than the one God has made you. Follow him with all your heart and soul and mind and strength, and trust him that you are neither worthless nor useless. You are a beloved blessing to many."

"Thank you, Mother," said Veril softly. "I love you."

"And I love you, Veril," said Imranie.

Ilohan, looking at them as they looked at one another, saw in Imranie's face a deeper love for her daughter than any words could convey. After a long moment Veril turned and looked into Ilohan's own eyes. "You have truly forgiven me?" she asked.

"Yes, Veril," he said. "Truly and forever. Save that I do not consider that there was anything to forgive."

"I thank you," she said.

"It is a joy to see you comforted," said Ilohan, and then in the silence he thought, "The world is reeling, and the future is unknown beyond my imagining. Savior, do not leave me, and let my heart belong to you. I feel balanced on a pinnacle between loss and blessing, and I do not know which way I am falling. Yet even that does not describe it. Without your leading I would be forever lost."

Imranie stood and resumed her own chair, leaving Veril alone on the bench. Lady Eleanor rose and sat beside her. Her face was very pale, and the remnants of her tears were not hidden. "Will you forgive me for allowing you to carry out the test?" she asked Veril.

"Of course, Ella, – I mean, Lady Eleanor," said Veril, slipping in a kind of reaction of relief into the children's way of addressing Eleanor. "Indeed, I nearly forced you and Father into it. I forgive you with all my heart!" Then she looked more closely into Eleanor's face. "My Lady – I am sorry – I had forgotten – you were telling them the story, and I burst in upon you. Ah! What part had you reached?"

"I had just told of his death," said Eleanor, "and now I must go on to tell of what came after. But it will be less hard with you here beside me."

"Oh, Eleanor," said Veril, putting her arms around her, "If anything I can do makes it easier, tell me of it!"

"That is very good, Veril. I thank you! Stay here, and you will indeed help me. There is joy after the sorrow."

Mudien got up, replaced some of the low-burnt candles with fresh ones, added more wood to the fire, and returned to his seat. In the silence before Lady Eleanor began, Jonathan reflected that her power with stories was no less dangerous than the power of a warrior with a sword or bow. What she was about to say, like what she had said already, would tear his heart as the same stories told by a poor raconteur could not have done. He would never be able to forget the story, even if he wanted to. He was glad that he had not known, when he had held the split skull of the prince of Karolan in his hands, the story of his end. It had been easier, then, to think of it simply as gray bone, the skull of a man he did not know. Now he shuddered because he knew the man, a man who had lived and loved, walked and talked vibrant on the green earth, and whose immeasurably precious life had been destroyed at the height of its nobility. Leaving nothing but gray bone in the mud. The candles that Mudien had not replaced burnt out, and all except their corner of the room was sunk in darkness.

"The princess ran," said Lady Eleanor, "far beyond what she had thought was the limit of her strength. She tried to think only of running, only of escape, only of obeying the command she had been given. The Norkaths had horses, of course, and they reached the crack before her. But she would not give up hope, or believe for a moment that her beloved had died for nothing. She kept out of sight behind the blowing swells of grass, until she was quite near the cliff. Even when the soldiers saw her they stayed by the crack. In their arrogance they thought she was captured already, and they did not at once give chase. Before they suspected her plan she had tied her son securely to her back using the corners of his blankets, and had begun to climb the cliff-wall of Luciyr. They had barred the pathway through the crack against her, but she was determined to find another way or die in the attempt. The Norkaths tried to climb after her, but she was light and strong and desperate, and they were afraid of falling. They threw rocks at her, but she was soon too high for them.

"Her legs trembled after her running, and she thought she would fall. She kicked off her shoes so that her feet might grip the rock, but soon they were battered and bleeding from the hard edges of the stone. She prayed desperately time and time again for help from God. The heartless stone of the cliff was dampened with her anguished tears, and with the blood from her torn feet. Yet she did not fall, and at last as she got higher the rock became less steep.

"Night came upon her as she tried to work her way across the ridge and down into the valley where she and her prince had last camped with their retinue. It seemed to her that she was trapped up in the frozen sky, between the cold heavens and the brutal mountains of broken stone. She stopped in a sheltered but lifeless cleft of the gray rock, and nursed her child and moaned softly over her cold and battered hands and feet. Her son, the prince of Karolan, lay in her arms and looked up at her with complete trust. He did not cry any longer. He had been warm in the blanket in which she had wrapped him, and now she was caring for him as she always had. He did not know that all was lost, that in all likelihood he would never see the dawn.

"As her love of her husband had forged her desperate determination to escape Luciyr, so now her love for her child rekindled her flickering hope and resolve to live. Her life and her son's were precious, beyond all measurement of value. Her beloved had died to save them. Would she now lose them, those treasures that he had considered of such worth? No. A vow formed in her heart that somehow, if the uttermost strength of her will and body could accomplish it, she and her child would live. She prayed that her vow would be kept, that God would give her strength. She carried her child against her breast, trying to keep him warm, wound his blanket around them both, and went on.

"Of the rest of that night she would not speak, save that she came down the cliff to Karolan in moonless darkness, and that although she was saved from death it seemed to her that God had deserted her utterly and left her in a shadow-world containing nothing but horror and pain. The child was nearly dead of cold, and she in her hunger had no warmth to give him. Even the sun did little to warm them when it rose over the mountain forest where she was walking, gasping in pain with every step.

"She reached at last the place where she and her beloved had camped before venturing into Luciyr. The servants were dead, lying cold in their own blood around the slashed tents. The horses and provisions were gone. Yet no Norkath soldier awaited her there. She was sick, kneeling weakly on the ground and vomiting bile from her empty stomach. She took one thick blanket that had somehow been left, and the shoes of one servant, and went on her way. With the death of the servants she was sure her last hope had perished. But her vow remained.

"She was half delirious when a Norkath rider thundered up from behind and drew his sword to kill her. 'No,' she gasped, 'I am too precious. Can you know the value of my life?'

"To her surprise he did not kill her, but lowered his sword and dismounted. He looked at her, and the look on his face was horrible. 'That is true,' he said. 'Your life is precious to me. For how often has a common soldier had a chance to rape a princess? Afterward you will die.' She cried out, but he only looked yet more vile, and pulled her against himself in his unthinking lust.

"Her baby screamed, and he started in surprise. Then another Norkath voice shouted, 'Kill her, fool!' A Norkath leader rode up and jumped down from his horse with a drawn sword. But the soldier who had found her first was so maddened by his lust that he released her and raised his sword to protect her.

"'Scoundrel!' shouted the leader, 'Will you protect her? Kill her, I say!'

"'Wait. She is as good as dead already, indeed. Do not waste her.' His words were thick with the lust that takes a man and makes of him a beast. He actually dared fight his superior. The princess remembered her prince, and his mighty death.

"'Assassins die by murder, and the lustful by their lust,' she cried. 'But I shall be a princess to the last.' And for a moment her heart gave thanks, for she was free, and she saw a bag of food stolen from the servants hanging unsecured by the Norkath's saddle. She grabbed it and ran like the wind. She did not feel her sore feet or her weariness, but she ran through the woods, nearly blindly.

"The Norkaths came after her on their great horses. The trees hindered them, but despite this she was sure they would soon catch her as her strength failed. She did not see the cliff ahead of her, hidden as it was by brush, until suddenly she felt nothing beneath her feet.

"As she fell, she saw with terror that this was no earthen bank, but a high stone cliff. Yet somehow even then she did not give herself up for lost. With her child and the bag of food clasped in her arms she could do nothing to break her fall, but she tried to land as best she could, with her feet beneath her.

Branches whipped past, snapping beneath the terrible force of her fall, their broken ends scraping her as they passed. She hit the ground, crumpled, and rolled. Even in the instant before there was any pain, she knew somehow that her battered feet were shattered, and that the bones of her ankles were also broken. The pain stabbed through her like a spear, and she crammed a corner of her child's blanket into her mouth to keep from screaming. But she had survived the fall, and so had he. She crawled into the deep woods, knowing that the Norkaths could not come down that cliff without falling.

"They hunted her, but she was faithful to her vow. She hid using every forest skill she had learned as a girl running wild through the woods around Castle Britheldore. She had food for a few days, and she drank from the trickling streams that she found here and there in the forest.

"She bound her feet with strips of the blanket, and made crutches out of branches. Every step was an agony of grinding bone and lightning bolts of pain. She dared not move except at night, and then paused often to listen for the Norkaths who sometimes came near. The days were terrible, when she cowered in some concealed place, wondering how much longer she could carry on, and whether her baby would die this day or the next. The pain of her broken ankles never ceased. She seldom slept. Time and time again she prayed that her hunters would despair and turn back, but still she would hear their cries and their footsteps as they searched for her. Time and time again she prayed for some man or woman of Karolan to find her, and take her to Aaronkal and safety, but it seemed that God had abandoned her. She clung to something, too small to call faith or hope, but somehow she did not give up or curse God. She did abandon hope, and she clung to her vow in agony and despair.

"Those days shattered her. They broke her – spirit, body, and mind – as she had not known she could be broken. Everywhere she turned there was agony, and nowhere comfort. Nothing she could do, either good or evil, could bring her peace or healing. God was silent, the prince was dead, her child was dying, the sky was heartless, the sun cold, the night sleepless, the hearts of mankind loveless. She had thought the world a place of deep joy, but now she plumbed the depths of its pain, and found that in them even the memory of joy could not be found.

"Each day her pain grew worse. Her ankles and feet swelled and grew hot. Her thoughts wandered and she saw things that were not there. A time came when thinking clearly or deciding anything required an immense effort of her will. She found herself still walking as morning came, on a huge open field of high grass. She knew she would be caught and killed, since there was no shelter and it was day. But it was beyond her power to stop, or choose anything. Darkness closed in around her and swallowed her.

Chapter 16

The Purpose of the Quest

SILENCE REIGNED IN THE ROOM AFTER ELEANOR'S STORY was ended, broken only by the soft swish and ripple of the brook in its channel in the floor. She had said the last words with finality in her voice, as if she never intended to speak again. Her head was bowed, but there were no tears upon her cheeks.

Jonathan wished he had not heard the story, for it came near to breaking his faith. Could living be worth its price? Could he bear to live in exultation in a temporary joy that could be so utterly shattered? What would suffering do to him? For a moment he was terrified, for his life seemed to him to have no anchor. In that moment he cared nothing for the story, for the princess and her agony, but only feared for himself in a world where ruin such as hers was possible. Then he declared himself immune, and said that he could never thus be shattered. He knew that what he had done was false, but in pretending it was true he could love and help, love Ilohan and wonder what this night was bringing him.

For his part, Ilohan wished with all his heart that it had not happened – that the world had not been so marred nor God so slow to help. Yet the knowledge that the princess and her son were dead gave him a strange comfort, for it stilled certain wild and unbearable thoughts that had been stirring in his mind. He laughed at them internally, and was ashamed of them. But then he swallowed both his laughter and his shame. If the princess had died, how did Eleanor know her story? And if the child had died, why would he be told of it tonight? He did not know. But he was afraid. He covered his face in his hands and shuddered. Then he felt something brush against his arm. He lifted his head and saw that Mudien was handing him a parchment. He took it silently, began to read without speaking, then bethought himself of Jonathan and Veril, and read aloud.

"I, Thomas, son of Konder, king of Karolan, write with sorrow in the Castle of Dilgarel this account concerning the death of my son, Prince Kindrach of Karolan:

"He went toward Luciyr with his beloved and child. Riders from Fingar of Norkath were sent to me bearing tidings that he had been captured at Luciyr and abdicated his throne to Fingar. They said also that he was killed afterwards as a fit reward for his treachery. As I wear the crown or the heavens last forever, it is false. The riders found me near Carrah. I raised an army of a thousand men, and met Fingar at his capital of Guldorak. I sought an audience with him, and he basely imprisoned me. Metherka and others bargained with him. He agreed to permit me to walk unrestrained on the parapet of Guldorak once a day. On the fourteenth day I wrested an axe from one of the guards and knocked Fingar against the battlement with the butt. I threatened him with instant death, and he bade the guards leave us.

"I demanded from him the truth concerning my son's death. He told many false tales of his betrayal. He revealed his own vileness. Each tale concerned the prince betraying Karolan to save not his own life but his beloved's. So Fingar admitted his baseness: he admitted to threatening the princess and her child. I asked where the princess was, and he said she was dead. I asked how and he did not say. I demanded the crowns of the prince and princess as the ransom for his life, and he said the prince had thrown his crown into the lake, and the princess had been found without hers. At last I drew his own dagger and cut a blade thickness into his neck.

"He looked at me with terror in his fickle eyes. He told then what I believe to be the true tale, as best he could past my dagger. He said that he had come upon the prince and princess at Luciyr, having learned from spies that they were there. He had given Kindrach the choice either to abdicate or be killed, along with the princess and her child. The prince refused both, and actually secured the escape of the princess before his death. However the princess and the child were soon recaptured and killed. Neither was wearing a crown, and their dead bodies were burned at Luciyr to hide the evidence of their violent deaths. I asked him if it was all true. He swore it was. I swore he would die if it was ever proven false, soon or late. I leaped up on the parapet, plunged off into the moat and so escaped. As I fell he denied the story's truth, and said that Kindrach was a traitor. As the mountains stand and the sun rises he was not.

"We escaped Norkath at terrible cost. God forgive me for the lives of those who perished. The story I won from Fingar was not worth that price.

Ilohan finished reading. There was a silence. "My Lady..." he said to Eleanor, hesitating.

"What is it, Sir Ilohan?" she asked.

"I ask to know what became of the princess," he said. "Fingar lied concerning her, clearly, for you have said she traveled far from Luciyr before she perished. Yet if she died alone, you could not tell her story."

"A farmer of far eastern Karolan found her in his field. She barely clung to life, as did her child. The farmer brought them to Aaronkal in a cart, with all speed. King Thomas was then a captive in Norkath, but Queen Sarah received her, and cared for her and her child with her own hands. Thomas knew nothing of this when he wrote the account you have read, when he had just reached the border castle of Dilgarel in Karolan after his escape." Here Eleanor stopped. Ilohan could not read her face, unless its blankness meant that she was patiently waiting for his next question.

"Did the princess live?" he asked.

"She lived," said Eleanor, "but she did not love her life. She lived, and at Aaronkal she recovered enough to speak a little, and to think, but she did not heal. Sarah's power was great, but it could not heal her brokenness.

"The child lived also, and soon was well. The princess saw him, one day while King Thomas was still a prisoner, laughing and smiling in Sarah's arms. And she said to herself, 'I have been shattered, but he has not. It is a victory. But shall his life be lived in the shadow of my darkness? No.' And she told Sarah to send her away, and keep her child, that he might never come to know or understand his mother's ruin.

"Sarah, the humble queen, admitted her lack of power to heal the princess. She sent her to Ceramir, where lies a deeper power, by way of the foothills of Cembar, far from Luciyr. Sarah and Thomas raised her child as a humble squire of no lineage, believing this was the best way to make him at last a faithful prince. The child grew, and was happy, and knew nothing of his mother's pain. But as the years passed the princess herself found that God was good, and had still the power to heal. Her shattered life was bound up and finally healed. With her healing, her longing grew to know her son. Yet she knew that far more than her desire for his love was at stake.

Eleanor stopped. Ilohan looked straight into her face, and it was shining with joy. He was afraid, deeply afraid, yet he would have accepted twice the fear rather than dim that joy. The traces of her tears of grief were gone, and only tears of joy shone in her green eyes in the candlelight. She was beautiful, more beautiful than anyone he had ever seen, and beautiful in a different way. She loved. She had waited, and at last it was right to have what she had so long desired. Imranie, the Mother of Ceramir, stood behind her and shared her joy.

"The name of the princess?" he asked softly.

Eleanor bowed her head modestly, and Imranie's careful fingers quickly slipped the white ribbon out of her light brown hair. When she raised her head again a silver circlet set with diamonds shone entwined where the ribbon had been. "Eleanor," she whispered.

"And of the child?"

"At his birth we named him Prince Niran. But when Sarah knew he must live at Aaronkal unknown, as a ward, she gave him a new name. That name was Ilohan."

She stood with swift yet patient care, and he as if he were going to fly. She hugged him, and he her, and he knew that his life without a mother had been like a land without rain. And Eleanor, the faithful princess of Karolan, held her son as she had not been able to for nearly a score of years. "I thank God," she wept, "I was shattered in protecting you, but it was not too high a price to pay for your protection. I know now that the deepest pain in the world cannot destroy the deepest love, and that as long as there remains anything to cling to, even a withered and unrecognizable seed of faith or hope, it is certain that dawn will come."

"Mother," he cried, "so long you have waited, and so long I have lived without knowing you! And yet you loved me so much – a tiny child who had not even learned to speak. You were shattered in saving me, and then hid from me your pain. What can I do – what love could ever be enough to repay you?"

"Love knows no payments and no measurements, Ilohan," she said, "and at last you have come, and are true, and rejoice that I am your mother. It is enough."

"Father," she continued, looking upward while still hugging Ilohan, "it is ten thousand times enough. How I thank you. You have brought me my son at last."

"You are wonderful, Mother," he said. "Had God come to me and said I had a mother, and told me to imagine her the best that I could dream, my hopes would yet have fallen far short of the truth. I do not want to let you go. I wish it was in my power to wipe away the darkness through which you have passed, and replace it with light and joy."

"Do not wish that, Ilohan, for through it God has brought me strength, and by it my love for you was proven. It is passed, and you are here, and are faithful. I could not have dreamed of greater blessing." They sat down together on the bench, which Veril had left for them.

"You will journey on to a small village to meet a certain person," said Ilohan, quoting the king. "When you have stayed there some days the person will send you back, and you must make all speed back to Karolan and report to me what you have found." Ilohan paused. "And this was what he meant.

Had I a dream for every star above the desert, not one of the dreams would have touched the truth."

"Alas for a world in which you come at last and I must soon send you away," said Eleanor. "Yet I shall not dim my joy nor wrong my God with grumbling. Forever I shall be your mother."

"And forever I shall be your son, Mother," said Ilohan. "But why did the king command my swift return?"

"And why did I wait so many longing years while you grew up at Aaronkal another's child? Alas, my son. You are the prince of Karolan, and your land will soon have need of you."

A shudder went through Ilohan. Finding that he had a mother had been a shock of great joy, but finding that he was the prince was a shock at which his mind rebelled in terror. He was Sir Ilohan, a Knight of Karolan – one of the weakest of the Knights of Karolan. He could not be the prince, could not be Kindrach's son, the son of a mighty warrior and a hero. It was impossible. As well – better – to make Jonathan, or Joseph, Barnabas or Karlak or Rangol the prince of Karolan. He could not be the prince – it was impossible, terrifying, inconceivable. But it was true.

"I wish I could be your son and yet not be the prince, Mother," he said.

"Yet you cannot, child," said Eleanor. "Often I wished your father need not be the prince."

"Yet he was worthy to be a prince of Karolan," said Ilohan, "and I am not."

She looked at him lovingly. "My son," she said, "in all the years of your father's life he never considered himself worthy of his crown. And no one else in all Karolan considered him unworthy of it. Courage, Ilohan. Never abandon your humility, but do not turn back from the path to which you have been called. You were born a prince, and a prince you are. You have passed the test, and if your father's crown can ever be recovered from Luciyr, or Norkath, none but you will be held worthy to wear it after him."

"May we speak, yet, of what we found at Luciyr?" asked Ilohan.

Eleanor shuddered in her turn. She was not ready, she discovered, to learn what they had found. Even after all the years she was not free from the horror of the last sound she had heard while running desperately away from the rock at Luciyr. She put an arm around Ilohan's shoulders and gripped him tightly, knowing how near he had come to sharing his father's fate, and fearing yet that a Norkath blade might take him. "The reason for silence is passed," she said, "but let us not speak anymore of Luciyr tonight. Later we must speak of it, and hold the council of our war."

Ilohan saw her eyes go cold when she spoke of the war, but the chill soon passed, and they were lit again with her joy and love. She spoke to him of her prince, and of the happy times at Aaronkal before their lives were shattered. Ilohan listened attentively, trying to form in his mind a fuller picture of the man who had been his father – Kindrach whom all Karolan had loved, and into whose place he was now unwillingly thrust.

Though Ilohan thought himself not at all like his hero-father, Princess Eleanor saw in her son many, many things that reminded her of her beloved prince. She was sure beyond a shadow of doubt that if he lived, he would be all that they had hoped and more, a king for Karolan to remember forever. She would have liked the night to last forever, but at last she rose and bade Ilohan and the others seek their beds.

When Jonathan and Ilohan reached their room, Jonathan drew out the great sword from the bag where it was hidden. He held it up before Ilohan, gleaming in the dim candlelight. "Broad and long, made of a metal stronger than iron," said Jonathan. "The hilt overlaid with gold, and a ruby set in each end of the cross-guard. In the pommel, five diamonds set in gold in the form of a cross. The Lady Eleanor described it perfectly, though I have concealed it with the greatest care ever since you handed it to me on our arrival at Harevan."

Ilohan reached out and touched the blade reverently. "My father's sword," he said.

"Now I understand," said Jonathan, "why the king bade you conceal whatever you had found. It was so that you might know with certainty that Princess Eleanor's story was true – that she had not invented it to match what she already knew you had seen at Luciyr. Little did she and King Thomas know how strong the evidence would be, thanks to the care with which you searched – and made me search."

"In any case, I could never have doubted her," said Ilohan. "Surely you saw, all night, how truthfulness shone in her face."

"Yes, I think I did see that," said Jonathan. He carefully replaced the sword, blew out the candle, and slept.

Prince Ilohan slept also. He dreamed of having a mother, as he often had before. Yet this time there ran through his dreams not the feeling of unbearable longing for Sarah, whom he had lost, but the irrepressible, singing joy of loving Eleanor, whom he had found.

* * *

Princess Eleanor lay in her bed for a short time, utterly happy, but far from sleep. Then she gathered a light cloak around her, and went out into the cool moonlit night. Her lameness seemed to matter nothing, for in the still night the whole world was unhurried. She wandered among the trees, silver in the moonlight, and came out upon the fields and gardens of Ceramir, close against the great black shadows of the mountain cliffs.

She walked quietly to where a lonely bush stood among the open fields. There she gave four sharp, strange cries, and waited. A great eagle seemed to detach itself from the looming blackness of the western cliffs, and swoop down to her, the moonlight gleaming dull gold on his broad wings. He perched in the bush beside her, and she drew out of a pocket a small piece of parchment.

She reached out her hand to tie the parchment to the eagle's foot, touched the hard skin of its strong talon, but then drew back, folded the letter, and put it away. "No," she said, "there is no need to rush the days. When the council is over, then I will send word."

She turned back toward the south and the sleeping house. Her joy was deeper than the mist-cloaked lake and brighter than the stars, yet she mourned the shortness of the days. "Oh Ilohan, my son, would that you were not also the prince. Yet this is our fate: it is my loss, and the gain of thousands. In these few bright days I will rejoice, and it will be as though Norkath had never been. Each day lived shall be a treasure that cannot be taken away. I have had other days that were like that. Perhaps, if we lived truer, we would find all days thus."

She brought a few strips of dry meat from one of the sheds against the cliff, and fed them to the patient eagle. "Peace for tonight, Skykag," she said. "Another time I will send you where only you can go."

The eagle quickly swallowed the meat, and then with a strong shrill cry took wing. It mounted up against the shadowed cliff in mighty spirals, and Eleanor marveled as she often had at the strength and beauty of its flight. She had a moment's fear lest it fly over the mountains to Karolan unburdened, but then it swooped into the shadow of the cliff and did not return, and she knew that it had gone back to its aerie.

She returned to her room and slept. At first her dreams were of the eagle's flight, winging high and strong through the icy vastness of the mountain skies. Then she danced in Luciyr, with Kindrach her prince, and it was in a deeper sense as though Norkath had never been. Ilohan stood by, grown, strong, and faithful as he was in truth, and shared with them their joy.

Then a nightmare came upon her, and again she was held by the Norkath soldiers while the prince was asked to give up his throne. Again he set her free and then fought them all alone. But as she looked at him she thought he was Ilohan, not Kindrach. And then again perhaps he was Kindrach. He did not ask her to fly, so she stood and watched in terror. But then she realized that their swords did not wound him, even those that touched him. And they cried out in terror and could not stand against him, and he fought with chivalry and honor and great skill. They fell and broke ranks and were utterly vanquished before him, and he stood unharmed, triumphant and joyful. She looked at him very hard to see who he was, but she could not, because someone completely unrelated to the story was talking to her eagerly and distracting her.

Then she realized she was waking up from a dream, and with an effort she told herself dreams meant nothing, so it mattered not whether it was Ilohan or his father who had defeated the Norkaths. It was dawn, and someone was speaking to her from the doorway of her room.

"Lady Eleanor, wake up!"

It was Karlak, with urgency in his voice. She sat up in bed, her blankets still wrapped around her. "What is it?" she asked. She could hear that others were astir, and the peace of the cool morning was broken.

"Brogal, returning from the desert. He brings a caravan of Cembaran slave traders. Some of the slaves have the plague. The traders care little for them, but fear the plague themselves. It is an evil thing, but we are not dismayed."

"No," said Eleanor briskly, now becoming fully awake. "I will come as soon as I put on the clothes this day will need. But do not wake Prince Ilohan. I would not have him brave the plague."

She dressed quickly in the dim twilight of her room, laying aside the beautiful white dress, and putting on ordinary brown clothes. She hid her beautiful diamond crown under her pillow with a sigh, and pulled a strange blue hat over her brown hair.

The sky was twilight blue and serene, with the orange moon just on the point of setting far out over the desert. Yet out beneath the shade of the lovely trees the night was not serene. There were torches, confused movements, and angry and frightened voices raised in more than one language. Eleanor wished this had not happened on the very first day that she was known to her only son, yet she accepted it. She had been given power through the darkness she had borne, and she must use it for whatever good it could accomplish. She would not hang back today. "Preserve me, Lord," she prayed, "for it has been nearly a score of years since I valued my life as highly as I do now. Yet I will follow you: whatever my life's value, it is yours."

Chapter 17

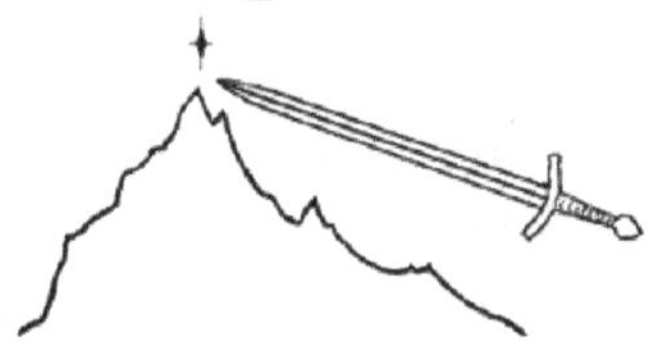

Choices and Safety

WHEN SHE HAD ASKED KARLAK NOT TO WAKE ILOHAN, Eleanor had not seen that he and Jonathan were already awake, standing a little away from the slave caravan and talking earnestly with Mudien.

"Whether you will help or not must be your choice alone," said Mudien to them. "I, Imranie, Lady Eleanor, and Karlak are bound to help: this is our station in the Cloth of Joy."

"But have you no way of protecting yourself from the plague?" asked Jonathan, astonished.

"None but prayer," said Mudien, smiling. "If we knew of another protection we would use it; though we do not we must still try to heal. Our Lord will not suffer our lives to be ended before their proper time."

"But if you fall, Ceramir will perish with you," said Jonathan.

"Ceramir has lasted well and faithfully from the time Kondoran, grandson of Nirolad, reigned in Karolan until now. Every one who has born the title of Mudien has risked his life as I will today, and the Valley of the Undismayed has not ceased to be."

"I would protect my life," said Jonathan, "though I do honor to your courage and confess it is beyond my own."

"It is upheld by faith," said Mudien.

"A faith I do not share," returned the blacksmith.

"Then your life requires more courage than mine," said Mudien. "It is a very frightening world that has no God in it. You are either brave beyond human courage – or blind."

"I will serve with you," said Ilohan.

"That will grieve Princess Eleanor," said Mudien.

"Yet she will help," said Ilohan, "and who is to say that my death would hurt her more than hers would hurt me."

"I say that it would," said Mudien, "and I say also that your life belongs to all Karolan and is not wholly your own to risk."

"Yet you have said yourself that this is my choice, and that God will preserve us as long as we were meant to live. Even if my life belongs to my people, it belongs first of all to God. If I do not use it willingly in his service, it will never be Karolan's with his blessing."

"Well spoken, Prince Ilohan," said Mudien. "I commend your choice."

"And I," said Jonathan, "although there is nothing I fear more than the plague, will not abandon my friend."

"I wish you would protect yourself, Jonathan," said Ilohan. "I would not be responsible for your death."

"You have nothing to say about this, Your Majesty," said Jonathan. "Do not ask me to break the Code that you yourself have promised to uphold."

"I thank you, Jonathan of Carrah," said Mudien. "Blind or seeing, your courage is very great. And we are in much need of a blacksmith, for there are many irons to be broken."

"That I can do with joy," said Jonathan.

* * *

Mudien and Rangol led the whole chained caravan of slaves, and the traders, into the central room of the house, the largest one through which the stream flowed. Jonathan went up and down the chain with a large hammer and a hard chisel. The slaves were filthy, and their stench filled the previously clean room. Many of them had the plague; some seemed already to be dead.

He knelt grimly beside the first man, and with one terrific blow of the hammer he broke the cold iron of his arm shackles. The man fell sideways onto the floor and lay there unmoving. One of the slave traders moved toward Jonathan angrily, speaking rapidly in a strange language and drawing a curved dagger from his belt. Jonathan raised the hammer.

Rangol stepped forward and spoke to the trader calmly in his own language. The great bow in Rangol's hands contained an arrow effortlessly held at the ready. Several more men of Ceramir, similarly armed, kept the room effectively under guard. The slaver let his dagger clatter to the floor, and sank back against the wall in dismay. Jonathan proceeded with his work unhindered.

He gently placed each manacled wrist against the floor, and then examined the crude irons for their weakest point. Finding it, he carefully positioned his chisel where the power of his blow would not harm the slave he was freeing. Then with a terrific blow, and often a bright spark, the cold iron would break, and the slave would be free.

Although his fear of the plague was like a huge weight in his stomach, it was a joy to him to see the iron break before his careful strength, and to set the miserable slaves free. Some of them were not sick, and could turn to him with deep thanksgiving in their pain-haunted eyes. There were women the age of his mother, and of Naomi, and there were young girls like Jenn. There were men of his own age, in some of whose eyes he could see burning the deep anger he himself would have felt in their place. There were young boys, and older men, all filthy, all slaves, all in great danger of the deadly plague.

When the last fetter was broken he stood back and looked about him, uncertain what to do. The chain lay in a dark, ugly line on the floor. The room was lit with an odd mixture of blue morning twilight from the partly opened windows, and warm firelight and candlelight. The slaves, who numbered perhaps a dozen and a score, stood, knelt, or lay on the floor beside the chain. Those who could looked around anxiously, wondering what would happen next. Their wondering was not for long; Mudien, Imranie, Eleanor and Karlak were already among them, talking to them softly in their several languages.

Jonathan marveled at the power of their love. It was beautiful but painfully moving to watch. The slaves listened to them, believed them, and trusted them. Their words brought hope and peace to anguished hearts. They calmed fear, stilled anger, pushed back despair. Even guilt and hatred wavered before them and were silent. It seemed that the slaves to whom those four spoke would do anything for them, obey any command they might give.

Ilohan saw this too, and tried to comprehend their power. He knew it came from God, but he sought to name it, and bring to his heart some understanding of its working. "Love unveiled, undismayed, keen as the blade of a sword," he thought, "from God, through those who love him. It makes them seem like healing angels. How rare this love must be, yet it is only what love is meant to be – pure and strong, and all unhidden. But is it so strong – or is it so rare? I am blind and without understanding. Yet I wonder – is love strong and deep more often than we know, but hidden because its glory is fully manifest only in the war with evil, in the face of death and sorrow? Let evil, death, and sorrow fall before this love until, confirmed forever, its glory shines unveiled without them, and all who languished in their darkness are set free."

Ilohan went to Mudien as he walked among the slaves. "Is there a task that you can give me?" he asked.

"Many," he said. "First, we need all the cleansing wash in Ceramir, perhaps more than we have. You will find the buckets of it in a closet on the roof. Bring all of them down, and ask Jonathan to help you."

After that Jonathan and Ilohan always had something to do, and the time for standing and wondering was over. Yet still Ilohan watched what passed around him, even as he worked, and he saw many things that moved him to joy or awe, or to deep and silent sorrow.

Jonathan also looked about him and wondered, but he wanted more than his friend always to be working, always doing something. He wanted to keep down his fear, and to use his strength in some way to fight the plague, which he deeply hated.

Jonathan helped Ilohan bring down the heavy buckets, amazed to see that the brilliant sun was already rising while the treetops kindled with its light. The wash smelled good and strong, of healing herbs and of some other, more caustic cleansing vapor. Mudien, Karlak, Imranie, and Eleanor washed each of the former slaves in the warm brook that ran through the room. They began with those who were well. Imranie and Eleanor washed the girls and women; Mudien and Karlak the boys and men. They stripped them of their clothes, and set them gently in the stream. Using the cleansing wash and a cloth, they sponged away all their filth, and though it stung them, the wash purified their sores. Once again it was a wonder to Jonathan and Ilohan how calmly the slaves trusted those who washed them. As they lay back in the warm stream, many of them bore on their faces expressions of utter peace. When they were clean and clothed in the bright garb of Ceramir, which Ilohan and Jonathan brought them, they looked like slaves no longer. Some went and stood near the bright fire, as its heat dried their damp skin and wet hair. Their eyes were bright with incredulous hope.

The four healers of Ceramir went on grimly to wash those who already had the plague. Imranie cried for them, and told them through her tears that all could yet be well. Some of them were unconscious, some were delirious, some were clearheaded but miserable and terribly afraid. They dressed them in the same clothes as the others, and then Ilohan and Jonathan carried them to beds that they had placed beside the clean stone walls of the big room.

Until now Eleanor had been too focused on the plight of the slaves to see that her son was risking the plague along with her, but now she suddenly looked in his face as he lifted a sick girl she had been tending. Instantly her eyes filled with tears. "No," she said in a whisper. "No... Go away from here, wash yourself in the lake. Oh, my son... Do not risk your life thus. Do not take from me the one I love best on earth. Please, Ilohan, please go where you will be safe."

"Mother," he said softly, "I am sorry to cause you hurt, deeply sorry. But surely I must do what I am called to do, and not seek a safety without the will of God. Do not say, 'Fly if you have ever loved me,' for I love you and I must not fly. Is your life less precious in my sight than mine in yours? I will not leave you to risk the plague alone. Please do not grieve so, for I am in God's hands just as surely as you are. Our love will last forever, and our lives will not end before he wills it."

Eleanor took a deep breath, feeling as though she were lifting a heavy weight. She could not smile, but somewhere within her there was a surge of something like joy or triumph. Her tears fell, and she could hardly speak. "You are Kindrach's son," she said, "the Lord protect you." She returned to her washing, but all her heart was in her prayer. She begged God to preserve his life, and felt no certainty that he would. Yet she trusted that his life as well as her own belonged to God.

When all the former slaves were washed, the slavers' turn came. They had not realized the power of Ceramir. It might save their lives from the plague, but the price they had to pay was high. Yet, between their fear of the plague on one hand, and Rangol and his archers on the other, they had little choice. They let themselves be stripped and washed, and they dressed themselves in the clothes of Ceramir. They watched with dismay as their evil-looking weapons were gathered together and taken away.

They watched with even more regret as Jonathan – obviously enjoying himself – piled up their chain in a great rusty heap on the floor, lifted it up with a mighty effort, and threw it with a crash into the fire. The iron glowed red-hot as it rested against the blazing logs, and all its filth burnt away. Gradually it fused into a weakly welded heap of metal in the coals, never to be useful as a chain again. Rangol and his archers bound each slaver's hands tightly but not cruelly behind him using rope and strips of cloth.

Then Mudien stood up in the big room and said, loud enough for all to hear who were not unconscious from sickness, "I give you welcome to the Cloth of Joy. I grieve that many of you are stricken with the plague, and all the rest are in danger. Yet by the power of God all of you may be healed, if he wills it.

"Everyone who has touched or been near a person with the plague must wear a blue hat for the next seven days. This is a warning to all in Ceramir that the plague is among us, so that they may protect themselves if they will. Anyone who touches or comes near a person wearing a blue hat must also wear one, for seven days. Do not approach a person who has not yet been exposed to the plague unless they ask you to do so. All who are well among you may wander freely in Ceramir, though you must not go among the cottages that are in the woods beyond the lake, which will be kept for those who have had no contact with the plague. There will be beds in this house each night for all who need them, and food whenever you are hungry. Whoever feels sick should come quickly to this room and seek for healing. All who are well and wish to remain in this room should be quiet and calm, out of courtesy for the sick who will be tended here. By the power of God, in whom we trust, none to whom life is a blessing will die, and within a score of days we will all be free of the plague.

"All who were once slaves I proclaim free. To the slavers I say this: we will use all our prayer and skill to keep you well or heal you. For three days only you will be bound. After this, if you pledge neither to plan nor to attempt hurt to any in Ceramir or Harevan, we will remove your bonds and you shall keep your freedom if you keep your pledge. We will not give you back your slaves, your weapons, or your chain, nor will we permit you to retake them now or ever. Yet we will show you life and joy as you have not yet seen them, and when the plague is passed we will set you free – well provisioned on the desert road if you wish it. The other choice, open to all who ever come to Ceramir, is to stay in this place at peace with all its children, and live among the undismayed.

Mudien repeated this speech in several other languages, and then sent Jonathan, Ilohan, and Karlak away to bring food. The freed who were well were starving, and ate the good bread and soup of Ceramir hungrily. Jonathan and Ilohan joined them in this. Brogal stood nearby, eating too, in the early morning sunshine just outside the house. Jonathan approached him.

"I thank you for the horse and supplies you gave us," he said. "You saved our lives, or very nearly did."

Brogal smiled. He was very tanned, and his eyes held a mischievous twinkle. "I need no thanks," he said, "but they are good to have nonetheless. I commend your courage in daring to help with the sick today."

"Do not so," said Jonathan. "I am a coward concerning the plague, and should be far away were it not for my love of Ilohan. How much danger are we truly in?"

"Courage love makes is courage still," said Brogal. "I would not say you are in much danger. You are strong, and love life deeply. Even if you take the plague I think you will not die. But let us talk of brighter things."

"How did you find these people?" asked Jonathan.

"I stayed at the church no longer than I could help – only long enough to earn a new horse and pay for the food I stole –"

Here Jonathan interrupted incredulously, "You gave us your horse and stole supplies from the church?"

Brogal grinned. "It was not true theft – I only put them to their proper use. They were supplies of God's church. Withholding them from you who needed them was theft, and I took them to give in proper charity. But the gatekeeper and the 'servant of God' who is his master called it stealing. They locked me up, but I have little regard for locks. I took the hinges out of the door the same night. I made the tower bell work, which it had not for a long time, and I cleaned the shaft of the latrine. I was so much use free and so much trouble jailed that they let me keep working. After two days, I asked for a horse and a week's supply of food, and they gave it to me. I think they feared what might happen if they did not.

"It was a good horse, and I know all the water holes in the desert, so I traveled at night, like the wind, and would have been here two days ago had I not noticed the signs of a caravan heading east toward southern Norkath. I followed them, found them soon, and wondered if I could free some of the slaves. Then I noticed that they had the plague among them, and saw a chance to free them all. I went to the slavers, and –"

Brogal was interrupted again, this time by a young woman of about sixteen years who had been among the slaves. Her dark-circled eyes shone with joy despite her former pain and present weariness. "– And you made them think their lives hung by a thread, with Ceramir their only ray of hope," she said, speaking the language of Karolan with a strange accent. "Had they left the sick – or all of us, perhaps – to die and be swallowed by the desert, they might have escaped with little danger of the plague, but you made them believe otherwise. You made their fear so strong that they could see nothing else, and they followed you blindly to Ceramir – where you freed us all and bound them! Free, free... My own life to lead, and hope reborn..." She looked into the bright blue sky as she said it, and lifted chafed wrists no longer encircled by fetters.

"Perhaps I did suggest their danger was rather deadly and immediate," said Brogal, his eyes sparkling more than usual. "When men make other men their slaves, they are more likely than ever to be enslaved themselves – in this case, enslaved to fear. It was a good jest, and a fair one. They hold their lives so tight, these men who are fools. A threat to them, well stated, will lead them to anything."

"You made a thing far greater than a good jest," said the girl, "and you should say it. Had your words been less well chosen, they would have seen the trap. Saving my life and a score and ten of others is no jest, Brogal of Ceramir. The prize you sought to win was real and precious, and only barely did you tilt the balance for our lives. Do not call that a jest, I pray, unless you would laugh at the thought of our death."

"And I would not, dear Rennel," said Brogal. "I laugh not that your rescue may seem a trifle, for it is not, but that my own pride may be mocked. For Brogal is a jester, one to whom the Lord gave laughter, not a hero to go out and rescue many slaves."

"Yet you rescued them!" she said, still nettled by his refusal to accept her praise.

"Thank God," said Brogal, "a score and twelve who yesterday were slaves today are free. But what shall we do, while we wear these odd blue caps and yet are well? Rennel, having walked all night, will want to sleep."

"I do not," said Rennel. "Freedom is too good, though you refuse the praise that I would give you. I do not want to sleep. Free hands... Green grass beneath my feet, blue sky above. A life to plan. No, I will not sleep."

"Are we not needed, to help with the sick?" asked Jonathan.

"I think not," said Brogal. "The most urgent need is passed, and there are many other willing hands. If you will," he said, including Rennel in his invitation, "come with me to the eastern side of Ceramir, and we will sit in the warm grass and talk or be silent – or sleep, for I am not as wakeful as a soul newly set free."

* * *

They talked long, on the warm grassy slope in the sunshine, mostly about things of no consequence, and Brogal dropped off to sleep as he had said he might. While he slept Jonathan and Rennel talked alone, and she told him of her home in far western Karolan, near the border with Cembar. Her mother was Cembaran and her father Karolan. She had many brothers and sisters, and the food on their isolated farm was sparse. She told the tale with bitter candor.

"So, because I am the oldest, my father sent me into Cembar to buy grain. He gave me a heavy pouch sewn shut, with the gold I had need of inside. In Cembar there is a law that any Karolan captured within the borders must be taken as a slave, but my father said that I, being half Cembaran, would be safe. I was captured just inside the borders, and all his comforts were proven lies. The pouch I carried was sewn around not gold but stones. Always I should have known he hated me. Always I did know it, but I looked for love like a child who searches for gold in a stream, and will not be told he has not found it."

"I am sorry," said Jonathan. "I have known love so well, I cannot imagine the pain of lacking it as you have. Yet perhaps this place will give you the love you search for. Surely Mudien is a father to any who have never known a father's love."

"Mudien?" asked Rennel. "The king of Ceramir? It is the queen I love, who cried and gently washed my tangled hair. What is her name? Imranie… Imranie… I have not known a mother's love yet either. But I will know it." She stretched her hands out on the grass. "Free…" she whispered, relaxed again, and was asleep.

Jonathan stood up, and looked through sleep-hazed eyes at the great mountains. He was thinking of Naomi, and of her measurelessly precious love. A thought whispered in his mind that he was giving Rennel her place. It was a stupid, feeble lie. His love for Naomi was like a bright fire roaring on the hearth; compared to it the compassion he felt for Rennel was a firefly's dim glow. They were different in character as well as mightily unequal in strength.

Yet somehow Rennel's fate made him tremble for Naomi. Where would he find her if the Karolan army was broken and the Norkaths swept through? How long might he, disguised, imperiled, search the masses of Norkath's new caught slaves before he found her? But the Karolan line would not break, and even if it did Naomi could run like the wind and find shelter in a thousand places. He was more likely to be captured than she was, but after the fight at Luciyr he scorned the Norkaths: they would never take him. Naomi would never have to search the captive ranks for him. He would come home to her free.

The sun soon shone on him, too, sleeping in the warm grass.

* * *

The day was cool and bright in Glen Carrah, and from high up in the glen Naomi could see that the farmers below were reaping the very last of their standing grain. The sturdy oaks that grew down in the village and along the road glowed red with autumn leaves. The sheep ate the dry grass of the glen hungrily, now and then searching out a patch where it was still partly green. It would be their last green grass for the year, for already a few cold mornings had covered the ground in frost.

Naomi exulted in the cool freshness of the day, and despite the sunshine she often ran, both for joy and for warmth. As usual, she had refused the warm leather cloak her father would have liked her to wear. She preferred to keep warm by running. The sheep were gathered into a tight flock today, for whenever one strayed very far she ran after it and brought it back – very surprised at being caught so quickly.

Often she looked with some concern back toward her father's cottage. She loved him deeply, and yet of late she had opposed him, and it seemed to her that all was not well between them. He had wanted to buy a fast, powerful horse for her from one of the farmers in the village, that she might fly to a place of safety if Karolan fell to Fingar. He had put it to her as a question, and she had said, plainly and emphatically, "No."

She knew she would have put his heart more at ease by agreeing, but she had not liked the idea of the great black horse tethered to a tree outside their cottage, or penned in the sheepfold. It would have been out of place, she thought. Riding it she would have felt that she usurped another's position: a happy peasant girl in the seat of a grave and anxious queen.

It was also very expensive – it would have cost all the gold they had, their savings over many years. Naomi, though she was a miser in nothing, thought that a more pressing need might arise. They had dreamed often of that gold, talking together about what great good they might accomplish with it, small in value though it was. Naomi was sure this horse was not the use for which they had reserved it, but Joseph disagreed.

She searched her heart, and considered carefully, in the long cool afternoon with the bright wind off the mountains swift and cold in her face. She came to the same conclusion as before: they should not buy the horse, and since her father had asked her the question he must accept her answer. She only wished it had not caused him so much hurt. He had wanted to ensure her safety, and she had valued it less than he did, and had prevented him. But no, that was not it. Neither the horse nor anything else could truly make her safe – no one was safe. Only God would keep their souls safe, his soul and hers. Slightly reducing the danger to her mortal life was not a good use either of the gold or of the horse.

She ran after a straying yearling lamb, caught it and carried it running back to the flock. Her foot caught in a tussock of grass and she and the lamb fell and rolled together on the soft grass. Neither was hurt, and Naomi got up laughing, wondering what the lamb must think.

The autumn sun was lowering brilliant gold over the western spur of the mountains when she led the flock down the long bright sweep of the glen, across the stone bridge over the Carratril, and into their fold beside the cottage. As she walked through the door there was a loud snap, and she saw that a crossbow bolt had snapped in her father's hands. She knew they were not easy to break. He flung the pieces behind him into a corner of the room.

"I will never be a soldier," he said, "but alas! Why must I always be harping on that? I thought I had accepted my fate, but I was wrong. It is like starting from the beginning again. And the road… the road was always so impossible… But this must stop – Daughter, I am sorry, forgive me."

"I forgive you, Father," she said. "And what I said before stands still."

"You mean concerning the horse?" asked Joseph. "I was not speaking of that."

"I also was not speaking of the horse," said Naomi, "but of an earlier thing."

"You called me a…"

"A hero, Father. I meant it then, and mean it still, though you are so far from understanding it that you will not even say the word."

Joseph turned away from her and set bread, milk and honey on the table. "These, at least, I have got," he said, "though I have done little else of any value today, or many days before. I am sorry for all that I have left you to do alone. I have tried to train and prepare..."

"Yes," said Naomi, taking her seat. "You have tried, and have not ceased to try, though it is harder for you than anything else in the world. That is what I meant."

Joseph looked at her. The light of the bright window behind her glanced on her hair and cheek. He thought of the danger that threatened her, and let his mind wander for a moment on the edge of the dark abyss that was the thought of losing her. "Not harder than anything..." he whispered.

He bent his head to pray, and perhaps did pray, though he found no words. In the end it was she who spoke. "Lord God," she said, "I thank you for the love that you have for us, and for the love that is between us. Let nothing block or weaken either love, and be with us whatever befalls us. I – we are afraid, and I ask that what we fear will not come to pass. Yet above all I ask you to be with us, and make us true to you, both now and forever."

"So let it be," said Joseph. "But what are you afraid of, Naomi?"

"I am afraid chiefly of the pain that you will suffer, but also of my own, for you will leave me and we have never parted before."

"And is there no deeper fear?"

There was a deeper fear, in her eyes, which seldom held anything of such darkness. "Jonathan," she whispered. "Lost forever."

He was silent for a while, and then said, "You understand I fear the same for you?"

"No!" she said. "You do not fear the same for me. Do you not understand? You cannot lose me forever, nor could I lose you." There was great love for Joseph in her voice, though her passionate words came near to anger, "You and I are on the same side of the chasm, Father. Jonathan and I are on opposite sides. Can two souls so bound be torn apart forever – further apart than the width of all that is, never to meet or touch in all eternity? Do you understand my fear?"

Joseph bowed his head. "You are right, my daughter," he said. "I am sorry. You have shown me my error and my folly. The love between us has all eternity to grow, and whatever hurts us here will only bring us greater glory there. My fear for you, however deep, must end in hope. I grieve that your fear for Jonathan has not this limit, and thus is darker yet."

He lifted his eyes in praise. "Thank you, God, that I shall never lose them nor they me, but we shall only meet in you unhurt and free forever." When he dropped his gaze to look at her again he caught his breath at her beauty. The open window behind her was filled with the soft glory of late sunset, and the fire and candles behind him lit her face.

"Yet, Naomi," he said, "should I not seek to protect your earthly life if I can? It is not as though it had no value, nor as if its loss would bring no grief."

"Certainly you should protect me, Father, as I will pour out my heart and soul to God in prayer for your protection. But my certain safety is a thing you cannot obtain, and there is a time where the protection of mortal life cripples life's richness, wounding a thing more precious than what it tries to save."

"But where is the balance? We are not to throw our lives to the wind. Would what I sought to do have crippled our life's fullness?"

"My heart tells me it would have, Father, and from where else could my answer have come?"

"From nowhere else, beloved daughter. But what will you do if the Norkath army marches into Carrah, hot to burn and pillage, rape and capture?"

Naomi shuddered. "That will mean you and Jonathan are dead," she said in a dull voice.

"Perhaps not," said Joseph, "perhaps only wounded or captured. But even if we were dead, would it not be your duty to escape if you could?"

"I suppose it would be," she said in the same tone. "But not on a great black horse, only on my two silent feet, in hiding and in mourning. And I would soon return, searching all the world for Jonathan, and for you. I would hide my beauty in a hooded cloak and dirty rags, and go among the prisoners, the wounded and the dead. That would be my place, Father, not some place of safety in the mountain crags, or some cave in the forest."

"Yet you yourself spoke of hiding just now. Would it not be well to know the ways to such places?"

She smiled, hoping her acquiescence would ease his heart. "If you want me to learn them, Father, I will."

His smile answered her own. "Thank you, Naomi. In the days to come, I will take you to them. The sheep will do well; already they have much hay. Four of the five places I have found lie within a half-day's journey, so we would be back by nightfall. Yet," his eyes twinkled, "we will need two borrowed ponies."

"As long as they are borrowed, Father," she said, with laughter in her voice.

They rose, and made for the doors of their respective bedrooms, yet before they parted he clasped her hand. "Regarding Jonathan I have little to say, except to tell you my sorrow and compassion for your fear," he told her earnestly. "Yet this one thing I would say: remember who is at the core of your heart. His love is worth the loss of any other love; his fullness heals the hurt of any other lack. I do not ask you to make your love for him greater than the love you have for Jonathan, for it would be a mockery to suppose it were not so already. Yet remember that it is so, and should be so, and let that knowledge rest deeper in your soul than all your fear. I know the darkness is great, Daughter. I am sorry."

He was gone, and she stumbled into the darkness of her sweet smelling room. Was he afraid for her soul, she wondered, fearing she was giving Jonathan the place of Christ? And if he was afraid, was he wrong to be? Surely she did not love Jonathan more than Christ – her father himself had just said so. But did he know? Did her love come near idolatry? "My Lord should be everything to me," she thought. "Yet if Jonathan were in Hell, could any place be Heaven for me? Is my love for Christ so incomparably stronger than my love for him? Yet it must be; it shall be – God will make it so if it is not so already. My Lord, I give myself to you; I have long been yours. Work your will with the longings of my heart. And yet…and yet…Will you suffer me to be so shattered as I must be if you do not carry Jonathan across the gulf?"

After a little while, the moon shone upon her sleeping form. In her dreams she lay in the arms of Christ, and knew certainly who was all to her, and felt the Savior bless his child.

Chapter 18

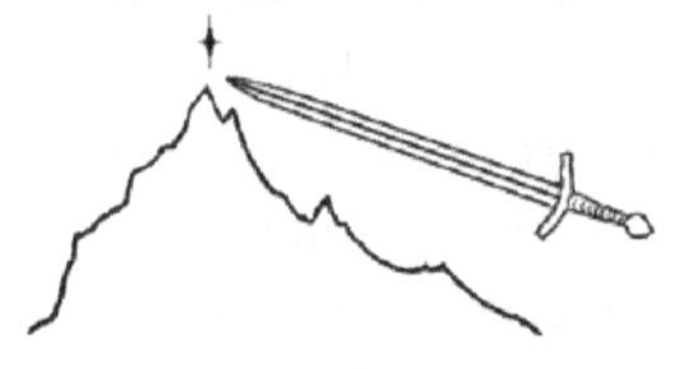

Inevitable Loss

THEY STAGGERED THROUGH THE DARKENING WOODS OF Ceramir, Jonathan and Brogal supporting Rennel between them. She shuddered and trembled, and would have fallen often but for their hold on her.

"I could carry you," said Jonathan.

"No, I will walk," said Rennel desperately but determinedly. "I will not be carried. Yet how terrible I feel! How horribly sick. I had hoped I might live…and love living. I die… like a mouse freed from a trap but then thrown to a dog, I die."

"No!" said Jonathan. "You must not die! This is a place of healing – who knows how great its power? They will save you. You will have the life that evil robbed you of." He spoke as though the warmth of his voice alone might save her, and tears were in his eyes who scarcely ever wept. There were things he wanted more than Rennel's healing, far more. But this was the first time in his life that he had come against something he desired so fiercely, without seeing anything he could do to make it come to pass. Even when he had fought for life in the icy lake beyond Luciyr, it had been his to fight, and something in him had never lost the confidence that he would win.

Now he knew Rennel might die – the life of love and freedom that she had longed for, that seemed to have been given her, might be snatched away even before she fully recognized its value. And there was nothing he could do. He knew nothing of the healing art of Ceramir, save that it was strong but could not always cure the plague. Not always. "Rennel," his heart cried silently, "Rennel – would that I could demand for you the life you hoped for! What a dreadful world this is, and how weak my strength and sword."

They reached the house, and Imranie met them at the door. She looked at Rennel, and Rennel returned her gaze.

"Yes, you have the plague," whispered Imranie. "But Rennel – Rennel!" she said, as the girl's eyes wandered, "Heaven will resound with my prayers for you, and I will beg my God in tears for your mortal life. But whatever his answer – Rennel, look at me, you must not wander yet – whatever his answer, he offers you in love a life that never sickens: a life that is endless, boundless, fearless, full of the Love of which all other loves are merely echoes." Rennel's eyes clouded and wandered, and Imranie felt a moment's self reproach that she had been able to say so little.

Brogal, watching, thought, "Who can say if anyone else, with the power of love alone, could have held her back from delirium so long? I could not have, not so late. More shame to me that I did not try sooner – but I cling harder to their mortal lives than does my mother."

Jonathan carried Rennel into the house, and laid her on a bed against the clean stone wall of the big room. Mudien came almost at once, to find her tossing and turning on the bed, delirious and miserable. He smoothed a blanket down over her, but it did little to calm her. He held a fist full of wet leaves above her, and crushed them until the green juice squeezed out between his fingers. The smell of the leaves was pungent and strong. Rennel quieted almost immediately. He lifted her head, and began to trickle a cup of something down her throat, using the hollow stem of a vine to guide it. Her eyes remained staring, and she did not come out of delirium, but she swallowed all the fluid easily without choking. Her face was ashen, and except for the slight, worried movements that sometimes passed over them her hands might have been mistaken for those of one already dead. They were gray and cold. Mudien tucked them under the blanket, and wrapped it tightly around beneath her.

"It would have been ten times better if she had come here at once," said Mudien. "The sickness has been coming on her since early afternoon."

"I swear by the stars we brought her here as quickly as could be as soon as we knew she was sick," said Jonathan. "Alas that we slept so long, Brogal and I. We had fallen asleep near her on the grass close to the eastern wall of Ceramir. She sickened while she slept. She did not become fully awake, I think, until the cool evening woke us, and we were alarmed at her appearance and roused her. She was not delirious until we reached the door of this house."

"I meant no reproach to you, Jonathan," said Mudien, "and for the one you felt I am sorry. That she fought off delirium so long shows the strength of her spirit, which bodes well; yet her body is not strong. If anyone is to be reproached it is myself: I should have stationed a watch over all who wear the blue caps, to make sure that any who sicken come to the house at once. This plague is more virulent than we hoped. Will you take the duty of watchman?"

Jonathan, who was kneeling beside the bed, looked up at him with pain filled eyes.

"You would rather stay at her bedside and wait?" asked Mudien.

"I would," said Jonathan. "Never have I wanted something as desperately as I want her to live."

"Do you love her?" asked Mudien.

"By the stars and the mountains, no – not in that way," said Jonathan. "I love a woman of Glen Carrah: Naomi, dearest to my heart of all who live. But Rennel never knew real life or joy, and now, just when she began to hope for them, they are snatched from her. I want her to live! How I hate death! I hate it more than anything else. I wish I could destroy it. And tonight I am so weak; my strength is so useless...I can do nothing."

"Nothing by staying here – save praying only," said Mudien. "If you will pray, pray! But if not, save others from Rennel's fate, while our prayers and labor go to save her from her own."

"My prayers would be a mockery, and I will not make them," said Jonathan. "If there is a God I – no, I will not say it. If there is a God, he is either evil, or very, very strange, otherwise he would have destroyed death. I will keep watch!"

He went quickly out into the night, not giving Mudien a chance to answer, for he did not want to hear a defense of the faith of Ceramir. He walked through the dark woods, looking for any who might have wandered there and fallen sick. As he walked, his thoughts ran on the very thing he had tried to prevent Mudien from speaking about. In Ceramir he had seen a mighty power and a brilliant, dauntless joy, and no one save himself alone seemed to doubt that the source of both was God. This troubled him. Could it be that he had found the evidence he had always said was lacking – evidence that would demand of him his soul? But no, the evidence was not enough.

He quickened his pace, pounding out the sentences of his thought with his heavy footfalls. "Not enough," he said. "What would be enough? What if God is real, and yet no matter how much evidence I see, I still say it is not enough? I hope that will not happen!"

He stopped suddenly, his hand on a tree. He hoped it would not happen? But hope was too weak a word. If God were real – if after all Naomi and Ceramir were right – then by rejecting the evidence, he was cutting himself off from the source of all beauty, justice, and honor. He was cutting himself off from the real purpose of the world, to follow a phantom – a faith of his own making. And there was another thing, seldom spoken because of its horror – though he had seen it haunting Naomi's eyes. There was Hell. "But would it not be Hell to me in any case?" he asked himself. "Even if there were no realm of fiery torment, yet it would be a torment to me to know I had rejected Naomi's God, the God of beauty, honor, and justice, when all along he was real. And when God sentenced me to the realm of torment itself, I could only approve his justice. It would be just as though I had slapped my king in the face and abandoned his service. Have I said I merely hoped to avoid this? Hope is no word for such a thing! I must be certain."

Even as he thought this he realized that he was calm and unafraid. "I am certain," he said to himself. "If I were not certain, I would not have this calmness. There is no God of goodness and beauty – not in this world where the goodness and beauty are always destroyed. What I have always believed is true: the essence of the world is heroic love and irrevocable loss." He left the tree and strode on through the forest, thinking that the question was resolved in his mind.

Yet it was not – not fully. There was the power and the faith of Eleanor, Mudien, and Imranie – of this whole valley of

Ceramir. A breath of fear touched him that by some impossible chance he had misunderstood it all, and Hell was real. Should he after all attempt to turn himself to God, to escape it? Should he try to take that precaution, against the unimaginable calamity of damnation?

He brought himself to an abrupt halt in a strange hollow of the woods, ringed about with low hanging branches. He wanted to answer his thought once and for all, for it seemed to him a great crime that he had even thought it. Should he turn to God and so find rescue from Hell if he were wrong? He spoke his answer aloud: "No! No, with every drop of strength I have. No again and again. No for every star that shines above, for every leaf on the trees! Shall I betray truth and turn to a faith I do not believe out of fear of Hell? Never, not for anything! Better honest in a false faith than a scared imposter in the true one – even if it is true as I know it is not! Fear is no foundation on which to build a life. Fear!" He spat the word. "The fear that holds love back. I will not yield to it. I will not drown my soul in hypocrisy."

He continued on, reached the sheet of vines and climbed it swiftly. There was a white-faced boy in a blue cap clinging in terror to the vines near the summit. Jonathan thought the boy had the plague, and hated the prospect of bringing him down the cloth of vines. If he were delirious, there was a very real chance he would fall. When he reached him, Jonathan realized with great relief that he was not sick, but merely frightened. Even so it was a difficult task to get him down the vines. It effectively ended Jonathan's philosophical speculation, and the young blacksmith found this, also, to be a relief. Yet the thought of Rennel dying remained, like a twisted chain in his stomach and an ugly veil over the moonlit beauty of the night.

* * *

Mudien leaned wearily against the stone wall beside the hearth at dawn. When the slave caravan had come in, fourteen slaves had been sick. Now a score of the freed, three of the slave traders, and two of the children of Ceramir had the plague. He had tended them in turn all night. Thrice he had knelt in sorrow while a soul left the loathsome, infected body his skill could not preserve. Three of the former slaves dead. Three for whom freedom had come too late, and been only a mockery.

He was weary as he had seldom been. This was one of the most virulent plagues he had ever seen. It came on quickly, and could kill within two days. He hated death, perhaps with even more intensity than Jonathan did, even though he believed that it could be a doorway into Heaven. He woke Karlak, Eleanor, and Ilohan, who had slept through the night while he tended the sick. He washed himself in the stream, then swam across the lake as the first red rays of dawn lit the top branches of the trees. He dried himself by the fire, and, committing himself to God's care, slipped quickly into sleep in a clean white bed in the house.

Jonathan kept the task of watchman far into the bright morning, and even through part of the afternoon. He was reluctant to ask for help, and his great strength of will and body helped him remain alert despite his lack of sleep. Also, though he did not admit this even to himself, he was using his duties to keep himself from thinking. Finally he realized he was becoming too weary to judge efficiently who was well and who was not, so he went into the house and explained this to Eleanor. She told him to go to bed at once, and assigned Ilohan to replace him.

Ilohan did not want to leave Eleanor, but he saw her joy at being able to assign the watchman's duties to him – duties that would keep him far from those infected with the plague. To please her, and because he knew the need was real, he acquiesced.

Eleanor watched him go, sighed long and softly, and returned to her rounds among the sickbeds. Despite her fear for him the hours had been sweet to her, and they had talked of many things in soft voices beside the suffering people they were working together to heal. Now she was alone – for Karlak worked by himself – and, oddly, her fear for Ilohan was no less than before. Her thoughts of him were troubled as she went from bed to bed, looking into drawn, ashen faces, feeling cold or fever-hot hands, and murmuring prayers bright with love.

Now and then she gave some medicine, but of it Mudien and Karlak knew more than she. Eleanor believed that it was the power of her love, received from God and freely given both to him and to those she served, that healed the sick. "Like a sword of light I lift up my love," she said. "Die, dark pestilence, die before it, stabbed by heavenly brightness." She smiled, for she stood leaning on her crutches beside the bed of one for whom the tide had turned. A woman, between her own age and Veril's, had passed through the nadir of her infection, and lived, and although her face was still ashen, Eleanor knew that joy would shine there again, and she would dance in Ceramir when summer came. This was the first victory; for all others the outcome was yet uncertain.

She limped over to Rennel's bed, and saw that Imranie knelt beside it, while Jonathan lay asleep on the floor nearby. The young blacksmith was obviously still well, yet she feared for him lying so near those deathly sick, asleep with no precautions taken.

"Should we not wake him?" she asked Imranie softly.

"No, do not wake him," said Imranie without turning her head. "He would sleep less soundly and less safely anywhere else. He loves the poor freed girl here, Rennel."

"Are you certain? Is Naomi of Glen Carrah not his beloved?" asked Eleanor.

"He does not love Rennel in that way, but he loves her in a very real way," said Imranie. "He desperately wants her to live, for he has seen both the darkness that came before and the light that might follow after."

"He does not understand that the brighter light is reached by passing through death," said Eleanor, "rather than by escaping it."

"Rennel does not believe," said Imranie, "so for her, death is unlighted fear." She shuddered.

"What do you think will be her fate?" asked Eleanor.

The mother of Ceramir looked up, with golden pity brimming in her eyes. "I think the plague will kill her, and I cannot let her go."

"Can you ever let anyone go, Imranie?"

"Never easily, I love them so. But often I can see Heaven opening to them and know that only cruelty would seek to hold them back."

"What of Mudien?" asked Eleanor.

Light leaped into Imranie's eyes, and she smiled. "In his power I still hope," she said, "but the time is not yet. Jonathan must waken first, and I will keep watch over her spirit until then."

* * *

The day was cool and bright, with a white cloud-haze in the blue sky and a fresh wetness in the air. The sun was golden on the smithy wall. Barnabas did not see it. Despite the cool air, his sweat fell in drops on the grinding wheel, where he was sharpening the eighth sword. He was more tired than he had been in years, and still he was falling behind. There were four more swords to make, and only eight days in which to make them. He was sure that somehow he would do it, but the weariness and the drudgery made every new step seem impossible. He must just carry on, and the impossibility would fade away before him as it had always done. How hard or uncomfortable it was, was not his to consider.

Hannah came out to him with a cup of cool water, and he smiled at her, and drank it gratefully. She went away without a word, but he felt more hopeful and less tired as he turned to his grinding again. His wife came back carrying a light wooden table that she had made, set it down, and went into the cottage again to emerge with two chairs. He stopped his grinding and looked at her, perplexed. "What are you doing?" he asked.

"Since you are going to work all day and into the night, and forsake your sleep, I will also," she said. "This is my right, and willingly I accept it as my duty. You will make four swords in eight days, working night and day until you are finished. I know, because I know you, that you will make them well, permit no slag in the iron and spare no pains in the tempering. This task is at the limit of your strength, so I will stay with you and help you until it is done."

Her strength was not a third of his own, but he knew her too well to doubt that she would indeed help him. She turned the grinding wheel for him, shoveled the charcoal, and pumped the bellows. He could see that showing her love so tangibly brought her joy – joy that he shared as he worked beside her, even though he wished she would not exhaust herself so severely, or strain so hard over the grindstone and the bellows.

When there was no work that she could help with, she sat at the table and made things of wood and leather as she always did, singing or talking to him as she worked. Hearing her voice singing, in between the great bangs of his hammer, warmed his heart and made him lift it up to God in deep thanksgiving for her love. When twilight fell she leaned long oak torches, soaked with oil, against the four stone corners of the smithy and lit them. Their bright yellow light illuminated the forge and wheel well enough for Barnabas to work as easily as though it were still day.

They ate a hasty but enjoyable meal at the little table, and then went back to work. Though his arms still ached, and his will still strained to uphold his careful skill, it seemed to Barnabas that his work had taken wing. When at last the late moon, waning a few days past its full, rose in a glow of silver cloud over the dark eastern mountains, he quenched a fiery blade in the tempering water and set his hammer down in the exultant realization that in a single day he had forged a new sword. Hannah came into his arms, and they hugged one another tightly in the light of the late moonrise, both exhausted, yet happy and thankful for each other's love.

Love was a mystery, Hannah thought, as they went into the cottage. Why was it so strong, so beautiful, yet by some never found and by others never given? She squeezed her hand in her husband's in the deep gratitude of her soul. Human love was beyond her understanding; God's love immeasurably far beyond that. Love was beyond her, but she was not beyond it. That knowledge held her, warm and bright in the safe darkness of their bed. In it they both rested, and their dreamless sleep was sweet.

*   *   *

Jonathan awoke stiff and sore from sleeping on the hard stone. Someone had thrown a blanket over him while he slept, and he was grateful for its warmth. Despite this, he cast it off and rose quickly as the hope and concern that had not left him even in sleep clarified in his waking mind. It was night; the room lit only by candles. He was alone beside Rennel's bed. He looked down at her.

He went cold, and for a moment he made no move. Rennel did not look like the girl he had known for those few bright hours long ago. Her mouth seemed open in a gasping cry, there were dark splotches on her skin, and a sick smell came from her that the herbs of Ceramir could not hide. But something in her face taught him that the horror of what had befallen her was more than merely the sum of her disfigurements. Hers was not the guileless face of the sleeping, nor the wakeful, watching face of the living – nor yet the blank, inhuman face of a corpse. If Jonathan had ever seen a man being tortured he would have recognized her expression. He had not, but still he understood.

The wave of his first distress fading, he stretched out his hand above her. Her expression remained fixed, frozen and still. Her hands, which somehow had slipped out from under the blanket, were oddly twisted, like the claws of a dead bird. Fear that she was already dead surged above his stunned pity, and he lowered his hand lightly across her dreadful mouth. He had an idea that what he was doing was extremely dangerous to himself, but in that instant he did not care.

For a long moment he felt absolutely nothing. Then the very tiniest warmth came to his fingers, and he knew she had exhaled. After another long wait, it came again. Yet it was so faint, not even breath enough to blow the petals of a flower, that he was sure it soon would cease – perhaps even now would never come again.

"Mudien – Sir! Please come! Rennel dies!" he cried loudly, not caring whom he woke.

Imranie came running. "Does she die so soon?" she asked. "Alas that I left her! I will fetch Mudien at once."

A bright lamp was in his hand when he came. It was nearly the middle of the night. He set the lamp on the shuttered windowsill above Rennel's bed. He looked at Imranie, and her eyes were pleading. "So let it be," he said. "If God will allow it, I will do as you have asked. It is no small thing, but then we fight for no slight cause."

He bowed his head, and knelt beside the bed. Jonathan stood by in wondering silence. He did not believe in prayer, but he had indeed some confidence in Mudien. If anyone could bring Rennel back from the brutal edge of death, Jonathan had a hope that Mudien could. Yet his hope was very faint, for it seemed to him an impossible miracle.

Rennel gave a short, inhuman groan, writhed suddenly on the bed, and was still again. Jonathan started forward, dismayed, but then stopped out of deference to Mudien. Mudien raised his head, his brow furrowed with concern, as if he also considered it possible that she had groaned her death. They watched her still form carefully, and saw that she breathed. "Hope yet," said Mudien in a low voice, and returned to his prayer.

At last his prayer was over. He lifted Rennel gently and propped up her head. He took a flask from a pocket of his cloak and trickled its contents into her mouth with great care, using a hollow reed. Even so she choked weakly once, and coughed. Imranie bound white cloths across Mudien's mouth, then Jonathan's, then her own. "Death comes into the air with their coughs," she said, "and those protections that we know, we often should use."

At last the flask was empty. Mudien unbound the cloth from his mouth. "She should not see such signs of protection," he said, "and it has been long since she coughed."

Jonathan's hope leaped as he removed his own cloth. He had not thought those lidded, black-rimmed eyes would ever again see anything. Mudien waited, watching silently, and Imranie prayed. The night was still save for the occasional groans and stirrings of the sick, the footsteps of those who tended them, and the unworried rippling of the creek in the floor. The waiting seemed endless. Jonathan took to counting his heartbeats, but lost track and gave up. He wondered exactly what they were waiting for.

Mudien's patient expression became alert. Jonathan bent over the bed. Rennel moved a little, and gasped softly. Her eyes opened slowly. They were bloodshot, and though they had been brown before they were now a sickly gray. Yet there was life in them.

"Ahhhhh," she gasped again, and then asked, after pausing to muster energy and focus to speak, "will I live?"

"Rennel," said Mudien gently, "unless God reverses the course of nature, you will die." Though he only paused an instant, each of his listeners had a reaction. Jonathan clenched his hands in anger and despair, knowing Mudien had no power to call her back to health or life. A shadow of deep pain passed across Imranie's face, but vanished, leaving only an expression of longing. Rennel's eyes kindled with intense terror, and a shudder passed through her failing body. "Yet God's love is not constrained by death, and not all who die cease to live," Mudien continued.

Jonathan stood by with his face set like stone, and heard Mudien tell Rennel that mighty, beautiful falsehood. He knew, now, that Imranie had hoped to save Rennel's soul more than her body. And he knew that, contrary to Imranie's belief, the soul and body were inseparably joined – so that when Rennel died, she would be lost forever. He despaired, but even in his despair his sense of honor pricked him. Should he try to tell the dying girl the truth? Should he seek to quench the false hope Mudien might give? He had to make that decision quickly, blindly, without guidance. He chose to keep silent. Instantly he doubted his choice – but it was made. Wrong or right, merciful or dishonest, he would abide by it.

Rennel's terror gave her a feverish energy, and though she was plague-stricken and dying she spoke clearly and quickly in a sort of harsh whisper, breathing hard and gathering strength before each sentence. "There is no God," she said.

Mudien's voice was gentle, yet Jonathan felt it carried enormous strength. He seemed to be speaking not to her ears but to her heart. "Rennel, you know that is not true," he said.

"You are right," said Rennel. "I do know... But God does not love me."

"Tell me why you believe that," said Mudien.

She breathed twice, barely equal to the effort of answering, yet driven by her fear. "I hate him... All my life he has hurt me... Evil parents... Slaved... Plague... In the desert in chains I... I cursed him." She raised herself a little with a terrible effort. "I will curse him again now... I—"

"Rennel!" Mudien's voice, though still gentle, was loud and strong. "Do not."

She sank back. Jonathan wondered how she felt; whether she was in much pain. "No," she whispered. "I will not... Yet I know he hates me."

"He loves you, Rennel," said Mudien. "The love that you feel here is only an echo of his love for you. Is our love for you true? His is truer."

"But... I cursed him!"

"In justice he cursed you in return, but in love he bent his own curses back on himself, that none would touch you. He bore their pain – worse pain, Rennel, than even you have ever known."

"He cursed himself... with the curses I deserved?" she asked.

"Yes," said Mudien. "Because he loves you, Rennel."

Tears came to her eyes, brown tears because of her infection, and they trickled down her stricken face. "Alas that I hurt him... And now I die... And never said, 'Forgive me.'" Frantic fear returned to her face. "I die!" she said. "Death is despair... Beyond it horror lies."

"You will die," said Mudien, "but God can bring you to love instead of horror, Rennel."

"Why would he?" asked Rennel.

"Because he loves you," said Mudien.

"Will he rescue... me from the horror? ...What if he does not?"

"He will if..." Mudien hesitated.

"If what?" asked Rennel desperately, her whisper growing weaker. "What does he... want me to do?"

"He wants you to say, 'Forgive me,'" said Mudien.

"Nothing more?" asked Rennel.

"Only trust that he is real," said Mudien, "and that he loves you, and will hear and rescue you."

Rennel's gray eyelids were flickering closed, and her whisper was desperately weak. Yet in it there was hope. "He can... hear me... even now?"

"Yes, Rennel, yes! He can."

"God... forgive me."

She opened her eyes again, and it seemed to Jonathan that their plague-ravaged gray had become brown again. "I trust him," she said.

She was silent for a moment, then fear crept back into her face. "Sinking... sinking," she said. "If he... loves me... why... was I hurt... so much?"

"Soon he will rescue you, and give you peace and understanding," said Mudien. "Soon you will see him. He loves you, and all that you should know he will tell you. Can you trust him with the mystery of your hurt until then? He understands hurt, and all it makes and proves, though we do not. He is worthy of trust, and through all pain his love still shines. Yet he wants you to trust him."

Her eyes closed again. "I trust... He loves me... Your love... is real... He is... real... He heard me."

Jonathan looked at her face, and fell without a word to his knees, not caring for the pain that shocked through him when they hit the hard stone. He buried his face in his hands, and through them his clear white tears fell, for he knew that she was dead, and though of this her face carried no word, he was sure that she had not received the joy she had been promised.

Yet Rennel was not dead, and although she never again opened her eyes she spoke again, very softly. "What... is... his... name?"

"He has many names, one of them known only to himself," said Mudien. "Yet when he came and lived among us, and taught us and bore our pain and curses and death on himself, we called him Jesus. He loves us, and he is stronger than death and stronger than any curse."

"I... know," she said. The blankets across her body rose once more, ever so slightly, and her very last shallow breath carried the whisper, "Jesus..."

Mudien felt almost as if he could watch her soul leave them, and the body on the bed cease to be Rennel. The eyes slid open, and were glazed, and in them there was no longer any hint of brown. Mudien's heart leaped, for he was sure she had gone to joy, and thus the failure of his healing was the victory of God's great love. The sadness that had gathered over his heart the morning before was banished. Then, three had died and gone to no certain fate, and he had felt that all of Ceramir was threatened – but now he delighted in God's rescue of a soul; a thing of measureless value, and a cause for great celebration.

Jonathan stood up. He saw the joy in Mudien's face, and Imranie's great thanksgiving. His anger burned, not at them but at death, and his sorrow felt like lead in his chest. "You think she has found joy beyond the reach of death?" he asked.

"She has," said Imranie. "It is what I longed for, and deeply feared would never come."

"Why could you not heal her?" he demanded of Mudien.

"God wished to give her a greater gift than healing," said Mudien, "and he would not let me keep her from it. I thank you for your silence, Jonathan, while I spoke to her. Yet I wish with all my heart that you shared our hope. It is terrible to see only death, and not the life beyond it."

Jonathan listened, his hand on the post of Rennel's bed. He saw only death, saw only that she was gone. Lost forever, her life a bud never blooming, a hope never fulfilled. Yet they thought she had received the highest good. His words came unguarded from the anguish in his heart. "There is no life beyond death. Ceramir is like a lovely dream, yet those who wake find it a brutal world. She is gone, there is nothing left of her. The joy and love she hoped for will never be. I have seen a treasure slip from the world. I had thought that in mourning there was some consciousness of noble sorrow. There is not; only deep pain and burning anger. Yet I scarcely loved her."

In the silence that followed his outburst, his own words echoed in his ears. "I scarcely loved her." He had meant he loved Naomi immeasurably more, yet even for Rennel the sorrow was this deep... If Naomi died... There were no words to describe it. His anger would blaze hot enough to burn the world; his grief would be dark enough to quench the sun. His love for her was the center of his life. Yet if it were taken from him he would not die. He was too strong: no grief would be enough to kill him. He would live on, in a world empty of all but agony.

His hand on the bedpost crushed it so strongly that the wood cracked. Rennel's corpse lay on the bed, horrible in appearance yet somehow at peace. Mudien and Imranie stood together looking at him with pity, but they said nothing. Their hair and faces glowed in the warm light of the candles. They were king and queen of the kingdom he had called a lovely dream, yet he knew that to them, the dream was more real than the brightness of the sun. "I am sorry," he said, and ran out into the night.

He ran like the wind to the edge of the lake, leaped out, and crashed through the surface of the black water. Its warmth closed over his head and he was swimming fast and strong. When he reached the other side he turned around and swam back. He went back and forth across the lake, until there began to be some comfort in the rhythm of his swimming, and in the increasing weariness of his body.

Finally, in the warm darkness of the midnight lake, a song began to form in his mind, shaping itself to the rhythm of his strokes, relieving his sorrow by releasing it into words. When he had the whole song, he stopped swimming and lay in the shallows far from the stone house. He remembered Rennel falling asleep on the warm grass, with words of hope on her lips, and in mourning for that lost hope he sang:

Your joy was beautiful;
Your hope was born.
Now, cold and pitiful,
You lie forlorn.

Tears bring no solace,
Truth I must face:
You cannot hear this;
Empty your place.

Lost, fallen, vanished,
Slipped from life's hold.
From love's joy banished,
Ne'er to grow old.

Did you dare ask for
Riches in lust?
Love, hope, but no more,
You asked in trust.

Grass in the sunlight,
Mother's warm love,
Eyes with life's joy bright,
Clear stars above.

Was she so wrong, Fate?

Proud or unjust?
She asked for love, late.
You made her dust.

Voice made for singing,
Feet made to run,
Heart made for knowing
Laughter and fun,

Lost, lost now, always,
Small flower crushed:
Ended her few days,
First hope-song hushed.

Death her has taken,
In filth and pain:
Bruised child forsaken,
All loss – no gain.

My anger, burning,
More than sun-bright!
Strong my soul's yearning:
Something to fight!

Death, hear my war cry!
March out in force,
Under the black sky,
On your pale horse!

Heedless of terror
Fierce would I fight
But there's no answer

Out from the night.

For death is formless:
No foe shouts loud.
Sudden, yet endless,
On each falls the shroud.

Swords cannot slay death,
Nor can love shield.
My cry is but breath;
My foe cannot yield.

There was no grand resolution in Jonathan's heart. There was only unexpected comfort, and increasing strength to carry on. Fate was a meaningless word, a fable to give false reason to what happened, not a being that could be fought. However hot his anger burned, his sword was weak and limited compared to the death that threatened all he loved. But life was his to live, not over now nor even darkened by great loss. He went into the house, found dry clothes and a bed prepared for him, and lay down in the darkness.

The room was very still and peaceful. The footsteps of those who tended the sick did not come here, for this room was for those who were as yet healthy. Jonathan lay still for a while, and then cried quietly but unrestrainedly, his tears falling down on the clean pillow. It was a simple action, the natural release of the sorrow of his heart. He was not ashamed by his tears, and did not try to hold them back. He was crying for Rennel, because he had wanted her to live. When his crying had spent itself he slept. His sleep was deep and good, benevolent darkness untroubled by any glimmer of a dream.

Chapter 19

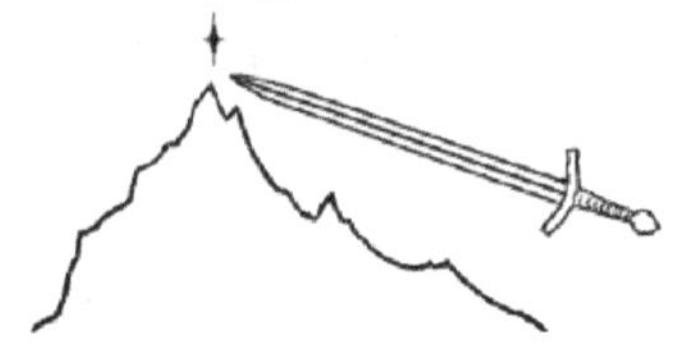

Hope and the Prince

ILOHAN LAY ON THE GRASS BESIDE THE LAKE, AND watched the high crowns of the trees catch the red light of the rising sun. He had not slept all night, and had been up through the previous day as well. He knew that if he closed his eyes he would soon sleep. His will, however, was fully given to his duty as the watchman, and it was strong enough to keep him wide awake. Soon he would wake Jonathan, to replace him, but not yet. Eleanor, also, had spent the dark night wakeful in her service of the sick – and he shared with her not only the bright love of mother and son, but also the bond of those who had fought together against the plague. While she woke and prayed and labored, he would not sleep.

He got up and began to walk around the lake to the north, with the idea of searching once more through the woods and then going back to the house. But he stumbled as soon as he stood, and the ground seemed to tilt beneath him. He put a hand on a tree, and still the world would not steady. His heart raced and the strength seemed to go out of his body. He was sure he had the plague, and fear took hold of him and seemed to force out his very breath. Then the fear sunk down and he thought calmly of what he should do. There was some strange joy in the doing of it, in the knowledge that the crisis of his life had come and his priorities were absolutely clear. He felt deep pity for Eleanor and the grief this would cause her, but soon painful weakness overwhelmed his thoughts, and only his duty remained, forcing him on.

He staggered around the lake to the house, and opened the door. Eleanor was in a side room to the right, giving a drink to a sick man who was recovering. Ilohan went in and fell on his knees beside his mother. The world seemed spinning around him as he heard his own voice speaking. "I am sorry, Mother. I love you. I do not want to leave you. I want to fulfill your hopes, but... But I am sorry. All that I did I thought was right to do."

She knelt before him and took his head between her hands. They were cool and steadying against his burning temples. "Beloved son, I forgive you," she said. "I love you and I know that you belong to God. You are a hero as your father was, and always heroism has its price. Yet you will live, Ilohan. If a mother's fervent prayer is heard in Heaven, you will live."

Then suddenly her anguish broke forth uncontrolled. She took him in her arms with a great effort, and held him up, his head on her shoulder as she knelt erect on the floor. "God!" she cried, "Will you give only to take, and heal only to wound? Will you build hopes in years to shatter them in days? Will you destroy the heart I gave you, broken, which still was yours when you had healed it? Will you break the hope of Karolan, where dwell fifteen score thousand people whom you made? Father! Was Kindrach's death, were my days and years of sorrow nothing to you?"

With an effort that was beyond her strength she stood and tried to carry him through the doorway to the other room, but her lame legs buckled beneath her and she fell backward.

Ilohan tried to break her fall, but he was dizzy and weak, and perhaps worsened rather than easing it. Eleanor's head hit the hard stone with a loud crack, and she lay there still.

Ilohan was horrified and confused. He hardly understood what had happened, but he knew that his mother was hurt, perhaps killed, and that he was to blame. All the world was a roaring confusion to his senses, and yet his thoughts and consciousness remained, to his torment. "Mudien!" he called. "Mudien, help us!" The Caretaker of Ceramir came running. Mudien said no word, but lifted Eleanor as though she weighed nothing and laid her in a bed in the main room. He washed Ilohan in the stream and put him in another bed, beside his mother's.

"Whatever has happened, have peace, true prince," he said. "Your mother will live, and so will you. You came in time, and God has not chosen to end here your pilgrimage upon the earth. Drink this."

The medicine was bitter, but seemed to Ilohan to be good in an elusive sense that was deeper than mere pleasant taste. When it was gone he hoped he would fall unconscious, but this relief did not come. Now and again his fear would rise in a terrifying, thought-confusing wave, but each wave passed and still he neither died nor slept. The worst torment to him was the memory of his mother's fall, and how he had failed to save her. He had been intensely aware of the depth of her love and anguish, and had been awed by the power of her prayer. And then, because of him, she had been knocked senseless, losing the ability to show her great love, or send her desperate prayers. Had he destroyed her, he who had thought he rightly risked his life alone?

He moved his feverish hand waveringly across the sheets, and it found hers, still cool and steady, lying on the sheets of the other bed. He held it, and even unconscious she seemed to give him peace. He remembered the Darkness in the chapel at Aaronkal, and rejoiced that he, at least, could still pray. The waves of deadly fear began to weaken, and his prayer for his mother's life, strength, and joy gained peace and power. It wavered only when his physical anguish overwhelmed him, and he cried out desperately to God to help him bear it. So the first morning of his sickness passed, but Ilohan lost all sense of time, for only at the end of each moment of agony did he find the strength to bear the next.

* * *

The king strode into his council room at Aaronkal, stern and confident as ever. His crown gleamed in the light of the fire and candles, and his knights and counselors rose to do him honor. He acknowledged them with a nod, and walked around the shining, dark oak table to take his seat at its head. The knights sat with him, and a smart clatter of swords rang in the room as they did so. He smiled, for he trusted their loyalty for the most part, and tonight he was able for once to believe that his long faithful rule had earned their allegiance.

His voice was grim, however, as he called the council to order. "Noble Knights of Karolan, and Counselors of Aaronkal," he said, "we have as yet no word from the prince."

"Thirty days it has been since he was sent," said the young Knight of Dilgarel. "Six to Luciyr, three searching, eight to cross the desert. That is only seventeen days in all. The eagle should have brought Your Majesty news of his arrival in Ceramir a week ago, at the very latest."

"Even if his travel was somewhat slower than Sir Dilgarel's guesses, he cannot have needed more than twenty days to find his companion and then journey to Ceramir by way of Luciyr," said Tulbur the Steward. "What has become of the rest? Surely he did not search at Luciyr for ten days."

"I am not certain of that, Sir Steward," said the Knight of Metherka. "Prince Ilohan would be reluctant to give up searching unless he had found something."

"Was there anything to find?" asked the Knight of Nildra, a castle in northern Karolan. "Your Majesty has revealed this plan to most of us but seven days ago. Before that I, like all in Karolan, assumed that Princess Eleanor and her son had been lost along with Prince Kindrach. Now we hear that Her Highness escaped from Luciyr on foot, and told Queen Sarah the story of the prince's death, while Your Majesty was a prisoner in Guldorak. But Princess Eleanor was sick and sorely hurt, and had lately been delirious. Can we be sure she understood what had happened? Even if she did, why should we think Fingar did not recover the prince's body from Luciyr? It seems strange to me that Your Majesty did not cause the valley to be searched many years ago."

"I gave my daughter to a prince," said old Sir Britheldore very slowly in his gruff voice. "For many years all have thought she died with him, and at the king's command I have not spoken. In silence and secrecy I have waited, and few and short have been the times that I have seen her. Long did she wish that she had died with her prince; then at last she triumphed. Let none mistrust her word." He was the only one present older than the king, and he spoke with a calm, forgiving sorrow that caused many to turn to him glances of surprise mixed with reverence.

"The plan has always been a strange one," said the steward. "The king is my witness that my counsel was against it from the first, yet I have served him long and faithfully in pursuing it."

"Peace," said the king. Although his voice was not loud, the firm command rang in the room in the sudden silence that followed it. "Long ago that choice was Eleanor's, and Sarah's, and mine. For long years it has been made, and irrevocable. We come here not to say if it was made for good or ill, but to say what new choices shall follow. Sir Britheldore, for your sorrow I am sorry. I will send you to Ceramir again before the war.

"Sir Nildra, you ask why Fingar left the body of Prince Kindrach at Luciyr. Consider, then, the moments after Kindrach's death. He had killed many of his foes, and wounded more. I believe he had even wounded Fingar – at least, that craven was limping from a thigh wound when I confronted him at Guldorak. The princess was fleeing. Kindrach, in dying, had fallen into the lake. Fingar had to secure the capture of the princess, and his own safety. Would he have commanded any of his knights to brave the icy water of Luciyr to recover Kindrach's body?

"You ask also why I did not order Luciyr searched to find Kindrach's body. Not to do so would have been folly – as foolish as your assumption that I did not. I sent out a party as soon as I reached Aaronkal and heard what the queen had to tell me – but my searchers did not find what they sought. Fingar the liar had said my son's body was burned; Eleanor the truthful that he had fallen into the lake. My men found clear traces of blood, the blood of more than one man, on the rock where Eleanor said the fight took place. They saw no marks of fire anywhere. They did burn a corpse themselves: that of the prince's horse, which the Norkaths had killed with an axe-blow and left to rot. Autumn had come on quickly in the high valley, and the lake was frozen: they could not search for a body beneath the ice. For a year I had all the approaches to the lake ceaselessly watched. Fingar never dared attempt to disturb the bones of his victim. In his eyes I have seen a murderer's guilty fear.

"Prince Ilohan is a true knight, dauntless in the face of hardship and diligent in pursuing his duty. I commanded him to search thoroughly. Unless some evil befell him on the road to Luciyr, I am confident that he has found what my old search did not. As is fitting, he has been the first to touch his father's bones, and to trace out the history of his last fight.

There was a silence, and then Britheldore's slow voice broke it gently. "Your Majesty, I thank you for saying that I may go to Ceramir once more. My heart longs to see Eleanor again before I die, with secrecy no longer needed. But I will not leave you, not now in the hour of your need."

King Thomas bowed to him. "I thank you, Sir," he said. "You are faithful beyond hope and duty."

In the long silence that followed, many searched the old king's face for any sign of his thoughts, but found it still and unreadable as a stone. The silence was broken when three loud raps sounded on the heavy oak door. "Enter!" said King Thomas.

A herald bearing a spear stood aside, and two men hooded and cloaked head to foot in dull brown clothes entered. "Bring chairs for them," said the king. "And bread and wine to refresh them."

They moved slowly, as if very weary; gratefully they took their seats and ate their bread with wine. At last they pushed back their hoods, revealing strong, bearded faces and calm, shrewd eyes. "What have you to report?" asked the king.

"The men of Norkath are mustering in every town and village to train for war," said the first of the spies. "The smallest hamlet in the nation yet supplies a few armed men for the conquest of Karolan."

"The men are armed poorly for the most part," said the other spy, "yet day by day we saw them with better weapons in their hands. Fingar is arming them from somewhere. Every forge in the land must be hot with the making of swords and spears, and many trees have been felled to build siege engines, and to make lances, bows, and arrows."

"Have you learned anything of the council of Fingar himself?" asked King Thomas.

The first spy smiled. "Many knights of Norkath, riding along the roads of the realm in twos or threes, paid no heed to the dusty, hooded paupers who trotted near them for protection. The paupers listened well. The knights talked of inspiring the men with tales of the gold, land, and women of Karolan. They also spoke of the king of Karolan, a dotard on his last bed, soon to leave the world."

"Fools!" said the other man. "They spoke of King Thomas as a feeble old man, and Karolan as a ripe fruit soon to fall into the iron-gloved hand of Fingar. Only a precious few (and they were scorned) advised caution, saying that the king might yet live long, and that the people of Karolan were never known for softness."

"And some," went on the first spy, "said that it mattered little if our people were hard or soft, our army large or small. They said that the force Fingar would muster would be the largest seen since Dradrag the Zarnith pillaged Cembar; that the men of Karolan would be swept away before it, regardless of their numbers or their strength. Some even dared speak against Fingar as a coward, saying he should invade Karolan without waiting for the news of the king's death. Most disagreed with these, however, saying (forsworn fools that they are) that Prince Kindrach's vow gave them the right to take Karolan only after the death of its king, and that justice required them to wait."

"How many swords could Fingar muster, and in how many days would they be ready to invade us?" asked King Thomas.

"In six days he could have ten thousand swords at our border," said the first spy. "He could get only so many if he raised his banner at Guldorak today. If he waits but ten days before issuing the call to arms, however, then in six more he might put thrice as many well armed soldiers on the road to Aaronkal."

"Have you anything else to report?" asked the king.

"Nothing," replied the spies.

"I thank you for your service. You may go."

The spies bowed and departed, and the herald closed the great oak door behind them. King Thomas turned to his knights and advisors. "You have heard the tidings of our enemies," he said. "Our danger is great. What do you counsel?"

"If it is true that Fingar will not attack while the king lives," said Dilgarel, "then we have nothing to fear. The army need not be mustered until the prince returns and the king abdicates his throne to him."

"We must have the army already mustered, and at the border, when the king proclaims his abdication," said Britheldore. "If we do not, we are fools."

"The Stone, Sword, and Star should be raised before Aaronkal at sunrise tomorrow," said Metherka. "When has Fingar's word ever been worth trusting?"

"Having the Army of all Karolan assembled before the gates of Aaronkal is a costly precaution," said the steward. "It is no light matter to feed a host of twenty thousand men. Our army might starve away before the war. I council an envoy to Guldorak, bearing the white flag, to ask Fingar for terms of peace."

"No terms that we could justly grant would be accepted, Sir Steward," said the king. "Fingar will not end his reign without another war."

"All hangs on one question." The voice of Britheldore, even more deep and slow than it had been before, brought silence to the room. "Where is the prince?"

"Why do you say that all hangs on that?" asked Nildra after a pause.

"Men fight when a prince leads them," said Britheldore. "His very sight brings courage and kindles will. A prince means hope, and hope is a thing worth dying for."

"It is true," said King Thomas. "The prince must come."

"Yet he has been gone for many days," said the steward. "It may be that he has perished."

"If he is dead, then all is lost," said King Thomas.

Britheldore looked intently at the king in response to these words. A swift shadow seemed to cross the king's face – swift, but dark, as though for an instant his iron will had failed. King Thomas recovered himself so quickly that Britheldore guessed that he alone had seen his brief despair. Yet what he had seen made the old knight wonder how wrong the Norkaths were who said that the king of Karolan had not long to live.

"Even lost men must live and act," said the steward. "If the prince is dead, Your Majesty must appoint a new successor, and make terms of peace with Fingar."

"Or fight him to the end," said Metherka fiercely. Britheldore smiled at the young knight sadly, and shook his head.

"I would draw this council shortly to an end," said the king. "Here are my decisions: I will not call the Army of all Karolan to assemble before the gates of Aaronkal, only to starve there. Before I raise my standard, I must have clear knowledge when the war will come. Our spies will inform us the instant Fingar raises the banner of the Fist of Iron at Guldorak, and at that moment I will gather the host of Karolan. Until then we will wait for news of the prince, watch carefully all the doings of our enemy – and pray."

"Surely my prayers will join with yours, Your Majesty," said the steward. "But we cannot wait for the prince forever, while the forces of Norkath grow ever stronger. Soon or late, we must take action."

"Steward, you speak beyond your right!" said the king sternly and sharply.

"It is my duty and my right to give you the wisest of my counsel in all things, Your Majesty," said the steward. "Yet forgive me if I spoke too boldly, answering a question you had never asked. I only meant to say that, though you end the council now, another will be needed soon."

"You are in the right, Sir Steward," said King Thomas. "It is my decree that this council will be held again, in seven days' time, if in that time there has been no word from the prince. If word comes from him, then of course the council shall assemble at once."

"May I have leave to speak once more, Your Majesty?" asked the steward.

"You may," said the king.

"I counsel Your Majesty to shorten the time until another council is held. It is my thought that seven days is too long. Things may be very dire indeed if nothing is heard from the prince, and we wait so long to act."

"You would have them shortened to five?"

"Yes, Your Majesty, or even four, perhaps."

"It shall not be so. My decree of seven stands." The king's words were imperious, and he rose from his place and stood regally beside his chair at the head of the table. "This council is ended. I thank you for your service, and I bid you all rest well."

The knights and advisors rose, saluted, and filed out of the room. Tulbur the Steward seemed inclined to linger, but when he glanced at King Thomas and was met instantly by the monarch's own stony gaze, he departed in silence.

The king was left alone in the council chamber. He drew his great sword, and rested its point flatly on the table before him. The lights of candles and torches gleamed and flashed from the polished metal of the keen blade. "Once again, I go to war," he said. "Whether I sheath or wield this sword, much that is lovely must perish, and much that is good depart from the world. Tulbur would have me be cautious, sue for peace at the cost of some great ransom. That price might well be less grievous than a war, but it would mean freely yielding to tyranny and evil. Must I not stand for justice, whatever the cost? God, I wish another had been king! Would that Kindrach held this blade. Then Norkath would tremble, with cause! But it cannot be; you have not chosen it to be, my Lord. Let my days on this earth end shortly, but let me first set this crown on the head of a good and mighty prince."

He walked with a swift, firm step to his bedchamber, took off his robe and crown, extinguished the candles, and lay down. His voice came through the darkness once more before he slept, yet had his knights and counselors heard that voice, they might well not have known it. "Ilohan... Ilohan, prince of all our hopes... Ilohan, last memory of departed Sarah, last echo of Kindrach's might. Oh, God, do not let him die. Do not let him fail… Do not…"

* * *

Eleanor awoke on the afternoon of the second day of Ilohan's sickness. Imranie was watching her then, and rejoiced when her eyes opened, for they were clear and focused. "Are you well, beloved friend?" she asked.

"I wish I were not," said Eleanor in a dull voice. That voice sent a dagger of cold fear into Imranie's heart. She had not heard it in a score of years. It was the voice of the shattered princess who had come to Ceramir so long ago, more deeply hurt than any other person Imranie had ever known. She knelt beside her bed.

"What is wrong, Eleanor?" she asked. "Ilohan is sleeping calmly, and will surely live, and your own injury did not seem to me severe. You slept so long more from the herbs we gave you than from the blow to your head."

"Ilohan is dead," said Eleanor. "All joy and hope has fallen from my world, and still my God requires me to live. I do not want to obey him or trust him. So all I have and am is lost."

Imranie was silent for a moment. She prayed very quickly about what she should do. "Does it matter what you want?" she asked.

"It matters if I find that all I thought I was, the burning faith and love I thought I had, is only a vapor that cannot stand the test," said Eleanor.

"But is it indeed a vapor?" asked Imranie. "You have spoken of what you want. What will you do?"

"I should carry on in faith, although I have no joy, and try still to serve and bless those who yet live," said Eleanor. "I do not want to."

"What will you do, Eleanor?"

Eleanor cried hopelessly and unrestrainedly for a long time. Imranie waited patiently. Yet when the tears had ceased the princess slept. Imranie looked at her pityingly, offered yet another loving prayer for her, and walked softly to the door of the house.

She smiled. Children were playing on one of the rope swings, and Veril was watching over them. The sunlight streaming through the trees made swirling shafts of light in the wisps of mist that rose from the warm lake. Jonathan was climbing the highest rope, already at a dizzying height above the water. Finally he pushed himself away from the rope and fell, to land with a gigantic splash that sprayed sparkling water high into the sunny air. Imranie smiled again. Jonathan had had little to do in the last two days, for Ilohan had been the last person to fall sick. Though he still kept watch, hope burned bright in Ceramir that the plague was now defeated. Six had died, but perhaps all the rest would live, and no more would catch the deadly contagion.

* * *

Jonathan stood beside Ilohan's bed in the late evening in Ceramir. He was tired with a good weariness, from his wild revels of the last two days in the Cloth of Joy. He had exulted in the growing hope, the rising tide of joy that flowed through Ceramir as its children realized that once again the plague had fallen before the onslaught of life and love. Yet throughout his playing, the thought of Ilohan, said to be certain of recovery, yet presently very sick indeed, and the thought of Rennel, said to be in Paradise but really lost in nothingness forever, had dimmed even his vibrant joy. He gazed pityingly at his royal friend now. The candlelight flickered over Ilohan's drawn face, and gleamed in the beads of feverish sweat on his brow.

"Can you hear me, Your Majesty?" asked Jonathan. "I wish that I could give to you my strength."

Ilohan spoke with difficulty, pausing often to draw labored breaths. "I thank you. I cannot thank you as I would for such friendship. Indeed my own strength is…" he laughed a short, bitter laugh, "…very little. Yet in God it shall be enough."

"They say you will surely recover," said Jonathan

"I cannot say if it is true or false, yet I trust them," replied the prince.

"It is true, and will be soon!" said Jonathan. "I will see you crowned at Aaronkal, with three score thousand voices roaring out approval, joy, and hope."

"I do not see how that could ever be," whispered Ilohan. "But let it pass… I have no desire for such a thing."

"So be it, Ilohan. You will receive it nonetheless. Yet now, sleep well. You will heal soon. I will trouble you with speech no longer."

"Sleep is now only a mockery of rest… There is no true escape in it."

"I am sorry," said Jonathan. "Do you not want to sleep, then?"

"No… Speak to me, friend, if you wish to, and though I will not answer, yet I shall be glad to hear. Tell me of hopes of good things… of, if you are willing, Naomi and Carrah."

So Jonathan sat beside his bed, and spoke in a low voice of the bright future he hoped for. He spoke of Aaronkal with the banners of Karolan waving bright in the sun from its towers, and of the great army spread out below it, bristling with swords. He spoke of the advance to the border, and the fearful onslaught of the Norkath foe, which despite its strength was utterly defeated, surrendering before half a morning's fighting had gone by, and while full a third the swords of Karolan had seen no blood. He spoke of the great rule of King Ilohan, during which all Karolan would flourish, and many wrongs would be healed, and many battles fought and won.

Ilohan listened, and the words seemed to him a bright fable, like a rainbow in a cloud, while the reality of what would happen was a hard, rugged mountain silhouetted black against the sky. He was sure that jagged shadow did not foretell that he would ever wear the crown of Kindrach or Thomas, and he doubted very much that any golden age for Karolan was outlined in its stone-hard realness. He liked it better when Jonathan spoke of Naomi.

Jonathan told how she and he ran with bright joy through the sweet smelling, golden grass. They dreamed of living, married, in a new cottage together at the very top of the glen where no other dwellings were. She was more worthy of love than anyone in the world. She was full of life, vibrant and pure, deep, real, and joyful.

Ilohan began to understand how deep was Jonathan's love for her. At first his heart rejoiced, even though sometimes his pain rose so strong that he could barely hear Jonathan's words. He saw more clearly than before how he and Jonathan were different. He delighted in the passionate intensity of Jonathan's love, and deeply desired for his hope to be fulfilled.

Then great fear fell on Ilohan, for he realized that Jonathan loved Naomi and desired her more than he himself loved and desired anyone, save, he hoped, God alone. And though he could not lose God, Jonathan could lose Naomi. When King

Thomas died, Karolan would go to war. A war to secure his crown. A war that could cost Jonathan his love, his hope, his life, his soul. The awful responsibility terrified him. Perhaps it would be better if he died. Yet would his death prevent the war that threatened? He did not know. The pain of his sickness made thought difficult, and even Jonathan's bright words were sometimes lost in his weakness and agony.

"God," he prayed, "do not let Naomi die. Give to my friend Jonathan the life that he dreams of. Do not let this war destroy the beauty he has known, or that he hopes for. Let them be married in a blessed land at peace. Do with me and my crown as you will, but please spare my people – oh, Father, it seems arrogant even to say such things... My crown... My people... How can they ever be? Lord, I give them to you; them and myself. Save my mother, I pray, and bring her joy."

He did not know how she was. There was so much he did not know or understand. His sickness had confused his senses and wearied his thought. He cried softly and brokenly for a long time.

Jonathan saw his tears, and stopped talking. When he stopped weeping, it seemed to Jonathan that he slept. Jonathan walked softly away, searched all through the Valley of the Undismayed once, reported to Mudien that all except those already in sickbeds were well, and went to sleep himself.

Mudien asked Brogal to take Jonathan's task, for although the danger was growing less with every passing day he did not think it wise to dispense with the watchman yet. He was weary as he walked the candlelit and firelit rooms of the house. They were winning, yes, as with God's help they had always won, yet the battle was long and hard. Many who were desperately ill now would need close tending for many days to come. Some there were, indeed, whose lives still hung uneasily in the balance. It might be very long before there was another banquet in Ceramir.

Yet he raised his large gray head, and looked with clear eyes up into the future. They were winning. The time was not far off when they would say, "Praise God, we have won!" They were not dismayed, and never would be. Ceramir rested in the hand of God, who loved his children.

He stopped by Eleanor's bed, where she lay not far from her plague-stricken son. She had been unconscious for far too long, he thought. The fall had not been severe; he had no fear for her on that ground. He knew why she had slept for two days and most of the third. She did not want to face the knowledge she thought waking would bring. She thought that Ilohan was dead. Why she thought this he did not know, but Imranie did. Imranie understood Eleanor better than he, and in this case that understanding was deeply needed. Eleanor stirred and groaned; Mudien thought she would wake soon.

He walked softly into a dark room where those who were well were sleeping, and laid a hand on his wife's shoulder. She was deeply and tranquilly asleep, and he did not like to wake her, yet he felt he must. He gently shook her until she opened her eyes. "I am sorry to wake you, Beloved," he said. "But Eleanor is waking, and I think you should be near her. You know better than I what she needs."

"Ah, my sleep was sweet," said Imranie. "Yet you were right to wake me. I will go to her, and God help me when she wakes. It is a dark path indeed that our princess is treading." Imranie stood slowly, and made her way out of the dark room and into the candlelit sickroom where Eleanor lay. She felt as she often had when sudden need woke her in the dead of night: as if she were cleansed of bustle and confusion, blessed with clearer vision and a more tranquil heart to face her task. She prayed deeply for Eleanor as she knelt beside her bed.

The princess was lying very still, but Imranie could tell she was awake. Her face held great, almost despairing sorrow, but also a kind of peace. Imranie put a gentle arm beneath her head, and, lifting back the clean white covers, embraced her compassionately. "Wake up, beloved friend," she said. "Let the love of God, and the love of those who love you bring you joy. Willingly I would share your grief."

"You spoke of a choice, Imranie," said Eleanor softly. "You asked what I would do. I have chosen. I do not know how to carry on, but I do not need to know. I trust. I will take the life that God has given me, and... and he will be with me to uphold me. But... but even now I do not know how to go on." Eleanor cried, calmly and without noise, for a long time. "I have given him up," she said at last. "I do not know how to carry on."

Imranie lifted her gently, and supported her in a sitting position on the bed. Ilohan lay before her. He was very sick, and often tossed or groaned in his sleep, but he was alive. "He will live," said Imranie. "Your joy has not been taken from you, beloved Eleanor. God loves you, and has not let your son be lost to you. Yet he has proved you and found you true, because you have not withheld from him your son, your only son. Remember that you have given Ilohan to God, and that he belongs to him forever. And rejoice – oh, Eleanor, rejoice! – that he is alive, and will be well. He will be the greatest king that Karolan has ever known. I know it."

"He is alive?" breathed Eleanor. "They told me a thousand times, a thousand ways, that he was dead. It was all lies? God has saved him? Oh, Imranie..." Imranie embraced her, and she cried long and freely on her friend's shoulder. Both felt they would have been content for that moment to last forever.

Eleanor was weak from having starved for nearly three days, and Imranie made her a bowl of warm, good soup. She ate it slowly and gratefully, sitting on her bed beside her friend, and never taking her eyes off the living, breathing form of her son. Imranie softly left her to return to bed, but Eleanor remained, watching her son until dawn began to glow dimly through the shuttered windows. Then she rose quietly and got a cup of water from a huge stone jar that was kept just outside the house.

The dawn twilight was cold and deep above her, and the mist off the lake seemed full of good mysteries as it spun and sailed up beneath the autumn trees to lose itself in the calm morning air. Eleanor drank deeply of the clean, cold water, before going inside to take up her forgotten task of tending the sick. But she found she was still too weak to work, so she sank gratefully down on her bed, and fell into a deep sleep free of lying dreams.

Chapter 20

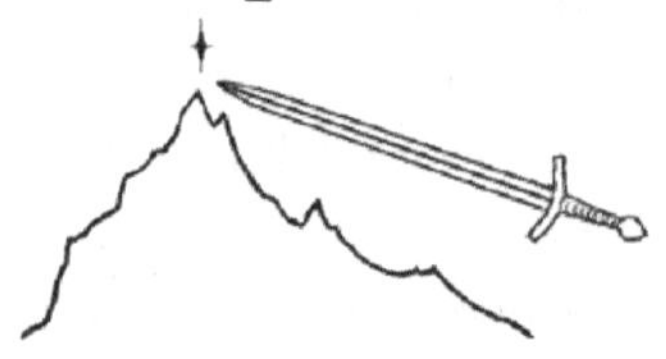

Joy of the Dawn

DAYS PASSED, DAYS OF BRILLIANT SKIES; OF BLUE, cloudless space; of cool winds; and of autumn leaves that fell in bright flurries to the misty lake. Jonathan reveled in them. His body never failed to answer to his will, and his great strength seemed to burn with a strong but harmless fire within him, bringing him joy as he exulted in it and in the Cloth of Joy. His frolics had no violence in them, only a great exuberance. Even Rangol could scarcely surpass him at swinging on the rope, or climbing the great trees, or swimming and diving in the warm lake.

He felt pity and sorrow for Ilohan's pain and sickness, but that only tempered his joy. Without it he would have felt that he was in Paradise, and would have mistrusted the feeling. No more people died or sickened in the Valley, and though he sometimes reproached himself for recovering so quickly from Rennel's death, he always found in the end that his joy could not be refused. He would not force her from his memory, and when he thought of her he let the thought sober him. Yet soon it would sink again beneath the current of bright joy. He was young, deeply in love, strong and fearless in a valley that was made for joy. For those few days he was among the

Undismayed, and seemed a son of both Ceramir and Glen Carrah. He wished Naomi could be with him, yet she was in his mind and heart, and he could not believe that she, who was so much a part of him, could fail to share in his joy.

* * *

On the seventh day of Ilohan's sickness, four days after the night when Eleanor recovered, Veril and Auria were standing together on the platform of the lower rope, watching the children swing in the bright cool afternoon. Neither wore a blue cap, for both had avoided contact with any who had the plague. Auria had been ordered to do so by Eleanor, and Veril had avoided the sick since Mudien had banned her from working as a healer. Thus they were able to watch over the children, without fear of bringing them disease.

Auria looked carefully at her sister Veril, with concern in her bright-eyed glance. "You look as though you have a stomach ache, Veril," she said. "But I know you do not. What is wrong? In your eyes I can see tears that you will not let out."

"Auria, will you watch the children alone?"

"Of course I will, Veril, if you wish, but will you not tell me what is wrong?"

Auria got no answer, for Veril was running around the lake toward the house before her sister had even finished speaking. She broke into a hurried walk half way around, and soon stood trembling at the door. It was Eleanor who greeted her. The princess looked at her an instant, took her by the hand, and directed her to a chair by the fire. Eleanor herself followed, on her crutches, and sat down in another chair facing her.

"Now Veril," she said, "tell me what is the matter."

"I wish I knew better myself. I... I am afraid you will not like it."

"Tell me, Veril. You cannot lose my love, and I pray I have not lost yours."

"No indeed, you have not, Lady Eleanor, it is only... I think I love Ilohan."

Eleanor's face became grave. "And you feared I would be jealous. That was no unreasoned fear. I had hoped, for these few days, my only son might be mine alone, that I might requite in days the futile longing of so many years. But Ilohan is not mine, Veril – he is God's. If you truly love him I would rejoice to have him love you, and to watch your friendship deepen in the few days given you. Yet..."

Eleanor was silent for a long while, and looked lovingly at Veril, who sat very serious and still with her hands folded in her lap. "You barely know Ilohan," she said at last. "How can you be sure you love him, and not some imagined picture of him that your mind has made?"

"The time has been short, dear Eleanor, but so much has happened in it that I think I do know him – more than barely. He is faithful, brave and strong, yet he feels deeply and is easily hurt. I want happiness and blessing for him more than for anyone else. I feel that I understand your stories as I could not before – that I know how you felt when you watched the sunrise over Castle Britheldore with Kindrach for the first time. I think... Oh, Eleanor, is it possible that I might bless him or bring him joy? I want to try to find out, to learn if he delights in me, if he might come to love me. May I watch by his bedside with you, and be with him when he awakes?"

Eleanor looked at her a long time. A thousand things ran through the faithful princess's mind and heart. She thought of the morning when she had given a stranger whom she had known for only a night the priceless sword that was her dowry. She thought of the starlit nights on the parapets of Castle Britheldore, and of their hopes and dreams as they walked on the crunching ice. She thought of her two years in Aaronkal as Kindrach's wife, the princess of Karolan. She had blessed her prince, and brought him joy, she knew, and their love had been worth all it ever cost or ever could have cost. She took Veril's hand between both her own. "You may watch with me, Veril," she said, "and God bless you."

* * *

"I am well, Ilohan, and God has brought me joy. Rest and recover, my son, and I will rejoice in your waking." Those words, spoken in Eleanor's voice, cut through the red fog of Ilohan's feverish dreamworld. A great peace came over his heart for an instant, and then he sunk again into agony and confusion.

A band of iron circled around his head, and it was hot, and burned him. He longed to take it off, but his duty to the stars was to wear it. The stars looked down on him, and did not care that their orders hurt him. They were so bright and high, and cruel and heartless, that his suffering mattered nothing to them. He wandered far, searching for something cool, to ease the burning of the crown of iron he wore, but he found only heat. Trees aflame arched over a boiling lake, and toads and rats, bloated and dead, fouled the roiling water and spun in the bubbling currents.

The desert was endless and waterless. The sun was dark red and dim, but still the land broiled beneath it. Slowly it sank below the castle wall, and the moon rose on the other side of the sky. But the moon was blue, and instead of light or heat it gave forth cold and darkness, and he was frozen to the bone. He tried to make his way to the castle, and he found it, and King Thomas was standing with Sarah on the steps. But before he reached them, he saw the king raise his hand and strike the queen, and she fell at his feet crying. Ilohan ran forward to help her, but the king kicked her and then went away, and when Ilohan reached her she was dead.

He felt a hand on his shoulder, and looked up to see Jonathan. He told Jonathan about the terrible cruelty of the stars and the king, but Jonathan only called him a fool and dragged him to his feet, telling him to keep walking or they would never get to Ceramir. But he could not walk. He was too tired, too hot, it had been too long, too long…

He felt a cool touch on his hand, and it seemed to him that new hope came to him. Perhaps he did not have to walk, perhaps this warm river that wrapped around him would carry him where he must go. There was a comforting, soft and gentle light above him, and a voice that he had never heard before was singing. The sound was a delight to hear, and the river kept carrying him, though now it seemed very strange to him that a river should be made of woven wool. The stars that had been so cruel faded a little, or smiled, and he began to hear the words of the song:

So long has the darkness been, all forget hope and the day.
The stars but a feeble hope give – dim and ice-colored ray.
We fear what lurks in the night, right indeed are we to fear:
They killed and hunted us hard, shattered many we held dear.

Tired eyes, look now over there, truth, is this hope but a dream?
Darkness has reigned for so long; say, is that vision a gleam?
Graying, it floods the black sky; softly, the faithful stars fade!
Wonder, a miracle glows! Oh! Let its loss be delayed.

Stars now surrender their beams, lost in a sky filling glow.
Tremble lest this joy should fade, lest the broad, bright hope should go.
Fade it does not, but grows more, hinting of color unknown:
Blue, deep blue upon blue, reap we hope where we have not sown.

Relent! – No more can we bear, lovely, so pure, and so strong,
Light we cannot comprehend, dark we have lived for so long.
Merciless, dazzling joy, still shall the brilliant light grow:
Color too deep for our words, bright beyond all that we know!

Yellow, the mighty east glows, bright blue the heavens above.
Piercing the blinding bright light, yet in its power is love.
Red, clear like water made fire, rises up now in the east;
Eyes that know night squint in pain, starved beggars balk at the feast.

Revel in pow'r that o'erpow'rs, dare to stare Dawn in the eye,
Naming the wonder at last, love it, in bliss live or die:
Made were our hearts for the light, see, feel the hope that it brings.
Hidden far from us, and light, now are all dark, terror-things!

Look, now the east blazes white, like a diamond set all aflame.
Crimson, yellow fade into the light, pure, brilliant, intense, clean, it came.
Brighter still grows the great east; dazzles the keenest of sight.
Cleft twixt two black mountain peaks, fills with star-core, molten light.

Beams in the air bending low, tell of the light soon to come;
Climax of climax draws near, herald needs no trumpet or drum.
Piercing light brighter still grows – brilliant, impossible, – done!
Bright, bright, now brighter than bright, glorious rises the sun!

Hope that we trembled to lose; joy that we scarce dared to gain;
Ending of night that we feared; day that brought light that brought pain:
Stand we now clean and bright, healed; fearless and strong, seeing clear,
Hope that we looked for fulfilled, Triumph of triumphs now here.

Ilohan felt that he was rising swiftly, through layer upon layer of delirious nightmare, until at last he broke the surface into reality and breathed grateful breaths of air. He opened his eyes. The windows were open, and the fresh air and sunlight of full morning in Ceramir streamed in. There was a bad taste in his mouth, but the air in his lungs was sweet. He breathed deeply and swallowed, and shifted his limbs in the bed. Their weakness astonished him, but so did his comfort. He lay still, delighting in his freedom from pain.

He felt a touch on his left hand, and looked up to see that Veril was standing beside his bed. She looked very pale, and there were dark circles beneath her eyes, but she smiled at him. He returned her smile, expecting her to speak. After a long silence in which she only looked at him, he spoke instead, not caring that his voice sounded like a croak in his ears. "Was it you I heard singing while I was still asleep?"

Veril looked puzzled for a moment, and then said, "I sang the song we call Joy of the Dawn just before sunrise, but now the sun is high and you have just awakened."

"The time must have shortened in my mind," he said. "The song was very beautiful, and brought me hope."

She smiled again, shyly. "I thought that you were too delirious to know. I am glad I was wrong."

"My dreams were very terrible," he said, and then stopped suddenly, startled by the shadow of horror that passed across her face. He went on after it had passed. "Is all well with Jonathan, and Thomas, and Sarah? Can you comfort me concerning them?"

"Jonathan is well, and rejoices in Ceramir," said Veril. "The children of Ceramir love him, and he has helped them in the fight against the plague. Thomas, at last news of him, was well, and very proud to send his grandson, the young Prince Ilohan, to Ceramir. Sarah –" Veril bowed her head sadly, and raised it with tears in her eyes. "Sarah is dead, and I cannot bear to think how much her loss has hurt you."

"How did she die?" asked Ilohan.

"She had been sick for two months," said Veril, "but she had hidden it from most, and gone about very cheerfully. One day the sickness overcame her, and she could not rise from her bed. A week later she died, with Ilohan and Thomas near her. They loved her to the last, and she them, and in her death, though it was not – though it was not easy, she was brave, patient, and kind."

Silent tears ran down Ilohan's face into his pillow, and yet he smiled. He saw that Veril also was crying, and the soft splashing of her tears on the stone floor told him more of her kind sympathy than the most eloquent words. "I thank you," he said. "As you have told it, so it was in my memory – but in the dreams of my sickness it was otherwise."

She wiped her eyes, and looked down at him, smiling.

Fear suddenly returned to him. "What of Eleanor?" he asked. "I heard her voice tell me all was well with her, but perhaps that also was a dream. Is she well?"

"Yes, Ilohan," said Veril. "She is very well. Her fall did her no lasting harm, and for three days now she has been tending the sick as she did before. She would have been here to see you wake, but she was called urgently away to pray for another whose recovery is less hopeful than your own. Soon she will come to you."

"Your words dispel the darkness of my fears, Veril," said Ilohan. "I thank you! But what of yourself? You are very pale and tired, so that I even fear the plague for you. But even if you are well, you must soon sleep – see, you have just now wavered on your feet."

Veril steadied herself, a hand against the stone wall behind her. "I am well," she said, "only weary."

"As indeed she should be," came the voice of Eleanor, accompanied by the cheerful sound of her crutches on the hard stone floor. "She has stayed up all night long, and wept, and prayed, and hoped. She was never made to tend the sick, for their pain hurts her too deeply, and the good that she can do them costs too much. Yet she has watched by your bed from the afternoon of yesterday till now." At the sound of his mother's voice, Ilohan's joy soared like an eagle in the sun.

But Eleanor turned to Veril, and saw that she leaned heavily against the wall, and her head was bowed. "Dear child," said the princess, "though your heart rejoices in the moments, and regrets to let them pass, you must sleep. You do not know the depth of your own weariness."

"You are right," said Veril. "Lead me to a bed, please, Lady Eleanor."

Eleanor led her into another room, gave her a drink of something warm, and put her to bed. She returned to Ilohan's bedside with her heart singing. She took his right hand between both of her own. Unable to trust her voice, she whispered. "God has saved you, Ilohan. God has restored you to me. He is very good."

He smiled at her, but his smile faded. "Mother, I cannot bear the knowledge that I made you fall," he said. "I tried to save you, but only pushed you down yet harder. Can you forgive me?"

She knelt carefully beside the bed and took him in her arms. "Beloved Ilohan, you wrong me that you ask. It was my frantic despair that made us fall, and my grief would have been the greater if you had been injured rather than I. All that matters is that you are alive, and soon will be well." She hugged him tightly, and he embraced her with his weakened arms.

Finally she laid him back on the bed, and looked long into his face. Dark circles were around his eyes, and his bones stood out far more clearly than they had a week ago. She could still see in his features and his eyes traces left by delirious nightmares and relentless pain. The pain had been intense, and his danger real, yet he had borne the pain, and escaped the danger. She had surrendered him to God, and he had blessed her and given him back. "I love you, Ilohan," she said. "Thank God that I have you to love!"

"And I love you, Mother," he said. "The worst of my nightmares were those in which I found Mudien had lied to me, and you were dead. Now in truth you are alive and happy!"

"Is there anything you want, Ilohan?" asked Eleanor.

"I would like to eat," he said, "if that can be, and also to lie in the sun outside and talk with you."

Eleanor called for Karlak, and Ilohan felt the young man lift him gently. He carried him out to a couch beside the lake. Ilohan lay there looking up at windblown treetops framed by the immeasurable depth of the sky, and knew that he was healed. Eleanor brought him a small bowl of soup – very difficult for her to do with her crutches – and sat down on the grass beside him. He ate the soup slowly, enjoying it with a humble, awed intensity, as if eating were a new, unheard-of privilege and pleasure. Talking with his mother seemed the same to him; her presence at his side a miracle beyond all dreams. They talked quietly and happily, long into the bright cool afternoon.

* * *

Ilohan's rising, healthy hunger woke him very early the next morning, while Veril and most others were still asleep. Eleanor was awake. She came to him carrying a basket, carefully and slowly with her crutches, and sat down in a chair beside his bed. When he saw that she had brought him a hot breakfast, he thanked her gratefully and sat up in bed with an effort. There was a large bowl of soup, and thick slices of fresh, soft bread, which he ate with great enjoyment.

"You have labored to prepare this," he said to her. "Did you sleep at all?"

"I slept enough," she said, and indeed, with her sparkling eyes and cheerful face she looked as though she had. "I guessed, however, that you would wake early, and wanted to have food ready for you when you did."

"I thank you, Mother."

They sat together awhile in silence, while the cool morning brightened from blue to gold outside the half-shuttered windows. Finally he broke the silence. "Why did Veril stay with me?" he asked.

"She thinks she loves you, Ilohan."

"Do you think she does?"

Eleanor was silent for a moment, and Ilohan guessed she was praying for wisdom. "I think she almost loves you now, in the sense that you mean," she said at last, "and that she will soon, if you let her. What are your thoughts toward her?"

Ilohan was silent awhile in his turn. The question was not easy to answer. "I want to believe I love her," he said. "But I remember that my first desire for her was in lust, and I am afraid, lest my feelings now be only lust disguised as love."

"Was your first desire for her in lust?" asked Eleanor. "Was it not another thing?"

"I suppose my first desire was for her rescue, that is, to help her," he said. "I did not lust for her until later. Even then I fled temptation swiftly. But I was vulnerable to it, and am still."

"That does not mean you are incapable of love, Ilohan. Indeed, you have proven that you love her in one sense, for you have mourned her hurt and sought to spare her when you could."

"That is the sense in which I ought to love everyone." He lay back and raised a trembling hand to open wide the shutters and gaze up at the morning sky. "I want to know if I love her as a man should love his wife," he said. "I am afraid of fixing my heart too soon, on the first young woman that it finds."

"Be patient and compassionate, Ilohan," said Eleanor. "Your caution is wise. You cannot know yet if you love her as a husband should; you do not know her well enough. But you can seek to know her better."

"That I have great desire to do," he said.

"Then your desire matches her own," said Eleanor.

"I am glad," said Ilohan. He stretched in bed. "How good it is to feel my strength returning! I wonder if I will be able to walk today."

Princess Eleanor smiled. "I think you will, beloved son. Your hope is strong, and you have much to live for. Soon you will walk with Veril in the lovely woods of Ceramir, and I will stand beside the lake and watch with joy and prayer."

There was a patient sadness in her voice, and Ilohan looked intently into her face to find out why. He learned it quickly. "You would give these days you hoped would be your own to Veril, Mother, would you not?" he asked. "I will see to it that they are yet almost fully yours – if you want them, for I do not know why my presence brings you joy."

"I love you, Ilohan, and these days when I can speak with you seem to me to have fallen out of Heaven. Yet you must do what seems best to you, what, before God, you think is good and wise."

"Mother, I will."

They talked a little longer, and then she brought him fresh clothes and a towel. He crawled cautiously into the warm brook, and washed himself carefully there, then dried himself and put on the clean clothes. It was wonderful to him to be free from the filth of his sickness, and he sat gratefully on the hard stone floor beside the fire, reveling in the living heat that beat upon his clean, damp skin. Finally he looked up at Eleanor, who was leaning against a corner of the room. He took a deep breath. "I think I can stand now, Mother," he said.

"Be careful, Ilohan," she said, "you may be weaker than you know."

He was weaker than he knew. It cost him a concentrated effort to raise himself, but he did it. At last he stood on the hard stone floor, before the warm fire, trembling and breathing hard. He did not fall, and as he waited, his balance became surer. With wondering steps he made his way across the room to her, and then they walked together out into the early sunshine on the warm grass. They leaned against a small tree that grew there; Eleanor dropped her crutches and they embraced. Then they sat back on the soft green grass and laughed.

Veril and Mudien came out to meet them. "I am just going to bed, Lady Eleanor," said Mudien. "I imagine Karlak and Imranie will care for the sick today?"

"Yes indeed," said Eleanor. "Today I am called to other labors."

"To which I leave you with great joy," said Mudien. "I will send out breakfast for you all."

Veril sat in the grass with Ilohan and Eleanor, and they watched the morning brighten with joy. Karlak brought them breakfast: the second for Ilohan, which he did not mind, and the first for Eleanor and Veril.

The day passed delightfully. They talked, and slowly walked, and laughed, and stood in awe of Jonathan's stunts on the ropes and trees. They swam in the warm, shallow water at the edge of the lake, and talked on the green lawn beneath the eastern cliffs of Ceramir. Ilohan learned more of Veril, and his fears fell away without being replaced by any passionate love. He liked her, and wanted to bless her, and enjoyed being with her, and in these facts he was patient, happy with them as they were, calmly waiting for them to grow if they would. Veril's feelings toward him were stronger far, and she was sorry that he did not seem to share them, but she, too, hoped in peace.

Chapter 21

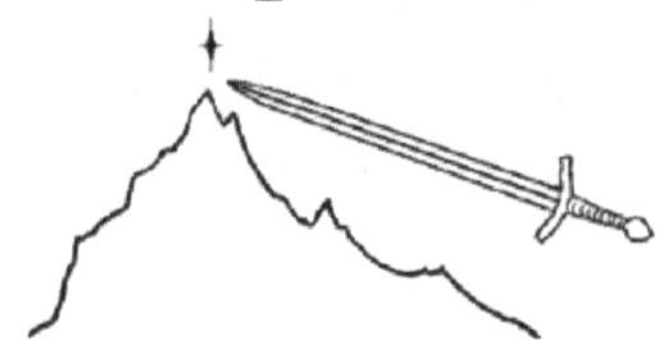

A Game of Chess

THE COUNSELORS AND KNIGHTS FILED IN TO STAND behind their seats. They stood still for a moment, straight and noble, a splendid sight worthy of the wisdom and valor of Karolan that they represented. The king, who had already taken his place at the table's head, nodded to them. They saluted him smartly and took their seats.

But the crisp, beautiful pageant had been little more than acting. This was no calm gathering of knights and advisors to plan the sure defeat of Karolan's enemies. It was a desperate meeting of a divided council, trying to save a tottering realm. The knights might be brave, but their boldness was to different ends. The counselors might be wise, but their wisdom led them to conflicting conclusions. None had confidence that either courage or wisdom could save them.

King Thomas sat at the head of the table, as regal and strong as ever, but the lines of worry in his face had grown deeper in the seven days. Only he knew the mighty effort of will required to maintain his poise and his stony calm. "Knights and counselors of Karolan," he said, "yet another week has gone by and still there is no word from Prince Ilohan. With every day the might of Norkath grows, but Fingar has not raised his standard yet. The people of Karolan require a prince to lead them, yet it may be that the prince is dead. We can muster the army, but who would lead it? We can wait, but how great will Fingar's forces grow? My friends, our danger is great. We have prayed much, and now we come to talk and choose our course of action. What do you advise?"

"Muster the army at once, Your Majesty, under the command of your knights. If Fingar musters an army also, we fight him at the border and defeat him. If he does not, we send a message offering our terms of peace, and threatening to sack Guldorak if he does not accept them." Thus spoke Sir Metherka, with battle-longing in his face.

"He would muster at once, and with no prince to lead us we would fall," said Sir Britheldore. "The prince must come."

"If he does not, we lie down and die, I suppose?" said Sir Nildra. "What would you have us do, Sir Britheldore?"

"Your discourtesy is reprimanded, Sir Nildra," said the king.

Nildra bowed his head, ashamed, "I ask your pardon, Sir Britheldore," he said, "but, with all respect, my question stands. What would you have us do if the prince is proven dead?"

"If the prince is dead, two bitter paths are before us," said Britheldore sadly. "We can fight, with near certainty of defeat, and the death of thousands. Or we can sue for peace, knowing that Fingar will perceive his strength, and set the terms accordingly. The second path is the sweeter, but both are bitter indeed."

"What terms would Fingar demand?" asked a counselor. "He will not make them light. Might he not demand the crown?"

"No," said Britheldore. "Only a great ransom for it."

"He might accept a lesser ransom rather than confront our armies," said Tulbur the Steward. "But he might not be content with anything less than the crown. Let us offer him the ransom first, and see if his cowardice and greed can refuse it."

"What would you give in ransom, Sir Steward?" asked the king.

"A thousand horse loads of gold, the provinces of Nildra and Idranak, and one thousand slaves of Fingar's choice, but not from among the nobility or knights."

"Fool!" said Metherka. "Would you have us sell our peasants to the greed and lust of Norkath churls? I would sooner see all Karolan in flames!"

"Bridle your tongue, Sir Metherka," said King Thomas. "That may well be the choice we have to make."

"The peasants will be slaves in any case – or dead – if Karolan falls to Fingar," said the steward.

"Nonetheless I would rather lose our people in battle than give them up without raising a sword," said Metherka. "I would rather lose a true cause than win one that, by my doing, had ceased to be true."

"There are times when one must look to results, with caution and prudence, rather than to one's desire for truth and honor," said the steward.

"I deny that," said Metherka. "I say that honor and truth are never to be abandoned."

"They are never to be abandoned," said the king. "Or, at the least, I will not suffer Karolan to abandon them while I wear the crown. But where, now, do they lead?"

"Are we sure we cannot win without the prince?" asked Metherka. "Prince or no prince, the men will be fighting for their homes, their families, and their lives. Will that not be inspiration enough?"

"A prince brings hope," said Britheldore, in his slow, gruff voice. "Without hope, the men will die."

"Is there no other way to bring them hope?" asked Nildra.

"Only the appointment of another prince," said a counselor.

"There is another way, if Fingar musters soon," said the king. His words fell like solemn drumbeats in the suddenly still room.

"What is it, Sire?" asked Britheldore.

"I could lead them one last time. I know I have it in me still to stir my people on to hope and glory. The last flicker of the strength my God has given me could kindle such a flame. If I die in battle, yet Karolan is saved, you, Sir Tulbur, must gather the knights in council to choose my successor."

Britheldore looked long and hard at the king. The old knight's eyes were piercing, but he said nothing.

"Are you strong enough for that, Your Majesty?" asked Tulbur. "Would it not be wiser to appoint a younger man as your successor, and send him to war?"

"I ask the council," said King Thomas, "whom do you favor as my successor?"

There was a long silence, finally broken by Sir Nildra.

"The steward," he said.

There was a collective intake of breath. Many faces looked anxious; some looked horrified. The king stared straight at one, who looked more horrifed than any. His voice cut through the air like a sword, cold and hard. "Speak your concern, Sir Idranak."

Sir Idranak opened his mouth and moved his lips, but no sound came. The tension in the room tightened. Finally another man spoke, deprecatingly, almost hysterically. "The writing in the Book of Secret Records," he said. "The steward is... I mean to say, in the reign of Konder, at the time of Your Majesty's...

At the request of Sir Grandor, may he rest in peace, it was written..."

"Yes," said Britheldore, his calm, deep voice unchanged. "In the Book of the Secret Records of the Knights of Karolan it is written that Tulbur, the cousin of King Thomas, has been cast from the Royal Succession."

The silence that followed was as deep as if shame, fear, and consternation had turned the whole assembly to stone. None dared to look at the steward or the king. Most had read that book, which was open to all Knights of Karolan but to no others. Most had pondered the strange words recorded there during the reign of Konder, the father of King Thomas – the words that cast Tulbur from the Royal Succession, but did not make the reason clear. For decades the writing had been there, often read, but never spoken of for shame. All the Knights of Karolan had known Tulbur could never take the throne – all, apparently, except Sir Nildra: Nildra from an outlying province; Nildra who was bold but young and inexperienced; Nildra, who had never read the book.

At last the voice of the king broke the agonized silence. "The king has authority over that Book," he said. "The steward has never breathed a word requesting any change in it. But now I, Thomas of Karolan, say this: Let the Book not be considered."

A gasp of surprise and a sigh of relieved tension shuddered through the room. But to one man the words meant more than to any other. Old Sir Britheldore's eyes were fixed on that man: Sir Tulbur, the Steward of Karolan. It seemed to the old knight that light and life and openness came into Tulbur's face that had not been there since his early youth, but that suddenly these were swallowed up and replaced with a shrewd bitterness that was merely an intensification of one of the habitual attitudes of the man. Britheldore was troubled by this, and pondered it, but then reminded himself that he was an old man, and the room was lit only by candles, and perhaps indeed the steward had felt only the king's kindness and mercy.

"I have spoken," said King Thomas. "I ask the council again, who should succeed me?" Since the king's own words had reversed a decades-old decree and placed the steward on the list of possible successors to the throne, few could consider any other possibility. As the steward, Tulbur had been the king's own choice to have charge of the realm when he was away at war. Yet still no one dared to speak, so strong was the long-held prohibition from the Book of Secret Records. At last the king's eyes went around the room, seeming to draw out an answer from each man they fell upon.

"The steward."

"The steward."

"Sir Tulbur."

"Sir Britheldore, if he were younger; now, the steward."

"The steward."

"I yield to the majority."

"The steward."

"The steward."

At last King Thomas's eyes fell upon old Sir Britheldore, so long his faithful and well-trusted friend. Britheldore smiled. "Metherka," he said.

King Thomas smiled wryly. "Sir Tulbur, you are the favorite of the council. Could you lead a score of thousands into a hell of fear and blood, and bring them out again victorious?"

Tulbur smiled. "If such were your desire, Your Majesty, I believe I could. It would not be the first time I marched at the head of many thousands."

"No," said King Thomas, "and neither I nor Karolan forgets it."

A long silence hung in the room. The candles and torches burned steadily. The strong, cold autumn wind moaned in the towers of the castle, and the sound came muffled through thick stone walls even to the council chamber. King Thomas again looked carefully into the face of each of his counselors. Especially he lingered over the wrinkled visage of Sir Britheldore, who alone had cast his vote against the steward and for young Metherka, a knight the king had never trusted. The king stared at last into the flame of one of the candles, his face as motionless as the stone wall behind his chair.

"So," he said finally, "we have gathered to make a dire decision, and now it shall be made. The laws of Karolan decree that the weight rests on my shoulders alone. Hear that I will pay Fingar no ransom."

The king let the stern words ring in the room. He gave the men who had advised him time to understand that he had chosen war, that he had judged the price of peace too high. Safe though they were for the moment, some shuddered, and the wind seemed to moan more loudly. The merciless, tearing monster called a war would be unleashed upon them, and there was no longer any hope to hold it back. King Thomas continued, explaining why he had made the dreadful choice.

"I will not save the realm by giving other men's wives and homes up for slavery and occupation," he said. "War is indeed terrible, and high though Fingar's price would run, it might yet be less brutal than a war. Even so, we will not pay it. In honor and justice we cannot. We will put our hope in God, to help the truer cause. I will draw my sword, and if one begs for terms of peace it will be Fingar."

In the silence that followed he looked around the table, his searching eyes probing each advisor. Would any dare to dispute his agonizing choice? No. Some wished to, but none would. So it was done. He dropped his gaze a moment to the smooth oak surface of the table, glistening with its oiled finish. He looked up, and spoke once more.

"So, how shall we fight this desperate war? First, let it be known that I do not believe that Ilohan is dead. If you ask me why, I give but three reasons. His father was Kindrach. His mother is Eleanor. His God is the God who lives. Let any dispute my reasons who will.

Because I believe that Ilohan lives, I appoint no successor in his place. If Eleanor sends word that he is lost, I will reconsider. We do not have the hope the prince would bring, but my old torch can ignite one last fire. If our army is gathered before the prince comes, I must lead it. Sir Tulbur shall be regent in my absence. If I fall but Karolan is saved, and Ilohan is not found or heard of alive within a year, then Tulbur shall call the council, and their vote shall decide the next king. This vote is a formality, clearly, but it is a formality worth observing. Thus the choice is made."

Tulbur looked at the king in the light of the candles and torches. "He is still a leader," he thought. "It may be that what he says is true, that his words could once more stir the hearts of thousands, bringing them hope and courage, like a raging fire before which the Norkaths would tremble and die. It might be so. But, with a strange, unlooked-for sorrow, I doubt it will be."

"Leave to speak, Sire?" asked Britheldore.

"Indeed, friend," said the king.

"If you die in battle, who will lead?"

King Thomas looked very hard at Britheldore, then at Metherka, then at Tulbur, then at Nildra, and finally back at Britheldore again. "Metherka shall lead the army if I fall," he said at last.

"May I speak, Your Majesty?" asked Tulbur.

"Certainly, Sir Steward."

"With great respect for Your Majesty's wisdom and courage, I wish to remark that eight of the last ten kings of Karolan died at a younger age than Your Majesty has now attained. Though you are strong, you do not ride to the far limits of your kingdom often and swiftly, as you used to do. If exhaustion comes upon you in the war, Your Majesty will be hard pressed to light the torch of which you have spoken, and however great a man's wisdom, he finds it hard to choose wisely in the midst of great weariness. I counsel you to choose a younger leader – but one known for wisdom as well as courage."

"You mean yourself, Sir Tulbur," said the king. "You believe my mind may lose its wisdom through exhaustion, so that I can no longer command, inspire, or prudently lead my men."

"I would never speak so bluntly, Sire," said Tulbur, "but I cannot hide from your wisdom. You have named my true wish and counsel."

The king stood, slowly and stiffly, but at length as straight and regal as a mountain pine. "The council is at an end," he said. "My decision, for the present, stands. Yet, in acknowledgement of Sir Tulbur's misgivings, I will put my choice to a contest – a contest of wisdom and of will. All who wish may stay and watch, but only in silence. Sir Metherka, bring us the chess."

The knights who had stood and prepared to leave froze for an instant in surprise, then managed a ragged salute and sat down again. Metherka departed, and returned soon with three pages carrying the large, heavy table set with the royal chess pieces. The pages, with the aid of some of the knights, moved the great council table to the wall of the room, and set the chess table in its place. Sir Tulbur and King Thomas took their seats facing each other across it, and the other knights gathered round and waited in absolute silence. Bright candles lined the sides of the chess table, and cast their clear light across the board. The rest of the room seemed to fade into darkness in comparison. The pieces in their orderly rows each wore a tiny crown of candle flames reflected in the polished wood of its head. There was a dead silence in which all eyes were fixed on the chess board where the fate of Karolan might be decided.

"Sir Steward," said King Thomas, "do you accept my challenge to an honorable game of chess?"

"With pleasure and awareness of the high honor, Your Majesty," said the steward.

They progressed through the opening moves of the game, utterly absorbed in their play. Each man's strategy was flawless. Though they had played many games in long, varied years, still they gave even the simple moves a moment's thought. They knew each other well: Tulbur had been Thomas's friend and advisor even before his marriage to Sarah. They reached the central part of the game, tangled and complex, every move a careful balance of many risks and chances.

The knights watched in deep silence. Some thought that Tulbur and Thomas might be considering the great stake for which this game was played. Others understood: to the steward and the king, the game had become the whole world, and if the thought of the great stake intruded, it was only to focus their minds more intensely on their play.

The intensity of their focus wearied and drained them. A time came when both were moving slower, and thinking longer, than they were wont to do. Their minds wandered, and were held to the game by force of will.

Tulbur glowered down at the white ash pieces that made up his army. They were disposed in a flawless, intricate pattern of mutual protection and attack, but despite his most ingenious moves he could make no inroads on the king's defense. The steward controlled some frustration. The knights who watched could feel it too. The king was not attacking. His strategy was so defensive that it put him at a slight disadvantage, as Tulbur controlled a larger portion of the board. Yet, restrained though Thomas's forces might be, they appeared utterly unassailable. Even old Sir Britheldore's eyes betrayed the ghost of perplexity as the game went on in the same vein. It was like the king to venture boldly out, to sacrifice pieces, and win by daring strategy – or lose by failing to see one slight, subtle trap. He was not a foolhardy player, but he was not usually a cautious one.

Tulbur moved a knight against Thomas, catching a bishop and a critical pawn in a fork. The king could protect one, but must lose the other. The atmosphere in the room was tangibly changed; even this relatively minor attack was a change from the long sequences of moves that never led to anything more than shifting networks of protection and the taking of a few outlying pawns. The ghost of a smile came to the king's face: Tulbur had made a minor error, the first such event in the game. He brought out the other bishop and rapped it down just across the center of the board. Now it covered one of Tulbur's own guard pawns, and behind the pawn there was a rook – if Tulbur moved to save the pawn the rook would be unguarded.

The steward made a quick motion of disgust and, after a long moment of thought, brought his knight back from attack and set it to guard the rook that Thomas threatened. The pawn he could not save, though the network of pieces around it seemed ominous, ready to close in on a foolhardy attacker. Thomas looked at it long and hard. He was weary, and his head hurt with the long effort. His hand leaped up unwilled to press against his aching brow, but he forced it back before it got there. He moved the bishop back to safety, and did not attack Tulbur's pawn. The disappointment of the watching knights could be felt in the room. More than one mind formed the question, "Why will the king not play like the king?"

Tulbur, who, as one of the players, was at liberty to speak, gave his sovereign a wry smile and asked, "Where is the fierce, bold chivalry against which I have so often had to warn you in true life?"

The king raised his head as if it were too heavy for him, but the eyes that met the steward's were penetrating and bright. "It is hidden beneath the prudent caution that years of pain, hopes deferred, and your own wise council have taught me."

"Hidden, but there nonetheless?"

"Yes. There nonetheless."

The game dragged on, and still King Thomas made no attack. Finally, Tulbur sat back behind his front line and brewed a grand assault. It burst through the line of pawns to attack the king's left flank, and the steward's splendid, careful strategy swept Thomas's defense before him. King Thomas lost a knight, and that disadvantage loomed very large in the careful, evenly matched game. The Knights of Karolan looked on in awe as the king's magnificent defense fell into disarray. Would he lose? Would he actually reverse his decision and put Sir Tulbur at the head of the Army of all Karolan? Most of the watchers found it hard to believe, for they had had an implicit certainty in their minds that the king would win and knew it, else he would never have staked his decision on the game. The fact that he was losing made them feel as though the castle itself were reeling beneath their feet. Yet every move seemed to make it more certain.

King Thomas played on, his head filled with aching, intense thought. He must win; he knew it. He had dared to stake everything on this; he must lead the Army of all Karolan with the full confidence of all his knights, and therefore he must win. His mind was in turmoil, weary, aching, confused, yet held to the game by his iron will. His prayers were tattered shreds of thought, offered up with faith, like poor wilted flowers offered to a mother who loves the giver, and therefore despises not the heartfelt gift. He was losing, and he must not lose. He had come to the climax of years of plans, and desperate hopes; he had done all in prayer and prudence, and now was a critical part of a dire plan to be lost because of a foolish game of chess? It was his own idea, after all; if it were foolish it was he who was the fool. Was it his move? Yes, and once again his thoughts had been wandering. What could he do? Tulbur had his back row on the left flank. His own forces were huddled back on the right, trembling before Tulbur's attack. "Father, help me! Do you will that I shall lose? Surely, surely in your mercy I will not fail!" He calmed the trembling of the hand that reached out to move a rook, and with the other hand he steadied upon his head the crown that felt like a band of dull, hot iron. He might be losing, but he was yet only one knight and a pawn behind, and the time for heroic recklessness had come at last.

It was two moves later that he saw it, cutting through the turmoil of his weary thought like a sword through muddy water. Three moves. The first looked wise, but let his queen be trapped. On the second move she would be taken. On the third – if only Tulbur did not see it coming – his rook would check the steward's king. It would then be one move until checkmate – one move with his one remaining knight – but by then there would be no escape. Tulbur would not see it coming. He would too gladly trap the queen, and the attack was too obscure, too strange, and too wildly foolish, to be seen except by the most incredibly observant player. That Tulbur was not, not now when he was weary and closing in for his own kill.

Thomas reached out his hand to move the queen. He was so tired from concentration that nothing seemed real, and dreams floated through his mind, now and then swallowing up what was true as his eyelids momentarily closed. Now a terrible, reasonless delusion struck him, and it was all he could do to fight it off. He was sending that queen to certain death. "The queen is not Sarah," he said to himself. "It is a chess piece well carved in black walnut. The queen is not Sarah. It means nothing. It symbolizes nothing. Move it. You must move it. Fight, do not give in to the mad lie. The queen is not Sarah. Sarah is safe forever. Move. Move now..." He did, and withdrew his hand shaking. The delusion washed over him with terrible power, and then it was gone. It left no feeling of safety or comfort behind it, but only the trembling consciousness of a fragile hiatus in an onslaught.

The satisfaction of the rap of wood on wood with which Tulbur closed the trap around the black queen woke King Thomas up a little, and with renewed alertness came renewed power to control his thoughts. He scanned the board again, coolly and carefully, and his hope leaped, for the conclusion was the same as before. A preposterous trap awaited Tulbur's king, and he had only to spring it. He made the next move.

The moments that followed seemed to last forever, a dead silence in which even the moaning wind held its breath. Finally Tulbur made his move, and he did not take King Thomas's queen. He blocked the planned attack. King Thomas saw his brilliant plan ruined, thought for one moment only, and then slid his queen cleanly out of a hole that Tulbur's move had opened in the trap. The steward moved to guard the knight that was threatened by the queen. Thomas made a move. He met the steward's eyes. "Check, Sir Tulbur," he said.

The steward looked carefully over the board, and an expression of awed dismay washed across his handsome, bearded face. His move had reopened the king's attack, and Thomas had used it. There was no way out. He had one move, but nothing he could do with it would save him. He took a deep breath and looked over the board again. He stared at it for a long time, and the moaning of the wind came low and clear and eerie through the stone walls to the ears of all the watchers. At last Tulbur settled on a move, and made it. He took Thomas's queen. The king did not even blink. He examined the layout very carefully one last time, and slid his knight into place. There was a silence, as all present considered the board. Finally it was Britheldore who spoke, free now to do so since the game was over. "Checkmate," he said.

King Thomas stood, and Tulbur rose with him and looked him in the eyes. "I thank you for a good game of chess, Sir Steward," said the king. "I will lead the Army of all Karolan if we muster before the prince has come, and in two days I will address the people. Send messengers to the nearby towns to proclaim this before you sleep."

Tulbur spoke very quietly in reply. "All shall be as Your Majesty has commanded it. Yet I would know one thing. Was it by your great wisdom and thought that you defeated me today, or was it another thing, a thing we did not mean the game to test?"

"What does it matter?" asked Thomas of Karolan. "The other thing, too, shall not fail when Norkath comes. I bid you goodnight."

His keen memory did not record his exit from the council chamber, or the walk up the torchlit stairs to his tower room. He was trembling when he threw off his crown and robe, and collapsed on the firm softness of his bed. His will had been enough, by the grace of his God, and he had won. He had won the right to lead the army that could not win in a war without hope, which nonetheless must be fought. Tulbur was right. The prince was dead, and he, Thomas, had not strength enough to lead the army. He looked around the candlelit room through hazy eyes before which the solid objects wavered. The window was open, and the fuzzy stars shone dimly, overpowered by the candlelight. He saw only one thing clearly. Skykag had not come, and there was no hope. He slipped out of his bed, and came to rest painfully on his knees on the stone floor, but could find no words to pray. At last he blew out the candles and dragged himself back into bed. Words seemed to fit themselves into his dreams as he sank into darkness: "You are there still when hope is gone. Save..."

*　　　*　　　*

Frost was on the autumn grass in Glen Carrah that morning, and the footsteps of Barnabas and Hannah crunched crisply through it as they went from the well into the smithy. The month, that had started so long ago on the day that Jonathan left, was now ended, and the twelve swords were made. They had been finished on time, two days before. Today the blacksmith and his wife merely wandered into the smithy to sit together at the table there, and enjoy the peace that their long labor had earned them.

The swords lay in a shining stack against the far side of the smithy, and the snowy mountains were just visible above the wall behind them. It seemed a wonder to Hannah that she and Barnabas had made those things, out of so much leather, glue, and ore. They looked magical in the misty morning light, their polished surfaces shining so much smoother and harder than anything natural. Yet still she was pained by the sight.

"I know the evil of them," said Barnabas, following her gaze. "Yet there come days when men set out to do a thing so vile that it is better for them to die than to accomplish it. For such times swords are rightly made."

"Yet men – perhaps, Beloved, even you – seem to want such times to come," said Hannah. "How can that be?"

Barnabas thought for a while, and the edges of the mountain peaks glowed brilliant white as the rising sun struck them. He took his wife's hand, and they rose together and walked out of the smithy and into view of the full glory of the morning. They walked a short way up into the crunching, ice-gilded grass of Glen Carrah. The slight morning breeze was crisp and bracing in their faces, and their breath smoked in the air. The frosty grass and soft, blue mist made the glen look like fairyland. The mountains towered above the fog that blanketed the upper reaches of the glen, and the piercing brilliance of sunlight on snow outlined them in white fire.

"How could anyone want war in a world as beautiful as this?" asked Barnabas. "Should I desire a thing that might take away this life I live with you, Beloved; our bright love shining amid the glory of this life-filled land? And yet you are right when you say that some men long for war, and that the longing is not wholly absent from my heart."

"Because war tests your courage, and teaches those who do not understand the truth of life and death, and cowardice and courage?" asked Hannah. "Is that worth its cost?"

"I do not know, and cannot say," said Barnabas. "But those who fight justly in a war, who are not shattered by it nor slain in it, are tempered and taught by its horror. They learn to value more deeply those they love, and to understand the value of their life and hope. They learn to prize as highly as they should their homes and lands, and not to boast too highly of their courage. They see their souls laid bare, and learn what they will do when terror strips away hypocrisy. Afterward some give up their hearts to God, knowing their fault and weakness, and ask him for healing and for making right. I cannot measure the value of this, nor can I compare the value with the cost."

"Are there no other possibilities," asked Hannah, "none for whom such blessing does not come?"

Hannah saw a look of horror pass across the face of Barnabas, despite the autumn morning's loveliness. "I think there are," he said. "Men may be shattered, and have a good and fragile part of them destroyed. Others may raise shields against the horror that they can never afterwards take down, and so become hardened and blind to much that is good and beautiful. To all, I think a healing may come later, but it is a dark and bitter road they must follow."

"Yet neither you nor Jonathan will be among these?" asked Hannah.

"I will not," said Barnabas. "I have seen war, and I know that the only thing it can take from me is my mortal life. All else that is within me has been proven already, and is safe. As for Jonathan, the vibrancy of his life protects him, yet I do not know to what end that strength might turn if the war proves very terrible to him. I do not know, and I fear."

"I will pray for both of you, with all the strength I have, and God will protect you," said Hannah, looking up at her husband. "For Jonathan, we have one great hope, and that is

Naomi. She will hold him back from evil, and soon or late his doubt must fall before her faith. Hers is a hard path, but she is strong and faithful, and hers will be the triumph in the end."

"I hope so," said Barnabas, "I hope so with all my heart! And yet it comes to me that God has given us another good hope for Jonathan."

"Sir Ilohan?"

"Yes, beloved Hannah. I think that timid young man has a very great faith, and that he may in time gain courage and wisdom to empower it. It is a blessing to us that Jonathan should journey with such a one."

Hannah shuddered and squeezed her husband's hand, which held her own in a firm, warm grip. "It has been so long," she said. "So long and still they do not return. The journey should not take so long."

"Do not fear, Beloved," said Barnabas. "They might stay long at Luciyr or Harevan, and even if they had stayed but a few days in each place, they would scarcely have reached Carrah by now."

A high, clear trumpet sounded behind them, on the path before their house. A voice called, "Payment and commendation from His Majesty Thomas of Karolan. Open, of courtesy, to perform your duty and receive your due."

Hannah and Barnabas turned quickly to see the banner of the Stone, Sword, and Star waving over the roof of their cottage, catching the new-risen sun. They went hastily back to open the door for the king's messenger. After exchanging the appropriate courtesies, they led him to the smithy. They waited in silence while he inspected their work. He held each sword before him, and watched the sun glance along its polished surface. He tested the firmness of its grip, and sliced a braided cord to test its edge. Finally he swung it with moderate force against the wooden target to try its strength. Every sword was smooth, polished, well hilted, and sharp. Every sword rang true.

"May I have leave to speak concerning the quality of the king's swords?" asked Barnabas.

"Indeed," said the messenger, "such excellent work gives you the right to say much."

"Just over a month ago a Knight of Karolan came here, and asked my son to accompany him on a mission from the king. Before they left I tested his sword. It shattered. Not all of the king's smiths are working well, and some of the swords are not well tested. May I test these for you, to prove once more that all is well?"

"Yes indeed," said the messenger, standing back.

Barnabas took each of the swords in his hand in turn, and struck a mighty, ringing blow at the wood target. Chips flew, the target swung, and the messenger gaped at the force the blacksmith was using. "A polish is for beauty that stirs hearts to courage," said Barnabas. "An edge can always be mended with a stone. But the strength of forged iron is the heart of a sword, and by it Karolan may stand or fall."

"Well said," said the messenger, "and well made! Would that all smiths made such swords as these! Yet I fear it will be all the king can do to put a sword, however strong, in the hand of every man who musters to his call. We will take the work of every smith, though we will do what we can to set right those whose work is poor."

"What you must do, you must do," said Barnabas. "Yet, when the king at last raises his standard, let the messengers who go forth to muster the army order every man to gather any sword that he may easily find, and bring it, and it may be that you will not lack for weapons after all."

"I thank you for your words," the messenger said to Barnabas, "I will heed them well, and bring them to higher ears than mine. Now," he went on, turning to Hannah, "as I am here, may I also buy the arrows and bows you have been making?"

"I have not made bows," she said, a little downcast. "I work only in oak, not yew. Yet stay here and I will bring the arrows out."

She brought them out in great leather bags of her own making; large stacks of neat, well made arrows. "Here are ten score and eight shafts," she said, "and nineteen score eleven bolts. The oak is firm, the feathers straight, and the points sharp, though heavy was the heart that made them."

The messenger examined a few of them, confirmed her words, and counted them. Then he carefully selected a pile of gold coins for her, paying exactly for each arrow according to the king's price. Barnabas looked at that little pile of gold, and thought of all the sorrow it had cost his beloved wife. He saw that the messenger was already counting out the gold for their swords. "May you not pay something over the standard rate for them?" he asked. "They are good, and cost us much toil and long labor, since our son is gone."

The messenger looked up, surprised. "You did so much in one month, alone?" he asked.

"Not alone," said Barnabas, smiling. "We worked together, Hannah and I, and together did what seemed impossible. But for her I should never have finished. Still, our toil was hard and long, especially hers as she is not accustomed to such brutal labor."

"I admire you both," said the messenger, "would my own wife and I had the love you must share! Willingly I would give more than the standard price, and my king would not dissuade me, save that his treasury is very low and he will not tax the people more. I can give you no more than His Majesty's set rate."

"So be it then," said Barnabas. "But could not good King Thomas, in his need, speak to the miners of Petrag concerning the great store of gold that is hoarded there?"

"The hoard of Petrag is but a legend," said the messenger. "The king has sent messengers there, and they find that the miners possess a charter signed by King Corzogad of Karolan, sixth ancestor of Thomas, stating that henceforth the gold from the mines is theirs alone, and none need come to Aaronkal. There is no gold there that is rightfully the king's."

"Take them at the set rate, then," said Barnabas. "May they be used well, for the defense of what we love and the defeat of evil that would destroy it. Would you have eight more by this month's end?"

"We would indeed," said the messenger, stowing the swords and arrows in his saddlebags. "I thank you both on His Majesty's behalf, for you have worked beyond expectation and duty. Farewell." He rode away, the Banner of Karolan snapping in the morning air above his galloping horse.

Barnabas put most of the money in a leather bag and gave it to Hannah. He went to his large iron anvil, knocked in a square of solid metal on one side of it with a huge blow from his hammer, and slipped the rest of the gold into a recess behind the block of iron. He heated the block in the forge, and hammered it back into place, sealing the gold invisibly and almost inextricably into the heart of the anvil.

Hannah smiled as she looked again at the sunlit mountains. She held the bag of gold in both hands. "Thank God we have enough to live on, and more besides," she said. "Yet for what are we storing the gold in the anvil? What might we do with it some day, Barnabas?"

She turned to him as she spoke, and he came out of the smithy and stood beside her. "I do not know, beloved," he said. "But it seems good to store it by, since the times are uncertain. There is no greed in my heart, I think, though surely I value highly what we have earned with so much labor. Maybe we ourselves will need the gold some day, or perhaps God will send us another who would find it a great blessing."

"It will not be for us, I think," said Hannah. "Another will have greater need. Have you more work to do today?"

"Not if there is something else that you would have us do," said Barnabas.

Hannah smiled at him again and took his hand. "Will you walk with me in Glen Carrah?"

"With joy."

They walked together, as the last of the mist blew away and the sun shone bright on the golden grass that still gleamed with frost. The keen wind that whipped down out of the mountains was icy-cold, but their clothes were good and the sun on their faces was warm. It was a free, bright and wild day. They passed the great piles of rocks along the Carratril and went yet farther up into the glen. Nearly at its height, where the grass began to grow sparser as the steep rock of the mountains drew near, they halted and turned around to look at the glowing land below them.

They stood there long, with the wind and the sun at their backs and the golden sweep of Glen Carrah stretched out before them. Far away at its foot they could see their cottage, and Joseph's, and the whole village. The Carratril ran on their right, a shimmering ribbon, sometimes frothy white and sometimes rich royal blue, like liquid sky flowing along the ground.

"Soon winter will come," said Barnabas, "and it will all be pure and piercing white."

"I love all its times," said Hannah, "and all its beauties."

They were silent another moment, and then she spoke again, and Barnabas turned to her, surprised at how her voice had changed. "Who knows if we will see it shining white? Who can say what this winter brings?"

Barnabas looked at her with love, and felt the terrible strangeness of the world. Its beauty shone, so flawless and so bright, and their hearts rejoiced. Yet even at the height of the joy, they might feel, like icicles against their skin, the evil that had marred the good Creation. Their hearts were tugged one way and then another, by delight, or by cold, hard fear. Their trust in God was firm, but the winds of the world were tempestuous and strong.

"I think about what you said before, beloved," said Hannah, "of war and what it brings. Do you think that other things beside battle could temper men and women thus? Can other things prove them; humble and refine or shatter and destroy them, as war does?"

Barnabas thought for a moment, gazing at the blue Carratril running through the golden grass. His voice was shaking as he answered her, for the thoughts her question had raised were new and powerful to him. "I am sure, sure beyond a shadow of a doubt, that there are such other things, Beloved," he said, "yet I had not thought of them so before. It is strange that I should be so blind, for surely war is not the only dreadful thing that tries and tempers."

He looked at her a moment, and then suddenly he was afraid, and hugged her close, so tightly that it took away her breath. "I fear, beloved," he said. "For you may be tempered too."

She rejoiced in his love and strength. His arms around her comforted her, and she knew her presence brought him peace. "We will be tempered, both of us," she said. "The days that come are dark, but God will not leave us. He will hold us when we cannot hold each other. How I love you!"

Chapter 22

The Eagle Flies at Last

JONATHAN MARVELED AT THE WAY THE GOLD GREW SOFT in the fire, nearly as soft as butter when he drew it out dazzling yellow and sparking with intense heat. It was not like iron, which still had to be formed with a heavy hammer even when it was white-hot. He had to find out all that he needed to know alone, for at present there was no gold or silversmith of Ceramir to teach him how to use the little forge at which he worked. He rejoiced in the labor, the wonder of forming the soft, precious metal with light blows from a small hammer, or with only the strength of his hands on a chisel. Would two gold coins weld if he heated them and then pressed them together? Yes, they did: it was a solid weld, as though he had one coin of double thickness.

Jonathan tried a few more experiments, entranced by the ease with which he could form the brightly glowing metal. Finally he took a deep breath, and set to work on the crown – his charge from Eleanor, who had asked him about it privately. He heated it and gently smoothed and straightened the twisted metal with his cold chisels. When that was done, he set the halves of the crown together on the anvil. They fitted well, leaving only small, even gaps between the smooth flat edges.

He heated them as hot as he could, and then set one side of the crown against a hollowed stone, and forced the other half down onto it. It made a good weld, but at the contact points the gold widened a little, so that the band was no longer smooth and even. He took a sharp chisel, and cleaved off the excess gold, leaving a smooth, bright surface beneath. After a long moment of intense, careful work, the circlet was as smooth and even as he could make it.

When the crown cooled he took it in both hands and carried it out into the light. The forge was in a hollowed cave up in the western rock wall of Ceramir, and the whole southern half of the valley stretched out below him, flatly and beautifully lit by the westering sun. He tossed the crown high in the sunlight, and its rubies flashed fire. It was perfect, a flawless circle, as though it had never been cut. He caught it and carried it inside. As he passed out of the sun, his eyes caught the marred inscription on the inside of the crown. He studied the letters, unable to read them, but wondering at the skill that could translate the speech of men into silent written shapes. But the letters were not his task. His task was done, and now came the payment he had asked.

He leaned back against the wall, facing the glowing forge, to think what he would do. It was difficult. He closed his eyes, and his mind wandered to Glen Carrah. Sudden longing for Naomi fell on him with such intensity that he was near to calling out her name. His arms ached to hold her. He had given her his heart, and without her he was not whole. Finally he opened his eyes and looked at the forge again. He must ache, and would, until he saw her again, but even now he could show his love. He threw himself into his project, and suddenly it did not seem impossible.

His hands on the chisel cut from a rod of bright-hot gold small shavings the size and shape of grains of wild wheat. He welded a thin, small band of gold into a perfect circle, just large enough to fit his smallest finger. He laid the wheat grains on it, and in response to the furnace's hot breath and the careful pressure of his chisel they joined with the band beneath. The pattern was regular and staid, so he cleaved them off, reformed the ring, and tried again. Again he deemed the result unworthy, and again and again he tried. The slivers of cut gold welded onto the ring one last time, and he withdrew it from the fire with a trembling hand. He took the very sharpest chisel, and gently touched the delicate ring all over its surface, until it gleamed with countless tiny facets of cut gold. He took it out and up into the sunlight and gazed at it as it lay in the callused palm of his hand. It seemed a wonder to him that that large, rough hand could make something so perfect and so small. The ring was like the wild grain of Glen Carrah – exactly like it, only shining with the gleam of gold.

"Naomi, Beloved, child of Glen Carrah," he said, "your wedding ring is made, and the day will come when I rejoice to put it on your finger. Yet our love is deeper than the most beautiful symbol hands could ever make. No darkness in the world will keep me from returning to you." He fastened the ring around his neck with a thin, strong cord made in Ceramir, and tucked it underneath his clothes. He took the crown and the sharpest chisel, and made his way down to the trees as the last rays of sunlight gleamed golden on their tops.

*   *   *

The council that Eleanor had called met in the same room where she had told her story, and revealed to Ilohan that she was his mother. It had lately been filled with sickbeds, but now, as many of the plague-stricken were recovering, it was restored to its previous state.

When Ilohan entered the room, Eleanor, Jonathan, and Mudien and Imranie were already there, sitting on wooden chairs in a circle, as before. Veril soon arrived, and slipped quickly into a chair, looking around anxiously as if uncertain of her place there – though Ilohan knew that both he and Eleanor had separately invited her.

They were all dressed in banquet clothes, and they had laid aside their blue caps, until, leaving the room, they should go from the hopeful but weighty deliberation of the council back into the long battle against the plague. Most beautiful in Ilohan's eyes was his mother. She wore again the pure white dress, and her shining diamond crown was entwined in her gray-brown hair. She looked as lovely as she had on the night of her story, but the air of happy expectation she had had then was replaced by a calm gravity. A light shone in her eyes, as though she saw things far away and sought to move them with the intensity of her prayer and desire.

"We have a war to fight," she said, her voice soft and clear, "and it is time to choose what part we shall play in fighting it. King Thomas's plan, Ilohan, is to abdicate his throne to you when you return to Aaronkal. Fingar will attack Karolan as soon as he can after hearing of the king's abdication, and you will lead the Karolan army to block the invasion."

There was a silence. Ilohan opened his mouth, found he could not speak, and closed it again. He reeled under the shock of learning he was expected to lead an army to save Karolan in a few weeks. Weakness left over from the plague made it worse, and even though his strength had been recovering rapidly, the room seemed to waver around him. At last he took a deep breath, swallowed, tried to smile, and said, "What is there for us to decide, then?"

Princess Eleanor also found herself unable to speak for an instant. Yes, he would make a king. He might not have the strength of Kindrach, but he had his courage. It cost all her effort not to weep. "We must decide the path you are to take back to Aaronkal, beloved son," she said. "And we must also consider whether a different plan should be adopted. I fear that there is treachery afoot, something neither Thomas nor I imagined."

"The evidence of treachery being the fact that Jonathan and I were attacked on the journey?" asked Ilohan.

"Yes," said Eleanor, shifting suddenly in her chair with the horror that realization still brought her. She steeled herself for what must follow. "Prince Ilohan, will you give a careful account of your journey, so that we all may know what happened? Perhaps all our thought and knowledge together will reveal the traitor."

Ilohan told the story as clearly and completely as he could. He noticed Jonathan frowning at some points, but on the whole his companion seemed to approve. Eleanor turned pale at his account of the attacks by the archers and the knights of Norkath, and tears formed in her eyes as he spoke of Kindrach's bones, but when the story was finished, she smiled at him.

"Do you yourself have any guess at the identity of the traitor?" she asked him.

"I may be a trusting fool," Ilohan replied, "but I cannot bring myself to think it was Sir Benther. He did violate my friendship, but he was under some strange stress and terror, and I do not think he meant to kill me."

"Someone meant to kill you," said Jonathan. "They laid good plans and came very close indeed to success. They would have had us both at Tharral's cottage had you not fought bravely despite an arrow through your arm." Pain shadowed Eleanor's face, and Jonathan saw it. "I am sorry, my Lady," he said, "yet your son has far more courage and strength than he told of, and he exaggerated mine."

Eleanor looked at Jonathan, and smiled. A long silence fell, while all faces were still and stern with concentrated thought. Finally Mudien said, "Fingar may have a spy at Aaronkal, who overheard the counsel of the king, and thus he may have plotted to kill Prince Ilohan."

"Yet that would not explain the fear that hung over Benther," said Eleanor quietly. "There must be something else."

"What could make a man attack his friend?" asked Jonathan. "And what did he hope to accomplish?"

"Something made him afraid," said Mudien. "Could he have been blackmailed? Or could a life he holds dear have been threatened?"

"There were few that he held more dear than me," said Ilohan sadly, "or so I thought. His betrayal was a strange, unlooked-for evil. And yet I think he repented of it."

"What could his plan have been?" asked Jonathan. "Did he want to kill Prince Ilohan some night while he lay sleeping?"

Ilohan winced. "I cannot believe that of him," he said. "I do not think any threat could have made him kill me."

Veril said, "I have an idea, but it may have no truth."

"Speak your thought, beloved daughter," said Mudien.

"Prince Ilohan said that the first assassins did not know him on sight. What if they knew Sir Benther? They could have been ordered to kill the man traveling with Sir Benther. Benther might not have known anything except that someone pressed him strongly to make himself Sir Ilohan's companion."

"My heart rejoices to think that might be true, Veril," said Ilohan. "It would mean my friend was not a traitor." Veril smiled shyly at him. She had wanted to bring him that hope, but she looked anxiously at her father and Eleanor to see if they thought it could be the truth.

"It is the only thing we have heard yet that makes sense of everything that has happened," said Mudien. "You have thought well, Veril."

"That is true," said Eleanor. "Still, we must not think we understand too soon. It seems strange that mercenary archers would know one Knight of Karolan well, and not another."

"Strange, yes," said Mudien, "but there are ways it could happen."

"It seems to matter little who the spies or traitors are," said Imranie. "We know there are spies and traitors. Assassins have twice been sent and have perished, but whoever sent them is surely still alive and dangerous to us. What shall we do in that knowledge?"

"There seems nothing to do, except go back to Aaronkal as King Thomas commanded," said Ilohan. "We must go in stealth, of course, and camp in hidden places away from the road. We will make it back to Aaronkal. We must."

"There are parts of the journey where there are no hidden places off the road," said Jonathan.

"Rangol and Brogal would rejoice to accompany you," said Veril. "They know the desert well, and are strong and fearless."

"I would spare them – though the thought is selfish –" said Imranie, "they are very dear to me, and to all Ceramir. And yet," she looked at Eleanor with love and fear in her face, "and yet, perhaps we must send them after all."

"If we are attacked again, surely it will be with overwhelming force," said Jonathan. "Twice we have escaped what, by any expectation, should have killed us. If there is a third time, they will send so many assassins that neither escape nor victory will be possible. It will matter nothing whether we are two or four."

"If there is a third time, you say," said Ilohan. "Perhaps there will not be. Little enough word has come back from the other two attempts. Even the archers who lived may have been too disgraced and wounded to make their report."

"We should not talk ifs when your life is in the balance, Prince Ilohan," said Mudien. "Being attacked again on the Luciyr Road is not a thing you should risk."

"But it is the only way back to Karolan, is it not?" asked Ilohan.

"There is another way," said Eleanor, a shadow of fear passing across her face as she spoke. "Through Cembar."

"A safer way?" asked Jonathan, incredulously, and then, "I am sorry for my swift words, Princess Eleanor, but is not the path through Cembar even worse than the Luciyr Road?"

"Not certainly," said Mudien. "It is true that the Cembarans have a law that any Karolan captured within their borders must be taken as a slave, and that they would rather err by capturing a few of their own occasionally than by letting Karolans escape. It is also true that very few who are not native to Cembar can speak its language without an accent, and thus Karolans are easily recognized. But the population of southeastern Cembar is sparse, and it is not impossible to make it through without being accosted."

"Especially," said Eleanor, "if one keeps to the high foothills. Nothing mattered to me when I was carried there, and the world was cold and dark and hopeless. Yet I remember, as from a dream, our stealthy march, and the fast ride into the desert at last after we had been seen."

Ilohan suddenly realized what she meant, and his heart acted before his mind thought. He was on his knees before her chair, holding both her hands in his. "Of course!" he said. "You came to Ceramir by that road, when you had left me at Aaronkal. Alas, even more fear and danger, after all else that you had suffered!" He looked around the room, as if in reproach to all the world that such things had happened to her. "I am so sorry, Mother. So sorry. I wish your life – and mine – had not brought you so much pain. So much... I am sorry." He kissed her hands, and his tears fell upon them.

She gently took her hands from his and raised his head between them. "Do not count it, beloved son," she said. "Do not count pain, and do not count love. They are beyond measure, and God alone can judge their worth. Here I am, with life and joy within me, because God has loved me. I do not understand the hurt I took, or the healing I received, but I trust. Trust also, and love also, and whatever happens I will count the joy beyond the hurt. How could I think otherwise, when you love God, and love me, and are faithful? It is," she looked up, with tears gleaming in her eyes, "worth all the cost."

The room grew absolutely still, as if all felt that holy love had descended and wrapped them in its spell with the words that had been spoken. At last Eleanor herself broke the silence and the spell. "We must carry on the council, beloved son," she said, "and choose what our acts shall be in these lives which we commit to God." Ilohan arose and returned to his chair.

"How long is the road through Cembar?" asked Jonathan.

"Six days' journey in the desert," said Mudien, "then seven to cross the foothills, and then five or six more from the Cembaran border to Aaronkal."

"Even longer than the Luciyr Road," said Ilohan. "Have we so much time?"

"I think we have enough," said Mudien. "We have no reason to think your return is needed earlier. In any case there is no other certain road."

"No other certain road?" asked Jonathan. "Do you mean there might be another way?"

"To Ceramir come legends of many things," said Mudien. "I have heard of another way, but not from any who had traversed it. It is not a better road than Cembar."

"May Brogal go with them, on the road through Cembar?" asked Eleanor.

"Indeed, I hope so," said Veril. "He knows the language well, and has been there often before."

Imranie smiled. She had little fear for Brogal in Cembar, for she knew her son well. He had no fear for himself. He passed through life with hope that nothing would keep him from the good he desired, and found that it seldom did. "Certainly Brogal should go with you," she said. "He will protect you better than an army could, and none of you will come to harm."

"Indeed," said Mudien, "Brogal has escaped so many dangers, and is so sure that none will ever catch him, that I begin to think none ever will."

"He would delight to be your guide," said Veril.

"Veril speaks the truth," said Mudien, "and he is one of very few who can speak the tongue of Cembar well enough to convince Cembarans that he is one of them."

Ilohan was very thoughtful. "Still I am not sure," he said. "Does even the Cembar road promise safety from the traitor? Suppose that after all he were waiting for us at Aaronkal?

Suppose he simply stood on the battlements with a good bow?"

Eleanor shuddered. "That is what I fear," she said. "When we laid our bold plans, and dreamed our great hope, we thought no traitor could find the secret. Now one has."

"Is there no way we can warn the king of a spy or traitor?" asked Ilohan. "I think we must simply do that, if we can, and then set out to go through Cembar."

There was a silence, and Eleanor looked into one of the flickering candles with a strange look on her face, half grave, half smiling. "There is a way to warn him," she said. "And beyond that, we must only pray. You are right, Prince Ilohan. God has given us a dream, a hope, which we must follow. We must take the road before us." She turned to Jonathan. "Please to bring us your handiwork."

"With joy, Lady Eleanor." He unwrapped a brown bundle he had carried, and lifted its contents out into the clear candlelight. The ancient crown of the prince of Karolan shone in the room, its rubies glowing redder than the fire. The princess took it in her hands. She was solemn and silent for a long moment while she held it.

"Rubies are the only stones in the crown of the prince of Karolan," she said. "Do you know why, my son?"

"No," said Ilohan.

"Thomas did not want you to be over-interested in the prince or princess before the appointed time," said Eleanor. "But the red rubies stand for blood, the blood of Christ, the great Prince of Heaven – the blood he gave to redeem his people, his bride. The blood of an earthly prince could never have such power. But with the rubies of the crown goes a charge: to offer your blood, of whatever worth it may be, for your people or your bride, if it is needed. Do you accept this charge?"

"As my father did," said Ilohan. "If it is needed, I will offer my blood to the last drop."

Eleanor's eyes filled with tears, and she groped for a place to lay down the crown. Jonathan came to her, gently took the crown from her hands, and held it firmly against a small table near her chair. He laid a chisel beside it. When her eyes were clear again, she took up the chisel in her hand. In clear, even letters, she re-carved the old inscription. The strokes of her beautiful script gleamed in the firelight, tracing out the words, the ancient blessing.

"Sir Ilohan, kneel before the Princess Eleanor," said Mudien. Ilohan obeyed him, and knelt where he had once before that night, with far different thoughts in his mind. He looked up into his mother's face, and he saw her great joy. She held the crown in both hands, a shining ring of bright gold and gleaming red jewels.

"This is the crown your father wore," she said. "As an inheritance, you have received not only his crown, but also his faithfulness, and in this I rejoice. Always be true. Remember that the deepest darkness is not dark to God, and that he holds to you even when you feel your shattered being can no longer hold to him. Remember that all you have, you have been given." She stopped a moment, and joy too deep for words shone in her face.

"As every mother of a crown prince of Karolan has blessed her son for years uncounted, so I bless you," said Eleanor in a clear voice. "As your days, so shall your strength be, beloved son. He who gives you strength will never forsake you, and no day will be dark enough to quench his light."

He bowed his head, and felt her crown him. The crown fit perfectly, and it felt somehow right, despite his countless thoughts that he could not be a good prince. It was not too heavy, and the coolness of the metal was comfortable. "Rise, Prince Ilohan of Karolan, and live the life you have been given!" said Eleanor. He obeyed her, and then helped her to her feet to stand beside him.

Jonathan looked at them together, and rejoiced. It was strange to see Ilohan, still looking thin and pain-weary from his sickness, standing there crowned as His Royal Highness, the Prince of Karolan, and yet Jonathan also thought it somehow deeply fitting. Ilohan was a man, his friend, whom he had fought beside, journeyed, worked, and starved with, yet he was also the prince. He was a real, flesh and blood prince of Karolan, who lived and breathed, who would not be a vague crowned idea to the people of his realm but a person who loved them, cared for them, and blessed them in reality. And he was his friend. Jonathan suddenly knew that, if he had to, he would die for the prince. He stood up, knelt to Ilohan and Eleanor, and rose to speak.

"I know no God by whom to bless you, Sir Prince," he said, "but I pledge to you my service and my love as long as I can give them." He turned to Eleanor. "Princess Eleanor, your pain has won you more than I can understand, and you are worthy of such a son. I will be faithful to him, and no harm will befall him if I can hold it back."

"Your love is of great value, Jonathan of Glen Carrah," said Princess Eleanor. "I could not wish my son to have a better friend."

"Nor could I wish for one," said Ilohan. "My only sorrow is that I fear your love will lead you to great danger, and I do not feel certain that we will see the hope of this night fulfilled."

Eleanor trembled with the fear that they would not. It was the deepest darkness left in her bright soul. She valued her son's life immeasurably more than he, and knew it might be lost. His fear could be at most only a shadow of her own. She longed once again for God's assurance that her prince would live, but she did not receive it. Swiftly she turned and embraced him – desperately tight at first, but her desperation quickly passed. "For us there is no night without a morning," she said. "Never forget it, and I will try to do the same. Now we must tell the king of what has passed."

Her hand was steady as she held a quill, and wrote their message to King Thomas on a piece of parchment:

All is well; he is safe and true and crowned.
He starts by way of Cembar in two days,
if you approve our choice.
Beware of a traitor; someone knew his errand and his path.
Hope and pray.
Eleanor.

They walked slowly out into a starry night with no moon. The cool air had a smell that told of life and freshness. Their footfalls, and even Eleanor's crutches, made little noise in the silent darkness as they walked slowly up through the trees and into the fields in the northern part of the valley. There was hardly any breeze, and the stars were very bright when they gathered close to the brooding cliffs. Eleanor gave three unearthly cries that shattered the stillness and echoed in the rocks: it was the eagle's call that only she could make.

Her imitation was soon answered, strong and wild and even more unearthly, like the scream of a falling star. The great eagle was silhouetted black against the shining Ceranim as he approached them, and finally with the sound of huge wings he lighted on a large bush nearby. Eleanor wrapped the parchment around a talon, and secured it with a piece of twine. After feeding the eagle, she gave one last imitation of his cry, and made a swift strong gesture as if she were throwing something over the mountains to Karolan.

Skykag took wing instantly and spiraled up until they lost him among the stars. One final shivering scream fell to them from the north at some tremendous height, and he was gone.

Weariness fell heavily on Eleanor as they walked back to the house. She could hardly believe that it was done. Her heart and mind could not encompass all the things that had happened. When at last she lay down in her clean bed in Ceramir, she knew she did not need to comprehend her life, and was thankful. She fell into a profound slumber, dreamless and sweet.

Ilohan and Jonathan's room was dim and quiet, but the wonder of the day was too strong in both of them for sleep to come quickly. They left their candles burning, and sat on their beds talking softly.

"Your Highness said before," said Jonathan, "that you would have trusted Eleanor's story, or King Thomas's word, without the proof the crown, sword, and bones have furnished."

Ilohan stood up to stare down imperiously at his friend. "On pain of my highness's extreme displeasure, you must not call me that again," he said, and burst out laughing.

"Well then, Prince Ilohan, for that title at least I will give you when I please," said Jonathan.

"Yes, of course I would have trusted them, as I said before," said Ilohan. "Yet though I know the truth, I still feel it is impossible I could be the prince! How strange this life that God has given us!"

"Ilohan," said Jonathan softly, "was there then no other purpose in sending us to Luciyr than to prove to you that you were the rightful prince, when you would have believed the word of King Thomas or Princess Eleanor without proof?"

"Yes," said Ilohan slowly, "yes, I think there was. I can scarcely feel even now that I am truly the prince, but it would be harder still if I had never been to Luciyr."

"You have touched your father's bones with your own hands," said Jonathan, "and by your will and diligence his sword and crown were recovered. You have stood where he stood, and fought where he fought. You have felt your mother's arms, heard her story, cried the echoes of her tears and known the shadow of her pain. No word from King Thomas could have taught you what you know now."

"No," said Ilohan, "none could. You understand it well, and say it better than I could myself."

"It was a privilege to share your journeys and your labors," said Jonathan.

"I chose my companion wisely, when I passed over all the Knights of Karolan to seek for you," said Ilohan. "But your journeys with me are not yet over."

They were silent for a long time, and the candles burned low and went out. Jonathan's mind wandered over the things he had heard that day, and filled with thoughts of the dangerous homeward journey to which Ilohan had referred – and the war that would surely follow it. As he drifted nearer sleep, his thoughts became less ordered. One that recurred oddly was the thought of the mysterious third way back to Aaronkal that Mudien had spoken of, a path of which even he had heard only rumors. "Ilohan," he asked in the darkness, "what do you think

Mudien meant when he spoke of yet another road back to Karolan?"

There was no answer: Ilohan was asleep. Jonathan was left to wonder alone as he slipped into the land of dreams. His heart was full of adventure, and he walked in sleep down a thousand fantastic paths of breathtaking glory, and mysterious wonder and danger. His adventures so far had neither crushed nor sated his desire to see things he had never seen, and do things he had never dreamed of doing.

* * *

The afternoon was warm in Glen Carrah, as Joseph and Naomi rode over the western ridge and across the golden expanse of dry grass. The day was like a last blessing of the departed summer: still, bright, and balmy. For both father and daughter it had been idyllic, a lovely, peaceful time that set war as far away as the dark roots of the mountains. The hiding place they had visited, a sheltered earthen valley a morning's ride west of Carrah, had been so calm and lovely that the very inviolate depth of its peace had seemed a protection. Shepherd and shepherdess had eaten there, in a hollow amid an abundant confusion of impenetrable brambles. Joseph had been comforted concerning his daughter's safety, while Naomi was reassured about Jonathan by the caring beauty of the handiwork of her God. God, who ruled and cared for the delicate perfection of sunlight glowing in the tracery of autumn brambles, would not let two souls joined as she and Jonathan were be torn apart by the great gulf between Hell and Heaven. She was sure of it.

This peace was still with her when she saw their home ahead, and knew that the short journey was nearly over. A golden haze seemed to hang across the Glen and the land below it, like a tangible emblem of the peace she felt. Naomi glanced at her father as they rode, content and untroubled. He smiled at her, and she knew that all was well between them.

A cooling breeze ruffled her rich brown hair, and she delighted in the free feel of it, but then looked up in surprise for until then the day had been very still. Up in the east an autumn storm was coming: the ghost of long warm summer was fading, falling away as autumn came with winter on its heels. The dark clouds rose quickly, and had covered more than half the sky before Joseph and Naomi forded the Carratril and turned down the glen toward their home.

The wind blew in fitful gusts, cool and strong, but Naomi found no more joy in its wild freedom. A bowshot from the cottage they dismounted, as if by one unspoken impulse, and stood together facing the dark east. The golden grass, autumn-red trees, and gray rock glowed in rich color against the blackness of the clouds. The feeling Naomi had had long weeks ago under the threat of a similar storm returned to her, intensified and made more clear. The threat rose, a threat of dire calamity – but all that was good shone unafraid, at the height of its glory in the last rays before clouds would cover the sun.

"Isn't it beautiful?" she whispered in awe.

Her father's hand found hers as he stood beside her, and the strength of his grip comforted her as he answered. "Yes, beloved daughter. It is beautiful." In his voice she heard the feelings of her own heart. Beautiful, yes, and unafraid. While the sun still shines.

Thunder boomed and crashed, echoing off the hills and rocks, and suddenly Naomi found herself in her father's arms, as though she were the frightened child she never in truth had been. They hugged each other tightly.

Far away across the Glen, Hannah was drawing water from her well. She looked up suddenly and saw them: two clear, tiny figures in the distance, embracing. She watched while the shadow covered up the glowing world behind them, until they alone stood bright against the storm. Then she turned away, and never saw the darkness take them.

Here ends the first book.

IF YOU ENJOYED THIS BOOK…

-Tell your friends! This is a self-published book without the advertising budget of a big corporation behind it. If you think it's a good read, spread the word!

-You can order a copy for a friend or family member from http://www.hopewriter.com/Karolan.html, or by contacting the author directly (ariheinze@hotmail.com, or (832) 622-1114). *Bright Against the Storm* may also be purchased as an e-book from Amazon.com. Additional new options may be announced on the website soon.

-Look for the release of the other books in *The Epic of Karolan*! Book two should be released in the first half of 2010, with books three and four following in late 2010 and early 2011.

-Check the website, http://www.hopewriter.com/Karolan.html for interesting background about Karolan, and for additional news as the release dates for books two through four approach.